BY EDWIN O'CONNOR

THE ORACLE

THE LAST HURRAH
(*Atlantic* Prize Novel, 1955)

THE LAST HURRAH

THE LAST HURRAH

By

EDWIN O'CONNOR

An Atlantic Monthly Press Book

Little, Brown and Company . Boston, Toronto

LIBRARY OF CONGRESS CATALOG CARD NO. 55-11224

Published February 1956
Reprinted February 1956

ATLANTIC—LITTLE, BROWN BOOKS
ARE PUBLISHED BY
LITTLE, BROWN AND COMPANY
IN ASSOCIATION WITH
THE ATLANTIC MONTHLY PRESS

Published simultaneously in Canada
by Little, Brown & Company (Canada) Limited

PRINTED IN THE UNITED STATES OF AMERICA

FOR

HOP and NIALL

PART I

One

It was early in August when Frank Skeffington decided — or rather, announced his decision, which actually had been arrived at some months before — to run for re-election as mayor of the city. This was a matter about which there had been public speculation for a good while: for, in fact, four years, ever since he had been inaugurated for what his opponents had fondly hoped was the last time. Since the beginning of the current year, however, the speculation had increased, not alone because the deadline was drawing nearer, but also because there were no other elections of importance coming up — the municipal elections took place in off years politically and so did not have to share the spotlight with national or state contests. Thus interest had mounted, and as it had, so had the hopes of Skeffington's opponents. For while he was admittedly among the most durable of politicians, he was just as admittedly getting older, and in recent speeches and press conferences he had expressed little interest in continuing his long political career. On one memorable occasion he had gone so far as to speak with a certain dreaminess of the joys of retirement, of the quiet time of withdrawal which would follow a lifetime spent in the service of the public.

"Far from the madding crowd," he had said, gazing at the reporters expressionlessly. "The declining years spent in solitude and contemplation. Possibly in some rustic retreat."

This hint had not been received without a measure of cynicism; one reporter from the chief opposition paper had led the questioning which followed.

"Tell us, Governor," he had said (for, as Skeffington had twice been governor of the state, the courtesy title lingered long after the office itself had been lost), "just how would you propose to adjust yourself to this rustic life? Wouldn't it be pretty quiet? What would you do?"

"Read," Skeffington had replied promptly. "And reflect." At this his pale blue eyes had closed, and an expression of extraordinary benignity crossed the full, faintly veined and rather handsome face; the long, heavy head inclined perceptibly forward, and the reporters found themselves looking at the silver crown of his hair. It was almost as if, in anticipation, he were paying pious tribute to the time of ultimate retreat.

The reporter had coughed. "We know you've always been a great reader, Governor," he had said, a trifle sardonically. "Any idea of the kind of books you'd take with you?"

Skeffington's reply, made with eyes still closed, had been characteristically elusive. "The great books," he had said.

The reporter had been persistent. "Which great books, Governor?"

Skeffington's eyes had opened, the silver head had lifted, and once more the reporters met the deadpan look. "I don't know whether you'd know them or not," he had said thoughtfully. "The Bible, which is a book composed of two parts, commonly called the Old and the New Testaments. The poems and plays of Shakespeare, an Englishman. And during the winter months I would also take the paper which you represent."

The reporter had said warily, "Thanks for the compliment, Governor. I suppose there's some special reason?"

Skeffington had nodded. "During the long winter months a glowing fire might be welcome," he had said, "and I have found from long experience that your paper burns very well. Makes grand kindling. I don't imagine, by the way, that most people are aware of that. If they were, your paper's very small circulation might be substantially increased. Any more questions, gentlemen?"

It had been a typical enough interview, save for the suggestion of retirement. None of Skeffington's opponents quite believed in this, but on the other hand, neither could they afford to discount it. On the whole, any hint of this kind was felt to be encouraging rather than otherwise, especially when related to certain other signs. For example, there were the heartening rumors of Skeffington's ill health: among the true optimists it was confidently whispered that a mysterious disease was devouring his brain bit by bit, so that now there occurred intervals in every day during which he reverted to the habits of his childhood and expressed a desire to play marbles or hide-and-seek. The newspaper for which his nephew, Adam Caulfield, worked — the same newspaper whose combustibility Skeffington had praised — offered support of a more oblique kind. It began to run editorials reminding the voters that while the life span of man undoubtedly had been prolonged, the problem of senectitude had by no means been conquered, and that aged men in positions of public trust could constitute a definite hazard (Skeffington, at this time, was approaching his seventy-second birthday). As the year wore on, obituary notices of well-known septuagenarians had been given increasingly prominent display. The paper conducted this campaign with some circumspection, as Skeffington was notoriously quick to strike in all matters of suspected libel, and in the past had actually secured two judgments against this very paper. But as the months went by he paid absolutely no attention to the partially concealed attack; this, taken with his own statement and the persisting rumors, was thought to be all to the good — and hopes which at first had been merely wistful now ripened and grew strong.

But Skeffington smashed them all in a matter of minutes.

On his seventy-second birthday Frank Skeffington had lunch with his nephew, and over the meal told him of his plan to run again. He then swore him to secrecy, and, following this — and almost as an afterthought — revealed the reason which, more than any other, had determined his decision to stay in public life.

"I want to," he said.

That night, at a birthday dinner given him by the party leaders, he made the announcement public. It was substantially the same announcement that he had delivered in private that noon; only the reason behind it had been suitably modified.

"My decision represents a submission to the will of the populace," he said, "and is against my every personal desire. I had hoped, at the end of my current term, to retire to a well-earned rest, but unfortunately one look at the names of those who have declared themselves as candidates for this office forced me to change my decision. Why, the mind positively boggles at the presumption of these men! As one looks down this bold list one would think that the only qualification necessary to run for mayor of this great city was to be without any qualification whatsoever. This is a time for experience, for leadership; I cannot abandon this fine city to the care of such fumbling hands. And so, dutifully if reluctantly, I submit my name to you once again, realizing full well that while my own health and rest are important, it is far more important that this city of ours should not be allowed to revert to Government by Pygmies!"

This announcement had been carefully timed so that it would appear in the city edition of all morning papers; in this way — Skeffington had explained to his nephew that noon — the maximum desirable effect would be achieved; the majority of his opponents would learn the bad news over their morning coffee. It was a thought which appeared to afford him a virtually limitless satisfaction.

"I hesitate to appear vindictive," he said, chuckling softly, "but what a pretty picture it makes: all those red and angry faces sputtering over the coffee cups! The day ruined before it begins . . . I don't mind telling you that that's the kind of thing that warms the cockles of an old man's heart on his birthday. . . . Have some more lobster."

The next morning Skeffington awakened early, as he always did; for half an hour he lay in bed, waking slowly, watching the first pale flush of daylight. He knew that the day would be exactly like the great majority of his days in its routine, yet coming as it did at the beginning of both his seventy-third year and the start of another campaign, he found it particularly exhilarating and even significant. An omen, he said to himself. A happy augury.

He rose, said his morning prayers, and had his breakfast brought up to him. He breakfasted lightly on tea and toast, for although in earlier days he had been something of a gourmand, he had of late become more prudent in his diet. Over the past few years he had slowly modified his regimen of living to conform to the requirements of his age; he did this without hesitation or regret, for he was a realist who meant to keep alive for some time to come, and he knew that at his time of life the list of permissible pleasures dwindled steadily, year by year.

After breakfast he picked up a book and settled down by the long front bedroom window to read; this had been his morning custom for nearly fifty years. When his wife was alive, much of the time he had read aloud to her; for the last ten years he had read silently to himself. He read poetry for the most part, and he read chiefly for sound, taking pleasure in the patterns of words as they formed and echoed deep within his brain. His taste was highly personalized and uneven; if, in the reading of a morning, there was likely to be "I have been half in love with easeful Death," there was just as likely to be "Let me live in my house by the side of the road, and be a friend of man." Adonais and Sam Walter Foss, yoked in uneasy fellowship: both were old favorites of Skeffington, and he read them again and again.

It was an incongruous picture: the aging political boss, up shortly after dawn, preparing for the daily war of the wards by reading a volume of verse; it was a picture from which Skeffington — who was capable, at times, of great detachment — derived considerable amusement. He knew that the widely publicized habit had given rise to indignation, even fury, among his opponents; in several campaigns it had cropped up as a major issue.

Twenty years before, it had been the principal target of Festus "Mother" Garvey, a crafty little volcano of a man who, in middle life, had been given his nickname because of his habit of carrying his mother about with him for purposes of endorsement. She would appear by his side at political rallies; the opening dialogue was unvarying:

FESTUS: Good evenin', Ma.

MA: Good evenin' to ye, Festus me son.

FESTUS: Ma, I'd like to have you meet all these grand folks out in the audience who came all the way here to see what I had to say for myself this evenin'.

MA: Well, God love them all, Festus.

FESTUS: And I'd like all you grand folks to meet the lovely

mother to who I owe everythin' I have and ever will have. You'll always be my best girl, Ma!

Ma: Thank ye, Festus. And I'd like to tell all of yez that me son Festus has always been the grandest son in the world to me, and if yez vote for him yez'll be makin' no mistake!

The preliminaries over, Festus would leap into battle. Skeffington, who had shared many a platform with him, now recalled vividly his little antagonist racing up and down the stage, red-faced and screaming, hurling his charges of abuse, mismanagement, and corruption. Eventually and inevitably, he would come to the poetry.

"Here we are in this grand city of ours, payin' the highest tax rate we've ever paid, and the garbage hasn't been collected for weeks!" he would cry. "Our back yards are bein' turned into vertable *bedlams* of nauseous perfumes, and where is the mayor while all this is goin' on? I'll tell you where he is; he's up in his mansion on the Avenue, *readin' pomes!* The city smells to the high heavens and Frank Skeffington's got his nose in a book! Not a one of us dares to take a deep breath for fear of bein' killed off by the poisons around us, and our mayor is readin' how Louisy May Lovebreath thinks vi'lets has a dainty smell in June! Oh, shame upon him, dear folks! Turn this shameful scoundrel out of office, him and his pomes both!"

And Skeffington recalled, too, his own rebuttal:

"I have sat here this evening and been warmed by the sight of this good mother, speaking so eloquently on behalf of her son. It was touching. Moving. Mother love is always edifying. Seeing her here tonight by her son's side, I cannot avoid thinking of those beautiful lines:

And 'mid the cheerless hours of night
A mother wandered with her child."

He had smiled benignly at the fierce, diminutive old lady who, hard by the side of her fifty-five-year-old child, sat glaring at him; then, in a thoughtful tone, he had added: "Still, we must not get carried away by emotion. We must remember one thing:

everybody has a mother. Creatures of the field have mothers. The despised reptiles have mothers. The viper, the scorpion, the asp, all have mothers. Presumably their mothers believe in them. All of us would doubtless admire their tender trust; we would not necessarily share it. And so, this evening, while I'd like to congratulate my opponent on possessing such a loyal parent, I'm afraid I can't congratulate him on much else. You heard with your own ears what he had to say. It only proves what I have long suspected: that while responsible civic leaders are preoccupied with grave and serious problems, Festus Garvey continues to think of municipal affairs in the terms of the simple device he loves so well — the garbage pail!"

He had beaten Mother Garvey handily; he had been beating him handily for thirty years; but Mother, himself motherless now and Skeffington's age, still clung on, an undying enemy whose ferocity had mounted with the years. And Skeffington knew that in the coming campaign he could depend upon few things as surely as he could upon the unrelenting, frenzied opposition of his ancient foe, coming at him from street corners, from the radio, from television.

It was a prospect which, at this stage of the game, did not alarm him greatly.

The morning poetry reading, regarded with rage by his enemies, had been championed by his supporters: they saw the habit as an awesome and barely attainable ideal, like celibacy or telling the truth, and they were proud of Skeffington for his dedication to it. And he, for his part, had continued to read — primarily, if by no means exclusively, for pleasure; as in most of his activities, there was in his reading a strong secondary purpose. His memory was both accurate and retentive, and thus his reading had provided him with a ready reservoir of quotation and epithet which had served him handsomely through numberless campaigns. Long ago he had discovered the rich potential in the mother lode of classical invective; properly used, it was a weapon to elevate and decimate the foe. (One had only to roar suddenly, "Ingratitude, thou marble-hearted fiend!" at perfidious Martin Hooley of Ward 2, and poor dumb Martin, anticipating abuse but of a more prosaic kind, would stand gaping and abashed; the crowd would shout its delight, and from isolated throats would come the proud, identifying gasp: *"Shakespeare!"*)

It was a valuable technique, but one which could backfire badly if misused. Skeffington, who understood his people thoroughly, knew their virtually bottomless capacity for suspicion and ridicule; he had seen other leaders, popular men all, who, when suddenly suspected of pretension, of getting a bit above themselves, had been turned on with a savagery which could scarcely be believed. The trick was, he knew, to space the grand phrases properly, to use them always with an air of winking complicity; to suggest, in other words, an allowable erudition untinted by the dangerous streaks of self-inflation. It was quite a trick, but Skeffington could say, without conceit, that it was one which he had mastered years ago.

He read for half an hour. Then he bathed, dressed, and went downstairs, and there, with two young men from his secretarial corps, he began the day's work. In addition to the routine correspondence, there was this morning a flood of congratulatory telegrams and telephone calls to be acknowledged. Skeffington and the secretarial pair worked swiftly and expertly, as letter after letter was dictated, each with precisely the right touch, each mirroring in every line the exact degree of cordiality, warmth, or restraint that obtained between Skeffington and the individual well-wisher. All this, while handled rapidly, was done with great attention to detail, for Skeffington had built his political life upon such personal contact, carefully established and just as carefully preserved. In correspondence as well as in the face-to-face encounter, one had to remember the minute details that made all the difference: the salutation to old Mrs. Lothrop always to read "My dear Lady" rather than "Dear Julia," and in the body of the letter a solicitous inquiry about the "indisposition" of her dipsomaniac nephew; T. F. Casey always to be addressed as "Old Friend Tim"; the patriarch of the vast Esposito brood to be called "Signor" and to be complimented upon the hideous grotto he had donated, twenty-five years before, to Our Lady of Loreto Church; the favored diminutive of E. Myron Goldfarb to be spelled "Myque" rather than "Mike," and E. Myron himself to be consoled on the death of his cousin the rabbi.

Of such small things was success compounded; this Skeffington firmly believed and allowed none of his subordinates to forget. In maintaining his elaborate web of tactful response, his own extraordinary memory was fortified by a comprehensive card-index system; and as a result, although slips had occurred from time to time, they had been few in number, and had done him relatively little harm.

He had come downstairs at 8:30; he and the secretaries worked on the mail until 9:45. Then the doors of the house were opened, and the people who had been waiting outside — there were perhaps twenty of these, some of whom had been standing patiently in the warm August morning for as much as two hours — were let in.

This too was personal contact. For decades, Skeffington had made himself among the most accessible of public figures, and he had made a ritual of receiving the public in his home. Promptly at 9:45 each morning he held court, and all who came to him were ultimately received.

"I'm available to every man and woman in the state," he once said to his nephew. "All they need is a little patience." As an afterthought he had added dryly, "And, of course, the vote. I find that may help."

This morning the supplicants arrived bearing congratulations. In joyous chorus they commended his decision to run again; they promised him the undeviating support of themselves and their families during the campaign. Skeffington, although a man of thoroughgoing cynicism, nevertheless did not discount these promises; he knew that for the most part they would be kept. He had no high opinion of the intelligence of the electorate, but experience had taught him that it quite adequately grasped the fact that all successful political activity was based on *quid pro quo*. In the light of benefits to be conferred, he thought it unlikely that those who came to him this morning would consider themselves as uncommitted on election day. Moreover, the sensible man helped to perpetuate in office the leader from whom he was able to secure assistance, and Skeffington had no reason to believe that these visitors would be less sensible than those who had gone before.

The courteous preliminaries over, they came down to business. Skeffington sat at the head of the long library table, one secretary at his right, the other at the lower end of the table filling in the blank information cards given to each visitor. Many of the group had come for the first time this morning; most, however, were occasional repeaters, with two or three hardy veterans, perpetually down on their luck, who had been coming to this door for decades.

The interviews were conducted, as always, with politeness, efficiency, and some privacy. . . .

"Mrs. Rocco Santagata," Skeffington said, glancing briefly at the card before him (*Age: fifty-six. Widow. Owns Atlas Road variety store. Boy in school trouble*), and then at the plump, gray and tearful Italian woman herself. "Well, what can we do for you, Mrs. Santagata?" The deep voice had never been mellower; it became mildly jocular as he turned to the secretary. "Are those tears we see, John? What do you suppose a good woman like Mrs. Santagata has to cry about on a morning like this? You don't think it's because she heard I was going to run again?"

There was no faint responsive smile; the round eyes grew wide with horror. "Oh no no, Mista May'!" she gasped. "I'ma no cry for dat. I'ma *glad* you run. Honest!"

She began to snivel dangerously, and he quickly patted her on the hand. "I know you are, Mrs. Santagata. Don't give it another thought. Tell me how I can be of help."

"My husban', he'sa dead. But he tol' me, long time ago, somet'ing goesa wrong, come to see you," she began — and the words poured out in a torrent while Skeffington searched automatically through the great file of memory for the name of Rocco Santagata. He could not place it, and so he said: "Your husband was a fine man, Mrs. Santagata. An exemplary character. That splendid lodge, the Sons of Italy, is the poorer for his absence."

It was a dead hit; he was not surprised.

"You know Rocco in da Sons?"

"Everybody knew Rocco, Mrs. Santagata. A man to be proud of." She nodded in vigorous assent, and he pressed on to business. "Now what's this about your boy? What kind of trouble is he in?"

"Joey," she said, the tears threatening again — "my poor Joey." The story was resumed, and from the tumbling mass of words and sobs Skeffington quickly pieced together the familiar pattern: a series of conflicts between a teacher and a fourteen-year-old boy, truancy, the boy apprehended, threats, more truancy, the threats intensified. Probably a hellion, he thought: of late, life seemed to have become increasingly full of little Joey Santagatas. Aloud, he asked the necessary questions.

"Has the boy ever been in trouble outside school?"

"Oh no no, he'sa *good* boy, Mista May' — "

"Never been mixed up with the police? Never been to court?"

"Oh no no *no!* Nota my Joey!" The eyes had grown round again, and Skeffington smiled at her.

"All right, Mrs. Santagata, we'll see if we can't do something for Joey." He said briefly to the secretary: "Letter to Danny O'Brien, School Committee. Have the boy transferred to another teacher. If necessary to another school. Right away." Another case for the Grievance Committee of the Teachers' Union, he thought: *Skeffington interferes again.* There might even be a protest meeting in a Unitarian church hall. "That ought to fix things up, Mrs. Santagata," he said. "Go home now and tell your boy to keep out of trouble. Tell him to behave himself, and tell him I said so."

"Oh t'ank you, t'ank you, t'ank you!" The woman was in tears again; she grabbed his hand and kissed it wetly. "You're a nice-a man, Mista May'. Like-a my Rocco say. T'ank you so much. I do anyt'ing for you someday!"

"You don't need to do a single thing, Mrs. Santagata. Only too happy to be able to oblige a fine mother like yourself." He half rose, eased his hand out of her grasp, and smilingly edged her away from the table. *"A rivederci,"* he said.

She smiled in delighted recognition. *"A rivederci.* God blessa you, Mista May'!"

She went off, and the others came on, one at a time. In every case something was needed: a job, a letter of introduction, medical care for an ailing wife, a low rent house, a pair of glasses, a transfer from one city department to another, a lawyer, a hardship discharge for a son in the army, money. It was the purest routine; Skeffington handled them all easily and with no hitches. The last one was old Timsy Coughlin.

"Oh by God Frank it's grand news, grand news," he said rapidly, slipping with great familiarity into the supplicant's chair. He alone of the visitors had no information card, for in his case none was necessary. A toothless, pale prune of a man with a thin evasive mouth and deceptively candid eyes, he had known Skeffington since boyhood and for decades had been one of his retainers: an ingenious deadbeat who came regularly for his handouts, each time bearing a fresh and highly fictional account of disaster. "Grand news indeed," he repeated. "What I stopped by for Frank was to give you the word that Timsy Coughlin's with you all the way in sickness and health. You can count on Timsy every blessed inch of the way, Frank."

"Glad to hear it, Timsy," Skeffington said, glancing at his watch. It was late; unquestionably it would be better to give Timsy the money straightway and leave. But there was the expected ritual to be gone through: after all the years it still amused him and he felt that Timsy, if deprived of it, would be bitterly disappointed. He gave him a slow look of appraisal and said solemnly: "You're looking well; I've never seen you looking better. You're a splendid figure of a man for your years, Timsy. I envy you your excellent health."

"Ah well now, what the hell, for the love of God, I'm not all that well!" Timsy said in sudden alarm. "Not by a damn sight Frank, oh by God no. I have some terrible bad days yes I do. I wonder should I tell you what it is?" He leaned forward confidentially, his wide blue eyes expressing an apparent anxiety and doubt: "Because what I mean is, it's not the sort of thing a man goes gassing around about himself, do you see?"

"Then I advise you not to say a word to a living soul. Keep your counsel, Timsy. Share these private matters only with your Maker."

"Ah well now, what the hell, I can tell *you* Frank. You're the boy can keep the secrets, yes you are. Don't we all know that now?" He paused to look engagingly at Skeffington, then lowered his tone. "I'll tell you how it is with me Frank," he said. Here's just how it is: *I'm not able to pass water!*"

"Prostate," Skeffington said unfeelingly. "Glad you told me, Timsy. We'll whisk you over to Memorial Hospital and Jack Ahern will take it out for you first thing tomorrow morning. You'll be skipping around like a boy in a week."

"Oh by God, do you want to kill me off Frank?" Timsy cried. He waved his arms up and down; his head ducked and bobbed in agitation. "It's not the prostrate at all, the prostrate's got nothing to do with it! What I got is something else entirely, something else altogether, Frank. What I got is the same thing my Uncle Jim died of. You remember Jim, Frank?"

Skeffington nodded. "I do. The man lived to be nearly a hundred."

"Ah yes; well the hell of it was he died at the end a terrible death. A fine living man all his life, still he couldn't pass water at the end. And do you know what it was, Frank? I'll tell you what it was: *It was the bladder kept shrinking up on him till it shrunk up to nothing at all!* You're a goner when that happens to you Frank. Watch out for the bladder. When the bladder goes you go. That's what happened to my Uncle Jim, Frank!"

"A tragic end," Skeffington said. "And you feel that something of the sort awaits you, Timsy?"

"I do. God knows I do, Frank. You might say it's in the family so to speak. Because of what happened to my Uncle Jim. So what I need," he said carefully, "what I need, Frank, is the medicine. That's what can save me Frank. The right sort of medicine."

Skeffington nodded again. "The bladder medicine."

"Oh by God you've put your finger on it Frank!" Timsy cried, delighted by such comprehension. "By God if you haven't! The bladder medicine is the thing all right. It's grand stuff, there's none better. A man's all right with that stuff inside him. But the pity of it is," he said, suddenly relapsing into woe, "the pity of it is this, Frank: How's a poor man to get it? Answer me that, if you can!"

"Very costly, I imagine," Skeffington said. "Doubtless compounded of rare old herbs, priceless ingredients."

"Ah costly's not the word Frank not the word at all. It's *dear* that's what it is. Terrible dear. And suppose a man only wants a bit of it it's still too damn dear if he's a poor man that is."

"The natural desire of the vast bladder medicine trust to mulct the suffering public," Skeffington said. "I've been fighting them all my life." He looked at his watch again; it was 10:45, and he could delay no longer. "Listen, Timsy," he said abruptly. "I've diagnosed your case. I think a man in your condition needs about ten dollars' worth of this medicine. What do you say to that?"

"Oh by God Frank I say fine. Ten dollars' worth that would put me back on my feet. I'd be a new man Frank that's what I'd be." He quickly took the extended bill and put it in his pocket without looking at it; this was not his normal practice, but he trusted Skeffington. "God bless you for this Frank," he said, getting to his feet and moving backwards towards the door. "God bless you for helping a family man and a good Democrat back to health. You're a grand man Frank, and I'm with you all the way."

"I know you are, Timsy. Take care of yourself now. Good men are scarce."

"Ah ha ha ha, by God isn't that the truth now Frank? *Good men are scarce:* you've put your finger on it. Good-by now, Frank." He was out the door and then his little head popped back in. "Mind what I said Frank. *Timsy Coughlin's with you all the way.* I mean that Frank!"

"Fine, fine. Good-by, Timsy." Skeffington got to his feet; the morning interviews were over. The secretary at his right said, "Where do you suppose he'll go with it, Governor? The nearest bar?"

"No," Skeffington said, "not the nearest bar. Timsy is a man of habit. He'll walk three miles, over to Charlie Donegan's place on the Causeway; he's been going there for fifty years. He'll have three Jamesons and he'll offer to fight anyone in the house who dares to say one word against Frank Skeffington. He'll have three more Jamesons, and then he'll tell Charlie what a hardhearted scoundrel Frank Skeffington is for not putting him on the Civil Service thirty years ago. Then he'll begin to cry and say that the Irish are the most wonderful people in the world, but too sentimental for their own good. Finally he'll pass out and Charlie will see that he gets home. And about three o'clock this afternoon someone will come running into the Hall eager to tell me that at noon today Timsy Coughlin was over in Donegan's place slashing me up the back. That's the way it will happen, my boy; Timsy's way of life may not be exemplary, but it's very regular."

"And Mrs. Timsy — what about her?"

"Dead and buried," said Skeffington. "Easily twenty-five years ago."

The secretary, who was relatively new to his job, expressed his sympathy for Timsy in his ancient trouble. "I imagine that's really the reason for it all?" he said.

"I imagine so," Skeffington said. "She was the meanest woman who ever drew on a skirt. Timsy's been drunk ever since out of sheer joy. Come along, we've got to be moving."

On the way out he thought suddenly of his son; he stopped and said to the maid, "Has Francis come downstairs yet?"

"No sir. I think he's still asleep."

A growing boy needs his rest, Skeffington thought sardonically; the only question was whether or not Francis Jr., at the age of thirty-seven, might properly qualify as a growing boy. For years Skeffington had been baffled and badly disappointed by his only son. Francis Jr. was virtually a physical duplicate of his father — the resemblance was so astonishing that Skeffington, looking at his son in recent years, could only groan at the unkind mockery of the mnemonic shell, smiling emptily at him across the dinner table. For some important if not quite definable ingredient had been omitted from the boy's make-up; he had been a pleasant, well-mannered, lazy youngster who had grown placidly into manhood without betraying a sign of ambition or, indeed, of intelligence. He had skinned through high school, preparatory school, college, and law school, gaining in this educational passage but a single distinction: in his junior year at college he had been voted Best Dancer in his class. It was an honor that Skeffington had failed to appreciate.

"I've sired a featherhead," he had said to his wife. "A waltzing featherhead. Or am I doing the boy an injustice? Perhaps he fox-trots as well."

"Ah, Frank, you expect too much," she had replied. A gentle woman, she knew and in part shared his disappointment in the boy, yet she had kept herself the buffer between the uncomprehending father and the smiling phantom son. "You want him to be like you and the simple fact of it is he can't be. It's not fair to expect it of him."

He had shrugged. "I don't expect it. I merely expect him to be like some recognizable adult. He's not like me, he's not like you, he's not like anybody. Possibly he's a throwback: a throwback to some dancing ancestor. He claims he wants to be a lawyer; do you suppose he plans to dance his way into court?"

She had persisted. "He's very young yet, after all. It's much too early to pass judgment. And he *is* a good boy; that's no small thing, surely?"

"He's good, he's moral, he's likable," he had agreed, "but he's also a puffball. No weight at all. Twenty-one years old, and everybody still calls him Junior; they'll call him Junior when he's ninety. I don't find that particularly encouraging, Kate."

She had returned to a long-cherished ambition. "I don't know, I always thought that one day he might surprise us all by going to the seminary. He still might, I suppose. I wish he would; I think he'd be happy there."

"Well, he's made a grand start," Skeffington had said dryly. "I understand the seminaries want only the best dancers. No, Kate, the boy will go through law school. He'll go through without too much trouble, I think I can promise you that; the good Dean Gillis is a fine old-fashioned scholar with a healthy respect for his own skin. Then when he gets through he'll get a place in a decent firm; it's barely possible I may have something to do with that, too. But what's to happen to him after I'm gone I haven't the least idea. Maybe he'll be all right as long as his legs hold out."

Now, sixteen years later, Skeffington's bleak prediction for the most part had been fulfilled. At thirty-seven, his son, unmarried, still danced; he could be seen nightly at any one of the city's numerous night clubs in the company of any one of a number of young women who danced well, laughed immoderately, and were remarkably similar in appearance. He was a thoroughly agreeable, well-tailored man, with a face as unlined as that of a child, who perhaps drank a bit more with the passing of each year, but whose behavior had remained untouched by scandal or disgrace. He was by occupation a practicing attorney, although the practice was largely limited to routine and undemanding labors in the offices of the city's Corporation Counsel, a department of government which had been for some years under Skeffington's control. And, by friend and foe alike, he was still called Junior.

The two men, father and son, lived in the big house on the Avenue, but now Skeffington saw his son at fleeting intervals, for the younger man returned to the house each night long after Skeffington had retired, and he slept well into the following day. And so, this morning, Skeffington was not surprised by the maid's answer to his question; he merely said to her, "When he does come down, tell him I'd like to see him in my office this afternoon."

Then, with his secretaries, he left the house and was driven down to City Hall. The passage was swift and unhesitating: the siren on the big gleaming Cadillac warned off lesser vehicles and traffic lights were ignored. Skeffington disliked wasting time en route, but more than that he knew that nothing could be counted on to annoy his opponents so unfailingly as these fast, flamboyant, raidlike arrivals, occurring regularly each morning, and serving to remind them, as they sat grimly at their desks, that their old enemy still survived and was among them for another day, living, breathing, smiling, poised for the possible kill. It was the kind of knowledge from which Skeffington derived no inconsiderable comfort.

Two

EARLIER that morning, in the home of his nephew, Adam Caulfield, Skeffington was the principal subject of discussion. Adam and his wife were at breakfast. It was, as always for them, a leisurely meal: as Adam's working hours were of his own making, the day was apt to begin late rather than early, and there was seldom need for haste. They breakfasted in the kitchen, an agreeable room washed by the midmorning sun. Adam was reading the paper; Maeve, who had already read it — or, rather, had read that part of it which interested her most this morning — was standing before the stove, her hands busy, her face quiet and faintly troubled. She was a lovely young woman, with the slender body of a girl, dark and softly curling hair, and large and rather astonishing hazel eyes in the clear, vivid oval of her face. She was twenty-two, and this morning, as she moved about the kitchen, clad in sweater and skirt and flat-heeled shoes, she looked even younger. After a year of marriage, she still had about her something of the bright untouched innocence of the schoolgirl; looking at her, one could almost peer through the years and see the knot of young sodality girls chattering happily over Cokes in the cafeteria of the convent school, while at the far end of the room the steel-blue eye of Sister Mary Charles roved in cool supervisory survey.

But now she was a married woman, a happy and remarkably untroubled married woman; still, every once in a while, she would read in the papers the name of her husband's uncle in some new, outrageous connection, and then she would see the small cloud on the horizon and hear the thunder in the distance. For, in Skeffington, she sensed danger. It was true that, so far, the danger had remained remote: Skeffington had never entered their married life, and he seldom even saw his nephew, yet all the same, she felt the danger to be there. . . .

She brought more bacon and fresh coffee to the table; seating herself, she glanced once more at the account of the Skeffington dinner. She read on for a moment, anxiety touching the great, lovely eyes; then she said suddenly, "Darling, does he mean it? Do you think he really does?"

"Mean what?" Adam said. "And who?" He looked up and saw what his wife had been reading. "Oh," he said, with a smile. "Uncle Frank. Sure, I think he means it all right; at least he seems definite enough about it. Why?"

"Oh, I don't know," she said vaguely. "Only all this time everybody was so sure he wasn't going to run, and then all of a sudden . . . Do you think he's going to win?"

"Well, I know *he* thinks he is, and he's supposed to be pretty good at things like that, isn't he?" He smiled again, but this time to himself. He was a tall young man with heavy, slightly unruly brown hair, a bony, quiet face, and dark, intelligent eyes; he was eleven years older than his wife, he loved her very much, and in moments such as these he was fondly and secretly amused by her. He knew quite well her feeling towards Skeffington; he knew, too, that she could not understand his own lack of passionate opinion on the subject of his uncle. He said, "As for me, I haven't any idea which way it will go. How about some of that coffee?"

She poured, rather abstractedly, and said, "I was talking to Daddy yesterday. He said that even if your uncle did run this year he was sure to be beaten. And beaten very badly."

"Ah well," Adam said diplomatically. For, with the introduction of Maeve's father, they had reached the heart of the matter. It was from Roger Sugrue, rather than from any political awareness of her own, that Maeve had derived her disapproval of Skeffington: it was an inherited prejudice passed on to her by this preposterous parent. Roger spoke frequently of Skeffington, especially when his own advice on municipal matters had gone unheeded. It was at such moments that, diverted temporarily from the main stream of his major monologues — *The Irish in America; The Church; Himself* (*A Poor Boy Succeeds*) — he would speak of *Frank Skeffington's Crime.*

"Frank Skeffington's crime," he would say, his tough little

vegetable head tilted wisely to one side, "Frank Skeffington's crime — and I mean no offense to you, Adam: I'm speaking purely as a citizen about an elected official — is not what most people think it is. No indeed. It is not simply that he has let down the community. Oh, he's done that, all right, but in my humble opinion he's done much worse than that. He has let down his community, yes, but first and foremost he has let down his inheritance, his people, and his religion! That's what he has let down, and that is his crime. It's what he'll have to answer to his Maker for!"

Pronouncements of this kind, uttered over the years, had had their effect on Maeve. Her mother had died shortly after her birth, and she had been raised by this singular, opinionated father; she was loyal to him, and worse, thought Adam, she revered him. All her life she had listened to him on Skeffington; as a result, she thought of the elderly politician as a kind of cartoon character, the bloated figure in a frock coat, symbol of treachery and corruption.

She had met Skeffington only once, and this had been at her wedding. It was a meeting which had proved unsettling to her, for Skeffington was a great charmer when he chose to be and, sensing her resentment and because Adam was his nephew, he had made a special effort on that day. So successful had he been that Maeve had been perilously close to succumbing; then, barely in the nick of time, she had remembered her father and Frank Skeffington's Crime, and withdrawn in something very close to panic. Skeffington, not unaccustomed to startled flights of this kind, had been amused; so, to a lesser degree, had Adam; but Maeve, when she later reflected upon the encounter, decided that she rather held his charm against Skeffington as an extra piece of sinister equipment about which she had not been warned, and for which she had not been prepared.

Now, beneath the polite surface of her husband's comment, she thought she detected the note of doubt; she said stubbornly, "Daddy's very good about things like elections." She regarded her husband for a moment, then, reproachfully, she said, "You don't believe him, do you?"

"About Uncle Frank being defeated? Well, it's a pretty doubtful article of faith, isn't it?" he said. "Even coming from your father." Scrupulously, he avoided irony in the final words. From the earliest days of his courtship, more than two years before, he had accurately assessed the strength of the bonds between Maeve and her father; he had decided upon a rule of prudence in the interest of domestic harmony. This rule, if formulated, would have read as a warning to himself: *No Frontal Assaults on Daddy*. At least, he thought, not yet. Still, the temptation was often hard to resist; it was really extraordinary, he reflected, how perpetually provocative his father-in-law could be. Even the mildest of his dicta, delivered in that nasal, all-knowing voice, could be relied upon to stir Adam from inertia into belligerent if unspoken opposition. Indeed, looking back on it, Adam was sure that when he had returned to this city, after his absence of so many years, it had been Roger's smug, unflagging attacks upon Skeffington that had left him determined to know and to like this uncle of whom he had heard so much, but to whom he was literally almost a stranger.

"You see, with all due respect to your father," he said, "there are some fairly good experts working the other side of the street. Or at least so it seems from the talk downtown. They're not all boosters of Uncle Frank by any means, but they think he's going to win."

"I'll bet Daddy's right all the same," she said loyally. Then, suddenly, irrelevantly: "I *hate* politics, I really do. I mean, especially this kind of politics with all those awful men who smile and smoke big cigars and put ads in the papers telling you to vote for them because they used to be altar boys. It's so *cheap!*" The clear young face glowed with indignation as she thought of cheap politicians in general, and of their leader in particular. She said, "Why does he want to run again, anyway? Well, no, I don't mean that, exactly; I guess I know why, but . . ."

Adam chuckled. "All that graft and everything," he said helpfully.

"You see, you're just making a big joke out of it," she said unhappily. "You won't be serious about him. . . . Anyway," she said, suddenly shifting — "will you be mixed up in it?"

He looked up from his coffee, genuinely surprised. "In Uncle Frank's campaign? Not unless we've both lost our minds. For heaven's sake, what put that in your head?"

"Oh, I don't know," she said vaguely. "I mean, you've never been around when he's campaigned before, have you? And I thought that maybe because he's your uncle and everything . . . and anyway," she said triumphantly, "I *know* you're glad he's running."

"Whoa!" said Adam. He put up both hands. "Slow down. Give me a chance to catch up." He spoke good-humoredly, but he felt a touch of the mild exasperation that arose when he heard, in his wife's voice, his father-in-law's convictions. "Let's take one thing at a time. First, I suppose I am glad he's running. He's my uncle, it's his life's work, he's physically fit, and I'm rather against compulsory retirement. Second, although I don't know too much about it, he certainly seems to be better qualified than any of the other candidates; so far as I can make out, everybody takes them as so many jokes. Whatever else Uncle Frank may or may not be, he's no joke; I think even your father would admit that. And finally, as far as my being mixed up in it is concerned, isn't that a little out of the question? In the first place, I don't want to, and in the second, you can bet your bottom dollar Uncle Frank doesn't want it, either. He's a professional politician, honey, and professional politicians don't go around asking their amateur relatives to jump into their campaigns. Not if they want to win, that is." He reached out, took her hands lightly in his, and smiled at her. "That being the case," he said, "can counsel for defense rest?"

She smiled back at him. "I *am* mean," she said, in sudden contrition. "I didn't mean to nag you about your uncle. I'm sorry, darling. Forgiven?"

"Forgiven," he said lightly. "No trouble at all. Now, let's get down to important matters: What's the story on dinner tonight?"

And so, for the time being, both politics and Skeffington were forgotten, as husband and wife discussed, with pleasant anticipation, the evening to come. . . .

Adam went to work. In the corridor leading to his office, he met the managing editor, who raised an imperative hand.

"Half a minute," he said. He was a small, bald, alert man with an enormous nose and a curious snuffling speech. By inclination and training, he had been an accountant; but a deep and ever-growing suspicion of his fellow man had led him naturally into journalism. He snuffled quickly and said, "I see where your uncle is going ahead with it."

"Yes, yes, so I see, Ralph."

The managing editor uttered a sharp barking sound which might have been a laugh. "You know what?" he said. "He's going to get his ay double ess beaten off this time, my friend."

"That could be, I suppose," Adam said. "I'm not sure he'd agree with you, though. He says he's going to win, and he isn't such a bad prophet, is he? At least he hasn't been in the past; he really has won most of the time."

Again the bark, closely followed by the snuffle. "Every old horse goes to the well once too often," he said. "This is it for your uncle, my friend. He might as well save himself the expense and head for pasture right now. You'll see."

The two men parted, then Adam was halted once more, this time on a note of economics rather than politics.

"Half a minute," the managing editor said, frowning. "Someone's always leaving the light on in your office. After you've gone home for the night. I walk around the building night after night and I come to your office and the lights are still on with no one there. Who's responsible for leaving those lights on?"

"I don't know, Ralph; I've never thought about it. Either Burbank or myself, I imagine; we're the only ones in there."

"Right!" he said darkly. "Either you or Burbank. You know what that means? It means that either you or Burbank is costing the paper money *unnecessarily*. In the future, watch it!"

Even in a community renowned for the economical character of its journalism, this paper was conspicuous for its frugality. The managing editor shook his huge nose at Adam as if to underline the warning, then moved away briskly along the corridor, intent upon his next task. He was bound for the city room: there, in a distant corner, lurked a copy boy whom the managing editor suspected of stealing pencils. Unobtrusively, he would watch him; with luck, he would catch him. Experience had taught the managing editor that it was the little leaks one had to watch: a pencil here, a pencil there, and before one knew it, bankruptcy and The Jews.

Adam went to his office, where he found Burbank already at his desk, reading about Skeffington, a smile of savagery upon his small, faded, effeminate face.

"I'm glad," he said defiantly. "I'm terribly glad. I can't begin to tell you how glad I am. Oh, how those dreadful bastards upstairs will start to squirm now! As a matter of fact, the squirming has begun: I came up on the elevator with our beloved top brass this morning, and you could positively feel the depression, my dear boy!"

He was breathing hard, he was so happy. Adam knew that bad news for the paper could be counted upon to leave Burbank exultant, for he had been with the paper for more than twenty-five years, and had come to regard himself as its chief, indeed its unique, victim. He had started well: he had been successively reporter, city editor, chief columnist and even — for one brief and deliriously happy interlude — theater critic. But this had passed all too abruptly, and quite without warning the period of the long decline had set in and Burbank's hour of glory was over. He had been demoted steadily, becoming in turn high school sports reporter, radio editor, women's correspondence editor, art editor, and now, at last, contest editor. This was the final humiliation, the bottom of the barrel, for while the contest itself was of the greatest importance to the paper, the contest editor was of no importance at all.

The contest was the backbone of the paper; it had been so since before Adam had joined the staff. There had been a time, long ago, when news had been considered as the prime ingredient, but for years now it had been felt that to base a newspaper on so capricious a prop was a great mistake (for every heartening outbreak of rape and hatchet murders, there were the corresponding intervals of disconcertingly tranquil human behavior); that if steady circulation were to be maintained, a steadying force was needed. Accordingly the contest had come into being, and now each day the paper contained an entry blank of one kind or another to be filled in by the reader and submitted in the hope of eventual reward. In the course of the average year there were actually several contests, one following hard upon the other, and each varying but slightly from its fellows in nature: Fifty Famous Faces, Do You Know Your City? and Scrambled Letters. The duty of the contest editor was to read the mail as it came in, sort it according to geographical origin, and forward it to the judges. It was, in short, a job of purest routine, a job for a file clerk, a job, unfortunately, for Burbank. He resented it bitterly.

He resented it all the more because at one time the contest editor had been a figure of greater dimensions, almost a personality. The position had been occupied by men who had been allowed a certain latitude, who had even been permitted to suggest new contests by way of variation. Burbank's predecessor had been the last of this great line. He had invented a contest called Boys Afloat, aimed at attracting new subscribers through their young: he had encouraged boys under sixteen to build small craft for the purpose of racing in a great Water Derby to be sponsored by the paper. The response had been little short of sensational, and on the day of the Derby the shallow basin of the river had been clogged with a vast assortment of homemade vessels. All of these were hideous; most were leaky; some had capsized in an instant. One small and weeping Armenian boy had been drowned.

The drowning had embarrassed the paper; it contained within it the dangerous potential of the lawsuit. As on all occasions when damages threatened, the paper had gone into a panic of placation. Old Amos Force, the owner and publisher, had made one of his rare sorties into the outside world: he had called upon the bereaved mother in person; he had talked with her and told her that God was Good; he had even given her a pewter medal. (A handsome *memento mori* this, as large as a saucer and embossed with a child's head under which ran the legend A LOVABLE BOY.) The paper's staff poet had written a commemorative song of requiem; to be sung to the tune of "The Rose of Tralee," the words began, "Your city will mourn you, small Mourad Nardesian . . . "

It was loving-kindness, but it was not enough. The paper's worst fears had been realized: *the woman wanted cash*. Shrewd though disconsolate, she had sued, she had won, and — far worse — she had collected. In this endeavor she had been assisted by Frank Skeffington, who, temporarily out of office, had offered his legal services to her. He had spoken, in court, of "cynical barons of the press who, no longer content with the mere assassination of character, now work their evil will upon the lives of our young!" He had spoken, apparently, more in sorrow than in anger; it had been most effective.

From start to finish, Boys Afloat had been an unqualified disaster; unlike Fifty Famous Faces or Scrambled Letters, it had never been repeated. The contest editor had been dismissed, and old Amos Force, wounded, had screamed like a panther and had prescribed the new qualifications for the next contest editor.

"No more creative men!" he had cried. "I don't want anybody in there with ideas or imagination or intelligence. I want a man with *no* ideas, who *doesn't* think. Is that quite clear? What I want is a man to pick up the mail and pass it on. He should be barely literate and that's all. What I want is a dolt. I employ a great many dolts on this paper; find me one of them!"

And so Burbank had been appointed contest editor.

Now he said, "I hope your uncle wins by a fantastic margin. I've always liked him, in a way; it's not just that these dreadful people around here hate him. When I was a reporter he was always extremely courteous to me. He had a certain manner, if you know what I mean."

"I know what you mean, Burbank," Adam said. He had found that most of the reporters who had covered his uncle over the years were apt to like him; even those who did not had at least a grudging regard for him, if only because he was always good copy and so made their work easier.

Burbank reminisced. "I remember him very well from the old days. That was twenty-five years ago, of course," he said, with a touch of bitterness, "when I was just a wee bit more important on this rag. It was during his first term as governor; I used to follow him night and day around the state. As I've never been the meaty, muscular type it was all rather fatiguing, but I can't honestly say that I didn't enjoy it. Because I did; somehow, it was all extremely exhilarating, if you know what I mean. Something was always happening. Your uncle was never really popular in the western part of the state — he belonged to the wrong party, for one thing, and then of course those people out there are absolutely depraved, far worse than anything in the South: all inbred, you know, from living together for centuries in those hills — so it was all most amusing and sometimes quite violent. In his younger days your uncle could play very rough, my dear boy. Oh yes indeed! With all that charm and that mellow voice there were always those two extremely hard fists. I remember one night at a rally in Derrford when the home folks and their lawfully constituted authorities were giving your uncle just a *teensy-weensy* bad time of it; before the evening was over your uncle had broken the chief of police's nose and had run his hat up to the top of a flagpole. There was very nearly a great scandal, but by the time tempers had cooled and certain *quite* necessary sums had been distributed, it was all very difficult to prove anything. Or at least to prove it in print, which was what we were interested in. Oh yes, my dear boy, I remember your uncle vividly. I wonder if he'd remember me? Even in my fallen state?"

"I'm sure he'd have no trouble at all. You're rather a memorable figure, you know, Burbank."

"You think so? I'm sure you don't, but how nice to say so, anyway. However, your uncle just might remember me at that. I like to think there was a certain mutual respect existing between us. He was obviously so many cuts above that dreary gang of anthropoids at the State House, and I flatter myself that I did stand out rather clearly among my brother journalists, even to the casual eye. For one thing, I had the positive *temerity* to appear in public with creased trousers. This, I can assure you, struck my dear colleagues as the unforgivable affront. However, your uncle was always something of a fashion plate, and every once in a while he'd come over to me and exchange a few words on the niceties of costume. Our clothing created a surface bond, if you know what I mean." He looked at Adam with a sudden slyness in his light eyes. "Which was, of course," he said, "nothing compared to the bond that arose later. When I wrote the article, I mean. The one that libeled him."

It was an unexpected piece of information and Adam looked up, startled; at no time previously in their association had Burbank hinted at having played a part in those ancient battles between Skeffington and the paper. Burbank observed this reaction with some complacency; he gave a dry little chuckle. "You never knew, did you?" he said. "No. Not many would suspect that the fallen Burbank was once a hatchet man. But he was, my dear boy, and his little hatchet once chopped away at your uncle. And that is why the dear man does owe a very great deal to me: forty-five thousand dollars, to be exact. That was the sum finally awarded him."

Was it the truth, Adam wondered, or was Burbank merely embroidering upon the past? He said, "Fill in some of the details, will you, Burbank? I know very little about the history of these things. For example, weren't there two separate suits?"

He nodded. "One was long before my time. Just at the start of your uncle's career, I should say. I really can't remember much about it; it was settled out of court, and I don't believe he got too much out of it in the way of money. Not nearly so much as with my piece. Still, he *did* get reams of publicity—very important to the rising young politician—and he *did* nick the paper in the pocketbook, where, I need not tell you, every nick is a mortal wound. Apparently they were just as cheap then, my dear boy, as they are now. Have they spoken to you about our collective crime, by the way? Our failure to turn off the lights?"

"Yes. Go on with your story."

"*I* intend," he said proudly, "to leave our little office a blaze of electricity, every night from now on. If they say anything to me I propose to blame it on either you or the scrubwomen. You have such broad shoulders, my dear boy, and the scrubwomen, being Polish, are used to being abused." He whinnied happily. "Anyway, fifteen years later there was the second suit; and that, my dear boy, is where I came in. That one, I'm happy to say, really hurt. You see by that time your uncle was mayor again, and our Mr. Force — somewhat younger then, to be sure, but in every other way quite the same miserable, vindictive, bastardly figure that we know and love today — had determined to 'get' him. At the time, the city was building roads all over the place; and there had been a little matter of a few hundred tons of traprock sold to the city at an exorbitant figure. A few very unkind people suggested that the real owner of the traprock prior to the sale had not been the little Portuguese whose name was on the contract, but had been none other than — guess who? Your dear uncle himself! Can you imagine that?"

Adam said nothing; Burbank continued:

"Well, Mr. Force decided to make an issue of it, and I must say that he finally gathered a great pile of rather impressive evidence, which he then turned over to me to handle in my own inimitable waspish style. The object was, you see, to send your dear uncle to the *clink* for the rest of his natural life. If I do say so myself, the story was extremely well written — and even, I thought, quite convincing; unfortunately, some months later a nasty old man in a judge's robes decided it wasn't quite convincing enough, and ordered the paper to pay damages. They appealed, of course, but that was no good; in the end they had to pay up. I remember that your uncle made quite a ceremony out of receiving the money on the front steps of City Hall; he even delivered a most entertaining little speech, explaining that a part of the money would go towards the painting of an enormous portrait of Mr. Force." Once more Burbank whinnied in reminiscent pleasure. "One of the reporters asked him what he intended to do with the portrait and I remember your dear uncle's reply. 'It will be mounted in the center of Municipal Park,' he said, 'there to be used as a dart board by the underprivileged children of the community!' "

He sighed. "Of course, my dear boy, the story has its humorous overtones, but you must realize that that was the beginning of the end for me on this paper. To be perfectly fair about it, *I* wasn't to blame. *I* hadn't originated the grand exposé; *I* hadn't dug up all the evidence which wasn't quite good enough. All I had done was to work with the materials given me. It was hardly *my* fault that they couldn't do the job. But someone had to be blamed, and I was the logical choice: after all, I *did* wear creased trousers, and I could eat a meal without sucking noisily on each tooth. There was the feeling, you see, that I was somehow leading the life of a sybarite while the paper had just lost a hatful. Accordingly I was disciplined. I need not add that the disciplining has continued through the years: my current role as contest editor is a rather compelling reminder that the Forces of this world neither forgive nor forget, especially when they've been touched in the pocketbook. And so you see, my dear boy, why I remember your uncle, and why I think it just barely possible that he may remember me."

He sat crouched behind the huge pile of unopened contest letters, the ever-renewing symbol of his ruin; his faded little face was lit with rare triumph. Clearly, Adam thought, he had enjoyed this recollection of his days of glory — and he had enjoyed too the novelty of an interested audience; normally it was the lot of the contest editor to be heard briefly and with manifest impatience. But now, reminiscing, he had held Adam, and again the question arose: how much was truth, how much invention? Adam rather thought it was the truth; the words had the ring of authenticity, and Burbank had unquestionably spoken with more feeling than was his custom. But parts of it were strange, and he said: "There doesn't seem to be much proportion between the punishment and the crime, does there? I mean, twenty-five years ago there was the old original sin, and today you're the contest editor. Does even Amos Force carry a grudge that long?"

"My dear boy . . ." said Burbank. "Oh, my dear boy! Let me see: you are — how old? Thirty-five?"

"Thirty-three."

"Yes. And you have been a member of our happy little family for how long? About three years, isn't it?"

"Just about, yes."

"Ah. Now *I,*" he said, "am *fifty*-three, and I have been with this paper for more than twenty-five years. So you see I am your senior in experience, both in the ways of the wide and wicked world, and in the ways of our dear little paper. And I can assure you that twenty-five years is a very short time indeed for some people to hold their cherished grudges. According to Mr. Force's standards, my punishment was more than just, it was merciful. Because, you see, I committed a crime for which there is no atonement. I lost him forty-five thousand dollars, or so he chooses to believe, and that's all there is to it. Life is really a very simple proposition, if you care to look at it in the right way."

Poor Burbank, thought Adam; aloud, he said, "What about my uncle? Did he know who wrote the article?"

"Oh yes indeed. Your uncle is an extremely knowledgeable man, dear boy."

"Did you ever see him about it afterwards?"

"No. But then, why should I have? I really don't follow you, my dear boy: what was there to see him about?"

"I'm not exactly sure. I thought that at one time or another you might have run into him and explained the circumstances under which it was written. I rather got the impression that while you wrote the piece under orders, you didn't necessarily believe that he was guilty."

Burbank clucked reprovingly. "Now that I did not say at all. You see, we may have had insufficient evidence to put your dear uncle away — and that, as I say, was definitely *not* my responsibility — but I've always considered him guilty as sin. But then you see I happen not to be a very moral man, and so when he got off scot-free I wasn't in the least disturbed. Your uncle is in many ways a likable and a most engaging man; I've always found him *simpatico,* if you know what I mean. The paper — and our dear Mr. Force — I have never found in the least *simpatico.* So there you are. All of which, however, hasn't for one solitary moment kept me from believing, my dear boy, that your uncle, on and off throughout the years, had been a perfectly outrageous old crook!"

From Burbank this was strong talk. Adam stirred, and Burbank, anticipating rebuttal, hastily raised a forestalling hand.

"Now now," he said. "No outbursts of moral indignation, *if* you please. Just consider, my dear boy: is it really worth your while to get angry at poor old Burbank? What does his opinion matter? Still, you did rather prod him for it, didn't you? And so he gave it to you; isn't that perfectly fair? You understand, of course, that I hold nothing against your uncle; on the contrary I wish him well, especially this November. Of course the paper is hardly disposed to be so generous. At this very moment our loving-kindness friends upstairs are in solemn conclave to discuss their strategy for dealing with him. Will it be the rabbit punch, I wonder, or the knee to the groin? Because, my dear boy, your uncle has cost them money. That's the reason they foam at the mouth whenever his name is mentioned. Not because he happens to be a Democrat while they happen to be Republican. Not even because he's Irish-Catholic while they've been Yankee-Protestant from the beginning. Most people think those are the reasons, but quite definitely, my dear boy, they are not. No indeed. The real reason is deeper, far deeper: *he has cost them money*. For that he must pay with his blood, or at least with a good stiff term in the pokey." The little eyes shot up slyly towards Adam once more. "And isn't it fortunate, my dear boy, that your little job on this paper is *such* a nice one, not even *remotely* connected with editorial policy? Because if it were, your position might become just a *wee* bit untenable, mightn't it? Wouldn't you agree? Or would you?"

It was the sudden flick of malice, but Adam said nothing, for he knew that it meant nothing: it was the breath of a ghost, the weakly venomous echo of the Waspish Burbank, Hatchet Man of Long Ago. The ghost now smiled and rubbed his hands, as if the lengthy tour through memory had left him cheered and warmed.

"Well," he said, "we have had a good talk, haven't we? At least I have; it has been quite a treat for me, a very rare treat indeed. I hope, my dear boy, I haven't bored you too much? No? I'm *so* glad. Burbank the Conversationalist is not in great demand these days. One day, if you happen to think of it, you must mention my name to your uncle. Purely for old times' sake. Because of my present station in life, I think it highly unlikely that our paths will cross again."

"I'm going to see him this afternoon," Adam said. "I'll give him your best, of course. Shall I add, by the way, that you're with him, though convinced of his corruption?"

"By all means, my dear boy, despite that little touch of irony which poor old Burbank is just clever enough to perceive. You'll find, of course, that the qualification will have no effect upon your uncle at all. Not the slightest. Some of his most ardent supporters have been convinced of his corruption for years. And your dear uncle, being the realist that he is, knows all about it and could not care less. A very cynical person might even say that he was far more concerned with their votes than with their convictions. Yes indeed." He sighed and spun around in his chair. "So much for the pleasures of civic affairs," he said, reaching for a letter and slashing it open viciously, "and back to my labors with Scrambled Letters and our charming, unlettered public! Such a pleasure! Such a great, *great* pleasure!"

And Adam, who also had work to do, turned to his own desk, thinking as he did so of this latest chapter in his uncle's extraordinary story, so surprisingly revealed from such an unlikely source. Poor Burbank, he thought again, and then he reflected that on one count, at least, Burbank had been dead right — that of Adam's job. Had it been in the least editorial, had it been even faintly connected with the shaping of public opinion, then, as Burbank had pointed out so maliciously, his position would have been delicate indeed. There would have been talk of divided loyalty — for Adam had discovered that on this paper, as with most organizations which were strong for the minimal salary, much was made of the virtue of loyalty.

As things stood, however, there was no such danger, for his role on the paper was unique in that it required no political attitude whatever. And then he reflected that while this was undoubtedly true, it *did* require work, and work which had to be done this morning. Accordingly he switched on the light, sat down before his desk, and began, with a few tentative pencil strokes, to sketch in the rough outline of his comic strip, Little Simp.

Adam had been drawing Little Simp for more than three years. It had begun as an experiment; it had met with a certain popular response, and then a curious and entirely unlooked-for development had taken place: old Amos Force had liked it. The precise reason for this liking Adam had never been able to learn, for, now in his eighties, Amos Force was crotchety, unpredictable, and suspected of being half mad. Nevertheless, something in the comic strip had appealed to the simple appreciations of this ancient tyrant; he had become a Little Simp enthusiast. This, in turn, had brought to Adam a mild prosperity. Not that Mr. Force himself paid him more money — his enthusiasms seldom led him in this direction — but he had arranged for the syndication of Little Simp in a respectable number of other papers. The arrangement had resulted in an increased income for Adam at no cost to Amos Force; thus for Adam it was a welcome arrangement, and for the paper, the ideal.

Little Simp! The name, Adam reflected, was perhaps the one master stroke of the whole business. It invited sympathy and affection for his little hero by recalling the bitter days when Simp's guardian, Mrs. Snip Snard, cruelly capitalizing on the extraordinary vacuity of his countenance, had dubbed him so ignobly. But Adam had brought his Simp a long way from those derisive beginnings; things had all turned out well. Mrs. Snip Snard was now in prison, a gibbering wreck broken by penitential toil; Little Simp — a small, orphaned boy, round, smooth, relatively easy to draw — cheerfully roamed the far corners of the world, a chipmunk named Daddy perched upon his shoulder.

In the beginning, Adam had been troubled by the selection of the proper pet for his little boy. A dog he regarded as commonplace; a cat, treacherous; a guinea pig, filthy; a parrot, by tradition associated with sailors and all sorts of nautical depravities, as hardly the suitable companion for an innocent. He had settled upon Daddy the chipmunk, a spruce, wise rodent, bright of eye and economical of speech, who said *Chrrk, chrrk.* In moments of acute danger to Little Simp, Daddy said CHRRK!

(There had been a day, early in the life of the comic strip, when Adam had explained the naming of the chipmunk. A kindly old man, in whose house Little Simp had found refuge while escaping from Big Boris, had asked him why he called his chipmunk Daddy. In the final panel of the strip Simp had simply stared out of the window and replied wistfully in the simple patois that had been devised for him:

"Gollicky-Moe, Uncle Dan-Dan," he had said, "I guess it's just mostly cuz he's the only Daddy I ever did know!"

This was considered by many Little Simp fans to be the most affecting panel that Adam had ever drawn.)

In plotting the story of Little Simp, Adam had been from the beginning a traditionalist. Not for him the sudden, improbable leaps into the outrageous; Little Simp adhered to a conservative pattern, one long-established in the world of the comics: the twelve-year-old American child successfully pitted against the powers of international evil. Adam had found, rather to his pleasure, that the problems involved in this special type of art were few, chief among them being that of supplying variety in catastrophe. He was forever faced with the need to destroy in a different yet diverting manner. Guns, knives, and bombs were old-hat, unacceptable weapons for the savage worsting of those who matched wits with Simp. The secret venom which contorted as it killed; the odorless vapor which left its victims slack-jawed and permanently disfigured; the man-eating monkey; the adversary lowered into a tun of sweet, viscous fluid — rather in the manner of a honey-dipped doughnut — then removed and left bound on the sands, to be devoured by giant tropical ants: these were Adam's methods. Unfortunately, no device, however ingenious, could be repeated, for his public was a discriminating one. Any duplication of disaster brought swift letters of indignation and contempt.

For the day-by-day perpetuation of this ridiculous story Adam was very well paid indeed; it was a state of affairs at which he never quite ceased to wonder, but which he accepted without complaint.

At the moment he was working well. Little Simp and Daddy, accompanied by the vagabond poet, Mr. Yeats Keats, were in Argentina; there, in an obscure Buenos Aires café, they had stumbled upon adventure. In this café was a waiter: a short, stocky man with a drawn, hysterical face. He had a comic mustache, and an oddly combed forelock dripped down onto his pale forehead. His speech betrayed his Germanic origin; his manner, for one in humble station, was so imperious as to be astounding; by both his employers and the habitués of the café he was accorded a cringing respect. One night a customer, startled by a peremptory reprimand from this waiter, had leaped to his feet, saluted, and yelled, "*Heil!*" There had been feverish attempts to cover up this monstrous *gaffe,* but Little Simp and his companions, seated at a nearby table, had seen and had tumbled:

SIMP: Gollicky-Moe, Mr. Yeats Keats, you don't s'pose it sure nuff could be . . . ?

YEATS KEATS (tight-lipped): Careful, Simp. Nasty little beggar. Mustn't let him get the wind up. It's my guess we're on to something BIG!

DADDY: CHRRK!

It was an ideal situation, one which easily could be sustained for weeks. Adam drew in Little Simp's eyes: twin circles of unimaginable vacuity. Then the lean, famished poet's profile of Yeats Keats. He had one of the sudden temptations which periodically assailed him while he was engaged in his work: this one was to reduce, almost imperceptibly, the dimensions of Yeats Keats, and to continue doing so day by day; he wondered just how long it would be before the first of the angry letters arrived, complaining that his poet was shrinking. He resisted the temptation.

He worked until shortly after noon, then left for his uncle's office, curious to see what the first post-announcement reaction had been. As he left, he saw that Burbank was still tunneling unhappily through Scrambled Letters, his face set in a mask of unrelieved woe. In response to Adam's farewell he gave only a peevish grumble; the petulant eloquence of two hours before had been drained from him by the relentless tide of idiot correspondence. Burbank at his labors was invariably Burbank tacit; it was precisely this, Adam felt, that lent him his peculiar value as an office companion.

Three

CITY HALL was a lunatic pile of a building: a great, grim, resolutely ugly dust-catcher which had been designed eighty years before by the then mayor, one Clement "Nutsy" McGrath. An ebullient man of antic behavior, he was the only mayor of the city ever to be kicked to death by a camel. This had happened in Egypt; he had paused there while on an ill-advised world tour. Wandering about Cairo, he had encountered his first camel—hitherto, like the roc, a creature of fable to him. This high-spirited and slightly demented man could hardly resist teasing such an odd beast; the response of the camel had been savagely disproportionate, and that had been the end of Nutsy.

It was from this man's unskilled and laboriously drawn plans that the present City Hall had arisen, and for generations it had been decried as the prime eyesore of the community. Despite this, the building had its defenders, and intermittent suggestions that it be razed had met with howls of protest from those who had worked long within it and who, with a certain rude poetic vision, saw in this inefficient, tangled warren the perfect symbol for municipal administration.

It was a noisy and an active place. In its old, high-ceilinged chambers the elected and appointed officials of government slumbered, mused, or conducted the affairs of the city; in this they were guided by the opportunities afforded them and, to a somewhat lesser degree, by the strictures of conscience. Along the endless, outmoded corridors, hard by elevator shafts and water coolers, ranged little bands of political guerillas; having no perceptible tie with the management of the city, they were nevertheless perpetually busy with concerns of their own. Red of face, shrewd of eye, agile of tongue, they continually nodded, winked, and flashed the cabalistic signs of confederacy, all the while regarding one another with a surreptitious if unremitting attention.

Skeffington's offices were on the third floor. Normally well-filled, this morning they were jammed to the doors, for with the announcement of last night the band wagon officially had begun to roll, and the crowd was rushing to get on board. It was a sight familiar to Skeffington; he had seen it often before, this quick parade of the professionals to the post; and as often as he had seen it, he had felt the same undimmed flush of joyous anticipation. Much as he loved to win, he loved the fight to win even more, and in his appraisal of his own strengths he put in first place that of the born campaigner.

This morning, once within the Hall, progress had been slow: there were more well-wishers lining his path from the outer door. He had greeted them all, addressing the majority by name. At length he reached his reception room, where the process was repeated; in addition to the individual greetings, he made a short speech, thanking all those assembled for their anticipated support in the campaign to come. Under cover of the cheers that followed this, he bowed, waved, and disappeared into his office.

Here three men waited for him: his chief secretary, Tom Lacy, and his two principal advisers, Sam Weinberg and old John Gorman.

"Gentlemen," Skeffington said. "A grand day to start the ball rolling. As well as heads. What's on the schedule, Tom?"

"Everything's fairly routine this morning, Governor," Lacy said, planting a small pile of papers upon the great mahogany desk. "These are all for your signature: the notices to all heads of departments about the collection for Tom McCabe's widow, the Easter Proclamation, thank-you letters to the K. of C. and the Polish-American War Veterans. Then there's the press conference, after which you're giving the keys to the city to Fats Citronella. Then lunch with the members of the Highway Safety Committee."

Skeffington held up a hand. "One moment," he said. "A little amplification is required: who in hell is Fats Citronella? And why am I giving him the keys to the city?"

"He's a piano player, Governor. He's coming here this week for an engagement at the Poli, and the theater people were anxious to have him officially welcomed. Cuke Gillen set it up."

"And I agreed?"

"Yes, one day last week; Cuke caught you on the run. Actually," Lacy said, "it may not be bad from the standpoint of publicity. Citronella's apparently quite well known."

"I imagine he is. It's been my experience that most of our great musicians are called Fats."

Lacy smiled. "No, but this one seems to be the latest fad among the teen-agers. He's what they call a bop-musician."

"Better and better," Skeffington said. "A bop-musician. Sam, you're a knowledgeable man. What do you know about bop-musicians?"

"It's nut stuff," Weinberg said, in a hoarse, uninflected voice. He was a small, lumpy man in his fifties, with a gray, slumping, unmistakably Jewish face, and great dull brown eyes, over which heavy lids blinked with a slow regularity, as if responding to some inaudible metronome. Crumpled in the huge leather chair at the far side of the office, he looked as if in the most desperate physical circumstances; in point of fact, he had never known a day's ill-health. Nominally a lawyer, his talents had for years been displayed in neither courtroom nor law office; his place was close by Skeffington, lingering in the background, an alert, tough, unobtrusive wraith, ready to slide out of the shadows and into action upon an instant's notice. Most of Weinberg's associates in the Skeffington camp regarded him with a mixture of deference and active dislike; they found not much in the make-up of this ruthless little cynic to inspire camaraderie. Skeffington, for his part, liked him and considered him an aide of singular value. He respected his knowledge of the minutiae of ward politics, his shrewdness at assessing trends, his ability as a tactician; he was one of the few people to whom Skeffington listened with attention and to whom, indeed, he almost gave his trust.

"Nut stuff," Weinberg repeated. "You know what it is, this bop? A bunch of hopped-up coons in purple suits blowing horns at a mob of high-school nitwits. The kids wear tight pants and run around screaming 'Crazy! Crazy!' "

"Oh, to be a boy again!" Skeffington sighed. "Sam, you're my bridge to the wonderful world of youth. Where does this go on?"

"A couple of joints up by the ball park."

"What kind of joints? Liquor?"

"Yeh, but no dough. The only ones who buy the booze are the musicians and a few clowns who come in to get warm. The kids are all under age. They buy Cokes and hamburgers and yell at each other. I give it six months."

"And I'm to greet the idol of these splendid young people," Skeffington said dryly. "Charming. Still, it's logical enough. A bop-musician: the Lord knows I've given keys to everyone else. Acrobats, aviators, professional wrestlers; I remember that on one occasion I even gave them to a dog."

"A water spaniel," Weinberg said, gloomily reaching into memory, "from Hollywood. An acting dog."

Skeffington nodded. "Trixie the Spaniel. In my opinion one of the most intelligent actresses then residing on the West Coast. She was the property of an avaricious Mexican, whom she subsequently bit; I think the man died. All right, Tom, we'll give the keys to Mr. Citronella. Have the photographers stay around. What time do the reporters get here?"

Lacy looked at his watch. "In about twenty minutes."

"Fine. Then we have time to get down to business." He pushed back his chair and looked steadily at Weinberg and Gorman. "All right," he said. "What do you think?"

Weinberg shrugged slightly. "I think just the way I thought a month, six months ago. It'll be a tough one."

"John?"

Gorman spoke for the first time since Skeffington had entered the office. "I don't know, Frank," he said. "I don't know will it be so tough or not. They've no one good man to beat." He spoke softly, his voice still holding the accents of the Galway of his nativity. He was a tall, superlatively erect old man, seven years older than Skeffington; he had come to his new country as a boy, he had made politics his life, and so conspicuous had been his talents and so assiduous his application that for nearly fifty years he had been a ward boss of unchallenged authority. In all these years this withdrawn, celibate, soft-spoken man had never once held public office, and he had rarely so much as appeared on a public platform; but from a single dusty room in an old waterfront building he had ruled his ward firmly, efficiently, and with an inflexible adherence to the rules of party discipline. It was he who found jobs and homes for the recently arrived, who supplied funds in time of distress, who arranged for hospitalization and the payment of medical bills, who gave the son of the family his start in life and the subsequent necessary pushes up the ladder, who built the playgrounds for the children of this populous district, and who, in these days when the aged, the helpless, and the indigent had come to depend increasingly upon government beneficence, saw to it that the baffling complexity of preliminary paper work was solved and that funds were ultimately secured. He had won for his efforts the devotion and obedience of most who lived within the ward, and this in turn, as it was the largest ward in the city, had given him an extraordinary political significance. Although it was possible for a candidate to be elected to municipal office against Gorman's wishes — it had, indeed, happened, on a few widely separated occasions — it was not easy; all aspiring politicians recognized his immense power, and all, at one time or another, had sued for his favor.

Skeffington had paid tribute to this power when, many years before, he had declared war on the ward bosses.

"They must go, every last one of them!" he had rumbled. "Little men who hold the destinies of thousands within their corrupt hands, minor barons who stand between the citizen and his elected representatives, greedy filters through which everything must pass and be soiled in the process: I intend to get rid of them all!"

No one had doubted that he intended to do just that, for his opposition to the ward bosses was well known. This opposition, despite his frequent pronouncements, was not a moral one, for he did not object to such bossism in principle; it was rather that he considered it to be superfluous, a quite unnecessary intermediary between the voters and himself. He was against the purposeless fragmentation of power, and his aim, like that of Peter the Great when contemplating the position of the boyars, had been essentially a simple one: that of eliminating the middle man. In this, with but a single exception, he had succeeded; the exception had been John Gorman. He had not eliminated

Gorman; he had not even tried. Skeffington was a confident man, but confidence alone had not brought him survival; he was also a practical man who could calculate the odds. Because he was himself of the paternalistic type of political leader, he knew well the fierce loyalties which Gorman commanded, and while he knew that Gorman, unlike himself, was a man of severe limitations, concerned only with his ward and the problems that affected that ward, he knew that in this very narrowness of concern there lay a highly concentrated strength. Skeffington was reasonably certain that in any city-wide struggle for power he could have defeated Gorman easily; a ward campaign, however, conducted in the very homeland of this formidable warrior, was something else again. To have waged it would have amounted to political insanity.

And so, because he was faced with the hard fact of Gorman's position, because he knew that Gorman's ambitions were in no way rival to his own, and because, too, he entertained a warm feeling for the older man (this was an important reason, only slightly less so than the other two), he had not fought him, but had joined him. The two had been allies now for almost four decades; it was an arrangement that had brought profit to them both.

Skeffington said now: "It's true they're in a bad way for candidates. Who *is* their man this time? Here they have all that shining armor left over from the last campaign and no knight to put in it. Charlie McGlinchy's a dying man; he can't run, and I doubt that he would if he could. Frank Collins is their only other bet and he's going to sit this one out."

"He could still come in," Weinberg said. "A tricky guy, that Collins."

"He's out," Skeffington said with finality. "We've reached an understanding, our Attorney General and myself. He wants to be the next Senator and I've promised him our support. Between ourselves, I gained the impression that he'd just as soon be our next mayor, but apparently there's a nigger in the woodpile in the form of the gracious Mrs. Collins. That good lady is tired of being gracious on a local scale: she wants to be gracious in Washington. And so Frank will run for the Senate next year."

"The man's a lunatic," Gorman said. "He can have all the help we'll give him and it'll still do him no good. Even should he get by the primaries they'll murder him upstate."

"Yes," Skeffington said comfortably. "They will indeed. He hasn't a chance; he'll lose and lose badly. He'd be far better off running against me for mayor, the circumstances being what they are. But Mrs. Collins wants to go to Washington. It's a vivid demonstration of what the love of a good woman can do for a man. In the meantime, however, he's out of our race, which leaves us with our present group of opponents. Seven good men and true." He gazed at the typed list he held in his hand. "Not a man among them ever won an election in his life, and Sam is worried about a hard campaign. I wonder why?"

"O.K.," Weinberg said. "So they're all dogs. Who's arguing? All I say is, even a dog can be tough if everybody gets in back of the same dog."

"A consolidation of the ungodly, born of weakness," Skeffington murmured. The possibility seemed to give him pleasure. "Is that what you think will happen, Sam?"

"It figures. What else can they do? You take guys like old man Force, that little ginzo Camaratta, Mother Garvey, even the Better Government League: they're no dopes. They don't want to run these dogs. They know they're dogs; they're only running them because they got nobody else to run. So what happens? One morning somebody gets real smart and says, 'O.K., let's face it: nobody's got nothing. Maybe we got to get together.' So then if they got any brains they get together, they make up their minds which dog is the best dog, and they start to kick him home. And they got plenty of stuff to kick him home with. Namely, the cabbage."

"Ah well," said Gorman, mildly objecting, "there's the possibility, yes, but I don't know as it's much more than that." He sat regarding his colleagues with calm blue eyes; a snowy veteran of every conceivable combination of political circumstance, he did not think highly of this last suggestion.

"It's all very well," he continued, "all this talk about I have nothing, you have nothing, he has nothing, so let's be pals together and maybe we'll grab it all. But I wonder does it work that way? I wonder does a man like Amos Force jump into the same bed with Mother Garvey? And would Mother have him? You don't get a man to go up to another man who's been kicking him in the behind for forty years and say, 'Put your arms around me, I'm your chum today.' Many's the time in the ward and in the city too I've seen the boys all split up and all without a chance to win, and still you couldn't get them to join hands. And that's because no man is willing to give up his enemies unless he's a saint or unless he's sure of the payoff." His pale old lips twitched slightly and he said, "I don't know but what we can eliminate the saints from our discussion here today. As for the payoff, there'd be no payoff unless they won. And together or apart, the man they'd be running against would still be Frank. Would they care to bet too much on that, d'ye think?"

"Nevertheless," Skeffington said, "there remains the possibility." He leaned forward and placed both hands on the desk; the heavy handsome face changed slightly and the deep voice became less casual. Swiftly and unmistakably, Skeffington took charge. The maneuver was accomplished without abruptness; both Weinberg and Gorman saw it as the natural consequence of deliberation, and it occurred to neither to question or resent it.

"I've been thinking about this for some weeks now," Skeffington said, "and it seems to me that Sam is on the right track. Our trouble is that we're operating in an economy of scarcity: we're faced with an acute shortage of opponents. It's always been a truism that there was nothing like having at least two strong opponents with substantial followings. It splits the vote, they knock each other out, and we come in free. This year things seem to be a bit different. To divide the house of the foe you have to have a couple of good dividers: that's what's lacking at the moment."

"A great ad to put in the papers," Weinberg said. "WANTED: *two red-hot candidates to run for mayor.*"

"It's a pity Roosevelt isn't still alive," Skeffington said. "If he were, I might request emergency aid from Washington in the shape of a pair of distinguished rivals. He'd be only too happy to supply them. More than that, he'd supply a few hundred thousand cash just to make sure I was defeated. Franklin was like that to his old friends. But as it is, it looks as though we face a vacuum, and I'm inclined to agree with you, Sam, that our vacuum might just possibly be filled by a single candidate, backed by everybody. That could be dangerous. I don't know that it would be as dangerous as you seem to think, but dangerous enough to warrant our taking a few precautions."

"Ah," said Gorman softly. With one thumb he delicately massaged the polished, almost transparent skin above one cheekbone. "You're sold on this, then, Frank?" he said inquiringly.

"No. I'm sold on nothing yet. Not this early in the campaign. I agree with you, John, when you say that they've never been able to work out a successful coalition in the past. You may even be right in thinking they can't do it now; I must admit I don't quite see Festus passing his days in perfect harmony with the elderly maidens of the Better Government League. Nevertheless it's their best chance whether they take it or not, and I think it might be sensible to assume they'll take it."

Gorman nodded. "They may make the try. I don't think so, but they may. And if they do I don't think it'll amount to damn-all. Still, as you say, there's the possibility, and it's always a good idea to plug up all the holes."

"We might begin by having another look at the field," Skeffington said, examining once more the list of names he held in his hand: CHARLES F. HENNESSEY, ENRICO NUCATOLLA, JAMES NUGENT, FRANCIS X. RYAN, J. J. FARINACCI, KEVIN MCCLUSKEY, WILLARD CHASE. At the last name he chuckled.

"Hope springs eternal in the thin bosom of Willard Chase," he said. "That's the best definition of an optimist I know: the head of the Planned Parenthood Committee running for mayor of this city. An Arab would have a better chance in Tel Aviv. And Charlie Hennessey!"

"He's soft as a grape," Weinberg said, "and getting softer every year. You know what he wears around now? A cap!"

Gorman said: "He's up there in the house by the reservoir, all alone with a couple of dirty old elkhounds and a ton of horse meat in the Deep-Freeze. I know damn well they all eat the same meals. Still, the man's a great talker, you can't take that away from him. Mother of God, what a gas-bag! D'ye mind his speech, Frank, at the dinner for Al Smith back in '27?"

"I do," Skeffington said. "One hour and a quarter without stopping, and all of it mush. I never saw the Happy Warrior unhappier." His eyes lit with reminiscent satisfaction, for while he had worked with and for Smith for a number of years, there had always been a conspicuous lack of warmth between the two men, and when, in the presidential election of 1928, Smith had been defeated, Skeffington, although he had campaigned dutifully in his behalf, had shed no tears.

"Charlie Hennessey," he said again, fondly. The memory of Smith's discomfort bred affection; then too, Charlie was a rival with no hope of success. "Now then," he said — "what about the Italian delegation; Nucatolla and Farinacci? Nucatolla's Camaratta's man: what's he got for support?"

"Only Camaratta's longshoremen," Weinberg said. "The other unions won't touch him with a ten-foot pole. On account of they hate Camaratta."

"Nucatolla's a great lad for playing the Church," Gorman said. "The little lickspittle is always pussyfooting around the ward after Monsignor Tancredi, whispering that what the Church needs is a few more Italians in tall hats marching at the head of the Holy Name parade. The Monsignor agrees with him but can't stand the sight of him, so it does the poor man no good."

"We can count him out, then, if all he's got is Camaratta," Skeffington said. "And while we're at it, let's count Camaratta out, too. For good. I'm tired of him. He's a double-crosser we've put up with for years just because he controlled that longshoreman vote. I've never liked him personally, but more important, I don't think he's as strong as he used to be. He's a nuisance: I say it's high time we froze him out permanently; I think we can do it with very little trouble. Any objections?"

The two men looked at each other, then shook their heads; Skeffington said, "All right then: we're agreed. Now let's take a look at Farinacci. I must say he's a new one on me. Apparently he's a new one on everybody: is it true that he's really a barber?"

"A barber for dames," Weinberg said. "He fixes their hair in a couple of beauty shops he owns."

"J. J. Farinacci," Skeffington said. "He has the courage of youth. I understand he's only a boy."

"Strictly a nut kid. Good-looking, wavy hair, melty eyes, about twenty-nine or thirty. He goes over big with the old dames."

"Too bad it's an election instead of a beauty contest," Skeffington said. "I'm afraid J. J. is in for a disillusioning experience. Where's the money coming from?"

"A buck here, a buck there from the old dames. But mostly it's his own, from the beauty parlors. I told you he was a nut kid. You want to know really how much a nut he is? He went two whole years to a chiropractor college."

"The most dangerous of all opponents," Skeffington said dryly. "An educated man. We'll see if we can't manage to further his education in the months to come. I hope, by the way, that he has the good sense to hold on to those initials. An Italian politician named 'J. J.' — what native Neopolitan heart could fail to respond to that appeal?"

Gorman whispered a little chuckle. "Jay Jay," he said. "Jay Jay Farinacci: oh, there's elegance for you! It's like one of our lads that comes up with the high-class middle name of a sudden. D' ye remember, years back, Frank, E. Claude Monahan?"

Skeffington nodded. "Eddie Monahan. A young man with a bright political future, until one day he decided to become E. Claude Monahan. He began to carry a cane and to bow from the waist. One Thursday night a delegation from the gasworks called on him at his home and found him all alone at the dinner table, wearing a tuxedo while eating corned beef and cabbage. He might just as well have been found going around the city streets with a rose in his teeth; from that moment on he was a dead duck. He had to flee the city; I heard later that he became a garage attendant in the Midwest and died of eating tainted fish. A humbling lesson to us all. Especially to Farinacci. And that leaves us," he said, looking at the list once more, "with three remaining candidates: Nugent, Ryan, and McCluskey. Which one do you like as a spearhead?"

The three men continued their discussion for a very few more minutes; there was the scheduled press conference to be held, and in any case, no progress was to be made in further elimination. Nugent, Ryan, McCluskey: it was agreed that if indeed there were to be a coalition with one of these at its head — and upon this point Gorman continued politely skeptical — then all were equally possible candidates. None was outstanding, and all were similarly qualified for election to the city's highest office; that is to say, all were Democrats, all were Irish, all were Catholics. It was not everything, but it was enough. As to their more special qualifications and comparative strengths, it was impossible to form an estimate at this time. All were relatively unknown and all shared the common disadvantage of political inexperience. Yet this inexperience was not exclusively a disadvantage.

"They have the strength of the stranger," Skeffington said. "They've never taken any pears because they've never been close to the pear tree. Whichever one it is — if it *is* to be one; I grant you that, John — the tactics will be more or less the same; therefore I don't think it matters a great deal which one it is. One of these three: we can forget the others. Meanwhile," he said, rising, "the ball has started to roll; let's keep on pushing it. John, you'll see the precinct captains?"

"I will," Gorman said. "We'll meet tomorrow night at my place."

"Good. Tell them we'll all get together Tuesday night. Sam, I anticipate the usual financial problems; maybe you'd better have preliminary conversations with our friends the contractors this week. All except Teddy Moran and Frank Ruffino; I'll take care of them myself."

Weinberg nodded and said nothing; Skeffington said, "Fine. A good morning's work. Now: any questions? Any difficulties?"

"There's one important thing, Frank," Gorman said. "The housing development in the ward: did you speak to the banks about the money?"

"Yes. Two weeks ago I invited them to submit their bids for loaning the money to the city."

"And . . . ?"

"And," Skeffington said simply, "there were no takers. It appears that we face a conspiracy. They're out to get us by claiming the city is a poor risk under my administration. Not one of them wanted to loan the city a red cent, even for so laudable a purpose. An inhumane group, bankers: ' . . . those whose hearts are dry as summer's dust.' Do you suppose Wordsworth ever had any dealings with the Consolidated Trust?"

"Now this is damn serious, Frank," Gorman said, with some impatience. He liked and admired Skeffington; he had never regretted his association with him; but there were occasional moments when he understood and even sympathized with Mother Garvey's rage at his colleague's affection for the poetic. The elusive reference, the high-flown quotation were all very well when applied to the great, nebulous issues of human rights and administrative conduct; but the matter of the new housing development was serious business: it concerned his ward. He said, "By God, Frank, we need that money."

"You'll get it," Skeffington said. "Don't worry. And you'll get it from a single source. I'm going to see Norman Cass of the Consolidated in the next week or so."

"If he's refused you once he's not likely to change his mind," Gorman said. "I know Cass: he's hard as nails."

"Well, we'll see if we can't soften him up," Skeffington said comfortably. "You'll get your money, John; the development will go up as scheduled. I give you my word. Now, if we're all set, Tom, let's get the gentlemen of the press in here. They're busy men: they have to hurry back to their papers, write their stories, and get out to the saloons. We mustn't keep them waiting."

Weinberg and Gorman left, and as he did, Gorman nodded his satisfaction; faith had vanquished skepticism. The habitual distrust he had of political promises was possible only to one who had lived long with those who made them; it did not extend to the promises of Skeffington. He knew that Skeffington would keep his word to him — although he did not know, nor did he particularly care, precisely how this was to be done — and this certitude was fortified by the further knowledge that it was very much in Skeffington's interest to do so.

Skeffington himself sat back in his chair and awaited, with pleasure, the resumption of the weekly pitched battle with the press. It was the kind of verbal infighting at which he excelled, and the fact that in such jousts his official position gave him something of an advantage did not unduly trouble him. He did not often think of politics in chivalric terms.

Four

ADAM arrived at his uncle's office as the press conference was concluding. The outer office was still full; most of those present were strangers to Adam, but some he knew at least by sight, others by name. He had no great acquaintance with any of his uncle's political associates, but because on occasion he had visited this office, because some or all of these familiars were usually on hand, and because he was his uncle's nephew, he had come to be known to them.

Adam had decided some time ago that these men fitted into two principal and rather obvious groups. There were first of all the professional politicians, the men who worked at the job of politics and produced, the men who spent their every day in watchful surveillance of the specific areas entrusted to them: the districts, the wards, each with its special and highly localized problems, each with its own ethnic base. Adam had gathered that these were the workers, the men of widely varying capacities and influence upon whose labors within the party Skeffington ultimately depended.

And then there were the drones. There were perhaps a dozen of these: middle-aged to elderly men, who held neither state nor municipal office, who seemed, indeed, to have no regular employment of any kind, but who nevertheless managed to exist and exist rather well; possibly, Adam thought, on some form of private dole supplied by his uncle. What they did for him, what they meant to him, was a mystery to Adam: their function appeared to be that of simply being around. All of them, in one way or another, paid Skeffington the doubtful flattery of imitation: some had chosen to duplicate his formal, old-fashioned style of dress; some the tones and accents of his speech; others his air of courtly benignity. These attempts at duplication were seldom entirely successful, but the total effect was often astonishing:

the sight of Skeffington entering a hall surrounded by his ring of imperfect mimes was not one easily forgotten. They seemed to amuse him, although Adam wondered if often they must not have exasperated him by their very persistence, their unflagging omnipresence, their relentless determination to prove that they were "with him" in every sense of the phrase. Still, he kept them around, and Adam suspected that in some strange way he depended upon them almost as much as he did upon those who toiled.

Workers, drones and total strangers were on hand today; it was the beginning of another campaign from which would come — or so it was profoundly hoped — reward of one kind or another for all. And if the reward were not perpetual, it was the best that could be expected upon this earth. It was a reward good for four years, until the next quadrennial election; no reasonable politician could hope for more.

Adam elbowed his way through the crowd, pushing, occasionally nodding in greeting, all the while making for the door to his uncle's private office. Almost at the door he came upon Ditto Boland, talking impressively to a group who, to judge from their rapt attention to his words, were utter strangers to him. Adam tried to slide by, but Ditto saw and stopped him.

"Ah, good morning to you, Adam," he said. He was a man of extraordinary appearance: enormously fat, with a wide, wrestler's neck and a tiny head. Because, more completely than any of his colleagues, he had patterned himself after Skeffington — in all aspects the master had been aped: the dress, the speech, the manner — he had come to be known as Ditto. The name, with its implication, seemed to please him; he answered to it readily, and the name with which he had been baptized was unused and in general unknown.

He held Adam firmly by the arm. "I'd like you to meet these good people, Adam," he said. In the hearty, important tones, issuing so strangely from the miniature head, every word rang with a fruity pomposity. "They are some of the excellent people who listened to the Governor's stirring address as of per last night at the banquet." With his free hand he pointed dramatically at Adam and said loudly, "Adam Caulfield here is the Governor's only nephew, gentlemen. The Governor's only nephew and the son of his only sister, since passed on to her reward. Adam is a splendid young fellow whom the Governor is very fond of. And with every good reason in the world, as I say as one who knows!"

There was a chorus of muttered acknowledgment; Adam smiled, nodded, and tried not to look foolish. He smiled rapidly and tried to edge away, but Ditto held on.

"All these good people, Adam, every blessed last one of them are 100 per cent behind the Governor. Even before the stirring address at the banquet. They have been great admirers of his grand qualities for years. They kindly came in this morning to pay him their heartfelt and wholehearted respects, as we say. I have explained to them that the Governor is naturally a very busy man with the affairs of state this morning, and so I have volunteered to pass on to him these heartfelt respects *personally*. Adam, this is Mr. Casimir Kowalski, a loyal tire dealer of the West End. And this is his handsome son Jules, also in the tire game."

The handsome son coughed nervously. "Jul*ius*," he said, and supplied a burst of immoderate laughter. "I mean, it's all right the way you say it, but the name is really Jul*ius*, I mean."

"I stand corrected, as we say," Ditto said. He rocked back and forth like some mountainous, balanced toy; geniality shone forth from the tiny head in the form of a capsule smile. "Jul*ius* Kowalski, of course. The name slipped my mind but only for the moment. It's a busy morning. That's a grand name you have there, my boy. Julius. He was no doubt named for one of the many Polish heroes, Mr. Kowalski?"

Mr. Casimir Kowalski cleared his throat and said, "I dunno. The old lady named him for his uncle."

"A grand people, the Poles," Ditto said, smiling at him. "A grand, grand people. They make grand citizens. I have always said that the Poles were some of our grandest citizens and always very loyal to the Governor. Every spring the Governor and I go down to the river and the Governor personally throws a beautiful wreath on the water in honor of that grand Polish hero Pilsudski."

Adam said, "If you'll excuse me . . ."

"One single minute more, Adam. I want you to meet *all* these good people." Recalled to duty, Ditto hurried through the remaining introductions. "This here is Mr. John Shanahan, also of the West End. And this is Mr. Danny Walsh and his brother Martin, and here is a most remarkable thing about these two gentlemen: they are related by marriage to Clam Carey of the South Side! Of course you met and knew the famous Clam, Adam?"

"The name," said Adam, "seems familiar, but . . . "

"The famous officer of the law," said Ditto, "who caught the Murphy brothers building cut-rate caskets that the bottoms would sometimes fall out of. As the body was being carried up the church steps by the bearers there was always the chance that the departed would come sliding out from beneath. I remember one time I had the honor to represent the Governor at Little Jim Callahan's funeral when it happened. I felt the casket getting lighter by the minute and when I looked down *lo and behold* there was Little Jim, slipping out through the end! He went rolling down the steps before any of us could stop him and wound up under a policeman's horse. That was the sort of thing that would happen with a Murphy Brothers' casket. They always hated the Governor, by the way, and it was nobody else but Clam Carey who put them where they belonged. In durance vile, as we say. Clam, Adam, is now unfortunately deceased himself."

"He died after eatin' a bad clam," Danny Walsh volunteered. "He was always very fond of clams, Clam was."

"A credit to his people and to the police force as well," Ditto said. "Yes, yes. Now this last good man you'll have the privilege of meeting, Adam, is none other than Mr. Thomas Jefferson, who was named after one of our great Presidents of the United States, and who will gladly tell one and all between now and Election Day just how he feels about the Governor. Right, Thomas?"

Mr. Thomas Jefferson was a Negro. "I am happy to announce that I stand foursquare behind the administration of Governor Frank Skeffington!" he said loudly. "And why? Because he has always been a great friend to my unhappy people! Who has been responsible for better housing for them? Governor Skeffington! Who has given them conditions whereby they are able to live better than the beasts of the fields? Governor Skeffington! Who — "

"That's fine, Thomas," Ditto said, slapping him on the

shoulder. "Save some of that fine spirit for the rallies. There you are, Adam. You heard how one of the leading spokesman for his great race feels about the Governor. The Governor can always count on the support of the grand colored folks who live amongst us. I intend to convey all their good wishes to the Governor personally!"

Adam was at last able to shake hands all round and withdraw; he wondered if the opening of every campaign called forth these specimen voters who seemed to compose a racial spectrum. He had gone perhaps three steps when Ditto caught up with him.

"One second, Adam. One single second. When you see the Governor you might tell him that I'm out here. You might tell him that I'm waiting to say hello on this day of days."

Adam said, "You mean you haven't seen him yet?"

Ditto lifted a pudgy forefinger. "Aha," he said darkly. "The big question is not have I seen him, Adam. The big question is this: *does he know I'm here at all?* I told Tom Lacy to inform him of that fact as soon as he arrived, but I doubt that he did. I doubt it very much. Tom's a good enough man in his way, but on a matter of this kind not a man to be trusted."

Poor Ditto, Adam thought; then, because he rather liked this preposterous man — in addition, he had once or twice used him, thinly disguised, as the model for a comic roustabout in Little Simp — he said soothingly: "I'm sure it's just an oversight. A considerable oversight, to be sure, but one perhaps forgivable in the light of the hectic morning."

"It's very important he understands that I'm here, Adam. Very important for all concerned, including among them Tom Lacy. The Governor's a grand man but he has a terrible temper when things go wrong. I wouldn't be a bit surprised if it didn't go very hard with Tom Lacy when the Governor finds out that I've been kept waiting at the gate, as we say."

"Well, I'll remind him that you're here, Ditto. And now — "

"That's the good lad, Adam. I will appreciate it and so will the Governor. I know the Governor from the ground up, as we say. He doesn't like to have his old friends kept waiting around. Some people will find that out to their unhappy regret. I mention no names. So you can tell him like a good lad, Adam, and tell him too that Ditto is out here waiting on his beck and his call. Until then, I will return to my mingling with the voters."

He went back to his group, and Adam, free at last, walked over and rapped on the private office door. He was admitted by Lacy, who said, with a slight smile: "He'll be a few moments; a ceremony is going on. Come in and watch."

Adam saw that Skeffington was standing in front of the big desk; by his side was a short, suety man with great horn-rimmed glasses, a crew cut, and a sparse goatee. He was clad in sandals and a suit of electric green; one small hand held a golden clarinet, while the other was less exotically occupied in plucking ceaselessly at the seat of his trousers. Opposite the two men the photographers had gathered in a semicircle; Skeffington, a large bronze key in hand, was preparing for the presentation.

"Always a great pleasure to welcome a distinguished musician to our midst. Music hath charms to soothe the savage breast. I would imagine, Mr. Citronella," he said, with the barest flick of a glance in the direction of the photographers, "that you run up against the usual quota of savage breasts in the pursuit of your profession?"

The fat man blinked his eyes, smiled with a cheery vacancy, and uttered a soprano giggle. "Reet!" he said. "*Reep* reet! You are strictly on the obbo-bobbo, Mister Mayor-man! But *real* strictly!"

"Splendid," said Skeffington imperturbably. Turning to the photographers he said, "I hope you're all listening, gentlemen: this is the way our English language is being constantly enriched. And now, Mr. Citronella, I give you the key to our fair city. Let it symbolize for you the entry into both the heart of our community and the affections of our people. I hope your stay here will be a source of mutual pleasure and profit; I hope you will see fit to return often."

Solemnly he awarded the key while flash-bulbs popped; Fats Citronella giggled again and gazed in admiration at the ornate and useless object in his hand.

"Lemme at that *crazy* lock!" he said. "Reet! I thank you one and all. Mister Mayor-man, you are but definitely with it! I mean, you make it!"

"Delighted to hear it," Skeffington said. Easily, naturally, unobtrusively, he placed a hand beneath Citronella's elbow, and together they began to move towards the door. "I understand you have a special appeal to the youth of the country, Mr. Citronella: a veritable Pied Piper in modern dress." Glancing at the gaudy clarinet, he said, "I implore you not to lure our young away with the magic music of your pipes."

A small, sharp-faced man who appeared to be with Citronella said suddenly, "Maybe you should give out with a few fast runs for the Mayor, Fats. A real snappy number. Maybe 'Pollywog Ramble'."

"No, no," Skeffington said. They had reached the door; he opened it. "That's a pleasure I must postpone due to the pressures of a busy schedule. Good-by, Mr. Citronella. Come back again and often. You and your handsome instrument are always welcome to our city."

"Reet!" said Fats Citronella, and gave a final giggle. The door opened wide and he went out, followed by the photographers and the newspapermen. As the door opened, Adam heard the noise of the outer office drop off sharply; he saw the crowd turn as a man in the direction of the partially emerging figure of Skeffington. Obviously they awaited some sign of recognition from this focal point of all their hopes; Adam wondered just what response such a situation demanded: the waving hand, the buoyant hortatory phrase, the lengthy address? Apparently, at this juncture, none of these, for Skeffington simply drew back into his private office without so much as a nod of the head; as the door closed, Adam saw Ditto frantically pushing his way across the room, eager to reach his goal before, once more, it was too late. But it was to no purpose; the door shut tight behind Lacy, and Adam was alone with his uncle. Skeffington pointed to a chair.

"Have a seat," he said. "Rest yourself. Most people seem to need a short rest after witnessing one of our official ceremonies for the first time. How did you like Mr. Citronella?"

"He seemed pretty unbelievable. I don't think I really understood just why he was given the keys to the city."

"A courteous gesture towards the distinguished visitor. A time-hallowed custom," Skeffington said urbanely, "although the word distinguished now takes in somewhat more territory than it did years ago. A necessary concession to the spirit of the times; even the British Government has been forced to give in to it. Their last knight over there was a jockey. Our problem is essentially the same, only instead of handing out knighthoods, we distribute keys. We used to give them to General Pershing, Lindbergh, Gertrude Ederle; now we give them to Fats Citronella. We've lowered our standards. Also," he said, "the quality of our keys. We're distributing a very poor grade of keys these days."

Adam laughed. "I see. Do they open anything at all?"

"Not a blessed thing. If they did we'd all have to head for the hills. I'm perfectly willing to honor our distinguished visitors; it's another thing entirely to trust them." He walked slowly back across the office and settled himself down behind the massive desk; absently he fingered an *objet d'art* of singularly macabre appearance: it was a small skull which seemed to have been converted into an ash tray.

"A recent acquisition," he said, in response to Adam's inquiring glance. "A souvenir sent in by an admirer. Said to be a relic of the first Republican mayor of the city: note the tiny cranial capacity. This place is full of heart-warming legends. But speaking of things that warm the heart, what's the mood in the camp of the enemy this morning? I don't want to tempt you to disloyalty, but how were they taking the good news? Amos was a vision of delight, I imagine?"

"I don't know about Mr. Force; we don't see each other very often. But in general, I think you could say that a certain lack of enthusiasm prevailed."

"I'll bet it did." He chuckled, picturing to himself the ring of glum faces around the editorial conference table. "I really think they felt all along I wasn't going to run. Amos should be rebuked for such groundless optimism; a man of his years should know better."

Adam thought suddenly of Burbank; he said, "Not everyone was unhappy, Uncle Frank. You have at least one ardent supporter down there."

"Oh? Who's that?"

"A man named Burbank. He says that years ago he used to know you quite well."

"Burbank? Not Edgar Burbank?"

"Yes. He wanted me to give you his best wishes for the coming campaign." In the interests of tact, Adam thought it better to omit the codicil to this message. "He didn't seem at all sure that you'd remember him."

"I remember him very well. A dapper man, rather effeminate. A venal little wasp, but on the whole not a bad fellow. I thought he died years ago; he seemed to be the kind of man who would die years ago. You say he's still on the paper?"

"He shares an office with me. He's the contest editor."

"Now that sounds impressive. Is it?"

"Well, not really." Briefly, Adam outlined the history and the present scope of Burbank's job; Skeffington listened quietly, his eyes lit with amusement. When Adam finished he nodded in comprehension.

"Now I understand why the man's so eager to have me win. Amos has been hard on him, and all for a small mistake made years ago."

"The libel suit?"

Skeffington expressed polite surprise. "He told you about that, did he? Yes, the libel suit. I never knew just how responsible Burbank was. In those days he was quite a good political writer; he had all the qualifications: full of innuendo and damaging hints, careless about little things like facts, not too scrupulous. When it came to the article that libeled me I supposed he had no choice in the matter; he wrote what he was told to write. Although," he added, "as I recall it, he seemed to be enjoying himself at the time. But then things went wrong and Amos cast him into outer darkness; Amos doesn't accept his losses with good grace. Especially when I'm the beneficiary. You might tell Burbank that I thank him for his good wishes. Tell him to drop around when he gets the chance and we'll have a drink in memory of happier days. Happier days for him, that is; I've never felt better myself. Don't add that, however; in his present position he might not appreciate it."

"I'll give him the thanks and the invitation, anyway," Adam said. "He's sure to appreciate those; I don't think either comes his way very often these days." Then, on another note, he asked curiously, "Was he right, Uncle Frank, in saying that the libel suit was really behind the paper's attitude towards you?"

Skeffington smiled slightly. "Is that what he said? Well, I think you might say that it was undoubtedly a factor; it didn't exactly put them in my corner."

"Yes, but was it *the* factor? What Burbank seemed to be saying this morning was that in back of everything else, all the other frictions, there was one spot that really did the hurting, and that was the loss of the money."

"I'm not so sure that Burbank is an absolutely reliable guide in these matters," Skeffington said dryly. "You have to remember a couple of things about a man like Burbank. First, if the libel suit was the big factor — which, by the way, it wasn't — it lends Burbank a certain importance, since he had something to do with it. It's been my experience that most newspapermen aren't averse to thinking of themselves as key figures. Second, while he did cover politics around here for a number of years, there's no guarantee that he really understood very much about what he was covering. The fact that he was a newspaperman would suggest that he didn't. It's a point of pride with most of our political journalists that they don't know a great deal about politics; if they did, it would interfere with what I believe they call their 'objective analyses.' The finest example of an objective analyst we've ever had was a reporter named Mulrooney who used to write a City Hall column. He was so objective that he didn't know where City Hall was. That was no handicap, however, as he wrote his column for ten years without ever leaving the house; they used to call him 'Mattress' Mulrooney because it was believed that he never left his bed, either. Towards the end of his career it was rumored that some informer had smuggled in some valuable information to him: facts about the size of the city, who the officials were, how many parties we had, and what year it was. Personally I never believed it; I think Mulrooney remained innocent until the end. It didn't matter. He was widely read and considered one of our leading authorities on municipal administration. I hope, incidentally, you don't think I'm prejudiced against the gentlemen of the Fourth Estate?"

Adam smiled. "I wouldn't say that they were among your favorite people."

"They're not bad fellows," Skeffington said, "but they write. In this city they write mostly about me, and one of the great advantages to reading a story about yourself is that you're in a pretty good position to check on the facts. I must say the most of our journalists don't seem to be too strong on facts; no doubt they have an occupational distrust of them. For example, take this business of the feud between Amos and myself. Burbank explains it on the basis of a lawsuit: that's the part of it he was implicated in, that's the part he knows most about, so naturally it has to be the explanation. And Burbank's fellow experts, most of whom have been trailing me for years, have their own theories: religious differences, racial hatred, party quarrels, even tax abatements — whatever you care to name, they've already named it. Now any numbskull who's been around the city for any length of time knows that all these things have some connection with the problem; they've all added fuel to the flames. But the point is that none of our profound friends have ever chased the story back to the beginning and found out what started the fire in the first place. Multiply this case by fifty or sixty others, and you can see why I have my doubts about Burbank and his colleagues as political seers. Well," he said, gesturing casually with his cigar, "so much for that. All brought on by the mere mention of an old friend's name. I didn't intend to bore you with a political lecture."

"I was far from bored," Adam said. Two thoughts, seemingly unrelated, now suggested themselves to him. It was surely remarkable that Skeffington, on what must have been among the busiest of his days, should have summoned him to the office for a leisurely, entertaining, but politically profitless talk. It was all the more remarkable because it was unprecedented; the two of them, uncle and nephew, were not that close.

Indeed, before Adam had come back to the city, he had known his uncle chiefly as a dimly remembered figure of his boyhood: a man who came to family dinners on an occasional Sunday and holiday. He remembered the big heavy man at the dinner table, his full face fixed in the familiar deadpan expression, while in a soft, musical rumble he told story after story at which the adults — even Adam's father, who had been notably cool towards his wife's older brother — had choked with laughter. Adam, sitting there, had wondered about this man of magic who could make his father laugh out loud.

After these boyhood days, Adam had been at home very little: there had been boarding school, then college, then the war; growing into maturity he had come to know the city only as a base to which he returned periodically for brief, interruptive periods in his normal day-by-day existence; he had come to know his uncle not at all. He continued to hear of him, for if Skeffington's operation was local, his reputation was not. For the most part, Adam had become rather skilled at avoiding the occasions of contention, and if he was not able to consider the assaults upon his uncle with the same equanimity as he was those upon the alien and the unknown — for there was, after all, the family tie, however tenuously held — he found it relatively easy to be noncommittal. In this he had been aided by his uncle's remoteness, plus the fact that he suspected that a good deal of what was said was very probably true.

It was only in recent years that the remoteness had contracted: a tragic circumstance had brought uncle and nephew closer together. During the war Adam's parents had moved to the Middle West, and when the war was over, Adam had followed them. Then had come, with terrifying swiftness, the accident: the skidding crash of automobiles on a rain-soaked highway, the death of both father and mother in a blinding instant. And so Adam, stunned, alone, had come home once more, bringing his parents for the last time back to the city where he and they and their parents in turn had been born, back to the city where he had spent so few of his years, and which he had not thought to see again.

After the funeral, he had decided, quite suddenly, to remain in the city. It was at this time that Skeffington had come forward with an offer of any assistance that he might need. It was scarcely an unprecedented gesture from an uncle to a mourning nephew, but coming as it had, it had touched Adam, and he perceived that the relationship between himself and his uncle had altered, however slightly. But it had stayed at that: there had been no steady burgeoning of familial warmth. The two men saw each other, but not often. Skeffington, an expert in the preservation of relationships, kept the contact with his nephew alive but not intimate. He called him at irregular and widely spaced intervals, and they would meet, usually in the city, for lunch; in the three years following the funeral, Adam had been to his uncle's home but once. At all their meetings, Skeffington behaved with courtesy and great charm; he talked amusingly and with apparent frankness, and Adam found him a tremendously entertaining companion. From each of these infrequent meetings he came away with the conviction that his uncle was both an extraordinary and a complex person, and with a curiosity to know him further. But months would pass before their next meeting; and under the pressure of daily concerns, the conviction grew dimmer and the curiosity weaker, to be brightened and reborn only when he again encountered his uncle.

And now, on two successive days, the very busiest of days, his uncle had asked him to call — it was this uniqueness of procedure that had, a moment ago, given Adam the first of his two simultaneous thoughts. The second was that the subject which his uncle was now discussing was proving to be of unexpected interest; when Skeffington had broken off in his narrative, Adam had felt a sudden impatience, a sense of having been let down unfairly. He said now, "Please go on, Uncle Frank. What *was* the beginning of it all? What did start the fire?"

"A social circumstance," Skeffington said. "Nothing but the plain fact that my mother — and your grandmother — was at one time a maid in his father's house. You know that, I imagine?"

Adam shook his head, then nodded in partial correction. "I knew that Mother's father had died when she was young, and that the family was pretty much up against it. And I knew that grandmother had gone out to work. But I didn't know it was in the Force house."

"The very house Amos lives in today: the ancestral manse. You wouldn't remember Amos's father, of course. Old Caleb Force: he was a banker. Physically he was quite different from his son. Amos always had that long, stringy look, while Caleb was small, almost to the point of being a dwarf. They made an odd pair walking down the street together; I remember someone once said that Amos being Caleb's son was like getting a rat out of a mouse."

Adam smiled. "That someone sounds familiar: it might almost have been you."

"Now that you mention it," Skeffington said, "I believe it might at that. Anyway, the years went by and as they did Caleb kept getting littler; in his final years the man weighed almost nothing at all. For his own good the family eventually had to put him on a leash. You see, he was in the habit of taking a morning walk down by the river, and this got to be dangerous: gusts of wind would blow him into the water, where he'd thrash around, screaming for help. Humanitarian strangers kept pulling him out. The family was sensible enough to realize this kind of luck couldn't possibly last. Sooner or later he'd be blown in and there'd be no one around but people who knew him, and that would be the end of Caleb. So they got him a leash and a male nurse to walk him up and down, and everything worked out fine. It was quite a treat to go down to the river a few years ago and watch the patriarch of one of our first families out for his morning trot. But before this, as I say, your grandmother had gone to work for him as a maid. Not for long, however; she'd been in the house for about a year when old Caleb fired her. For stealing."

Adam was shocked. Nothing in the casual, ironic semifable had prepared him for this blunt denouement. He had never seen his maternal grandmother, who had died before he was born; he knew her only from his mother's stories. She had been, apparently, a slight, pious, overworked woman, affectionate but anxious, a widow with more than her share of the immigrant's burdens and disappointments, who in later years had come with uneasiness and a faint distrust to the softened existence which her son, then on the political rise, had been able to provide for her. Adam rarely thought of this grandmother whom he had never known; when he did, he summoned to mind a dim, almost featureless picture of a good woman, touched with sadness and a mild heroism. That she might also be touched with larceny had never occurred to him, and the news that this monstrous charge had once been made stirred him to indignation.

"Didn't she do anything about it?" he asked. "Even then people must have had a few rights: couldn't she get some kind of redress?"

"Redress is always welcome if you can get it," Skeffington said. "Unfortunately, in your grandmother's case, there was a slight complication. She was guilty." He sat back and watched his nephew's face; what he saw seemed to amuse him. "Comes as a surprise, doesn't it? I wouldn't worry about it, however; your grandmother wasn't much of a hardened criminal. What she did was common practice in those days; you might even say it was a necessity. You have to remember the existing conditions: they weren't exactly all they might have been. Our people were immigrants and they were poor; the men worked on the docks and the women worked in the kitchens. Their employers were naturally eager to help them; they decided they could help them best by keeping them poor, free of the terrible temptations that torment the well-to-do. Maids and cooks were paid next to nothing; when they went home at night to their families, they'd sometimes take a banana or two with them. Everybody did it, everybody knew about it, and I don't imagine anybody thought it was one of the sins that crieth to heaven for vengeance. But Caleb Force was a rich man and rich men don't become rich by giving away bananas, so when your grandmother was apprehended by a loyal butler, leaving the house with a grapefruit and a small jar of jelly, Caleb decided to make an example of her. He did, too. He fired her himself, in front of his family and all the other servants, whom he had thoughtfully summoned for the occasion. He sent her packing, after first reminding her that in addition to being a thief, she was guilty of ingratitude to a fine employer who had used her well. As a Christian gentleman he naturally wanted to be sure she understood the enormity of her offense. As for Amos, he's never been able to forget that the son of the servant who committed this crime against his purse became mayor of his city and governor of his state, and in the course of doing so managed to make life just a little bit more difficult for him. Amos's life hasn't exactly been a bed of pain, but I think I can say with all modesty that it's been considerably more painful than if I hadn't been around. In any case, that's how it all started, and that's why your paper, even today, continues its splendid crusade for better government. Which is to say, government without me. Amos has a long memory, you see. I may add," he said impassively, "that so have I."

Adam was silent. The story of his grandmother's humiliation was a strange and painful one; having heard it, he was somewhat shocked to find himself not thinking of his grandmother at all. He was thinking, instead, of Skeffington, and of the light these revelations had shed upon his activities and possible motivations. For all his easy volubility, Skeffington in past exchanges with his nephew had proved to be rather circumspect on the really personal matters; Adam was oddly pleased and flattered at this unexpected confidence today. And as for the explanation of the beginning of the feud, it was absolutely astonishing.

"Reflecting?" said Skeffington. With an air of regret, he extinguished the cigar in the skull ash tray. "Until tomorrow," he said. "Well, I can hardly blame you for thinking it over. It's a peculiar story; not many people would believe it. On top of everything else it has the disadvantage of being true."

"I'm afraid I wasn't thinking too much about poor Grandmother," Adam confessed. "Which is fairly heartless of me, I suppose, because it must have been dreadful. But somehow I couldn't help thinking that the strangest thing in the whole story is that all this trouble between you and Mr. Force should have begun with such a personal matter. I mean, Mr. Force spends forty years fighting you in public all because, really, a long time ago Grandmother took a jar of jelly from his father's house. Wouldn't you say that was at least a little unusual?"

"You would indeed," Skeffington agreed. "Unless, of course, you happened to be in politics, in which case you wouldn't. Or if you would, you wouldn't be in politics for long. Your friends the journalists are responsible for this curious myth that public men fall out over public issues; I believe it's called division on a matter of principle. It's been my experience that it's just as easy to fall out over who said what to whose wife at a bridge party as over who voted which way on a harbor improvements bill. A good deal easier, in fact; most of our politicians have a sentimental attachment for their wives that they don't have for their civic waterways. Now, this kind of thing is true everywhere in public life — the friends and enemies of the dear departed F.D.R. can testify to that — but it's even truer in this city and with our people; everybody knows everybody else and everybody remembers everything. There are twenty men in that outer office right now who couldn't tell you at the point of a gun where I stood on the matter of low-cost public housing, but every last one of them would know to the day just when I moved from Devaney Street to the Avenue, or what year I took the trip to Bermuda with my mother, or what I said to our beloved Cardinal when he tried to grab a city parking lot as the site for a parochial school gymnasium."

Adam had never before been so aware of the possibilities in these conversational tag-ends thrown out so easily by his uncle; he said, "What *did* you say to the Cardinal? That is," he amended quickly, "if you don't mind telling me." He knew that there was no love lost between the two men.

Skeffington waved a casual hand. "I don't mind a bit," he said, "but we'd better make it another time. It's a long story, and naturally I'd want to do nothing but full justice to a man of His Eminence's stature. Besides," he said, in a tone slightly different, "it's not the main business before the meeting. I asked you to drop around today for a special reason. I have a little proposition to put to you."

A sudden impishness had dictated the use of the word "proposition"; like "deal," it was a word hardly calculated to disarm. He noted with no astonishment and with some secret amusement the quick bend of surprise across his nephew's face, as well as the barest flicker of suspicion. A grand word, he thought, full of unsavory connotations. Especially for the sensitive young men of the new generation who had learned in the classrooms something of the iniquity of their elders. He wondered if this intelligent, agreeable young relative, who had been listening so attentively to him, now suddenly imagined he was about to be offered dubious employment? Or, very possibly, a bribe? He chuckled inwardly, and then, because he was genuinely fond of the boy, and because he had planned this meeting with some care — too much care, indeed, to have risked it by this wayward desire to shock — he set about the task of quick reassurance.

Not, however, before Adam had a chance to say, with a certain wariness, "Proposition, Uncle Frank?"

For, as a matter of fact, Skeffington's reading of his nephew's reaction had been remarkably accurate.

"Proposition," he repeated gravely. "Just a little something I thought might be of some interest to you. Correct me if I'm wrong, but from our talks together, I've gathered that you've never been very much concerned about politics. You wouldn't be what might be called a political man?"

Adam shook his head. "No — "

"I think you're wise," Skeffington said, rather surprisingly. "I wouldn't think it would be too interesting to a young man today. Certainly not as a profession. Long hours, hard work, at the beck and call of every lunatic with a vote in his pocket, and in the end, unless you're lucky, you have a splendid chance of winding up with the assassins on your back and nothing in your purse. I don't say this is necessarily so; I've done fairly well, for example, but there are a number of reasons for that we needn't go into now. Anyway, it's the exception that proves the rule. And of course when I began it was long ago, and the situation around here was a bit different. I had no education to speak of, a good many roads were closed to our people, and politics seemed to be the easiest way out. I can't complain. But today that's all changed, and on the whole I'd say that a young man like yourself is far better off out of it."

"I suppose he is," Adam said, "unless, of course, he has some irresistible itch to get into it. I think I must be immune to that particular itch; at least I can't remember ever having felt it." The conversation had taken a bewildering turn; was it possible that his uncle had brought him here merely to urge him *not* to go into politics?

"Still," Skeffington said, "you'd be surprised how politics seem to fascinate people, people who wouldn't for five minutes actually get into the act themselves. They like it as spectators: it's the greatest spectator sport in the country. People begin as strangers and in a little while they know the names and numbers of all the players; a little while more, and they're telling the coaches how to run things. They wouldn't play the game for ten thousand dollars, but it's great fun to sit in the stands and look on. I must say I can understand how they feel; it *is* exciting to watch."

With a bluntness which rather surprised himself, Adam said, "And are you recommending that I take a seat in the stands, Uncle Frank?"

"I believe I am," Skeffington said imperturbably. "I'm even doing a little better than that: I'm recommending that you take the best seat. Which is another way of saying that I'm inviting you to drop in here at headquarters from time to time during the campaign, just to see how things are moving along."

He proceeded now to speak with a quiet, persuasive eloquence, yet with extreme care — he had no wish to frighten the boy off at the outset.

"You understand, I hope, that when I say drop in to *see,* I mean just that. I'm not inviting you in to play ball with politicians in smoke-filled rooms; to tell you the honest truth I haven't seen a smoke-filled room in years. I think they must have gone out of style. I'm not suggesting that you get mixed up in the campaign in any sense; I can't see how that could possibly benefit you. But what *could* benefit you is simply being an interested spectator during this campaign. And, I may say, rather an unusual spectator. The ordinary procedure is to follow the campaigns in the newspapers, on the radio, or on television; that's all right, but it's a little like looking at the moon through a ten-cent telescope. Still, it's the only kind of view most people get. What I'm offering you is a view that most people *don't* get; what I'm offering is a chance to see the whole shooting match from the inside. All of which brings us to an interesting point." He looked questioningly at Adam. "Why should you want to see it from the inside? Matter of fact, why should you want to see it at all? You've never bothered about politics before; why bother to be even a spectator now?" He lifted an eyebrow and said, "I imagine it's just possible that some of these questions may have occurred to you while I was talking."

"They have," Adam said, smiling slightly. "The trouble is that I don't seem to know many of the answers. Except, of course, the obvious personal one, that you're running and I'd be interested in seeing you win. And naturally I would be."

Skeffington's head dipped appreciatively. "Glad to hear it. I hoped you would be, but I could understand it if it were the other way around. We belong to different generations; we probably have slightly different ideas about the proper approach to politics. Of course there's the fact you're my nephew, but I've never believed that blood ties necessarily have to reach into the voting booth. I always think of Buster Mahoney in this connection. For years Buster was around town running for every office on the books; no matter what he ran for, on the night before the election an ad would appear in all the papers reading, 'Tomorrow I will vote for the opponent of Buster Mahoney.' It was signed, 'Buster Mahoney, Jr.' The boy had a certain sense of family feeling, you see. But anyway — and quite seriously — I do thank you for your support." More briskly he said: "However, I think you have several reasons which are better than the personal one for sitting in on this affair. Actually, you can approach it on a number of levels. First of all, purely as entertainment: a big political campaign, if it's run right, is one of the greatest shows on earth. I think I can promise you that this one will be run right; I think I can also promise that you won't be bored. Secondly, it ought to be interesting for you just to watch the people in action. You don't have to be interested in politics to be interested in the way people tick. And they're apt to tick a little bit differently in an election; something seems to happen to the average member of the body politic when he's being persuaded to cast his vote for what I modestly refer to as the indispensable man. Come along and have a look; you may get a few surprises along the way; I know I always have, and I've been at it a long time. Then too, I should think that the campaign might even have a certain historical interest for you: you'd be watching something that in a few years from now will be as dead as the dodo bird. That's the old-fashioned political campaign. Most of the boys coming along these days stick pretty much to radio and television; it's all nice and easy and streamlined. As for myself, I use all the radio and television I can, but I also go into the wards and speak in the armories and junior high school halls and on street corners. It can be a difficult way of doing things, but it's exciting, it's the way I've always done it, and, what's more, it's usually paid off. I find that to be of some importance. But there's no use kidding ourselves: it's on the way out. People can't be bothered doing things like that any more. . . . I suppose," he said reflectively, "that I'm about the last of the old-style political leaders who's still alive and moving around. All the others are dead or in institutions, held together by adhesive tape, bits of wire and plastic tubes. When I join them, the old campaign will vanish like the Noble Red Man. There simply won't be anybody around who knows how to run one. And, as this may be my last campaign, it may be your last chance to get into the act before it becomes extinct. It's quite an opportunity when you look at it that way, isn't it?"

"It seems to be quite an opportunity when you look at it any way," Adam said, "although, if it's all the same to you, I'd just as soon not look at it in the one-last-chance way." Once or twice before his uncle had mentioned, in the same detached and curiously joyous way, the decline of his contemporaries and his own approaching period of inactivity and eventual demise; Adam was never quite sure whether these words were intended seriously or not. Nevertheless, they managed to leave him feeling slightly uncomfortable, and now he said, "You don't mind if I say that the candidate's appearance defies such gloomy prediction?"

Skeffington chuckled. "I don't mind a bit. Matter of fact, it's good to hear such comforting words. They support my own secret conviction, which is that I'll live to be well over a hundred. As a reward for years of upright service. Still," he said, "you and I are optimists; the insurance people and the doctors, who don't feel exactly the same way about it, aren't. So I like to be prepared. And in any case, all this doesn't change the fact that both the old campaign and myself are at least somewhat on the wane, and that you ought to take a look while the looking's good. Besides which, it all might help you to know a little bit more about the place you live in."

He shifted in his chair; it was a movement dictated by the requirements of physical ease almost as much as by the necessity for glancing unobserved at his watch. He was notoriously unpunctual, and he enjoyed talking to his nephew; still, the day was wearing on, there were people to be seen and things to be done. Accordingly he decided that it was now time for the final stroke, the last persuasive push which should, he thought, do the job. Unless, of course, he had gauged the boy wrongly. It was an error which was possible, but not likely.

"Now look," he said, leaning forward, the deep voice increasing in resonance and conviction, "I'm suggesting this simply for one reason: I think you ought to know something about this city. It's none of my business, of course, but I can't help noticing that any time I talk to you about this place and what went on in the old days, and what still goes on today, you don't exactly turn away. You may not know a great deal about your native city, but I wouldn't mind betting a small sum that it interests you all the same. I can understand that easily enough. I admit to being slightly prejudiced on the subject, since in a way I've had a fair share in making the city what it is, but whatever it is, it's one of a kind. There's nothing like it anywhere else in the country, there never has been anything like it, and when it goes — as I expect it will go in a few short years — there'll never be anything like it again. A good many people will say hooray to that, but I'm not among them. I happen to think it's a grand city; it's fascinated me all my life, and I suppose it always will."

"And I can understand that," Adam said. In these meetings with his uncle, he was always prepared to be entertained, and he was never quite prepared for the occasional shift onto the plane where irony was suddenly abandoned and where, for an instant, genuine feeling came driving into unexpected view. It happened rarely, and always, as now, took Adam by surprise; because he was not an unduly sentimental young man — and because he was, in spite of his affection for his uncle, also just slightly suspicious of him — there arose, at such a moment, in some cool, distant questioning corner of his brain, a doubt. It was a doubt as to the sincerity of the emotion so abruptly if briefly revealed; it was, however, a small doubt and an ungenerous one. Adam balanced it against the vigor, the frankness, the appeal of his uncle's words; he banished it. "It is a fascinating city," he said. "And you're right, of course: it does interest me, the whole extraordinary setup. It must be completely unlike any other American city; in a way, almost a freak."

"It is indeed," Skeffington said, "but a grand freak. Mostly because of the way it grew. It changed overnight, you know. A hundred years ago the loyal sons and daughters of the first white inhabitants went to bed one lovely evening, and by the time they woke up and rubbed their eyes, their charming old city was swollen to three times its size. The savages had arrived. Not the Indians; far worse. It was the Irish. They had arrived and they wanted in. Even worse than that, they got in. The story of how they did may not be a particularly pretty one on either side, but I doubt if anyone would deny that it was exciting and, as I say, unique. Moreover, it's not quite over yet, though we're in the last stages now. For some time something new has been on the horizon: namely, the Italians. But when they take over that will be an entirely different story, and I for one won't be around to see it. I don't imagine," he said thoughtfully, "that it'll be too much fun, anyway."

The words were oddly wistful: it was the recollection of the great unnamed political comedies of the decades gone by, and it was, thought Adam, one of the stars of the show who was remembering. He said, "Still, for a story that's supposedly in its last stages, most of the main characters seem to be on hand. The city must have been kind to its chief *dramatis personae;* most of the people you talk about are still active, aren't they?"

"They are," Skeffington said. "It's a local phenomenon; the good die young here if nowhere else. We have a substantial company of the others still at last-legging it around the course. Amos Force, John Gorman, the Cardinal — I'm not exactly sure, by the way, that His Eminence would appreciate his inclusion in a group of politicians, but I'm inclined to believe he qualifies — Festus Garvey, even your humble servant — we all survive, if not for long. But as long as we do, why, the show goes on, and from it you can get a pretty fair idea of the how and the why of what you see around you today. Which is really why I invite you once more to have a seat and take a look during the next few months. I'm just a little bit serious when I say that it's a chance that may not come again."

"I'd like to," Adam said slowly. "I'd really like to very much."

"Well then," Skeffington said. He spread his hands; it was a gesture indicating that there was no more to be said. "In that case, do so by all means. What is there to hold you back? After all, there's nothing compulsory about it. We don't take attendance and it's not a matter of reporting every hour on the hour. It's entirely up to you. All you have to do is drop in whenever you want to — I'll let you know whenever anything especially worthwhile is due to happen — just to see how things turn out as the weeks go by. I wouldn't think it would interfere with your business or domestic life at all. Naturally, as a reader of your comic strip, I'd hesitate to do the former, and as an admirer of your lovely wife, I couldn't do the latter." He paused, and then said quietly but emphatically, "I should add that I'm not so dense as to be unable to figure out a certain question that may possibly — and understandably — be passing through your mind. I'd just like to make it perfectly clear that this is an offer from me to you, not from the candidate to the voter. In other words, there are no strings attached."

It was as he said: a sincere offer; he intended no strings. At the same time, it was strategically placed in the line of argument, and delivered with skill; and as Skeffington had figured, it did the job. Adam made up his mind.

"I wasn't thinking of strings," he protested. "And thanks again for the offer; I think I'll take you up on it."

Skeffington nodded. "Good enough." That was that, then; he was satisfied. It was what he had hoped for and what, indeed, he had expected, but one could never be sure. "I'm pleased," he said. "Delighted to have you aboard. We'll try to give you a good show; I think you'll enjoy it."

He shifted the conversation into more general terms; the two men talked for a few moments more before Adam rose to go. On his way out he remembered that he had been entrusted with a mission. "Incidentally," he said, "I have a message from your outer office. Ditto Boland asked me to tell you that he was there, ready and waiting."

"Ditto is always ready and waiting," Skeffington said. "The difficulty is to find out what he's ready and waiting for. Whatever it is, I'm afraid he'll have to wait a little longer. So that he won't waste his time, I'll have Tom entrust him with a mission of state.

Down to the drugstore for a box of cigars." He showed Adam to a door other than the one by which he had entered. "A better exit," he said. "The escape hatch through which one avoids the eager electorate."

Adam said, "Good-by, Uncle Frank. And again, thanks. I'll be in soon."

"And often, I trust," Skeffington said. "Or at least, as often as you wish. You won't wear out your welcome. Meanwhile, my very best wishes to your good lady. And will you be seeing your father-in-law soon?"

"Yes, tomorrow night. We're having dinner with him."

"The joys of table," Skeffington said. "He's liable to be a bit dispirited over the news that I'm running again. I'll tell you what: you may have my permission to tell him that I've had a complete physical examination and the result has been disquieting. It's a white lie, of course, but it might serve to brighten up his evening. Good-by again."

It was not until later, after he had left the building, that Adam thought of Maeve, and of her probable reaction to even this loosest of alliances with her old foe. The news of it, he felt certain, would only serve to upset her; therefore he would tell her nothing. It was the simple, the prudent, the *husbandly* solution; having reached it, he returned to the paper in excellent spirits, ready once more for Burbank and for the completion of his daily labors with Little Simp.

At this same moment, Skeffington, at his desk, was dictating memoranda of some confidence to Lacy; he was thinking of the interview just completed, the cause just won. All arguments, he thought, had been advanced, save that which really mattered: the fact that in recent months he had felt the growing desire to have someone of his own family observe him in the conduct of his last campaign. It was perhaps sentimental; it had the advantage of being the kind of sentiment that in no way imperiled his position. And it had to be the boy; apart from him, there was no one left. Except, of course, Francis Jr. At the thought of his son, Skeffington's lips tightened in an unpaternal grimace, and resolutely he put the subject from his mind.

Five

THAT night, all over the city, there were ceremonial gatherings, formal and informal, of varying sizes and tempers, which took note of Frank Skeffington's decision to remain in public life. . . .

In the home of Amos Force, two men sat at table. One was the managing editor of the paper. He had come here in obedience to a summons from his employer; he had come against his will. These compulsory visits to the Force homestead were rare, occurring perhaps twice a year; they sprouted from the singular emergency, and the managing editor feared and hated them. It was not so much the interruption of his own scheduled pleasures that he minded. It was not even the detestable food. It was Amos Force himself.

The managing editor ate with bowed head, his huge nose just inches above his plate; it was an uncomfortable posture but it gave him the illusion of avoiding the full force of his host's table talk. Mr. Force was very tall and very old. He ate rapidly and with enjoyment; as he ate he talked. His voice seemed to originate somewhere high in the back of his long, chalky head, and to emerge, finally, through his nostrils; it was like the ceaseless hum of some articulate bee.

To escape it, the managing editor tried desperately to concentrate upon the plate before him; it was a discouraging alternative. Months had passed since his last visit to this house and the blessed interval had dimmed his memory; the food, he knew, was appalling, but he had forgotten just *how* appalling. Now, face to face with the familiar menu once more, he remembered. There, on his plate, was the piece of codfish: it was dry, it was tasteless, it was inedible. There were the watery canned tomatoes.

There was the small, dull boiled potato. There was the bread but, as before, there was no butter. There was not even margarine. It was a meal fit for the workhouse and the dining companions of Mr. Force. The managing editor was a saving man, but the extreme frugality of his employer's table depressed him. Even I, he thought resentfully, even *I* eat better than this. It was his habit, wherever he ate, to calculate the approximate cost of the meal to the provider; tonight he knew that he was being fed for about twelve cents. It was a dispiriting realization.

The dessert arrived: this too was predictable. It was a pudding: a gluey gelatinous mess that was apparently indigenous to this house; the managing editor had seen it nowhere else.

". . . Good, plain food," Mr. Force was saying. He attacked the pudding voraciously. "Do you find this dessert enjoyable?"

"Very enjoyable, Mr. Force."

"You're quite right, it *is* enjoyable. It is a kind of tapioca pudding, but it is both less expensive and more filling than the regular tapioca. It is not only nourishing, it is faintly laxative as well. . . . I believe that Sidney Rogers has been committed to a mental hospital."

The sudden shift of subject within the monologue did not disconcert the managing editor; he was a veteran of innumerable conversations with his employer. At the paper, however, it was at times possible to escape; here, there was no retreat. And what was worse, it could go on for hours; he wondered again if the old man were really a maniac. Still, one could not count on it . . . there were always those terrifying, brutal, unexpected returns to lucidity. He said, "Ah?"

"One of my oldest friends," Mr. Force whined comfortably. "He tried to buy into my paper ten years ago. I refused to sell him so much as a single share. He was out to ruin me. He knew it and I knew it. Last year the boot was on the other foot. He needed money badly as the result of imprudent investments. He came to me. It was a foolish errand. He knew it and I told him so. It was shortly after that he began to lose his grip. And now apparently he has gone mad. Well well. Poor Sidney . . ."

He talked of world affairs. . . .

"The country is run by madmen. Madmen and Midwesterners.

There is only one solution to our present difficulties and that is the hydrogen bomb. It should be dropped on every major city east of the Iron Curtain tomorrow morning. The utter destruction of the enemy before he becomes the enemy: that is my philosophy. I want more editorials from that point of view."

Mr. Force talked of religion. . . .

"It is the crying need of our time. Our country was built upon religion. I am a deeply religious man, and I expect all my employees to be deeply religious men. There is an enormous lot of nonsense talked about religion. Religion in its highest sense — religion as I have always practiced it — is *brotherly love. . . .*"

He talked of modern medicine. . . .

"I no longer consult doctors. Doctors are a greedy group who have but one target: the rich man. In the past I have gone to doctors and purposely concealed my identity in the hope of escaping a ruinous charge. It was no use. One and all, they can smell out the rich man. And so today I am my own doctor and I have never been in better health. Health is simply a matter of eating the proper foods properly prepared. That is something you should remember for your own protection."

"Certainly, Mr. Force," said the managing editor, dispiritedly. He had been here for almost two hours; he had eaten horrible food; he had listened to the garrulities of a senile tyrant; and he had still received no orders on the only subject of importance. Skeffington's name had not been so much as mentioned. Perhaps it would not be at all. The worst thing was, one never knew. . . .

The two men moved to the library. Here there was a television set.

"This will be quite a treat for you," Mr. Force said, turning on the set.

The entertainment began, and it was now that Mr. Force revealed his softer side. He was like a child, enchanted by everything; the silence for which the managing editor had prayed was broken by little cries of delight: "Ah, see there! Did you see that? *He fell flat on the floor on his behind!* Ah ha ha ha . . . look look look! Oh this is a most amusing man: his name is Berle. He is dressed as a woman — Oh, my gracious! I believe he will be hit in the face with that bag of flour! This will be terribly funny. Watch carefully now. . . . Ah, THERE IT IS!"

After a very long time this comedy came to an end. It was succeeded immediately by a dramatic program, which offered a severely truncated version of *All Quiet on the Western Front.* Mr. Force sat spellbound, his long head bent forward, his mouth slightly open as the old story swirled by. Before such serious endeavor he was less vocal; only occasionally did the managing editor hear the muttered interruptive commentary: "You see this is a story of World War I. You can tell by the uniforms. . . . Now it is beginning to become exciting! The point seems to be that the soldier does not really want to fight at all. . . . We must watch him closely. . . . This is wonderful, truly wonderful. To see this in a theater would cost at least two dollars. And here we are seeing it absolutely free. . . . Ah, this is moving. . . ."

As the show reached its climax Mr. Force became emotionally agitated; when the soldier, reaching for the butterfly, was shot, he wept. When it was over he said, "That was an extremely sad picture. I was quite overcome. Men who are ashamed to show their emotions are indifferent to the fate of others. They have no brotherly love. That is what is necessary in the world today. . . . Ah, what is this we have here?"

The television programs continued. It was one o'clock in the morning before Mr. Force regretfully turned off the set.

"The programs are shut down now," he said irritably. "I don't know why they stop their programs so early. They are fools and idiots with no regard for the pleasures of others. Well, good night. It has been a nice evening out for you, hasn't it?"

"Very nice indeed, thank you, Mr. Force." That was that, then: the old lunatic had completely forgotten the main, indeed the only, purpose of the meeting. The night had been one of purest waste. Exhausted by the evening behind him, depressed by the thought of the long and expensive taxi ride before him, the managing editor shuffled wearily to the door; he was almost out when Mr. Force said sharply, "Now I hope you are clear on the matter of Skeffington. I want no mistakes."

The managing editor looked up quickly, just in time to catch the glint of malicious joy receding from his employer's eye. He knew then that the old man had really forgotten nothing; he had merely been playing another of his cruel and private games. Now the managing editor would have to play too.

"Ah," he said vaguely. "No mistakes. Naturally not, Mr. Force. Just to be sure, I wonder if we might go over it again?"

"Again?" The long horsy face registered mock surprise; it was the face of a *mean* horse, thought the managing editor. "Very well. If it is necessary." The garrulity, the aimlessness of his earlier conversation now suddenly vanished; the tender, emotion-swept Amos Force who had wept over the dying soldier in the film was nowhere in evidence. He said succinctly, "One: We will attack Skeffington every day until further notice in front-page editorials. We will begin with his repudiation by Roosevelt. I will give you the day-by-day procedure tomorrow. I will write the editorials. Two: No pictures of Skeffington are to be allowed in the paper for any reason whatever. Three: A detective is to be assigned to follow the movements of his son constantly. He is an imbecile; there may be indiscretions. Four: Our investigators will instigate an inquiry into Skeffington's income-tax returns from the beginning of his political career. You will get weekly reports from them."

This was an excessively costly business, so costly that it wrenched protest from the managing editor. "You'll remember that this was done twice before, Mr. Force? They were really very thorough but they couldn't turn up anything."

The eyes that had so recently been filled with tears now regarded him bleakly. "They will try again," said Mr. Force. "Five: On Sunday morning the paper will come out in full support of Kevin McCluskey. He is to be our choice for mayor. There will be a general statement of our position. On Monday we will begin his biography; it will run serially for several weeks. It will be warm, appealing. You will assign the reporters who will make it so. This is to be done thoroughly. I want immediate action. I want results."

"McCluskey," the managing editor repeated dully. He knew nothing about him. In some desperation he said, "This general statement of our position: just what *is* our position, Mr. Force?"

"You are losing your mind as well as your memory," Mr. Force said. "It is a sign you are growing old. Not too old for your job, I hope. Naturally our position is one of outright opposition to everything Skeffington stands for. We will say we believe this young man McCluskey to be the best qualified of the candidates opposing Skeffington. The reasons why we believe this we will reveal as we discover them. That will be your business. You will begin by conferring with McCluskey and his associates tomorrow morning." And here Amos Force paused to insert a warmer note: it was his own personal evaluation of the candidate of his choice. "I have talked with him," he said, "briefly. I was not impressed. He seems very little better than the usual lot. He is like the rest: trash from trashy stock. He is unknown. He is ambitious. He may be inoffensive. I suspect he may also be incapable. But since it is impossible in this city to elect a decent sort of person to public office, we must select the best of the trash to support. Therefore we will support McCluskey. Good night. It seems to be raining outside." With rare solicitude, he asked, "You have no raincoat?"

"No, I brought none with me, Mr. Force."

"It is just a short walk down to the gate. Your taxi will be waiting for you there. I do not allow them to drive up to the front of the house. The drivers throw cigars on the lawn. Good night."

And so the managing editor, his coat collar turned up in fragile defiance of the pelting rain, moved off down the sodden drive. Before he reached his taxi, he was very wet indeed.

The Ninth Ward Democratic Club — such was the homogeneous structure of this ward that there was no Ninth Ward Republican Club — was holding its annual Spring Dance. It had been planned months before; that it took place on this night of special significance was one of those gratifying coincidences which, arising as they do from time to time, serve to reassure the wavering politician of the ever-present possibility of Divine intervention. It was a conjunction, moreover, which had swelled attendance beyond all expectation, for with Skeffington's announcement the affair had been given another dimension. Middle-aged men, notorious nondancers, suddenly appeared at the edge of the dance floor, trailing bewildered wives; heavy-footed couples, they trudged around its perimeter, and in their agonizing progress they watched, they talked, they listened. For others, it was a gayer occasion; hundreds of younger couples danced beneath the bunting and the giant floodlit portraits of memorable Democrats: Jefferson, Jackson, Roosevelt, Skeffington. The bar was open; the buffet was formidable. At the end of the great hall sat the orchestra. It was large, it was expert, it was expensive; it played through its repertoire of dance favorites, interrupting only for the periodic insertion of the melodies of racial tribute so necessary to an occasion of this kind. Music strengthened fraternity; in the benign solvent of song, traditional animosities faded. Dr. Joseph Brady sang "My Wild Irish Rose"; Mr. Arthur Piccione sang "O Sole Mio"; the applause for the latter nearly equaled that for the former. It was evidence of the growing tolerance of the Irish; it was even greater evidence of the growing numbers of the Italians. The orchestra leader, in a burst of misplaced enthusiasm, signaled for "Chinatown, My Chinatown." It was a well-intentioned but entirely superfluous gesture; there was not a Chinese vote in the ward.

John Gorman sat on a small chair at the end of the hall opposite the orchestra. This quiet, motionless old man neither ate nor drank; he sat erect, receiving the steady procession of visitors who had been coming to him since the evening began. He was not interested in dancing, but he was greatly interested in the annual Spring Dance; he had, in fact, arranged it. He considered it a grand and useful affair. One got people together dancing and singing and eating and drinking, and sometimes, drugged by good spirits and the temporary feeling of fellowship, they said things and did things and agreed to things which, under more normal circumstances, they would have considered mad. It was politically very valuable. All one had to do was wait, sit tight, and keep one's wits; there was nothing like a nice dance, he often thought, for doing business. He sat and watched the circling couples; he knew all by sight and most by name. The majority of them had been to him for advice or assistance at one time or another; he sometimes felt that before he — or they — were through, they would all have come to him for the same. He did not mind. That was his function, his role in life. He was the ward leader.

Old Molly Riordan came up on him from behind.

"Hello, John," she whispered.

"Hello, Molly."

"A lovely party, isn't it, John?"

"Lovely. Were you dancing, Molly?"

"Ah, who'd dance with an old woman like me, John?"

"The men with sense," he said, and changed the subject. "I don't see Edward."

"*Edward,*" she sighed. "Ah, John, a fine lot Edward cares about his old mother these days, whether she lives or dies!" She went into the familiar story of her martyrdom at the hands of her wastrel son; Gorman attended politely, without interrupting and without listening. He had heard it all before and knew it all by heart; he could do nothing. The boy was a bad lot, always away in Japan or Nebraska or one of those places, and poor Molly was a bit foolish on the subject. But it was his duty to sit and let her have her way. It was no cost to him; if it wasn't Molly, it would be somebody else. At last the tale ended; he could tell by the familiar terminal sigh.

"Ah well, perhaps it's all for the best," she said, without great conviction. After a moment: "It's a lovely party." Then, after another moment, the subject of Skeffington. "You heard about Frank, I s'pose, John?"

"I heard, Molly," he said, without smiling.

"That's grand news now, isn't it? He's the best of them all, John, God love him. There's not a night goes by I don't say a little prayer for him. And as for those dirty little scuts that turn their back on him I hope they all burn in hell. I think they're all Eyetalians. There's a dreadful lot of Eyetalians here tonight, John."

"It's a big party, Molly," he said noncommittally.

"He's the grandest man that ever lived," she said fiercely. "If it wasn't for him and yourself I'd be walking around in my skin and no house to live in, for all my Edward would care. Will he be here tonight, John?"

"He will. A bit later."

"Ah, that's grand. There's months go by I don't see him these days. It's not like when he lived on Devaney Street when the mother was alive. But he's the same grand man all the same and I'll tell him so myself tonight." A few yards away, an old crony signaled to her; she waved back and began to move away. "Good-by for a bit, John," she said.

"Good-by, Molly."

A vote in the pocket for forty years, thought Gorman, watching her go; Skeffington could murder the Pope — or worse, he could even insult Edward — and she'd still be for him. And there were hundreds like her through the ward: it was the hard, untouchable core of his support. Gorman thought of them all with affection: they were good people. He sat, alone for the moment, watching the dancers, listening to the music; it made no more sense to him than the tribal rhythms of the Kikuyus. He did not care much for music: a little waltz now and again, or "The Walls of Limerick" — it was nice, but after all, of no great importance. He sat like this for perhaps forty-five seconds before being touched on the shoulder. He looked up and saw a heavy, laborer's hand, freshly manicured, extending from a handsomely tailored sleeve; it was the hand of Teddy Moran, the contractor. The two men exchanged the greetings of old allies; the bright blue eye of the contractor swept the room professionally.

"A big crowd. Twice as big as last year. You'll have a food bill on your hands for sure. How much, I wonder?" He named a figure and Gorman, with a slight smile, nodded.

"Near enough. A few dollars on the sunny side."

"Who's got the catering?" Moran asked. Details of this kind automatically interested him. "Jack Shea?"

"I split it up this year. Jack Shea for one and then I passed some along to Eddie Macaluso. He's a good lad and a hard worker, and he has all the Italian stuff: the pink cakes and the rainbow cookies and the likes of that. I like to keep everybody happy."

"Why not?" said Moran. "Why not? Listen, John: I was going to drop in on the Governor today but I figured all the clowns would be there hanging around. What time is he coming tonight?"

"In about an hour or so. He wants to see you, Teddy. Will you stay or come back?"

"I'll stay; the wife is with me. We might have a few dances. Pass the word along to the band to play a few fox trots; I can't do this Spanish stuff." He looked around the room again and said, "What's the story on the housing development? I heard today the banks won't come through with the money." As a builder and contractor, Moran had more than the layman's interest in the new project.

"There's been a bit of difficulty," Gorman said. "I wouldn't worry if I were you. We're to get the money from Cass at the Consolidated."

"I tell you what I heard," Moran said. "I heard he turned it down."

"Your hearing's good," Gorman said. "He did. But he'll turn it up again. These big lads change their minds now and again. Frank's to have a little chat with him one day next week."

"Well, Frank's a good talker. Does he say the money's good? For sure?"

"He does."

Moran nodded; as Gorman had been earlier in the day, he was satisfied now. He trusted Skeffington; he was his friend. Equally important — and looking at it more dispassionately — he was his strongest financial backer. Moran had been in politics long enough to imagine Skeffington's breaking a promise; he could not imagine his breaking one either to Gorman or himself. The ties of friendship fortified by finance were too strong. He said, "Good. Well, I'll see him when he gets here. I suppose there's some room where we can have a little quiet conversation."

"There is," Gorman said. "Back of the bandstand." Expressionlessly he added, "They call it the Trophy Room. It's the very same room where the axe fell down from the wall and killed poor Lumps McGuire."

"Better him than me," said Moran sentimentally. "I make it a rule never to turn my back on an axe. And now I'm off to do the light fantastic. Will you send up to those boys, John, and tell them for the love of God to play something that a white man can dance to?"

"I will, Teddy."

For the next half hour, Gorman sat and received those within his ward who, deserting the dance floor for a few moments, came over to pay their respects. All asked after his health; all inquired for Skeffington. One or two brought bits of insignificant information; there was a request for a temporary job; a young man presented his newly acquired fiancée. None of it vastly important, but all of it listened to with steady courtesy: one could never tell, after all, what might not one day come to be important. It was towards the end of this half hour that Camaratta approached him. Gorman had seen him come into the hall, accompanied by several colleagues; he had expected the visit.

"Hello, Camaratta," he said politely. This was the enemy; it was a fact, but it was not sufficient to move Gorman from the paths of normal behavior. The luxury of open hostility he regarded as being ultimately pointless.

"Hullo, John," Camaratta said. One large, dull-brown eye closed in a comradely wink. "Howsa boy?" Like Moran, he paused to gaze in appraisal around the hall. "You got yourself a real wing-ding here tonight, pal. You got yourself a sweetheart of a grocery tab, too." Without waiting for an answer, he named a sum almost identical to that named by Moran, but now Gorman slowly shook his head.

"A bad guess, Camaratta," he said. "You're miles off." One did not unnecessarily allow even token satisfaction to the enemy, and in any event, Gorman's rule in such situations was short and simple: *Tell them nothing.*

"Yeh?" said Camaratta. He laughed loudly in disbelief. "Well, it don't matter, anyway. It ain't Camaratta's dough. What time does the big fella get here?"

"Ah, that'd be hard to say," Gorman said vaguely. "The man has a busy night ahead of him."

"Sure, sure." Camaratta laughed again. "He's a busy fella. We're all busy fellas these days, hey? He's busy, you're busy, Camaratta's busy. I tell you what, John: maybe sometimes we all get too busy. You know what I mean? Maybe we could do just as good if we ain't so busy. Even the big fella."

He paused but Gorman said nothing; he was listening. Camaratta on The Necessity for Leisure was new; for this reason he suspected it. He felt that something was up. He waited.

"I tell you what, John," Camaratta said. "Maybe he should take some time off for a little talk sometimes. Like tonight, maybe. You know what I mean. So long as I'm here, I figure maybe the both of us could chew the fat a little, hey?"

He's ready to sell out, thought Gorman in surprise. He was not surprised by the duplicity — he had known Camaratta for many years — but by its speed. The candidates had barely had time to declare themselves; it was a record in quick treachery, even for Camaratta. There were other possible interpretations of the clumsily circumspect phrases, but in these matters Gorman trusted absolutely in his instinct, and he had not the slightest doubt of what was happening: Camaratta was about to sell his candidate down the river. Nucatolla's slight, swarthy, foolishly trusting body was even now on the slab, marked ready for delivery; to himself Gorman thoughtfully said: *Enrico, me bucko, out you go.* Precisely what had led up to this betrayal, he did not know; he had heard of no discontent in the Nucatolla camp. Still, there needed to be none; Nucatolla at best had no great strength, and the situation was ripe for the well-known Camaratta double cross. The bay was clogged with the bodies of innocents who had at one time or another put their faith in the laughing promises of this squat manipulator. And now it was Nucatolla's turn. Poor Enrico, thought Gorman; and then, because he was a practical man, he did not waste time in useless pity. Camaratta was here, he was ready to talk business, he could deliver the vote of the longshoremen. This early in the game it was an unexpected development, but one of which advantage might be taken.

"If you want to talk to him, Camaratta," he said, "there's no one to stop you. He'll be here and so will you. If you want to go up to him to pass the time of day, that's up to yourself."

"Sure," Camaratta said. He laughed again. "Like you say, pal: I'll pass the time of day. I tell you what we'll talk about: we'll talk about the weather."

"A nice quiet topic," Gorman said. "And how's your man Nucatolla these days?"

"A sweetheart," Camaratta said instantly. "A big vote-getter, pal. One of the biggest. And a real good boy, too. A sweetheart."

"Almost like a son to you," Gorman suggested.

Camaratta lit a cigar. "Yeh," he said. "That's it. Like a son, pal. So I'll see the big fella when he gets here. So long for now."

"Good-by, Camaratta."

Gorman, for the moment at least, was left alone. He had been thinking quickly; the more he thought, the more promising the outlook became. It was another grand coincidence. Only that morning, Skeffington had announced his decision to end, at long last, Camaratta's political career. It was a decision of which Gorman thoroughly approved, and of which Camaratta was pleasantly unaware. Yet here was the man himself, marching double-time to the hangman,; better than that, he was bringing his own rope. Gorman thought devoutly that it was all very close to being a miracle. He knew that Skeffington, who detested Camaratta, would see him tonight with pleasure; the situation was of the kind in which he rejoiced and in which he was at his best. There would be a few minutes of cordial conversation; then, if all went well, Camaratta, crafty though he was, would be pointed in the direction of the gallows, and in a little while that would be the end of him. And, thought Gorman, good riddance. He was not a vindictive man, and he had no time for the cherishing of personal resentments, but he did not like Camaratta. The man had no word, no word at all. That he was about to be rewarded for his misdeeds at this time was particularly suitable; Gorman had no special feeling for Nucatolla, but the old mother was a decent woman, and the family had been in the ward for years. The poor simpleton deserved to be beaten, but by the usual people and by the usual methods (Gorman had already planned a series of frontal assaults within the ward which would have destroyed him); he did not deserve the poisoned bit of the spider. And so it would all work out very well indeed: one candidate was eliminated from the race; he would be revenged on the man who had betrayed him; and the betrayer would be through forever.

In addition to which, he thought, they might even pick up the longshoremen's vote in the process.

Humming, smiling faintly, he began to beat time to the music with an old, light foot. He did not recognize the song the orchestra was playing; it was not at all important. It was a grand party. . . .

In his palace, situated superbly on a hill just outside the city, the Cardinal was seated in his study, an evening paper in his hand. He was reading; he was frowning; he was not in good temper. The day had been long and tiring and the Cardinal was an old man; too old, he reminded himself wearily, for many more days such as this had been. It had begun impossibly early that morning; after Mass, there had been the radio announcement which had informed him that Skeffington was to run again. Later there had been the courtesy visit of the young German bishop. Another disaster! The young bishop's native courtesy had led him to stay for lunch, a meal which the Cardinal, by preference and custom, usually ate alone; the visitor had talked with a solid, grinding zest of the progress of the Faith in Milwaukee; the Cardinal had been interested, but not for long. There had been the lengthy ride into the country to open officially a new convent for the order of nuns he had recently invited into the diocese; helpless before the overwhelming submissiveness of their gratitude, he had been conducted around the premises on a tour of paralyzing detail. There had been the usual routine matters of diocesan administration. And, at four o'clock, there had been the press conference.

The bumpy, richly veined surface of the Cardinal's round face darkened as he recalled the circumstances surrounding this catastrophe. Through some incredible blunder, the usual seating arrangements for the press had not been carried out; as the Cardinal had entered the reception chamber, he had seen, with horrified eyes, not the sturdy, humble, workaday chairs suitable for such an encounter, but an elegant, fragile semicircle of the ancient pieces he had brought back from Italy twenty years before. Purchased at great cost, imported with loving care, they were chairs for the great occasion. And now they were here — here, for the press! But it had been too late to remedy the error; the newspapermen had come barging in; they had seated themselves. One fat-thighed oaf had plumped down heavily and there had been an immediate sharp sound of splintering. The Cardinal had drawn in his breath in a hiss, and the reporter had looked down, then up, and had smiled the smile of an imbecile.

"Oops!" he had said guiltily.

"Why didn't you bring an axe?" the Cardinal had said icily. The press conference had not gone well.

And now there was Skeffington again. The evening paper carried a full account of his day; there was a large picture of Skeffington presenting the keys of the city to Fats Citronella. The Cardinal read and closed his eyes; he opened them again and was finishing the story when his secretary, Monsignor Killian, entered the study. The Cardinal threw the paper in the wastebasket.

"Only an illiterate can go to bed content these nights," he grumbled. "An illiterate who is also totally deaf. The papers, the radio, the television: all the news seems to be about war or murder or Skeffington. It's scandalous!"

The young Monsignor understood his superior; he knew that the source of immediate irritation had nothing to do with either war or murder. "Until last night I really thought he might not run again, *Eminenza,*" he said. Like the Cardinal, he had been trained in Rome; because of this, and because of the old man's personal fondness for him, he was permitted the familiarity of this form of address.

The Cardinal groaned. "Did you indeed? Then you're by no means as intelligent as some rather simple people seem to believe you are."

The Monsignor smiled. Almost alone among the clergy of the diocese, he was able to discuss, even mildly to dispute, matters with the Cardinal, whom age and sickness and pain had left liable to unpredictable bursts of crankiness. However, he did not at any time push him too far: charity and affection — and prudence — precluded this. He said, "I also thought that even if he did run, he had an excellent chance of being beaten."

The Cardinal waved one swollen, arthritic hand; the big ring on his third finger caught the light and gleamed dully. "And if he has?" he said. "I don't believe it, but if he has, what of it? He's had a lifetime to do his damage, and he's done it. Four years more, one way or the other, won't make the slightest difference. I'm not complaining because he may and probably will govern us for another term; I'm complaining because he was allowed to govern us at all."

"I suppose he came along at the right moment," the Monsignor said thoughtfully. "Just at the time when our people were beginning to flex their muscles and look around for a spokesman. And there was Skeffington, the man for the times. I guess you could say the wrong man."

"I guess you could," the Cardinal said grimly. "A scoundrel from the beginning. It *was* the right time, and our people *did* need somebody. Very well. The same thing was occurring in other cities at just about the same time. In New York, for example. The difference was that in New York they produced Al Smith, while we produced Frank Skeffington. We have been answering for it ever since."

"I remember some years ago doing research for a paper," the Monsignor said, "and coming across some of his speeches when he first became mayor. The funny thing was that I thought they were good speeches. I had the feeling that here was a man of exceptional ability who might really have been something, and that when you thought of what he might have been, his whole story actually became a kind of personal tragedy."

"You had that feeling, did you?" the Cardinal said, in sudden fierce derision. "You now support the Great Man Gone Wrong theory?"

The Monsignor said calmly, "I don't know about the 'great,' *Eminenza*. It's just that he seemed to be head and shoulders above the others at that time, and that he also seemed to have some extremely sound ideas on the management of a city."

"Yes. Which is why this particular city is on the verge of bankruptcy today. We have had your man of exceptional ability to lead us there. I heard only this morning that all the banks have refused to lend the city a comparatively small sum because it is considered such a poor risk. You young people seem to have the most wildly romantic notions about this man: he is supposed to be some sort of wayward giant, a person of charm, cultivation and administrative genius, who has somehow misused his great gifts. All this is nonsense. I've known Frank Skeffington all my life, and he is essentially a mediocre fellow, a cheap buccaneer with a talent for tricking the ignorant. Even leaving everything that is most important to one side, and taking him simply as a working municipal executive, he is haphazard, inefficient and dangerous. I know something about finance," said the Cardinal truthfully, "and I can tell you, Monsignor, that your man of exceptional ability is a financial irresponsible in addition to everything else. Never mind his early speeches; remember that the banks this week refused to lend the money. And if you want to read the record, read the last tax rate for the city. Better still, read the real tax rate instead of the announced one; that will give some idea of the abilities of this peerless executive."

And yet, thought the Monsignor, a record of mismanagement did not necessarily indicate incapacity on the part of the manager; it could just as easily indicate the unscrupulousness of an otherwise able official. The Monsignor was himself inclined towards this view. He felt that the Cardinal, for all his shrewdness, tended to sell Skeffington short; the long decades of cumulative irritations, of personal conflicts, of outrage over the latter's ceaseless maneuvering to use for his own purposes the Church of which the Cardinal was a prince — all these had bred in the Cardinal a contempt so deep and persistent as to forbid objective evaluation. The Monsignor, who had no such personal involvement, felt himself to be capable of greater detachment; Skeffington interested him and held his imagination. He felt, like the Cardinal, that the old politician was surely a scoundrel; but he felt too that he was a man of considerable parts. But now he did not press the point; instead, on another tack, he said: "What really is astonishing is the loyalty he commands. And all in spite of some rather serious scandals. Even when he's lost he's always managed to come through with a tremendous vote."

"You don't shoot Santa Claus," the Cardinal said wearily. "Isn't that what Smith said about Roosevelt? It's much truer of Skeffington. He plays Santa Claus in person every morning in his own home. The people come to him with empty stockings and he fills them: with jobs, dentures, eyeglasses, money — what have you. Every day is Christmas Day at the mayor's house; this good man gives to the needy out of his own pocket. The fact that all these personal gifts ultimately come out of public funds is neither mentioned nor considered. And it's these personal gifts, these favors, that have bribed and bought the people forever. They're good enough people and they're not immoral; they don't even begin to understand what's happened to them. And you can talk from now until doomsday and all they'll understand is that no power on earth — and no scandal, however serious — can turn them against the man who shakes their hand, inquires solicitously for each member of their family by name in that mellow actor's voice, and who does so much for them, day after day, year after year. They say, 'He's one of our own,' " he said bitterly, "and they say it with pride. He's the poor Irish boy who made good and came out of the slums to wear a frock coat and sit in the governor's chair, who puts ten dollars — ostentatiously — in the collection basket at ten o'clock Mass every Sunday, and who personally gives aid and comfort to the needy. They call him," he said with disgust, " 'a grand man.' "

"I don't know him at all," the Monsignor said, with perhaps a faint regret.

"That is your good fortune. I know him very well. And now, with your permission, or even without it, I think we can conclude this discussion. It disturbs me."

"Of course, *Eminenza*."

There was silence. The old Cardinal sat with his eyes closed, his lips slightly parted, his hands folded across the front of his soutane. He might have been napping, for he sometimes now fell off to sleep in an instant. The Monsignor rose and began to arrange the study desk for the next morning; as he worked he thought of the two old antagonists and their feuds of a bygone age. They were feuds now almost over; the Monsignor knew that he would one day inherit their fruits, and there were times — such as now — when he rather wistfully regretted that he had not been present, long years ago, at their beginnings. . . .

In the big frame house by the reservoir, Charlie Hennessey was entertaining Mother Garvey. It was unscheduled entertainment, for Charlie had not expected a visitor; he had been prepared for another of the lonely, lively, bustling evenings that he so enjoyed. He was almost always alone these nights, but he was never lonesome, for he was excellent company for himself, and there was always so much to do, so much to keep up with. Charlie liked to keep up with the latest developments in all fields. He was a sallow, happy tub of a man in his fifties with bulging excited eyes; every night he roamed about his house at a joyous half-trot, whistling loudly and tunelessly. He fed the horsemeat to the hounds, and if he thought of it he fed himself. Sometimes he hurled himself into a chair to read anything that was handy— this was a part of his "keeping up": he subscribed to twenty widely various magazines; he bought, borrowed, and even read bits of the latest books on synthetic fibers, bee breeding, miracle drugs, criminology in the New Japan, packaged waffle mixes— and sometimes he paused to switch on his tape recorder. He would talk into it without hesitation for a half-hour or more and then, returning to it much later in the evening, he would listen with appreciation to the words he had spoken.

"Marvelous, marvelous!" he cried aloud. He did a little skating dance around the room in his enthusiasm, his tartan cap tilted rakishly on his head. "Isn't it marvelous how we can preserve our thoughts for the ages, and all on a little spool of Scotch tape? The books of the future will all be on spools! Marvelous! We're living in an age of miracles!"

Sometimes he turned on the television set; he watched the President of the United States deliver a somber evaluation of the state of the nation, and as he watched he snapped his fingers happily and shouted at the television screen.

"No capacity!" he cried. "No capacity whatsoever! A square peg in a round hole! Great on a parade ground: hup, two three four! Oh, marvelous! But in the White House! Mother of God, save us all from Fort Riley, Kansas! Oh pitiful, pitiful!"

And he whistled again, loudly. Then, his eyes still fixed on the screen, he edged across the room and rather absently retrieved a valuable library book from the mouth of one of the hounds, who had been chewing it for some time.

But tonight Mother Garvey was a visitor, his small, truculent body sunk deep among the dog hairs that covered his chair and, indeed, every piece of furniture in the house. He was a single-minded man and he had come here tonight on a mission, yet the first sight of his host had startled him and momentarily diverted him from his purpose.

He said querulously, "Why the hell d'ye have a thing like that on your head, a man your age? And in the house too!"

Charlie took his cap off and examined it carefully. "You ought to wear one yourself, my dear man," he said, "for reasons of health. It's grand protection against colds; it keeps the temperature even on top of the head, a very vulnerable area. I have the best of recent medical opinion to back me on that. This is a marvelous cap in many ways, a tribute, you might say, to our day and age. What do you suppose it's made out of, my dear man?"

"I don't give a damn if it's made out of peanut butter," Garvey said irritably. "They'll be comin' for you with a net and I won't be the one to blame them. A cap!"

"Dacron!" Charlie said, replacing the cap on his head even more annoyingly: the visor now rested slight above his left ear. "That's what it's made out of, my dear man: *100 per cent Dacron!* Marvelous! I have all the available literature: the best of the new fabrics, the du Pont people down in Wilmington put it out, it's made from lumps of coal. It'll drive the wool people out of business in ten years. Think of the implications of that, my dear man! Put your brain on that for a while! A gigantic industry like the wool industry ruined by a chemist in Delaware! In fifteen years there won't be a sheep left in the country. Eat your lamb chops now while you can, my dear man! We're living in an age of scientific miracles!"

"For the love of God," Garvey said loudly, suddenly remembering his mission. "The whole entire city tied up in knots by the well-known pome reader on the Avenue, and you gas away about caps and lamb chops!"

"My hat's off to the poem reader!" Charlie said. "Oh, he has a grand technique! Marvelous, you can't beat it! A man who never read a poem from start to finish in his whole life, and half the city thinks he's the world's greatest expert on Shakespeare! And the fact of the matter is, my dear man, that he's abysmally ignorant on the subject. Oh, *abysmally!* The man never read a book: the whole thing's a legend. Up to ten years ago he thought that Shakespeare's first name was John! I had to put him straight on that one myself, just so's he wouldn't shame the city. John! Oh, there's no culture there, no culture at all, positively none! But a great technique!" Waving his arms up and down, Charlie slipped into an uncannily accurate reproduction of the famous Skeffington voice. " 'Good morning, ladies. On this lovely spring morning, I awoke to the music of the birds outside my window, and I couldn't help thinking, as I listened, of those magnificent immortal words of the poet who wrote, *Hail to thee, blithe spirit, bird thou never wert . . .* ' And the good women never suspect," said Charlie in his own voice, "that the man himself read the line for the first time half an hour ago on the back of a label for codfish cakes! Or on the side of a breakfast food box. He memorizes them while he eats; I know the man well. Marvelous! He's got them all buffaloed, yourself included, my dear man!"

"For the love of God, will you listen a bit!" Garvey cried, his combative face reddening further. The world's greatest living gas-bag, he thought, and getting worse by the day. But still, a man with a following and a murderer on a public platform, a man who could shout you to death at a rally, and a much better friend than foe. Less aggressively he said: "The pomes have no importance. The point is this, Charlie: Here's the city goin' over the hill to the poorhouse, arse over teakettle, and that dirty devil runnin' for four more years, just to make sure she gets there! And what the hell are we doin' about it? Answer me that! What the hell are we doin' about it while he sticks his big mush in the public trough and says, 'Stand back, nobody gets any o' this but me!' And by God they don't. Nobody else gets so much as a smell, whilst him and his pals is suckin' the city dry. My lovely mother, God have mercy on her soul, sized him up the first time she laid eyes on him. 'Festus, me son,' she said, 'the man's a greedy bastard!' And oh, wasn't she right though? The ma was always right. Here I stand, the man that give him his start, the man's that's give up his whole life to muni*cip*al service, the man that's made a vertible paradise of the whole damn city, the man who put in the Phil J. Rooney Memorial Macadam

Parkway, and today I can hardly get into City Hall to use the toilet! That's what the murderin' scoundrel does to them that helped him! He sits in his easy chair up in the mayor's office, smokin' cigars a foot long, handin' out iron keys that don't open nothin' to coon cornet players, gettin' rich hand over fist, whilst the man who made him what he is has to sneak in the back door to take a free pee! Oh," he shouted, the memory of personal indignities heightening his rage, "I say throw the rascal out of office! That's what's got to be done and what the hell are we doin' about it?"

Charlie examined him critically. "There's a big vein twitching away at the side of your head," he observed. "By the left temple. That could be a bad sign, my dear man. The blood pressure could be up very high, it goes with your age. I tell you what you do: never mind the doctors. Buy yourself a little kit and take your own pressure, that's the thing. Just strap it around your arm and pump it up, and whenever you feel yourself throbbing away like a motorboat tell yourself to calm down. Say prayers, suck on a Life Saver, take a warm bath: anything to keep the pressure under control, my dear man. Otherwise a man your age could pop like a balloon some fine day. Or there's a new drug out the Hindus discovered over in India: they make it out of a poison plant. I read about it the other day. One pill a day and you're in slow motion. I'll get the name of it for you tomorrow."

"Never mind the big veins in my head!" Garvey shouted. "Never mind my blood pressure! I didn't come here for that. For the love of God keep to the point, and the point is this: *Will you or won't you help us to lick that thievin' scoundrel who's gettin' rich on the city and on us all? Will you or won't you, Charlie?"*

"Sense, sense, sense!" Charlie said reprovingly. "Talk nothing but sense, my dear man! I'm surprised at a man like you paying attention to nut rumors! Frank Skeffington a rich man: oh, marvelous! And all nonsense! The man's not rich. He has no money, no money at all. It's all legend. He's stolen millions, but it's gone, all gone, easy come easy go, like slush down a manhole in March! Frank doesn't even want to be rich; he *has* to get rid of the money. It's a common psychological type, my dear man. You read about it all the time in the medical journals. He spends like the King of Armenia and he's the softest touch in the city. There's not a bum in town that doesn't park on his door-step in the morning and whine, 'Help! Help! I'm a dying man!' Now you or I, my dear man, would call the cops and let him die a decent death in a prison, but Frank is always there with the ten-spot. Oh, good-hearted! You have to say that for him. A crook and no culture, never reads a book in spite of what people think, but a grand heart. When he dies he won't have a quarter and the family won't even be able to pay for a casket. I'll have to bury him myself. I'll have to call up the telephone company and say, 'Good morning! This is Charles F. Hennessey. Have you got an old booth about eight feet long and two feet wide that you're not using today? I want to bury the mayor!' Oh, marvel-ous!"

Garvey felt weak. Fury had left him; he was drained of all emotion. It was the way, really, he had expected to feel; it was the way he always felt after the first few minutes with Charlie. He entered always with determination, with a purpose. Then came the anger. Then, floating towards him, came the words, the soft, thick, suffocating mass which moved irresistibly forward, growing ever larger as it moved, the cloud of nerve-gas dropped upon an enemy host to leave it bathed in lassitude and powerless to resist. It was without a doubt the greatest weapon in Charlie's arsenal.

"What the hell," Garvey said weakly. "All right, Charlie. All right. Only one thing, that's all I want to know: *Are you out to lick him?"*

"Of course I'm out to lick him," Charlie said. "Why my dear man, I'm running for mayor myself!"

"Charlie," said Garvey, "you can't win. We know that, the both of us. By God, all things bein' equal and fair bein' fair, you'd be in there come Election Day and I'd be by your side yellin' Hip-hip-hooray! There's no man deserves it more than you, Charlie. But what the hell, with this gang of double-crossin' murderers and their dirty money to buck, you haven't got a Chinaman's chance. The same damn thing will happen as last time and the time before — twenty thousand votes and no more, and what the hell use is that in a city this size? What I come here for tonight, Charlie, was to say: Come in with us. Come and join up with us like the smart man that you are. We'll lick the murderer together, the both of us, and carve him up like a Christmas turkey!"

"Ah my dear man, winning's not everything!" Charlie said. "No no no! The thing is to take the matter to the people, to let them know what's going on, to fight the good fight, to tell the truth! Marvelous! I'll be in my sound-truck on every corner in the city every night of the campaign, lashing away at them all! Skeffington and the rest of them! The big boys against Skeffington are just as bad and worse! I'll stand on the side lines and harass away, harass away! Marvelous! They fear it. They fear it more each year. One man telling the truth to the people! A time-bomb!"

As crazy as a bedbug, thought Garvey morosely, but still, a great man in the corner. Adopting the wheedling tones of diplomacy to which, by nature, he was so astonishingly ill-suited, he said: "But s'pose you could win *too,* Charlie? By bein' the power behind the man who's sure to win! I'm backin' a great lad this time, Charlie. A good, clean-livin' young man after your own heart. A young man, a college graduate, trained by the Jesuit Fathers themselfs. And smart as a whip, Charlie! A leadin' attorney-at-law, a former altar boy in his youth, a World War II vet'ran — by God I don't know but he might of been wounded in action; I see him walkin' with a little limp the other day — a fine family man, and the father of five at the age of thirty-five! And if that ain't enough, he's a handsome lad with a great personality, and he's way up there in both the K. of C. and the Elks! Now what the hell more could you ask of a man, answer me that, Charlie? Our next mayor, sure as God made little apples. Mayor Kevin McCluskey! D'ye happen to know him, Charlie?"

"McCluskey!" said Charlie. "Holy Cross College, Class of 1940. Georgetown University School of Law, Class of 1943. Into the Navy an ensign, out a lieutenant. No wounds, none at all, my dear man! I know all about him. I've made the usual investigation of all the rivals. Oh, thoroughly, my dear man! Very thoroughly. My own system, as good as the F.B.I. McCluskey! A nice pleasant lad, a good Catholic, and no capacity whatsoever! Oh, none at all, the poor boy!"

Garvey stared at him in speechless outrage; Charlie continued. He was slumped low in his chair, and his cap had slipped forward over his eyes. As he talked he snapped his fingers in peppy punctuation.

"Mediocre! Mediocre in school, in college, and in the law school, my dear man! I've seen the records, I've talked with the teachers! Oh, undistinguished! Poor in sports! I've talked to the coaches! Something wrong with the co-ordination: couldn't catch a ball if you threw it right at him! Slow in the reflexes! Slow in body, slow in mind! No capacity! Passed the bar on the strength of being a veteran! Oh, I'll have to tell the people the truth about him on the platform. I'll have to say, 'Dear friends, you're being asked to cast your precious votes for a good-looking youngster with nothing upstairs but a mass of floating custard. You're being asked to put at the switchheads of the city a handsome young fellow who wears hundred-dollar suits, Panama straw hats, and says, 'Pardon-me-Miss-did-I-step-on-your-foot?' at parish dances. Marvelous! Nice manners, dear friends! Nice! But when he adds up two and two he gets five and a half for an answer, and when he sued the city two years ago for Danny Dacey he lost poor Danny the case all because he thought all the banks were closed on Groundhog Day! He thought it was a legal holiday, dear friends! I refer you to the records! Oh, a grand young man, but simple! And last year — ' "

"You silly bastard!" Garvey yelled. He had risen in a fury and was standing over Charlie, screaming down at him. "Nearly sixty years old and sittin' in a chair, dreamin' up dirty fairy-tales about a clean-livin' young man who'll beat your arse off! The trouble with you is you lost all your buttons years ago! You're a loony! I don't know why I ever come out here to talk to the likes of you! You won't be elected garbageman when I'm through with you! Good night and t' hell with you!"

"Watch the pressure," Charlie said warningly. "The big vein is working again, pumping away, pumping away! And don't step on the dog's paw when you go out, my dear man. He sometimes lies in front of the door. And good luck in your campaign. May the best man win. You've got a grand simple boy there, my dear man!"

With a final shout, Garvey was gone; Charlie heard the front door slam. The interview had not left him in any way disturbed; in fact he had already forgotten about Garvey and his candidate, for now that he was alone he suddenly remembered a small experiment that he had intended to conduct earlier in the evening. It was something that he had read about only the day before. He closed his eyes, and breathed evenly, steadily; he placed three fingers of his right hand lightly on the inside surface of his left wrist. He was taking his pulse. Now, quickly, he inhaled deeply and held his breath; instantly the pulse decelerated and with delight he noted that it was fading, fading, almost to nothing at all. It might have been the pulse of a dying man, yet here he was, 100 per cent in the pink of condition. Healthy! The steady diminution of the pulse down to the merest whisper purely by holding the breath. Marvelous! A grand illustration of one of the little tricks the human body plays upon us all! The way the draft-dodgers had fooled the doctors in the last World War . . . He exhaled, breathed normally again, and the pulse returned to its strong, steady beat. Marvelous, marvelous! One more bit of up-to-date knowledge stored away for ready reference, for instantaneous production if and when required. *The pulse was important,* thought Charlie, *oh yes indeed!* He was happy. In his happiness he leaped up, playfully rapped the nearest hound across the muzzle, and made his way with rapid little skating steps across the room to where his tape-recorder lay. At a moment like this, there was only one thing to be done. He picked up the microphone and began to talk, rapidly and without pause; many minutes later he was still talking.

In the handsome eighteenth-century dining room of the city's oldest and proudest club, Nathaniel Gardiner was finishing his dinner. He was a bulky man in his seventies, with a large, pale and faintly freckled face; light gray eyes looked out steadily and pleasantly from behind old, steel-rimmed glasses which seemed slightly too small for the face they fronted. He was dressed neatly in neutral, inexpensive, anonymous clothing, for although he spent annually great sums of money, he spent very little on himself. He was a man of great wealth and even greater social position; he was an exceptionally able attorney; he was something rarer than any of these: he was, genuinely, a philanthropist, almost the last of a remarkable species that had once flourished in the city.

He lived alone now, in a room in the club. He lived so out of choice. His three sons were married and had homes of their own in the suburbs; separately they came in to dine with him every week, not out of a sense of duty, but because they wished to. None of them really quite understood their father, but they loved him, and they knew that he was a remarkable man. They knew, too, that from these weekly meetings came practical advantage, for they silently acknowledged that in the profession which they also had adopted this elderly man of placid appearance was still able to show them the way.

Tonight he was joined by his youngest son. Dinner over, they sat quietly by the tall windows, looking out through the near-darkness of the long August evening into the occasional traffic of the summer streets. The club dining room, at this time of evening and at this time of year, was almost deserted; save for the single old waiter, hovering inconspicuously by the door leading into the kitchen, the two men were alone.

"And now for the sixty-four-dollar question," the son said. He was a dark, lean, brisk young man with the face of a handsome horse. "I meant to ask it as soon as I came in, and then we began to talk about Ted and the Fabricant business. But what about this latest announcement of our esteemed mayor? Did you expect it?"

"Oh yes," Gardiner said calmly. "Yes, I fully expected it. I couldn't quite see Frank Skeffington doing anything else."

"Then you're not too disappointed over last night's developments?"

"I'm not disappointed at all," Gardiner said tranquilly. "I leave that to you young fellows. Are you disappointed, Dan?"

"I'm not overcome, no. But naturally the sooner we can get rid of him the better, and I really thought he just might finally decide to call it a day this time. There seemed to be a few rather definite signs that he would."

"So there were. I'm afraid, however, that they were signs he put up himself." Gardiner laughed gently. "He's a rogue. A complete rogue. And yet the most engaging rogue I've ever met. I admit to having a small soft spot in my heart for our mayor."

"Yes, I know you have." It was one of the strange streaks in his father that the son did not comprehend; he said, "Why? Charity's charity, but can't you push it a little too far?"

"Can you? I suppose you can. In theory, at least; I've never seen anyone who has. However, I wasn't thinking of charity at all in Skeffington's case. Do you know him, Dan? Have you ever met him?"

"No." Then, feeling the admission to be to some extent a damaging one, he added, "But I know all about him."

A fugitive, almost invisible smile wreathed its way across his father's face, but he said merely: "I've known him quite well for many years. And for two years, before you were born, I worked with him rather closely. During the First World War a Citizens' Committee was started and I was its chairman. We had meetings every month with Skeffington, who was mayor then too. I won't say that the arrangement was altogether satisfactory, but it worked out well enough for a bipartisan system. Eventually the inevitable conflicts arose and it was disbanded, but not before I found out quite a lot about Skeffington and even became rather well acquainted with him. He's really a most unusual man. Thanks to him our monthly meetings were considerably brighter than they might otherwise have been."

"The jolly thief," said his son. "Or are you saying, Father, that he wasn't such a thief after all?"

"Oh no. He stole. How much I have no idea; the estimates vary widely. I presume he still does, although I'm not in such close touch with these matters as I used to be."

"But in spite of that, you still have the soft spot?"

Gardiner nodded, smiling at his son. "I do. I hope you realize that doesn't imply an endorsement of his candidacy. Through the years I've been rather consistently opposed to Skeffington. I think I know him fairly well, and just about what he stands for. I don't think I ever opposed him because of who he was or where he came from or where he went to worship. These considerations never seemed to me terribly important in any case."

It was quite true. In the city, in addition to parks, to playgrounds, to gardens that had been quietly and freely bequeathed by Gardiner, there were the young men who owed, literally, almost everything to him. They were, most of them, poor, strangers to him, subscribing to beliefs and traditions alien to his own. He selected them regularly and carefully from the rosters of the secondary schools; he sent them through college and university; afterwards, if assistance was needed, it was he who supplied it. The work was one he had begun years ago, not merely because he was a generous man, but because of a curious, almost anachronistic sense of obligation. He had a deep ineradicable love for this city where he had spent his life, and which he and his family had helped to build; by underwriting the education of these young men of promise he sought to protect, in some measure, the city's future. It was largely an isolated labor, and one which so far had produced few encouraging results; nevertheless he was quietly convinced of its value in the long run, and in any case he could not have avoided what seemed to him to be no more than the duty of the citizen who could afford it.

Like all Gardiner's philanthropies, this one was unpublicized; few people knew about it. His sons, of course, knew something of the arrangement, but they did not know of its extent. Had they known, they would have been surprised, they would have been puzzled, they would not have been particularly sympathetic. Only their great respect for their father would have prevented strong objection. Gardiner knew this; he sometimes wondered, when he talked to his sons, whether they who seemed to have overcome so many of the old passionate prejudices of their ancestors had not also managed to overcome some of their old passionate virtues? In these neutral, tolerant times, did anyone really feel deeply about anything? Or was he, on the other hand, in the first stages of becoming an old fogey? He smiled to himself and then, looking at his son, he thought: *At least they feel deeply about Skeffington. . . .* Or did they? He contrasted this mild, automatic distaste with the violent shouts and empurpled faces that the name of Skeffington could occasion among his own contemporaries; he concluded that, even here, they swam in the new emotional shallows. In a sense, of course, it was a good thing; but still, he thought, but still . . .

"You have me wondering about that soft spot," said his son. "For example, would you even consider supporting Skeffington in an election?"

"Oh no. Not now. Although there was a time, very early in his career, when I did. I think he was quite surprised, and I know that several of our friends were." He laughed quietly. "I remember particularly the reaction here in the club. I didn't support him for long, to be sure, but long enough to be considered a bit of a traitor. I must say that it seemed a logical step at the time. The city needed a little fresh air and I thought that Skeffington gave some promise of providing it. He wasn't a man without ideas, you know. Some of his early proposals were farsighted, humanitarian, and most attractive."

"And these proposals," asked his son, "did they ever get off the drawing board? Did they ever become anything more than proposals?"

"Some of them did, yes. You know you really mustn't believe everything that Amos says about Skeffington in that newspaper of his. Amos is a decent enough fellow but he's not entirely rational on the subject of Skeffington. What should be remembered to Skeffington's credit is that our first substantial slum-clearing program, for example, was entirely his. And he was far more receptive than any of his predecessors to suggestions for providing facilities for the health and recreation of the public. He saw what needed to be done, and in more than a few ways he marched ahead and did it. He always had a certain fearless vigor which I rather admired. Along with this, however, he had a capacity for incredibly wasteful spending which I didn't admire quite so much."

"So no matter what you say," his son said, with an air of triumph, "you come right back to the important thing, and that is that he's a crook. No matter how many swings or seesaws he may have put up, didn't he line his pockets on every one? And didn't they make jobs for his loafer friends?"

"Oh yes. All kinds of public featherbedding and thievery began and continued. I don't really know to what extent Skeffington personally profited from all this — I expect it was rather less than most people imagine — but there's no doubt at all that he was chiefly responsible. I don't for a moment condone it; I agree with you that it was a disgrace. I think I said a few minutes ago that I considered Skeffington a rogue."

"An engaging rogue," his son said quickly.

"An engaging rogue," Gardiner agreed. "I don't wish to shock you, Dan, but I find that makes a difference to me. I know that it shouldn't, but unfortunately it does. It's rather hard to condemn totally a man with whom one has had an agreeable personal association. This is especially true when one considers that some of those who have condemned him most vigorously haven't done so with entirely clean hands. I won't go into the untidy business of naming names, but I know several reputable citizens connected with our banks and utilities who, with perfect legality, have stolen far more from the city than has Skeffington. The distinction between private and corporate theft is a neat one; I've never been quite able to accept it. Nor, I would imagine, has Skeffington. I recall, once, when he was the governor, that he addressed a small, influential, and extremely hostile group of men made up in good part of these same people. He wanted their support for some measure — I forget now exactly what it was — and here's how he set about winning it. He kept them waiting for three quarters of an hour before he appeared. Then he began to talk to them, stressing particularly the differences between them and himself: the differences in background, in political faith, in belief, and so on. And then, when he'd done this for several minutes, he announced that whatever their differences may have been, at least they were alike in one respect. 'We are united, gentlemen, in what is, when you come to think of it, a very considerable accomplishment,' he said. 'We've all managed to stay out of jail!' " Behind the small glasses, the light gray eyes twinkled. "The boldness of it!" he said. "The supreme impudence of the man! He absolutely took their breaths away. Oh yes, Dan, a most engaging man."

"I suppose so," said his son skeptically. "All the same, I don't quite square a story like that with the reputation he has as a clever politician. You say he wanted their support. Do you mean that after that he got it?"

"No. Indeed he did not. But I've always suspected that once he got inside that room that night and saw all those grim, disapproving faces staring at him, he may have decided that he wanted to get something rather than support. He may have decided," said Gardiner slowly, "to get a bit of his own back. And if so, he surely succeeded!"

The son said nothing. For a few moments the two men sat silently by the darkening window. Outside, the new street lights had been turned on; the weird bluish illumination soaked through the evening fog which had just begin to come in off the water. Inside the room, there was a sudden heavy metallic clashing as the old waiter dropped some silver; the sound was cut off sharply, the old man smothering it in shocked apology. Gardiner turned and regarded his son with fond good humor.

"Well," he said. "Finished?"

"All finished," the son said.

"Nothing more I can give you? Brandy?"

"No, no, not a thing, thanks, Father. I'm in fine shape."

"Good. We'll go into the library then. But before we do," he said, "I imagine I should define my position on Skeffington just a little more clearly for you. I can't have you going home thinking I'm altogether irresponsible." The son began a protest, but the older man smilingly waved it away.

"Bear in mind above all that I'm fundamentally opposed to Skeffington. Apart from his first campaign, I've never helped him. I think he did some extremely good and necessary things for the city — things which, but for him, would probably not have been done at all — but also some disastrous ones. I think that as an elected public official he has been dishonest, partial to his own, and vindictive towards others; but I should also like to remind you that perhaps there might have been some reason for all the partiality and vindictiveness. They didn't spring from a vacuum, you know. I know something about Skeffington's early life in this city; it wasn't very agreeable. He had rather a hard time of it, and so did his family and most other families like it;

I'm afraid some of us didn't help matters much. And so, because Skeffington has an excellent memory, there was a certain amount of revenge. I don't say this to excuse his conduct. A bigger man and a better man would have acted differently. But unfortunately we're talking about Skeffington and the way *he* acted, and all I'm attempting to do is to show you why, to some extent, I sympathize with him. He's a man with many qualities I like, even admire, and with many others that I deplore; I simply say that one has to look at both sides of the coin. To sum it all up, I should say that on the whole Skeffington has been a political misfortune for the city. But I should also say that he had — and has — another side, and when he goes, he will be missed by many, many people. Including, I'm afraid, myself. And with that confession of an old man's weakness," he said, pushing his chair back from the table, "I suggest we adjourn to the library and get back to business. I want to go over that Thayer case with you once more. I agree with you that it may prove to be somewhat trickier than it looks."

Together father and son left the dining room and went into the library; here, at least, in the discussion of legal procedure, they would meet on common ground. . . .

Adam and Maeve were at a party given by the Mangans. Like all Mangan parties, this was distinguished by noise, confusion, quite a lot to drink, and rather too little food. The principal dish at dinner had been a mysterious gray preparation, full of indigestible lumps, in a casserole. It had run out even sooner than had been expected; as it had not been very good, this had not mattered much. Despite the food, Adam was enjoying himself. He liked both Jack and Nancy Mangan, and he sat now talking to Nancy, who had folded herself onto the divan with a vast collapsing sigh, and who, in her mid-thirties, was just a little rounder and just a little blonder than when he had first known her, fifteen years before. She was also, now, slightly tipsy, or so Adam thought; with Nancy it was not always easy to be sure. They were talking about Little Simp.

"But it's so *wonderful!*" Nancy said breathlessly. She said everything a little breathlessly, each phrase given its apparatus of rapturous significance. Strangers, when first meeting Nancy, were often delighted by the dazzling attention accorded them by this handsome, full-bodied woman until they discovered, somewhat to their discomfort, that people and even objects far less worthy than themselves — a child toe dancer, a new recipe for an inedible dessert — received precisely the same attention. "I mean it," she said urgently. "I really do mean it, Adam. I love it. Jack loves it. Everybody loves it. Does Maeve love it? I'll bet she does."

"I'll bet she does too. She's a very loyal wife."

"I *know*. She's young, she's lovely, she's loyal: I *love* Maeve. Adam," she said dreamily, "how much younger is Maeve than you?"

He laughed. "O.K., O.K.," he said. "Any time you want to stop shooting it's all right with me."

She smiled slightly; they were old friends. "Anyway," she said, "you're a lucky man. Because she *is* lovely. Did you know there was a time when you could have married me? *Ages* ago, of course. Just by saying the word? Did you know that, Adam? You didn't, did you?"

Adam grinned. "You always kept your secrets well, Nancy. No, I didn't." And neither, he reflected, did anyone else, for this courtship had no relation to reality. Late in the evening, and under certain conditions, Nancy could be counted upon to view the past through the extraordinary prism of her own recollections; others who had lived in this past came upon the re-creation of it with something of the same sense of wonder with which they might have come upon the lost Atlantis.

"But it all worked out so beautifully, didn't it?" she said. "I mean, here you are married to Maeve and you're happy, and here I am married to Jack and I'm happy, and it's all so much . . . so much . . . "

"Happier."

"Yes, that's it. I really don't think, Adam, that you would have been terribly happy married to me. I don't know why exactly, but I don't think you would. And I tell you something else: *I don't think I would have been happy married to you.* Can you forgive me for saying that to you?"

"I can forgive you anything, Nancy. I can even forgive you your cooking."

"I know," she said, nodding. "The casserole. Was it awful?"

"Pretty awful, yes."

"Nobody seemed to want more and that was all right, because there wasn't any more. I don't know, I think either you're a born cook, or you're not a born cook, and I'm not, so that's all there is to it. And then I really don't *care* much about food so I don't suppose that helps."

"We might have been an ideal couple at that," Adam said. "Everything would have been in our favor: I have a digestive tract of cast iron."

"Lucky boy," Jack said, coming up behind the divan. He was a heavy, slightly rumpled man, with quick energetic movements; he reached over now and smacked his wife lightly across the rump with the flat of his hand. "Get going, sport," he said. "Mingle with the guests, attend to their wants. I want to talk to Adam for a minute. I want to tell him about the cook he could have married if he'd been really smart."

"Ha ha ha," she said lazily, pushing herself up. "And to think I have to leave, just when the conversation's going to become so *wonderfully* witty. And all about food, too."

"You see my unique problem as a host," Jack said, as she went off. "I'm faced with the constant imbalance between food and drink, the one needed to neutralize the other in order to avoid the final shambles. Yet ours is the only house in the city where after dinner everyone drinks on an empty stomach. Result: the possibility of chaos descending. Solution: the hell with it. Listen, I have a proposition for you."

"My second today," Adam said, and thought of Skeffington.

"What? No, never mind, I'll tell you what the deal is. It's about the comic strip, in a way. You could help me out, strike a blow on the side of the angels, and maybe turn a pretty penny for yourself. Interested?"

"I don't know yet. Some parts of the proposition sound better than others. I liked that bit about the pretty penny well enough."

"More details," Jack said. "Here's the scoop." The scoop proved to be a plan for a political comic book; it was to be sponsored by the veterans' group for which Jack was legal counsel, and in which he was a guiding spirit. The group was political, it was Democratic, it was liberal; the comic book was to be used as a weapon in the state elections of the following year, and the direct target was to be the incumbent Republican governor.

"A turd," Jack explained. "A well-born turd, but a turd nevertheless. A complete reactionary. The nineteenth-century mind at work, and not a good one at that. The abolition of the cat-o'-nine-tails marks the ultimate in progressive legislation. Anything after that is dangerous. On top of everything else, a social snob and stuffy as hell. Ridicule might be the best way of getting at him. Or so we think. A good job of derision."

"What do you want me to do: put Little Simp in the Civil Liberties Union?"

"No. What the hell, no jokes, sport. We don't want you to use Little Simp. You probably couldn't anyway. The paper would kick up a fuss; they'll be backing the governor up to the hilt. All we want is your ability as a caricaturist. We'll give you all the dope to work with. Looked at in a certain light, the governor's a first-class comic figure. All you have to do is shed that light. It might even be a lot of fun for you."

"It doesn't sound much like fun."

"Plus profit," Jack said. A figure was named, which seemed to Adam, if not generous, at least fair. However, he shook his head.

"I don't think so, Jack. The price is right, but the trouble is that all this business isn't exactly my kind of country. I don't want to get mixed up in it. And there'd be all sorts of complications with the paper and the syndicate. I wouldn't mind that too much if it were anything I really cared about doing, but it isn't. I'd just as soon you got yourself another boy."

"Right," Jack said briskly. "No bones broken, sport." He was a matter-of-fact man, not greatly given to emotion; he was sure of the value of his cause, but he was neither hurt nor surprised when his friends failed, as they so often did, to fall in with his plans. On the whole, he rather expected it, and if, suddenly, they had agreed with him, he would have been mildly pleased but also just a bit alarmed, and he would immediately have begun the re-examination of his own position. "The stuff is there to be done," he said, "and I thought you might want a shot at it. We'll pass it along to somebody else. Keep it under your hat for a while though, will you?"

"All right. And thanks again for the thought. By the way, this is just for next year's state elections? You're not using it in the city this fall?"

"No point in it, sport. We're out to knock off the Republican control; the city election is a one-party affair. A Democratic dog-fight all down the line. We're not interested in it, except secondarily. Which reminds me, how's your uncle? I haven't seen him in a couple of months."

"He seems in great shape. I saw him this afternoon in City Hall."

"What a place. They ought to burn the whole dump down and everybody in it. Except your uncle. He's the only really able man in the whole setup."

"So? Now that surprises me — I mean, that you think so."

"Oh hell yes. I don't like him but he's a powerhouse in that league. And pretty damn good in any league. A big-timer, your Uncle Frank, sport."

"I see." He said, "Look, I suppose this secondary interest of yours in the city election will extend to the support of a candidate, won't it?"

"Sure. Naturally."

"But you wouldn't say that candidate would be my uncle?"

"God, no!" He stared at Adam; the suggestion had genuinely startled him. It was rare, even among his friends, that his purpose and that of his organization had been so monstrously misunderstood.

"Well," said Adam, "why not? You're the one who's always talking about the logic of politics. I should think it would be fairly logical to support a man whom you regard as a big-timer."

Jack glanced at him with some surprise. "You really interested in this?" he said. "You really want to know what we think?"

"I do."

"An encouraging sign," Jack said. "Possibly the dawning of a political consciousness. We'll snake you into the group yet, sport. O.K. We've got all kinds of reasons, but three ought to do it for now. One, we can't count on him. He's able, sure. Just for your own information, he's probably ten times as able as the candidate we'll eventually wind up supporting."

"Oh, fine!"

"No, now wait. Ability's great, but there comes a time when you have to say to hell with it. When it's just ability, that is. Your uncle's the ablest politician to come down the pike in these parts in the last fifty years. O.K., what does that mean? It means that he knows what should be done and he knows the way to do it. What it doesn't mean is that he *will* do it. In fact we feel the evidence shows he won't. Judging by past performance, and so on."

"Corruption at the core?"

Jack shrugged. "Call it what you want. The fact is that he's just too tied up to do a good job. Tied up with too many people who lose out if changes are made, too many outfits to play ball with, too many old pals on the city payroll. To give the city a good administration he'd have to cut them all off. Nobody knows that better than the boss himself, sport, but he won't do it. First, because he doesn't want to, and second, because it's too close to the end of the line. It's not the way he plays. So there's the picture. We prefer to go along with our own boy. He's no whiz, but he's not a dunce, and he's got what the medieval boys called 'the disposition-to-the-good.' He may not know how to deal the cards too well, but he'll learn, and meanwhile it's a little safer to sit in with him than it is with Riverboat Phil."

"No names?" Adam asked. "Who is this object of faint praise?"

Jack shook his head. "Not yet. See me in a couple of weeks; we'll be ready to announce then. But about the second reason — you want to hear it?"

"Sure. Shoot."

"O.K. Well, we think your uncle's just a little out of date, sport. The world has passed him by. You're supposed to run a government today according to a few rules, a few laws. All that personal leadership was the thing around the turn of the century, but no more. Your uncle's one idea of government is old-hat paternalism. Nothing on the books, just one man passing out the jobs and Christmas baskets to the kiddies. So what we want to know is what happens when daddy dies, or if he doesn't happen to like one of the kids? And what we like is a few ideas, a few principles, a few guaranteed rights set down in black and white — minimum wage, FEPC, that sort of thing. That's the kind of talk we understand and your uncle doesn't. He may be for the underprivileged, but he wants to decide who they are and what they're to have, himself. The old boss principle. Government by favor, pre-Roosevelt style. Obsolete as the windmill, sport. So that's that. The election according to Mangan: the inevitable consequence of drink plus the inedible. Anyway, you've heard it all before, hundreds of times. All elementary college-classroom stuff, Government 3–A. But it's true, nevertheless. Or true enough to make us duck your uncle in the fall. So saying," he said, rising, "the host returns to his duties. Mobility is called for. Also, one drink. How about you?"

"Hold up a second," Adam said. "What about that third reason?"

"What? Oh, that. Well, in one way, sport, it's the most important of all. Practically speaking, that is. You see," he said, "we just don't think he's going to win."

"I see," Adam said thoughtfully. "Would you say that this reason was on a slightly different plane from the other two? A little less quixotic?"

"Sure. But then we're not entirely a quixotic outfit. We're all in big-boy politics together. What we have on our side, maybe, is a few principles, a little integrity, a few decent aims. That's all. And of course while we're at it we'd just as soon win."

Adam wondered, but he said, "One question more: you wouldn't care to tell me why you think he's going to lose?"

"It's too late in the day for him, sport. The Age of the Dinosaur is past. I'd elaborate," he said, "but for the fact that our cook of the evening has been giving me the hard eye for the last five minutes. Relief is required at the punch bowl. Coming along?"

"No, go ahead. I'll join you later."

For a few minutes, Adam was alone. He considered first what he had just heard: none of it was new, none of it had surprised him. Yet he had listened tonight to the old information with a fresh attention, and he wondered with some amusement whether this was the mark of the committed — of even the partially committed — man. True, he was to be only a spectator, but as such he was bound to have an increased interest in the spectacle itself. He wondered idly which candidate Jack would support; he thought that it would make little difference. Jack's organization was articulate but small; it had no considerable power. In the coming tug of war between it and Skeffington, Adam had little doubt as to whose pulling power was the stronger. And he had little doubt, too, as to which end of the rope his own sympathies inclined toward.

But now all thought was interrupted by the sudden sweep of hunger: Adam was ravenous. Somewhat resentfully he gazed across the room at Nancy, the irresponsible agent of his hunger; she was chattering away to a thin, pale, effervescent man who, like herself, presumably gave no thought to food. Adam looked for Maeve; he began to calculate just how long it would be before they could, in decency, abandon the party, and go somewhere, anywhere, where food could be obtained.

He had not long to wait. Maeve caught his eye and his signal; they left soon, and drove swiftly home, and there, in the kitchen, over a late-night supper of scrambled eggs and coffee, they slowly and sleepily and happily talked of the party, of the night and of the day. In this review there was one significant omission — they did not talk of Skeffington. Adam thought of doing so, then decided, looking at his wife, that there was, after all, no point in it at this time. It should be mentioned, certainly, and it would be — but later. There was no hurry. He would tell her in such a way that immediately she would see that his role was a harmless, even an amusing one; he was confident that this could be done. But later, later . . .

Skeffington was busy. Now a declared candidate, he wasted no time in beginning his campaign. There were, that night, four dinners which he was scheduled to attend; he would eat at none but speak at all.

He would speak longest at the most substantial of these. It was in one of the downtown hotels; he was driven there in the long official car, accompanied by Weinberg, Ditto Boland and Cuke

Gillen. It was Gillen who had arranged for the Fats Citronella presentation: he was an ex-vaudevillian who served Skeffington officially as the City Greeter — in which capacity he met important visitors to the city as they stepped down from plane or train — and unofficially as one of several court jesters. He was a small, spruce, agile man with a spike of gray moustache and thinning gray hair parted exactly in the middle; somehow there hovered over him, like a coat of invisible dust, the aura of a bygone age of entertainment: the Keystone Cop, the solitary banjoist, the Old Soft Shoe, and the man in the boater and the blazer singing "Shine On, Harvest Moon." He had a high, penetrating nasal voice, and told stories in a variety of dialects. Sometimes, in the tiny office in City Hall which he shared with the Director of the Division of Plant Pest Control, he would break into bits of his old vaudeville routine: a few fast shuffle-off-to-Buffalo steps, hat tilted rakishly to one side, palms slapping thighs in syncopation, while he sang "Yes, We Have No Bananas," which had been ingeniously arranged in the manner of the quartet from *Rigoletto*. Cuke sang all four parts; it was his proudest boast that he could do this while at the same time keeping constantly in motion.

His manner on official occasions, at airports and railway terminals, was somewhat more subdued; nevertheless, touring dignitaries were not infrequently startled and a bit bewildered by this spry figure in whose very approach, despite a certain strained gravity of facial expression and the civic uniform of morning clothes, there was contained the warning: GET READY FOR THE PRATFALL!

Now, as they drove from one dinner to the next, Skeffington relaxed, and Cuke talked. It was at such moments as these that he knew reminiscence was both permitted and welcomed; he reached deep into the pail of his extraordinary past. The touchstone had been Ditto's doleful complaint that, since lunch, he had had only a glass of milk.

"I knew a man who took a bath in milk once," Cuke said. "Out in Ashtabula one June, when we were playing a split week for short dough. He was my partner, Snapper Brady. You remember the Snapper, Governor?"

"The one who looked like a turtle?" Skeffington said. He was leaning back against the leather cushions, his eyes closed.

"The same. When he had his hair cut, that is. But he was a whiz on the musical saw and a great little guy. Well, this time out in Ashtabula, it's hot, and the Snapper is a great sufferer from the heat. Thin skin, the doctors said. So he has this skin rash and he's going around all caked up in vaseline. It's O.K., but he feels greasy and he smells like an oil well. Then, all of a sudden, one morning he reads about this foreign dame in the Follies who takes milk baths for her skin, so before you know it he gets the milkman up to the room, points to the bathtub, and says, 'Fill it up!' You could have knocked the milkman over with a doily!"

"Possibly he was a little short of bathtub milk that morning," Skeffington said. "It's always the first to go."

Ditto laughed loudly. "Bathtub milk!" he chortled. "Oh, that's a good one, Governor. Yes, indeed it is!"

"Anyway," Cuke said, "about two hours later I waltz into the room with a couple of dolls from the show. The bathroom door is wide open, and there's the Snapper, up to his armpits in Grade A. 'Come on in!' he shouts. 'It's O.K., girls, I'm all covered up. You can't see through milk!' So in we go, and the first thing you know, just for a laugh, the Snapper reaches out for a glass, swoops it down through the milk, and comes up with it full. 'Have a shot!' he says, handing it to one of the dolls. I'll be damned if she don't turn a little green and start to faint, and the two of them shoot out of the room and don't speak to either one of us for two weeks!"

"I wish I'd known the Snapper better," Skeffington said. "One seldom meets a really gracious host these days."

"A barrel of fun, the Snapper," Cuke agreed. "Anyway, I stick around for about half an hour while the Snapper splashes away in the tub, and pretty soon out he comes, all dried off. 'Snapper,' I says, 'how was it? Tell me the truth.' 'Cuke,' he says, 'it was lousy. I feel like a piece of cottage cheese!' And that was the last of milk for the Snapper!"

" 'Fare thee well, inconstant lover,' " Skeffington said. "The Snapper and milk, parted forever. Sad to consider. A blow at the vitals of the dairy industry. What's the Snapper doing these days, by the way? I hope he hasn't abandoned his musical saw as well as his milk."

"Sure he has," Cuke said. "He left the stage years ago, just about the same time I did. When vaudeville died. He's out on the Coast, some town in the south of California. He's got a city job: Director of Americanization."

"Director of Americanization," Skeffington said. "I hadn't thought of that one. It sounds good: what does a Director of Americanization do?"

"He teaches the young kids about their country. Kids and Mexicans up for their first papers. He teaches them about Paul Revere and his horse, and George Washington and the cherry tree, and how to pledge allegiance."

"The stage's loss is the Republic's gain," Skeffington said. "Both yourself and the Snapper have wound up in municipal service: a startling coincidence, Cuke. It speaks well for the vaudeville of yesterday as an incubator of patriotism."

"Sure thing," Cuke said. "Look at George M. Cohan."

The car stopped and Weinberg, who had been silent, now said, "O.K. We're here."

Skeffington nodded. "Right." He, Weinberg and Ditto got out of the car; Cuke remained. Weinberg leaned back into the car and said, "We'll be along in about half, three quarters of an hour. Keep 'em happy 'till we get there."

"Okey-doke, Sambo," said Cuke. He winked and spanked his collar with his forefinger; it was a jaunty gesture, the very same with which he had run onto hundreds of stages, his straw sailor at the familiar snappy angle, his luminescent tie firmly in place, and the orchestra playing "Glowworm." "Leave everything to me," he said. "I'll lay 'em in the aisles."

For Cuke was functioning tonight, as he would function throughout the campaign, as a political advance man. He would go on to the next dinner, where, until Skeffington arrived, he would hold the guests with his assortment of dialect stories: Irish, Jewish, Italian, Negro, and English. He told these stories well, although his repertoire was not now nearly so extensive as once it had been; Skeffington had pruned it ruthlessly. In pained astonishment, the raconteur had seen dozens of his most reliable party pieces discarded because of indelicacy or on even more incomprehensible grounds. An artist, he had protested; Skeffington's answer had been brief and final.

"We're living in a sensitive age, Cuke," he had said, "and I'm not altogether sure you're fully attuned to it. For example, if the Jewish Businessmen's Association was having a small get-together and you were to speak at it, I have the feeling that your first story might begin with the words: 'A little Hebe named Epstein was walking down the street one day. . . .' Now you may not realize it, but that kind of thing doesn't exactly bring the Jewish vote swarming to my doors. So while I like you as a storyteller, and appreciate your fine personal qualities, I don't think I'll give you your head. Unless, of course, you depart from the little program I've outlined for you and start telling stories on your own. Then," he said jovially, "I'll give it to you. On a platter. Better keep that in mind, Cuke."

Cuke had kept it in mind. As an added precaution, he had been given a short announcement to make as a preface to his public appearances.

"These stories are told purely in the spirit of good fun," he would say, "and no offense is intended to any race, creed, or color."

He had not understood the necessity for this, any more than he had understood the necessity for trimming his stock, but still, when it was a question of one's head, was understanding essential? As a practical man who had known his ups and downs, he had decided that it was not, and had obeyed without question. It was an obedience which Skeffington had fully expected.

Now Skeffington and Weinberg walked side by side up the walk leading to the hotel; slightly to the rear, Ditto automatically broke his stride, skipping to keep in perfect step with Skeffington. They had almost reached the doors of the hall when Skeffington sought from Weinberg the few details he would require for his address. Gesturing towards the hotel, he said, "Who's it for?"

"McLaughlin," Weinberg said. "Eddie McLaughlin."

Skeffington frowned. "*Eddie* McLaughlin?" He did not recognize the name, but he knew that it belonged to a younger man, and someone he had met fairly recently, for it was with names and faces encountered during the last few years that his celebrated memory was not entirely efficient. In his detached analysis of himself, he knew that this, like his restricted diet, was another of the signs of increasing age; it did not trouble him unduly. At this stage of the game, it was to be expected, and moreover, there were mnemonics that could be relied upon. He said, "Enlighten me, Sam."

"You know him," Weinberg said. "You remember the Legion convention in Chicago two years ago? The drunken smush with the squint eye that kept spitting on your lapel?"

"I do indeed," Skeffington said, with a grimace. "And that's our honored guest of the evening?"

"Yeh. He died, so they're giving him a dinner."

"That makes it easier," Skeffington said. "It's always easier to speak about a man like that *in absentia*. If he were there I'd keep thinking of my lapels. I presume the widow is to be presented with a memorial plaque of some kind? The usual enduring bronze?"

"Yeh. The head of the Legion makes the presentation. After you speak."

"Good. How old was the man when he died?"

"Forty-three."

"And what did he do for a living?"

Weinberg's gloomy face for just a moment lightened; it was almost a smile. "A vetinary," he said.

Skeffington's eyebrows lifted slightly. "A veterinary!" he said. "Well, well. I hope he finds his consolation in that Big Kennel up yonder. Come on, let's go in."

He and Weinberg entered the hotel, closely followed by Ditto. They were late, and intentionally so, for Skeffington was by design notoriously unpunctual. Early in his career he had discovered the dramatic value of the delayed entrance; as a consequence, he was seldom on time for any public function. Although this habit of his was known to everyone, and although he never failed to make his appearance, however tardily, his hosts invariably grew nervous as the moments passed, and when finally he arrived, as he did tonight, they greeted him in a flurry of nervous relief, born of the collapse of anxiety. Surrounding him, talking hurriedly, each one of the group eager to establish himself as one in intimate association with the Mayor, they hustled him into the dining hall; it was a noisy, hectic progression, and served to distract the attention of everyone in the room from whatever happened to be taking place at the head table. This was still another advantage of the delayed arrival; Skeffington often timed his turbulent entrance to coincide exactly with the spoken remarks of some valued opponent. In this way was the admirable effect of total disruption achieved.

Tonight, settled at the head table, the preliminaries over, he rose to speak. He waited until the room was absolutely quiet; in the instant of waiting, his mind reached back into the crowded day and hovered momentarily over selected high spots: the interview with his nephew, the conference with Gorman and Weinberg, the rage-filled countenance of a prominent merchant who, at lunch, had been wrathfully examining his newspaper for further news of the Skeffington candidacy, and had suddenly looked up to see the candidate himself bowing ironically in his direction. These were satisfying thoughts; among them was none concerned with either Eddie McLaughlin or the eulogy to come. This was a routine chore, accomplished almost without conscious effort. He had the few necessary details; he had sized up the head table in one quick glance; he was ready. And now there was silence.

"Mr. Toastmaster, Reverend Fathers, Mrs. McLaughlin, fellow Legionnaires, friends of Eddie McLaughlin," he began. The words, at the beginning, were pitched low deliberately; it was then that the ears of the audience strained to get what was being said, and the maximum attention was immediately secured. The aging voice which still retained its richness now flowed in easy unhalting music, for with negligible variations it had played the same tune literally a thousand times before. "When I left the house this evening I said to Tom Lacy, my secretary, 'Tom, it looks like we have a busy evening ahead of us.' He agreed. He said, 'Governor, you have eight separate speaking engagements, and all of them are important.' And I answered, 'Tom, I don't care if I have a hundred and eight. There's one I want to take care of before any of the others, no matter how important they may seem to be. And that one,' " he said, his voice now accelerating, growing in power and emphasis, " 'is the dinner the Legion is giving in memory of that valued comrade — more than a valued comrade, that valued and irreplaceable *friend* — EDDIE McLAUGHLIN!' "

He roared out the terminal words, at the same time cutting them short; this lent them the quality of a command from a cheerleader which could not conceivably be disobeyed. He was not disappointed; applause cracked in, shouts arose, and once again he saw that the situation was well under control. He continued, speaking in a more solemn vein, for the tone was, after all, one of eulogy. At least, he thought, for the moment.

"A tragic thing indeed that this young man was taken from us in so untimely a fashion. He was only forty-three, in the very flower of his manhood. There was still so much for him to do. Yet those of us who knew Eddie McLaughlin must be consoled by the fact of what he had already done. I think no one can deny that he has left his mark behind him, the ineradicable impression of his accomplishment. 'The evil that men do lives after them; the good is oft interred with their bones' — this could never be said of the man whose memory we honor here tonight. He did no evil, and with no difficulty whatsoever, we remember the good. But I almost hesitate to speak of his good qualities on this occasion. I feel it's very close to being an impertinence on my part, for there are others present," he said, bowing slightly towards the widowed Mrs. McLaughlin, "who know far better than I his worth — his dedication to the good life, his devotion to his family, his love for his community, his pride in his church, his boundless capacity for friendship — . . . " Here he thought grimly of the little drunken maniac charging at him across a Chicago hotel lobby, dripping spittle on his lapels; he added, "His sobriety."

He stole a glance at the widow; on her face were the marks of the familiar struggle between pleasure and an utter bafflement. She likes the words, Skeffington thought, but — is this her Eddie? He sincerely hoped not. He had often observed to his intimates that in these eulogies he accorded the departed their last and greatest favor: he rendered them totally unrecognizable to their relicts. One could do no more. And now, while the applause continued, the word "veterinary" clicked into place. He had not yet mentioned this. He would do so now; it was the next step but, more than that, it was the way to the exit for Eddie McLaughlin.

"And we mustn't forget, of course, the connection that existed between his splendid profession and his life. Eddie McLaughlin devoted his adult life towards helping those dumb friends of man who are unable to complain of their ills. I think it altogether probable that the many hours spent in their service — in the relief of the suffering of the helpless dog, the cat, the numberless other household pets who give companionship to so many of us — fortified his own humanitarian inclinations. They left him even more resolute in the pursuit of those noble ends to which every Legionnaire aspires. . . ."

He went on, but there was not much more to come. Already he had formed the phrases of transition which would take him from the memory of Eddie McLauglin back to the land of the living and, specifically, back to the fact of his own campaign. For although his memory was perhaps less effective than it had been in his younger days, he never came close to forgetting that he was running for public office. Accordingly he switched adroitly to Eddie McLaughlin, Political Man . . .

". . . Not actively engaged in the political arena itself, perhaps, but a lifelong and respected Democrat all the same. As such, he was profoundly concerned with the problems of the poor and underprivileged of our community. This is a noble concern, but I regret to say that it's not a universal one. I doubt very much if our good friends of the Republican party share in it to any great extent. Possibly a few of the shabbier members may; I've noticed that as soon as they get a bit down on their luck, they're apt to discover that the poor have rights."

The sudden ironic insertion, accompanied by the familiar deadpan stare, had the desired effect. There were smiles and there was laughter; the change of tone had been establishd; this was what most of them had come to hear. For one moment,

Skeffington felt the old impish temptation to shock: to tell, in this instance, a story of the departed veterinary having been called in to attend the cat of a wealthy Republican, and of having found it in a state of advanced malnutrition due to its owner having made inroads on the catmeat. But he resisted; such invention, in the presence of the widow, would be in questionable taste, and would, moreover, serve to reintroduce the name of Eddie McLaughlin.

"Still, we must remember that shabby Republicans are few and far between," he said. "The few there are, are carefully concealed from public view: they're smuggled around the city in the luggage compartments of Cadillacs. Most Republicans, however, don't even like to think about those less fortunate than themselves; it bothers them. I remember some years ago when I proposed building the public baths along the Strandway; I was greeted with a chorus of recriminations from the opposition party. They had a terrifying vision: hundreds of the poor would now be able to take baths regularly! For their part, they want our poor to be like Frenchwomen. A Frenchwoman, as you know, takes a bath but twice in her life: once when she enters it, and once when she leaves it. In between times she uses talcum powder. It's a well-known fact that the Republicans have a vested interest in the talcum powder industry!"

It was the kind of outrageous statement which his audiences expected from him and loved when they got. Everyone was now cheering and laughing, the spirit of the eulogy left far behind; even the widow, Skeffington noted, was smiling: there was at least the implication that her Eddie had had some share in the building of the poor man's bathtub. He kept on in this vein for some minutes, emphasizing the need for Democratic solidarity in the face of the Republican threat. A threat so grave in this city, he reflected sardonically, that for the last twenty years they haven't even bothered to field a candidate. Still, one had to proceed to the goal by the well-established routes of tradition; one flogged the Republican foe in order better to lacerate the opposition within one's own fold. He came, in this manner, to the focal point of the Eddie McLaughlin Memorial Dinner: the candidacy of Frank Skeffington.

". . . Successful opposition to this slumbering giant of power and privilege must depend upon a united party, under experienced and proved leadership. I can't help thinking in this connection of the names of some of those who apparently aspire to lead us in this fight. I think of these names with some difficulty, to be sure, as until quite recently I never heard them mentioned. I'm sure they're all fine men, good citizens, clean-living people who've never been to jail and who support their public institutions. But — are they leaders? That's the question nobody can answer because nobody knows. Can they run a city? Nobody knows that either. It seems to me that something new has been introduced into political campaigning: the voter is being asked to cast his ballot for the Great Unknown — and maybe not so great at that. It's a little like selecting the Unknown Soldier to be a general. He's a fine chap and everybody honors him, but who is he, and what does he know about commanding an army? I think most of us would prefer to trust our sons to those of proven ability. In the same way, we would prefer to trust ourselves and our city to those who at least have demonstrated capacity to take care of it. . . ."

In the next few moments he made it quite clear that the list of candidates so qualified was not limitless; that it included, in fact, but a single name. The point made, he did not dwell upon it. It was a reminder; the campaign was just beginning; they would see him again, and often. He mentioned, briefly, entertainingly, and with shrewd selectiveness, some of his political accomplishments; he mentioned them almost by the way, and that was enough. Then, his mission accomplished, he returned for the final token nod at the peg from which all things had been made to hang. He returned to Eddie McLaughlin.

"But we have strayed far afield," he said. His voice was faintly reproachful; it was as if he were gently chiding the audience for having led him into talking about himself. His heavy features assumed the mask of full solemnity that had marked the opening moments of his address. "In our zeal to urge upon you the necessity for experienced leadership in these troubled times, we may seem to have forgotten the primary purpose of our being here tonight. I assure you that nothing could be farther from the truth. What we've been talking about concerns the care of the underprivileged, the responsibilities of the good citizen, the proper administration of the city in which we all live and of which we are all so proud. I think we're agreed that no man among us was more aware of these problems than Eddie McLaughlin, and that no man gave more unsparingly of his energies for their solution. So then, to discuss these issues is, in the larger sense, to discuss Eddie McLaughlin and to realize more fully the measure of his accomplishment. It was a great accomplishment indeed, and tonight as we who are gathered here think of that accomplishment and of the generous, courageous man behind it, we're certain in our hearts that Eddie McLaughlin has long since gained his reward. We know, each and every one of us, that to his ears must surely have come those blessed words which he was born to hear: 'Well done, Eddie McLaughlin! Well done, thou good and faithful servant!' "

He inclined his head slightly in a gesture coincident with the ecclesiastical flavor of the concluding words; in the audience a slight reverential pause obtained, and then the room rocked with cheers and applause. Good enough, he thought, but it meant little, for the crowd had been overwhelmingly in his favor to begin with. A flick of an eye revealed that the widow had joined in the spirit of the moment; she was smiling at him and applauding. He smiled back; she seemed a pleasant woman, far too pleasant, surely, to have been saddled with the wretched little nuisance whom he had just commended so highly. The universally favorable reception continued to ring agreeably in his ears; although he gave it no special significance, it did seem a good omen: an auspicious beginning for a grand campaign. Success to be launched upon the bony shoulders of the deceased Eddie McLaughlin.

He did not sit down again; instead, as there was still much to do, he made his way from the head table to the nearest exit, surrounded by the same vocal congratulatory cordon that had escorted him into the hall. They saw him out into the corridor; they stayed with him in the descending elevator; they walked with him through the hotel lobby and down the front walk up to the door of his waiting car. It was not until the car pulled away from the curb that he was able to separate himself from them with a final wave. Once again he was able to relax against the cushions, flanked now by Weinberg and Ditto.

"A good talk," Weinberg said approvingly. "Right on the ball."

"Adequate, Sam, adequate," he said. "Eddie dead served us far better than Eddie living, that's sure."

"That was a very grand speech, Governor," Ditto said. "One of the very best I've ever heard you give on such an occasion." Inspired by the eloquence he had so recently attended, he said feelingly, "And I'm sure that the very same man in question you spoke in favor of tonight must be looking down on us right now and feeling proud of himself!"

"A sentiment like that does you credit, Ditto," Skeffington said. "There are times when you're a harbor of lovely thoughts. There's only one thing wrong and that's your sense of direction. I doubt very much that he's looking down on us tonight; I have a feeling that from where the good Eddie is, it's a hell of a long look up." He leaned towards the front seat and said to his chauffeur, "Pick it up a bit, Charlie. We have a lot of work to do before we go to bed. . . ."

Four hours later, Skeffington was in his home and in his bed. He had spoken at three more dinners following the one for Eddie McLaughlin, and he had gone to the dance given by John Gorman. Here he had conversed with Camarrata, and the memory of that conversation now caused him to smile, then to chuckle aloud. Shifting his position under the single lightweight blanket — for the August night was seasonably warm — he said softly, "Return to Sorrento, old friend Camaratta." Because after this election, the Italian would be politically dead, buried and forgotten in this city; tonight, all unwittingly, he had begun to inch forward on the terrifyingly short slide to oblivion. This was a thought which gave Skeffington some satisfaction. The day and the night had, in fact, been little else but satisfaction. From the moment of his rising until now, the sour note had been absent; fulfillment had exceeded anticipation in every detail. Even the interview with his nephew had come off without any of the small hitches which conceivably might have arisen, and this had given him the greatest satisfaction of all. The need to bring the boy into his corner by his side throughout the campaign had come upon him unexpectedly one day and had persisted; he thought now that it stood at least a reasonable chance of being satisfied.

He stirred once more; his eyes closed, and, in the utter midnight quiet of the big house, he prepared to go to sleep. He was tired. He was more tired than he had been in some time, and he did not try to fool himself into believing that he was not. His eyes smarted, there was an ache in his legs, and he was aware of the steady pulsations within his body, pounding away just a little too hard and a little too fast. The day had been too long and too full — but it had been worth it. Still, he knew his age, he knew himself, and he knew that prudence required a certain sensible curtailment; he would measure his activities with more care during the coming months.

And now, just before sleep, he thought, as he so often did, of his wife, and wished that she had been with him today. Then, in the final seconds of his conscious day, he thought suddenly of his son, and the fact that he had not bothered to come to City Hall, as he had been requested to. Skeffington frowned, sighed, and reflected that no day, however triumphant, could escape totally without a shadow. Then he fell asleep.

Two hours later, Francis Skeffington Jr. returned to his house to go to bed. He came up the stairs with a light, almost prancing step; he was singing softly to himself. He had been drinking, but he was not drunk. He had been drinking only enough to be happy, for he liked to be happy. Nearing the top of the stairs, he was singing an old favorite, in a new and unfamiliar rhythm. It was "Whose Honey Are You?" as done in the manner of Fats Citronella, the original words shot through with the primitive musical cries and grunts which had shot that gifted entertainer into fame.

"Whose honey are you?
Rootie va va vovity vop.

Whose tea do you sweeten?
Fumfy fo fo foti foop. . . ."

He had met Fats only an hour before; Fats had greeted him with enthusiasm.

"I met your daddy-daddy today, boy!" he had said, his great eyes beaming. "Reet! He gimme one of them *real* gone keys! Crazy crazy! Root!"

Junior had laughed agreeably. "Crazy crazy! Root!" he had said, right back. And then they had all laughed uproariously: Fats and Junior and Junior's blond girl. He had liked Fats.

Now, passing his father's closed door, he suddenly remembered that he should have gone to see him earlier that day. He had been asked to do so, but, what with one thing and another, he had forgotten. He wondered if it were anything important. He hoped not; he thought not. In any case, he had meant to go but now he would make it the next day instead. And he went to his room, still singing softly, "Whose honey are you . . . ?"

PART II

Six

THE weeks went by. Skeffington's campaign began to build, slowly and expertly; in its meticulous progression nothing was left to chance. All that was to be done had been done many times before, in previous election years, and there was neither desire nor room for the bold experiment. Skeffington was not opposed to innovation, but as an extremely successful politician he thought it unreasonable to abandon the techniques by which success had been gained. And so the campaign got under way. In these early weeks, the work was vigorous, routine, and — to the layman's eye — imperceptible. There were no great rallies, no mass meetings, no radio or television addresses; the time had not yet come for the visible, sustained bid to the electorate. It was a time of subsurface maneuvering, of putting the house in order. There were daily conferences between Skeffington and his chief lieutenants, regular meetings with the ward and precinct leaders, there was the careful outlining of strategy, and there was the establishing and renovating of the multiple connective lines with which each single city block was bound to City Hall.

Over all this preparation, Skeffington himself exercised a close and unbroken supervision. The labor was long, detailed and unexciting; he did not mind. He knew that someone had to do it; he knew that he could do it quicker and better than any of his subordinates; he knew, too, that in the final analysis it was all being done for him. This last consideration was one which occurred to him rather often; he found that it helped remarkably to preserve him from boredom or fatigue.

More than three weeks had gone by since the meeting between uncle and nephew in City Hall, and despite Adam's declaration of interest and commitment, the visit had not been repeated. The campaign might move onward and upward; so far, Adam had not moved with it. There were several reasons for this. The first was that Adam had re-examined his uncle's words and had found that, as always, they had been lent an extraordinary persuasiveness by his presence; considered later, in the cool reasonable shade of his absence, they were less compelling. They were by no means unconvincing: Adam was willing to believe that by following the campaign along the lines suggested by Skeffington he would come to know better both this man who had so attracted him, and the city which he found to be of steadily increasing interest. But what he did not now quite believe was that he could follow it unimplicated: the ringside seat which Skeffington had spoken of was all very well, but only if one could be sure of not falling into the ring. It was this certainty which Adam now lacked. His old distaste for becoming in any way involved in the subtle, incomprehensible machinery of politics began powerfully to reassert itself; he began to regret his promise to his uncle; he even started to wonder if, really, it had been a promise after all.

Moreover, there was Maeve. Eventually she would have to be told; it was an inevitable step which Adam contemplated without enthusiasm. Ordinarily the currents of his marriage flowed smoothly, almost ideally; the give-and-take between husband and wife was accomplished with a minimum of friction. Maeve was intelligent, she was adaptable; more to the point, perhaps, she was tactfully deferential to her husband's opinions. It was only that there were certain subjects from which could spring, full-blown, the argument, and these, while possessing no apparent relation to each other, were actually connected by the most infrangible of ties: they were the subjects upon which Maeve sought counsel from her father. The subject of Skeffington was chief among them.

Adam was not vindictive, but when he thought of his father-in-law it was almost with a grim wistfulness and a sense of regret that the problems of life did not lend themselves to the ready solution of those of art. How wonderful it would be, he thought, if his father-in-law could be treated with the ruthless, imaginative dispatch now reserved for the fictive enemies of

Little Simp! But this was only a dream. Roger Sugrue remained alive and mercilessly active, an untouchable oracle working away ceaselessly in the background, muttering, one after another, his incendiary platitudes. He was not a bad man, but he was worse: he was a self-made one. He had begun with nothing; he had put himself through Harvard; he had, in time, gained control of a large chain of women's specialty shops. From this exotic world of the chemise and the living-tissue girdle he secured annually a handsome income. Success among the undergarments had given him confidence, and he had begun to speak with authority on matters of graver concern: politics, life, religion. As an amateur theologian he had acquired the passion for nosing about through diocesan affairs which sometimes afflicts the well-to-do Catholic layman. Independently and unrequested, he called upon priests and their parishes; he conducted surveys; he investigated sources of strife and dispute; he passed his findings and his advice on to his ecclesiastical superiors, who received both with an increasingly ill-concealed reluctance. Skeffington had once spoken of this to Adam.

"The higher clergy in this diocese," he had said, "made the great mistake in the beginning of regarding your father-in-law as an ordinary pest. He is no such thing. He's a one-man plague. There they were, letting him putter around just like any ordinary run-of-the-mill nuisance with a couple of hundred thousand dollars that he's got to leave to somebody someday, and the next thing they knew he was chewing them up like a corn borer in a field of Golden Bantam. Poor Monsignor Flannery lived all his life in the diocese and his one wish was that he could spend his declining days in the parish he was born in. He would have made it, too, but he had the misfortune to be introduced to your father-in-law; six months later, at the age of eighty, he was clawing at the Cardinal's door, pleading for an assignment to the Foreign Missions. My heart went out to him; I've known your father-in-law a long time."

The Monsignor may or may not have been an apocryphal figure; Adam felt for him anyway. He too had known his father-in-law for some time; acquaintance had not bred affection. Only the preceding week he had gone with Maeve to Roger's home for dinner. After the meal they had gone into the library; there Roger sat and talked: a stocky, bald, verbose man of fifty-five who, every evening when the sun went down, slipped into the crimson smoking jacket with the Harvard seal on the left breast pocket. He was proud of his alma mater, so proud, indeed, that he had almost forgotten his misery as an undergraduate: the poor Irish boy on the make, socially and financially ambitious, forever subject to handicaps of poverty and the fact of being a representative of a race which had produced the young usurper, Skeffington. There had been sneers, an almost perpetual chill; Roger had never forgiven Skeffington for them. But now, long an alumnus, he had forgiven the college. The fact of his attendance had given him cachet; more, he reasoned that the secular academic background lent him additional distinction as a Catholic. It was a kind of proof of his Faith: he had been exposed to error, he had emerged intact. He was grateful to his school for having failed to defeat him.

On the night of the recent dinner the conversation for the most part had been devoted to the improbable turns of clerical behavior which Roger rather specialized in unearthing. One of the younger priests of the diocese, it appeared, had taken time out from his parish duties to enter and to win a country-club golf tournament. The simple triumph had fired him with ambition, and he had aspired to greater things.

"Why, he actually went to his pastor," Roger had said indignantly, "and asked if there was any provision in Canon Law to stop him from entering the qualifying rounds of the National Amateur Golf Championship! Imagine that if you will for a moment! A priest ordained for only two years, and wanting to be the golfing champion of the United States!"

Adam had departed from his usual practice of monosyllabic response; he had said, "I couldn't agree with you more. The danger of scandal is obvious. He must have had very little experience in actual competitive play; we would have no guarantee that he would win so much as a hole. He could be trounced by anyone: a Baptist, an Episcopalian, a rabbi. . . . "

Maeve had flashed him a glance that was at once warning and plea; his father-in-law, who, surprisingly, had for once listened to what had been said to him, added tolerantly, "No no, Adam, you're missing the whole point. I was afraid you might. The point is that it's not a suitable ambition. Ask yourself this question: *Where's the strength of vocation there?* . . . I intend to take it up with his bishop."

He had talked, that night, only briefly of Skeffington.

"He's overreached himself this time. He's gone too far, and at last he's been caught. Now I don't say this gloatingly. I hope I'm big enough not to seek revenge, or to wish any man hard luck, no matter how rascally he may have been in his public life. And of course, Adam, there's nothing at all personal in this. But the point is that Skeffington is running up against serious financial troubles. I have a good deal of influence in certain financial circles, as you know, and I heard only the other day on the very best authority — from Harvey Willet, who is Norman Cass's right-hand man — that the banks have refused point-blank to grant the city a loan under his administration. Well, you may say, that's not everything. And *I* say," he said, coming happily to what really mattered, "I say that it's something, and that something is the beginning of the end. . . . "

It was Maeve who, in hasty diplomacy, had turned the tide, by diverting her father into the path of autobiography. The possibility of conflict between these two men worried her deeply; she loved her husband, she worshipped her father. It was the blind spot in her which Adam could forgive but could not understand. Roger was the only parent she had ever known; as he himself said, rather often and rather sentimentally, he had been both father and mother to her. It was a claim that commanded a double loyalty; Maeve gave it willingly. She loved him, respected him, and was proud of his achievement. And sometimes, in their infrequent arguments, Adam seemed to see mirrored in the young and lovely woman he had married the urgent, opinionated figure of her father, spurring her on to disputation, reminding her not to let her parent down. This did not happen often; it was a condition which he thought that time or — more doubtfully — the demise of Roger would take care of. But he knew that if he told Maeve of his conversation with Skeffington and his resultant promise, she would be hurt, she would be angry, she would, finally, go to her father. That veteran pacifier could be counted upon to fan the flames. The alliance with his uncle, however loose, however understandable on a purely familial basis, would be misconstrued and would become the basis for a quarrel; it was an additional price that would have to be paid for the ring-side seat. This favored position, Adam thought ruefully, became more costly by the day.

Then too, there was the fact that he had not heard from Skeffington. Since the day of the conference Skeffington had been mysteriously silent. It was a neglect which Adam had not expected, and which — although he did not quite admit this to himself — left him more than a little disappointed. He did not fool himself into believing that he was in any way indispensable to his uncle; yet clearly, for whatever reasons of his own, Skeffington had been at some pains to urge him towards the campaign. In this he had been successful, and, this accomplished, Adam had supposed that the urgency would be maintained. He did not quite know how; he thought that perhaps there might be a series of telephone calls, informing him of opportunities for direct observation, possibly permitting him to choose from among them the occasions convenient to himself. In any event, he expected that contact, once established, would be attended to with constancy and care.

It was a swollen expectation, a measure of how little Adam really knew his uncle. It was true that Skeffington wanted Adam on his side; it was also true that he wanted to win an election. Between the two objectives there was no equation; the latter dominated his thoughts. He had by no means forgotten his nephew; he had merely allocated to him his proper position in the overall scheme of the campaign. At the moment, there were more immediate matters of concern, and one of these was the satisfaction of old John Gorman on the funds for the development within his ward. This was something which could not be postponed; it would have been an extraordinary circumstance indeed that would have led Skeffington to delay on any project close to John Gorman's heart. He was too close a friend; more, he was far too influential.

Accordingly, the previous week Skeffington had scheduled two unusual interviews. The first had been with Norman Cass Jr., the son of the banker. He was a blue-eyed man of forty, with a small, finely molded and faintly silly face; his hair, beginning to gray, was trimmed in a perpetual crew cut. He wore a narrow-shouldered suit of tan gabardine, a blue polka-dot bow tie, and a pair of old and much-scuffed white buckskin shoes. His appearance suggested that of a very old undergraduate. Possibly in apology for his costume he had entered the room saying, "I'm afraid I've jutht thith minute come up from the country."

The lisp was more than perceptible; it leaped out at the auditor so strongly that one became aware of it first, and Norman Cass Jr. second. It was a speech defect that had remained despite the resolute determination of Norman Cass Senior that it should go. From the first he had gauged his son's capacities; he had realized that these, plus a lisp, constituted an almost insuperable handicap. About the capacities he could do nothing; the lisp he could subject to remedial treatment. But nothing had availed, the lisp had hung on stubbornly, and now everything said by Norman Cass Jr. was given a comic dimension which, the contents of his words considered, could not have been more superfluous.

"Very good of you to drop in today," Skeffington had said. "To judge from your appearance, life in the country must be healthy. I imagine golf and tennis play their part in keeping you so bronzed and fit."

"Thailing, printhipally," his guest had replied. "In a thimply thuperb old thloop."

For just an instant Skeffington had had the suspicion that he was being made game of. *Thimply thuperb old thloop* — could such a combination be arrived at by accident? He looked sharply at the face confronting him, that distinguished family face which, in this instance, had been marred by the slight taint of boobery; he concluded that it was possible after all. He said, "A fascinating vessel, the sloop. Played a major role in the development of our fair city."

He talked for a few minutes about the maritime history of their fair city; only gradually did he lead the conversation into more pertinent channels. He then began to speak of men of opposite political faiths who found it necessary to subordinate their differences in a time of civic emergency; he suggested that indeed such an emergency was close upon them; he spoke of the Indispensable Man who sometimes arose to save his city; he at first hinted, then stated more explicitly, that the Indispensable Man in this instance was none other than Norman Cass Jr.

"In short, Mr. Cass," he said solemnly, "I'm saying that your city needs you. I'm telling you no secret when I say that the best minds of our community are agreed that our new Fire Commissioner should be Norman Cass Jr.!"

"Fire Commithioner!" Obviously, the suggestion that he could be of some service was both unexpected and unprecedented; dazed, he said: "There mutht be thome mithtake. I have no political ambithionth whatever. . . . "

"It's not a question of politics, Mr. Cass. I hope you understand that it's above that. It's a question of municipal need, of civic duty. I'll wager you already know something about our Fire Department."

"Well, no. . . . Not prethithely, that ith. Of courth," he said, with a small treble giggle, "I know that it putth out fireth."

"Exactly," said Skeffington, with a look of congratulation. "It puts out fires. You've put your finger right on the key to the whole situation, Mr. Cass, as I knew you would." He had gone on to explain that the Fire Department, at the moment, had been shaken in morale and, as a consequence, in efficiency; the present commissioner had proved a vast disappointment. What was needed, clearly, was an able administrator who could restore the department to its former happy state, a man who inspired public confidence and trust, a man who was above the concern of petty politics. In other words . . .

"I'm terribly flattered, of courth," Cass said. "But the truth ith that I know almost nothing about the workingth of a fire department. Ath you know, I'm a banker. . . . "

"What was it Clemenceau once said about war?" Skeffington said thoughtfully. "That it was too important a matter to leave in the hands of the generals? How well that expresses my own feelings about our Fire Department, Mr. Cass. It's too important to leave in the hands of professional firefighters." There had been more explanation; he had insinuated that although associated with his father at the bank, the junior Cass depended upon no family relationship for his reputation. There had been his work with the wonderful Boy Scout movement, had there not? And the Red Cross? From there Skeffington had gone on to stress, once more, civic duty, and the promise of freedom from all political interference. Norman Cass Jr. would be, indisputably, the boss.

"Well, really, I — " Again, there was heard the small giggle. "I'd like to do it. I hope I'm ath public-thpirited ath the average thitithen, but thtill — "

"Of course there are disadvantages too," Skeffington said casually. "I won't attempt to conceal them from you, Mr. Cass." Without appearing to, he kept a sharp eye on his visitor as he continued to speak. "First of all, I'm afraid you'd be extremely conspicuous. At every major conflagration you'd be present in a position of command, a recognizable figure in the commissioner's uniform of pure white. I have to admit to you that you'd be the cynosure of all eyes. And then in your day-by-day activities you'd ride in the long, maroon commissioner's car, equipped with a siren and two uniformed firemen to attend you; you'd be traveling at top speed at all times along our city streets; other cars would necessarily pull over to the curb to let you pass. I hesitate to tell you this because I realize that to a man of your reticence the necessity for traveling about in such a way as to compel constant and universal attention must be distasteful. Still, I tell you because I want you to know just what you'd be getting into; I want to be perfectly fair with you."

He had seen the blue eyes gleam with interest at the mention of "white uniform"; he had seen them grow brighter with each passing word; he knew that he had not mistaken his man.

"Well of courth," Cass said, "I thuppothe we all mutht make thome thacrifitheth. And thinthe you put it that way, I don't thee very well how I can refuthe. . . . "

"Excellent," Skeffington said. "I hope you won't." But he did not want immediate acceptance; he said, "Don't let me stampede you into anything, Mr. Cass. I'd never forgive myself if I rushed you into a hasty decision. I tell you what: why don't you sleep on it? Give it a night's consideration, talk it over with your good wife, sleep on it. Then, tomorrow, write me of your decision. Needless to say, I hope it will be favorable."

"Thatth ekthtremely conthiderate of you," Cass said, "but under the thircumthtantheth I feel thertain that I could give you my anther right now — "

"No, no," said Skeffington. Still talking, he rose and walked to the other side of the desk; duplicating his host's action, Cass rose too. Gracefully, the interview came to a close; Cass had left the office, reluctantly promising to defer his decision until the morning. Skeffington had returned to his desk well satisfied. There was some danger in allowing the overnight period of grace, but it was a necessary danger. The written acknowledgment was what he needed; this was the easiest way to secure it. And there was, after all, small chance that the junior Cass would change his mind. Not, Skeffington thought ironically, as long as it was possible to dream of a long maroon car *with a siren,* streaking along a crowded street in noisy splendor, while on either side motorists hastily came to a stop and watched in awed silence as the erect figure in pure white sped by, on his way to quell the flames.

" 'And visions of sugar plums danced through his head,' " he said aloud. He had little doubt of the answer he would receive.

It had arrived the following day. Skeffington had taken one look at it, then had made another telephone call. Twenty-four hours later Norman Cass Senior was in his office.

"You wished to see me," he said in a quiet, matter-of-fact voice. He was a short, compact, unobstrusive man, and in his face there was no silliness at all. A far different proposition, thought Skeffington, from the son. He was pleased by the visit; there was no one with whom he enjoyed going to the mat more than this shrewd, calm, tough financier, so well-born, so rich, so utterly ruthless.

"I naturally hated to intrude upon your busy day," he said, "but a matter of some urgency arose, and I thought we might be able to settle it in a few minutes of friendly conversation." Absently he fingered the skull ash tray on his desk, then lifted it for his visitor's inspection. "An interesting object. Said to be the skull of our first Republican governor. They seem to have had remarkably small heads in those days, don't they?"

"As you know," Cass said emotionlessly, "the first Republican governor of this state happens to have been an ancestor of mine. Since his bones, including those of his skull, are at present in the family vault at Mount Andrews Cemetery, I really don't think your story has a great deal of foundation in fact."

"Why bless my soul," said Skeffington, "I'd completely forgotten that there was a family connection." He seemed surprised, even contrite; he was delighted. It had been a fine opening gambit, a keynote to happy accomplishment. He said, "I seem to have been victimized by a charlatan. I've been sold the skull of a spurious Republican."

Cass nodded politely. "There was some specific matter you wished to discuss, I believe."

"I do indeed. A little matter of municipal finance. Hardly worth bothering you about under most circumstances, but we seem to have struck a few snags. Now, you're a busy man, Mr. Cass, and I don't see any reason why we should drag this out. To put it in a nutshell, I'd like to have you reconsider your position on that loan to the city."

Cass shook his head slightly. "I'm afraid that's impossible. We've already given it thorough consideration. Our decision was unanimous."

"So I heard. I was hoping you might make it a little less unanimous. You see, Mr. Cass, it's not an ordinary loan. I know that this doesn't come within the purview of the banker, but you're also one of our leading citizens, and I should think the fact that much of the money is to go for a children's playground might make some difference on purely humanitarian grounds. You know how crowded conditions are over in Ward Nine; every day there's an accident because little boys and girls are playing in congested streets. You can't blame them; there's nowhere else to play. Now I think our young people are important; I'm sure you do too. I think the city owes them a decent playground, with proper facilities indoors and out. But, Mr. Cass, we can't give it to them unless we have the money, and we can't get the money unless you loan it to us. That's why I want you to think of the purpose of the loan; that's why I beg you to reconsider."

"As you say," Cass said, "we're not, as bankers, primarily interested in the purpose of the loan. But, as you also say, we are citizens too, and I can assure you that this purpose of which you speak was considered. We agreed that the conditions in Ward Nine were deplorable. I believe we also agreed," he said, in the same tone of voice, "upon whose shoulders the blame for this must rest. We feel, as you apparently feel, that some sort of recreational project is needed. However, some of us seemed to remember that in the past loans were granted for similar purposes and the results achieved were hardly satisfactory. What work was done, was done at a prohibitive cost. More than that, as bankers responsible for our investors' money, we also remembered that we became considerably concerned about the risk involved. We feel that the risk is now greater than ever, and that it would be unwise to grant any loan at this time. While we sympathize with the need for such money, we prefer to wait until the municipal situation has changed to some extent before we gratify that need. I think that's about all I can tell you."

"What could be fairer than that?" Skeffington said, spreading his hands apart in a gesture of satisfaction. "I appreciate your frankness, Mr. Cass. And I'll even confess to you that up until now I'd been harboring an unworthy suspicion. I suspected that just possibly you might be doing this in order to embarrass me and my administration during an election year. There's no doubt that if the loan's refused, it'll do just that. So you see, Mr. Cass, I'm returning frankness for frankness. Would you believe that I had a suspicion of that nature?"

"I have no control over your suspicions, sir."

"As you have, apparently, over my destiny? Of course," he said thoughtfully, "if just by chance that suspicion were correct, I almost think I might be justified in taking the whole matter before the public. Properly put in the newspapers, I imagine a story like that could arouse considerable antagonism towards a man. Particularly if he were a banker. Speaking for myself, I like bankers: they're a fine, public-spirited breed of men. But the public as a whole doesn't share that liking; they're rather inclined to be hostile. And if the word got around that one especial banker was blocking a health and happiness program for little children, I suppose there might even be a hue and cry against him. What do you suppose, Mr. Cass?"

For the first time, the faintest of smiles appeared on Cass's impassive face. "I suppose," he said, "that this banker, knowing the people with whom he was to deal, would have anticipated such a possibility, and would have instructed his attorneys accordingly. I further suppose that any public reaction, if it should take place, would seem to him to be merely one of the expected hazards of his profession, and that it would not affect him too seriously."

"He'd be a brave man, your banker," Skeffington said. "I'd hope for his sake that he'd fully realize what he was doing. But enough of speculation, Mr. Cass: let's get back to you. Would you say your decision is final?"

"I would, sir," Cass said. He got to his feet.

"No possibility of reconsideration?"

"None whatever."

Skeffington sighed. "You're a hard man to do business with, Mr. Cass. I suppose that's the secret of your success. However, if that's your position, I don't see that there's anything more to say. I did my best; a man can but try. You seem to have won. I congratulate you."

For just an instant, a flickering part of a second, a light appeared in the small brown eyes of the compact little man who stood so trim, so immaculate, so victorious before him; then it died and Norman Cass said, "Good day, sir."

It was not until then that Skeffington released his bomb.

"One moment," he said. From his desk he took the letter written by Norman Cass Jr.; he handed it to the father. "I was so absorbed in your words I almost forgot to show this to you. Have a look at it. Have a *good* look at it; I think you might find it interesting."

Cass read the short letter swiftly. He looked up at Skeffington, then read the letter again. He said steadily, "What is this foolishness?"

"A major civic appointment is in the offing. This is the letter of acceptance from the potential appointee. You may keep it, if you wish." He added thoughtfully, "I believe I have several photostatic copies."

Cass continued to regard him with a fixed, emotionless stare. "What do you hope to gain by this?" he asked finally.

"Nothing but the valued services of a respected citizen who is the son of a respected citizen," Skeffington replied. "The boy was made for the job, don't you think?"

"Nonsense. You have no intention of appointing him. You know it. I know it."

"But does *he* know it?" Skeffington asked. "Apparently not; here's his letter of consent. It occurred to me that we might use it as a basis for our further discussion."

"We have nothing to discuss. I don't know how you got this. I don't know what use you hope to make of it. In any event, it's worthless. If you attempt to do anything with it, I can assure you my son will repudiate it immediately."

"But can he?" Skeffington asked. "Or even, will he? I wonder. I had a revealing talk with the boy the other day; he seemed to me to be rather eager to feel the spotlight's rays upon him. I suppose that's the natural consequence of having lived so long in the shadow of a successful father. You want to get out in the sunshine and grow by yourself for a change. And sometimes a kind stranger comes along to show you how that can be done. So then, maybe you could force him to repudiate it, and then again maybe you couldn't. I'm sure I don't know. But I'm equally sure I don't care, because it won't make the slightest difference what he does, one way or the other. The situation isn't exactly under his control any longer. Or yours either, if it comes to that." He leaned forward, partially supporting himself with his arms on the desk; it was the old familiar position of command. In a tone which was only slightly more businesslike, he said, "Have a seat, Mr. Cass. I think the time has come to talk a little turkey."

Cass said nothing. He remained standing; then, slowly, and still looking steadily at Skeffington, he sat down.

"Now," said Skeffington, "here's the position as I see it. I have this letter from your son. He says he wants to be Fire Commissioner. All right. I intend to appoint him. You don't believe that now, but you may in a minute. I intend to appoint him and leave him to his own devices. His own devices, Mr. Cass: you're fairly familiar with them, I believe. Now here's what I'm worrying about: How long will the boy last in a job which he doesn't know the first thing about, and where every politician in the city will be after him, first, because *he* got the job, and second, because he's your son? In some quarters, Mr. Cass, you are not a much-loved man. I'm very much afraid they're apt to put him in the bag so quick it'll make your head spin. Within two months of his appointment every paper in the city — with the exception of Amos's, of course — will be screaming for his resignation. There'll be charges of incompetence, even of graft — I don't imagine the boy, with his limited experience, will know how to protect himself against that one. Well, if that happened, you can see what my position would be. I'd have to step in and remove him from office. By that time, of course, the family name would be all muddied up, and then too, for my own protection — because this is an election year, as you may remember — I'd have to explain that I'd made a grevious mistake in the appointment, but that I had naturally assumed that a member of one of our first families would be above such behavior, and that my trust had been badly abused. And so, much as I hate even to suggest such an unhappy development, I'm afraid your son would leave office in disgrace. That wouldn't be so good, would it, Mr. Cass?"

Again a light showed in Cass's eyes. It was now a light of quite a different sort, and now it did not flicker and disappear. It remained, burning directly across the table at the heavy face whose features were still relaxed, but whose light blue eyes were as steady as his own. Still Cass did not speak. A lifetime spent on the politely savage battleground of his profession had given him a high opinion of silence and self-control as tactical weapons. He continued to listen. He had grasped, instantly, the desperate nature of his predicament, but there was still one way out. It was a way Skeffington now proceeded to close.

"There is the possibility that your son — doubtless at your insistence — might turn around and refuse the appointment. Or, as you said, repudiate his letter. In that case, I imagine there'd be nothing left for me to do but try to protect myself; I'd be forced into it. I might even have to tell a little white lie. Just to prevent anything like that happening, I might have to start a rumor circulating that your son had been offered the post. I suppose then that I'd have to come out with a denial of the whole thing, give the letter of acceptance to the papers, and explain that the boy had been the victim of a delusion, that the job had never been offered to him in the first place. I'd have to say something to the effect that he came to see me some time ago and offered his services to the city, specifying that he would like a position of authority commensurate with his position in the community. I might go on to say that while I respectfully and immediately declined this kind offer, he somehow acquired the fantastic notion that he was to be appointed Fire Commissioner, and that he wrote me a letter accepting what in fact had never been offered to him. This would be an extraordinary story, and you and I of course would be conscious of a little exaggeration in it here and there, but I think that it would be believed by the public. Particularly if I should point out his absolute lack of qualifications for the job, plus the fact that I'd hardly offer it to the son of an old political enemy. And then, of course, we have his own letter. So I suppose, Mr. Cass, that the result of this alternative would be not disgrace, but ridicule. I wouldn't be surprised if you, your son, and your family became the laughing-stock of the city an hour after the papers hit the street. And just by the way, I think I should point out that any attempt to forestall this by beating me to the punch — by going to the papers before me, for example — would unhappily fail. A little reflection will show you that there's no possible way of doing it without making your son out a perfect boob. So there you have it. It's a situation that gives me some concern; I don't quite know what to do about it." He looked solicitously at his old antagonist and said, "Got any ideas?"

And now Cass spoke. The light was still in his eyes, but his voice was perfectly controlled. "Typical," he said contemptuously. "Cheap and vicious and thoroughly typical of you and all that you represent."

Skeffington shook his head slowly. "It won't work, Mr. Cass," he said. "I realize I'm supposed to redden with shame at the thought of playing dirty pool against a distinguished opponent like yourself, but it somehow won't work. I don't know why. Maybe it's because I just this moment happened to remember who it is who every year delivers a bleak little statement about the pitiable plight of the people in our slums, but whose own large property holdings in those slums are shabby buildings not fit for dogs. Or maybe it's because I also remember that it's that very same man who engineered the merger of the Consolidated Trust with the old Mason Street Trust in such a way that one of his partners and oldest friends was driven to suicide. I guess you could say that this man has quite a pool table of his own, and after having watched the kind of game he's played over the years I don't believe I'm inclined to feel terribly remorseful right now. But I don't want to waste the time of a busy man like yourself in these little asides, Mr. Cass. The main problem before us right now is that you seem to be in a bit of a situation. I'm still waiting to hear if you've thought of any suitable way out."

For a moment Cass did not answer at all, then he jerked his head forward once and rose quickly. "Very well," he said. "We will re-examine the application for the loan."

"No," Skeffington said. "Not good enough. Try again."

"All right," Cass said sharply. "You'll get the money."

Skeffington nodded. "That's much better. Bless my soul if I don't think you've found the way out. For the second time today I congratulate you. And I'll leave it to you to explain matters to your son, may I? He's a young man of high spirits, eager ambition; he's bound to be slightly disappointed. You can soothe him by pointing out to him the error of his ways. I need hardly add that all evidence of that error will be handed over to you in the very near future. Say, for example, on the very day when the loan comes through."

Cass, during this speech, had turned his back on Skeffington and had walked briskly to the door; nothing was clearer than that he neither required nor wished an escort from this office. At the door he stopped and made his farewell.

"Very well," he said quietly. "You've got what you wanted. I tell you now that it is a victory you may regret."

"I have many regrets," Skeffington said. "One is that our little talk this afternoon didn't take place twenty years ago. So one more regret won't make much difference; it might even be something to look forward to. Good-by, Mr. Cass." He added urbanely, "And give my best to the family."

It was the final insult, but Cass refused to be baited. He closed the door quickly but silently; furious, he was nevertheless in complete command of himself. He walked briskly down the antiquated, ill-kept halls, and as he moved along the unfamiliar route he saw and passed the whispering confidential knots of beefy men. Instinctively his mouth tightened, for he recognized in them the marauders, the representatives of that boisterous, crafty and despised breed of latter-day Goths who had come to sack his city and had remained to enjoy their plunder. Yet despite his dislike of the Irish, Cass had not ignored them. He had studied them carefully, just as he had studied the Jews and, more recently, the Italians: like some lone defender of the human race unexpectedly confronted by an invading host of vermin, he had studied them in the interest of his own survival. The reported wit and charm of these strangers had completely eluded him, but he had found in them qualities he liked: sentimentality, intemperance, verbosity, and best of all, the lack of financial acumen. These were the little vices which, in others, became for Cass the useful virtues; like Skeffington, he was a realist. He knew that direct control of his city was no longer possible to him and his associates; the big immigrations had ended that forever. There was, however, the consolation of the indirect control: Cass had found that few things were denied him who held the purse. No one held it more firmly than he. A first-class financier, he regarded with a chill amusement the efforts of the newer group to intrude upon his domain, and for the individual members of this group he felt nothing but distaste and contempt.

About Skeffington, however, he had a different feeling. Here, alone among the invaders, was the dangerous antagonist. He was a man to be viewed with detestation, but also with respect. With his astonishing limitations and accomplishments, he was still, after all these years, something of a puzzle to Cass. It was a mystery, for example, how one so peculiarly maladroit in the ordinary ways of business — for whenever Skeffington, temporarily out of office, had ventured into the world of private enterprise, the results had been so calamitous as to often require a full term in office to restore him to his feet — should be so extraordinarily skillful in the management of his political affairs. Cass was not politically naïve. He was well aware that the talents and urges of the politician and those of the financier are not necessarily identical or even similar, and the recent history of his country had served as appalling confirmation that men of almost childlike simplicity in their business lives may wind up in the highest political places. Even so, he was impressed by the extent of Skeffington's disasters. He was even more impressed by the extent of his success; it had been attained through a combination of qualities to which Cass, putting aside the question of personalities, paid homage. He knew Skeffington as a superb practical psychologist with the instincts of a pirate, and since in his own aging veins there flowed the adventurous blood of the blackbirder and buccaneer of long ago, he respected this tough, intelligent and imaginative foe, from whom it was sheer folly to expect either scruple or mercy. And when he reflected, in cold fury, upon the outrageous, humiliating scene of a few minutes before, into his reflections there sneaked reluctant admiration for the maneuver itself: so bold, so ingenious, so incredibly inhumane. It was the kind of move which Cass was capable of appreciating.

But appreciation did not diminish rage. He had been defeated, a victim both to Skeffington and to his own idiot son. Defeat demanded retaliation; he would repay both, and he did not lack confidence in his ability to do so. As for Skeffington, there were the November elections; Cass resolved to get in touch with Amos Force immediately. He had been approached by the publisher, who had suggested that he lend his support to the coalition group now forming behind this young McCluskey. He had been cool to the proposal of his old friend, for while naturally he desired the defeat of Skeffington, he was attracted neither to the heterogeneous alliance which was to fight him nor to the young nonentity it was to back. To have committed his resources to such a group this morning would have been unthinkable; to do so now, in the light of the insupportable provocation, was unavoidable. He would call Amos Force within the hour; he would declare himself irrevocably in.

As for his son . . .

Arriving at the bank, he went directly to his son's office. Norman Cass Jr. was seated behind his desk, dictating the inconsequential memoranda with which he was habitually entrusted. At his father's unprecedented entrance he looked up in astonishment.

"Why, Dad," he said, "thith ith a thurprithe!"

His father said nothing; an abrupt motion of his head sent his son's secretary hurrying from the room. Then he said ominously, "I imagine I should call you 'Mr. Commissioner.' "

The long silly face flushed. "Tho you know," his son said weakly. "I hadn't planned to thay anything yet; I wanted you to be thurprithed."

"You were successful. I was surprised." And then, the stony self-control which had withstood the humiliating shafts of Skeffington broke down before the ogling vacant face before him. *This is my son,* he thought, in a spasm of agony; aloud he suddenly screamed: "You fool! You utter god-damned imbecile . . . "

For the next quarter hour, Norman Cass Jr. had a very bad time indeed.

In the mayor's office, Skeffington had summoned Weinberg and Gorman; with delight and with some elaboration, he told them of the satisfying conversation.

"By God, that's good, Frank," Gorman said. "That was grand talk. There'll be big doings at the bank about now."

Skeffington looked at his watch. "Unless I'm mistaken, a father-and-son chat should be in progress. There's nothing like a boy's own dad telling him the facts of life. In any case, I hope everything has worked out to your satisfaction, John."

The old man nodded. "It has, Frank. It has. We'll go right along with the development now."

"Couldn't be a better time for it," Skeffington said. "The progress of the development keeping pace with the progress of the campaign: I like that. It's a useful reminder that the present administration is constantly concerned about better living for the electorate. Meanwhile, what about our worthy opponents? Sam, you were dead right about the coalition; it seems to be shaping up nicely behind young McCluskey."

"Yeh," Weinberg said. "He's their dog O.K. The others we can forget about."

Gorman agreed. "Although I wouldn't have thought it would happen that way. They're a dreadful bagful of rascals. I still think they'll claw each other to bits before they're through. Can't you see them all together in the same room, each one smiling and promising the other he didn't bring his knife tonight? Every time Amos shakes hands with Festus he must think he's caught a terrible disease."

"At first, maybe," Skeffington said. "But then when he gets to know him better, he'll discover what a delightful companion Festus can be. I can't think of a better way to spend an evening than sitting back and listening to Festus give his talk on 'Celebrated Knights of Columbus I Have Met.' Of course, Amos can come right back at him with 'Happy Days in the K.K.K.' "

"Was he a Ku Kluxer?" Gorman said. "That I didn't know."

"Not many people do, including the people who gave him a Brotherhood award last winter. But he was, about thirty years ago. I never did know why he quit, exactly: I always suspected it was because he found out he was expected to buy his own sheet. Little things like that can drive a man to Tolerance. But to return to our friend McCluskey: I've looked over our reports on him pretty thoroughly. We don't seem to have come up with a thing, do we?"

Weinberg shook his head. "You don't dig up anything on a kid like that. He don't drink, he don't smoke, he goes home after work every night, he's in church every morning, and nobody ever told him any bad words to say. The kid's clean as a whistle."

"This is news to chill the blood," Skeffington said. "In other years I was up against mere men; now it seems I'm fighting one of the angelic host."

"He's a good enough lad, by all accounts," Gorman said reflectively, "but I wonder is he bright at all? I wouldn't think so. If he was, Festus wouldn't have his hooks into him. And then down at the Courthouse they tell me that as a lawyer he's not much. He looks good — tall, handsome, with the let's-go-to-Mass-together-on-Sunday voice, and the flower in the buttonhole — but he has a bad habit, it seems. He doesn't win many cases. I really don't know what he is."

"I'll tell you," Skeffington said abruptly. "He's a six-foot hunk of talking putty. Immaculate putty, to be sure, but putty nevertheless. So let's not waste any more time looking into his past; he has no past. He's not only never done anything bad; he's never done anything at all. All right. Let's go after him on that ground: the innocent do-nothing who's suddenly become the darling of a strange and rather ill-assorted group. We'll strip the armor right off this young knight in public, and show that he's really not Sir Galahad after all. He's Pinocchio. And right behind him is that well-known Gepetto, Festus Garvey, ably supported by that celebrated champion of the poor, Amos Force. There's no sense in attacking McCluskey for what he *was;* he wasn't anything. We have to get him for what he is. And what is he? A front man, a nice young spick-and-span front man with a shining face and clean hands who comes before the public wearing his First Communion suit. What we have to point out is that the nice young man is really the creature of the big bad boys in the back room. A puppet fallen among thieves. So we won't blast him: we'll blast the people behind him, taking care to show that they dominate him. As for the candidate himself, we'll make him an object of pity: the poor little lamb, with all his evil shepherds just waiting to wipe their dirty hands all over his nice white woolly coat. We'll take all this innocence and make it work for us, and I think we might be able to knock the pins right out from under this new wonder boy. What do you say to that?"

The white burrs of Gorman's eyebrows lifted in mild surprise. "By God, Frank," he said softly, "now that was a fast ride downhill you gave the boy. One minute he was up with the angels and the next he's Mary's little lamb." The old man smiled faintly and added, "It seems a grand idea to me. Only we'll have to take care not to make too much of a lamb out of him. There's always the danger he could pick up the sympathy vote. Everybody likes poor little lambs."

"Everybody likes the village idiot," Skeffington said, "which doesn't necessarily mean that they'd like him as the chief of police. But you're right, of course. We don't want to go too heavy on the pity or the ridicule; either can backfire on us and do some damage. Still, if we don't know how to gauge a little thing like that by this time we ought to quit and turn the whole shooting match over to the mayor of Boystown. I understand he's an efficient young man with a go-cart of his own. Sam, you're silent; does that indicate dissent?"

Deep in his chair, the slumped figure shook his head in negation. "Nah. I like it. It's as good a way out as any, maybe the best. You got this kid up there, you gotta do something with him, so why not make him out a dummy? He fits: the kid's a regular Charlie McCarthy. Only don't forget with all this talk about the poor little lamb that this one ain't so poor. He's got plenty of bucks in back of him. Garvey's got no dough, but old Cass'll deal himself in now. He would anyway but after today he'll do it on the double. And old man Force. And all those old dames in the Good Government bunch. They got nothin' else to do with their dough but leave it to cats. With a couple more like that behind him our dummy is sittin' on Fort Knox. And a rich dummy somehow don't look so dumb."

"Fair enough," said Skeffington imperturbably. "So we'll fight a wealthy little lamb instead of a poor one. There's nothing so different about that except that it takes a little more cash. I think we should be able to get it up without too much trouble. I haven't seen the latest organization figures, but I assume all good men are coming to the aid of their party."

In the financing of his organization, Skeffington had found it useful to duplicate the great men of the past: he had installed a system of tithes. It was based upon the ability to pay, and thus democratic: each party worker who had been given employment by the party gave to the party, in return, a modest portion of his annual earnings. Thus the party was in the enviable position of employer and employment agency. If, for any reason, an employed worker skipped a payment, he was visited by one of Weinberg's men and reminded of his dereliction. And if, after this, payment still lagged, the worker was subjected neither to violence nor to further reminder. He simply lost his job. This was efficient retributive justice; through its swift and impartial exercise did the organization perpetuate itself.

"No complaints," Weinberg said. "Everything's coming along O.K. Only one place is a little slow. Sanitation. I dunno about that."

"Why? Who've you got over there?"

"Charlie Ragazza."

"He knows the ropes. Why is he slow?"

Weinberg shrugged. "I ain't figured it out yet. Maybe collections are tough for some reason. Or maybe . . ."

"Or maybe Charlie's taking a little for his private purposes?"

"Maybe. Like I say, I ain't figured it out yet. He never took before. I got a few of the boys checkin' up on him."

"Does he still play the horses?"

"Yeh."

"Are the bookies into him?"

"Yeh. For how much I dunno."

"I'm told Charlie's been having his troubles," Gorman said meditatively, "but I wouldn't think he'd be taking. He might, but I wouldn't think so. He's always been one to play it straight enough."

"Yeh," Weinberg said. "Anyway, we'll know in a couple of days."

"We'll know before a couple of days," Skeffington said decisively. "Get Charlie in here the first thing in the morning. I'll have a talk with him. I'll find out in five minutes what's going on. He's a good boy and I don't want to hurt him, but if he's taking it's got to be stopped and stopped now. This is going to be the most expensive campaign we've ever run; the television costs alone will run it up sky-high. So we need all the money we can lay our hands on, and we can't spare any for Charlie. Or his bookie. Get him in here, Sam."

Weinberg nodded. "O.K. By the way, you talked with the truckers and contractors yet?"

"Yes. They're all right. One or two of them were disposed to be a little less than generous at first, but I had Teddy bring them in for a special heart-to-heart talk. I told them that parsimony was wicked; I also touched briefly upon the unpleasant things that could happen to niggardly businessmen whose livelihood depended upon the good will of the city. I think we parted in an atmosphere of understanding. No," he said, "I don't think we'll have too much trouble raising the wherewithal to fight your rich little lamb, Sam. We might even have enough left over to take a few good swipes at his shepherds. I must say it's a prospect to delight the imagination; I can hardly wait to begin!"

It was true. He sat there, smiling at his colleagues, an elderly warrior solidly rejoicing in the anticipation of still another battle. All preparations had been made, the ways had been greased, the campaign was now ready to be launched and taken to the public; it was from this moment on that Skeffington would fall to with special zest. It was the beginning of the hard, joyous, open toe-to-toe slugging match with old enemies; it was the wonderful, vigorous preliminary to victory and four more years of political control. For Skeffington, this was the moment above all others; it was truly the very best of times. He lit a cigar and said cheerfully, "We'll kick off on Thursday night at the rally at Davis Park; it's to be carried on radio and television. Your presence, gentlemen, is desired. Come early and bring your clippers; we're going to start shearing a lamb!"

Seven

IT was on the day following the Davis Park rally that Adam at last came to grips with the Skeffington campaign. Curiously enough, this came about not through Skeffington alone, but also through the somewhat unlikely person of Edgar Burbank.

On the previous evening, Adam had watched his uncle on television. Maeve had watched with him for a time; she had found the spectacle a source of the deepest discouragement. For one thing, it had been so extremely well done. Even the band, hired for the evening, had abandoned the standards of cacophony usually prevailing at political rallies, and had managed to play in tune. The speakers' platform had been heavy with dignitaries from state and city government, as well as from the military. Prominent among the latter had been Colonel Reuben Ballou, the city's only surviving veteran of the Civil War. Like the American flag, this feeble centenarian was an indispensable at all political gatherings. For some years now he had lived largely in his cot at the veterans' home, subsisting on chicken broth and custard; only during campaign time did he lead a life of whirling mobility. Then he would be trundled from his cot to one stage after another where he would sit, tiny, motionless, silent, and vague of eye; from time to time his dreams would be interrupted by the familiar prodding elbow, and then he would wave his toy cane in the general direction of the audience. The Colonel's services were in great demand.

Slightly to his left had sat the three clergymen: Catholic, Protestant, and Jew. (It was later revealed that a Greek Orthodox priest had been the victim of misfortune; invited, but less accustomed than his colleagues to the precise timing necessary to such occasions, he had arrived at the very end, too late to deliver his prayer and indeed, almost too late to be televised.)

Maeve had been discomforted by this supportive presence of Religion, but it was the crowd itself, standing before and around the platform, seeming to swell out into the farthest reaches of the park, that had sent her into despair. She had sighed, "But who *are* they all?"

"Gangsters, I imagine," Adam had said. "Smugglers, hopheads, and the lesser criminal elements from whom, as you know, Uncle Frank derives his support. Good Democrats all. Or, to put it another way, the very same people who crowded this park to see Roosevelt ten years ago."

"That was *much* different."

"No, it wasn't. *You* were much different, though. You were a little girl of twelve. And now look at you: a big, grown-up girl, fortunately married to the nephew of the man whom the multitudes honor tonight. Question: Did that little girl of twelve even then dream of one day basking in such reflected glory?"

She had made a face. "Ugh. You can sit here if you want to. I'm going out to the kitchen. Call me when it's over."

Adam had remained to watch his uncle in action. It had been impressive action; Skeffington had talked without a script and apparently without notes of any kind. Adam, although no connoisseur of the political address, had recognized it as a masterly performance. It had been a logical, powerful statement of administrative accomplishment, and of plans for the future; it had also been an entertaining if mortifying attack upon the qualifications of his opponents, with particular reference to McCluskey. When the speech was over, Adam had realized that the opening of this public campaign had been a brilliant success.

He had also realized, not without a touch of annoyance, that despite the earlier urgings and expressed desires of his uncle, it had been an opening to which he had not been invited. . . .

The next afternoon at the paper, he encountered the managing editor, plunging morosely along the corridor that led to his office. Adam had not seen him for several days, and he noted that the aspect of pinched harassment that hung about him always now seemed more sharply defined. He said pleasantly, "Trying times, Ralph?"

"Ha ha," the managing editor said tonelessly. He detected raillery; he said, "Save that stuff for your uncle. He'll need it. Just wait."

But it was a spiritless rejoinder from a spiritless man, for the managing editor was finding these trying times indeed. Difficulties assailed him from every side. There was first of all the union: a strike in the city room was in the offing; there would be discussion, there would be arbitration, there would be ultimately, he realized sadly, some raise in pay, however small. He was now busy considering the possible reprisals for this; they were lamentably few. He had already suggested, as a desirable inconvenience, the closing of the men's room on the strikers' floor. It was good, yes, but was it good enough?

Then too, there was his employer. Ever since the Skeffington announcement, Amos Force had been coming in to the paper daily, arriving early and staying late. The managing editor found his continued presence unnerving. Each day the old man wrote a new installment in his serial exposé of Skeffington's past: venemous in intent, it came out dull. Even the managing editor, who secretly approved of dull prose, found this to be singularly leaden. And all the while, from the massive ornate office where the aged tyrant now sat in constant residence, wearing the insigne of his office — a bottle-green eyeshade, incongruously perched on his long and bony brow — there came the stream of outrageous demands for increased speed, efficiency, and action, the endless questions which received no answers because, thought the managing editor wrathfully, they were unanswerable. Undeniably, Amos Force had taken the bit between his teeth; from now until the end of the campaign, the managing editor was miserably aware that every day would be a living hell.

Adam knew something of this, and there were times when he even felt compassion for the managing editor, but just now he was curious; he said, "Tell me one thing, Ralph: why McCluskey? What dictated the paper's picking him out?"

"Logic," said the managing editor swiftly.

"Yes, I suppose so, but that's what I don't understand. What was the logic that led to him?"

"The logic of the fact that he was the logical choice," the

managing editor said, rather snappishly. "That's simple enough, isn't it? You'll see, my friend. He'll take your uncle over the jumps, one, two, three."

But this too was spoken in the voice of duty rather than conviction, for the managing editor had just come from luncheon with candidate McCluskey; he disliked him intensely. They had eaten in Amos Force's office, and throughout the frugal meal the managing editor had covertly examined the subject of his editorial support with growing hostility. He was young, he was tall, he was a Democrat; worse still, he talked of "the Common Man." Once, just briefly, he had spoken of ". . . the possible extension of existing social services." The managing editor had found this alarming and so, thank God, had Amos Force. The old man's eyes had flashed and he had begun to talk violently of Thrift. McCluskey had hastened to reassure him, and there had been no more nonsense; still, the words had been uttered, and McCluskey had uttered them. Clearly, thought the managing editor, a dangerous man to support. But to Adam he said loyally, "A certain winner in November, my friend. Your uncle's going to get it right where it hurts." He seemed about to continue when, suddenly, he lifted his head, then whirled away and disappeared around a corner. Adam stared at the spot he had just left, mystified. Then, from a distance, faintly muffled by the intervening walls, came the sound: it was the soaring whine of complaint that had become so familiar in recent weeks; it was the cry of Amos Force, summoning his chief subordinate. Adam heard it; the managing editor had anticipated it. For not the first time in his employment on this paper, Adam felt distinctly thankful that his function was an innocent and an apolitical one.

He went to his desk and began to work once more on his comic strip. For the moment he was stuck, and so were Little Simp, Daddy, and Mr. Yeats Keats. The adventure in the Argentine was going badly. Momentarily incautious in the Buenos Aires café, the three chums had betrayed the signs of recognition; they had been seized upon orders from the hysterical waiter with the comic mustache. A series of frenzied commands in German had sent them to a stone fortress located some miles outside the city and here, chained to one another, they awaited their death. For food they were given each day a handful of local, inedible nuts; it was a diet suited only to Daddy the chipmunk, who waxed fat and whose fur grew glossy. But he was not happy, for his companions, unfortunately human, were all too visibly wasting away. Occasionally they were visited by their chief captor, who subjected them to maniacal bursts of Teutonic abuse; Yeats Keats drove him to further fury by responding with languid classical sneers, perfectly expressed in dactylic hexameter. The pseudowaiter foamed at the mouth; speaking through the froth, he had informed them of the method of their execution. They were to be fed individually into decorticating machines, the devices more normally used in Mexico for the stripping of hemp; once inside, they would swiftly be unhusked. This was not all. They would be buried; their graves would be marked by mocking cenotaphs made of mud. Looking out the tiny window of their prison, they could even now see these frightful objects in the process of construction. It was indeed a terrifying fate for the three chums to contemplate; it posed a problem of peculiar intractability for Adam to solve. To circumvent the designs of the malevolent German was imperative but not easy; Adam had already rejected three possible solutions as being unworthy of the dilemma. He knew from experience that such a situation required something new in ingenious fatuity, and of this he was, regrettably, in temporary short supply. However, he worked on, hoping for the best, and it was while he worked that Burbank, strangely absent all day, returned.

"Hello, dear boy," he said. But he did not enter the office, and Adam, looking up automatically, almost gasped in his astonishment, for the Burbank who stood poised in the doorway, one hand resting on the frame for support, was not the Burbank he knew. It was a different Burbank, a radiant Burbank, a — or so it seemed — slightly drunken Burbank. His faintly seedy wardrobe had been miraculously enriched; he now stood in clothes which were new, immaculate, elegant and *young:* the charcoal-gray jacket of cashmere, the pearl-gray doeskin trousers, the Tattersall waistcoat, the black loafers with the ribbon bows, the dark knit tie, and, just above the tie, the only familiar if discordant note — the tired, parchment Burbank face. It smiled proudly as its owner swayed slightly, and said again, "Dear boy, hello."

"I'm staggered," Adam said truthfully. "Who is this king of glory?"

Burbank smiled again, but said nothing. He walked into the office and over to his desk. The great unopened pile of Scrambled Letters mail awaited him; he reached out with both hands and, before Adam's amazed eyes, pushed it all into the wastebasket. Then, casually, he lit a match and dropped it into the pile; immediately the wastebasket began to blaze.

"Burbank!" Adam cried. He jumped up, crossed the office, and tipped over the basket. The burning letters fell across the floor; a few seconds of frantic stamping, and the fire was out. Adam said, "Have you gone crazy?"

"No," Burbank said. He sat in his chair and spun around to face Adam; carefully he centered the creases in his trousers. "No, dear boy, I am not crazy. And I am *not* a pyromaniac. This was just my little joke; I knew you would respond in positively *heroic* fashion. Although if you hadn't I must confess there would have been no tears. Not from Burbank, at any rate. Or should I say, not from Burbank the *former employee?* Because, dear boy, that is my secret: I resigned, bag and baggage, from our dear, *dear* paper, not five minutes ago!"

And he smiled again, more complacently than before. Adam was aghast; he said, "You're joking!"

"No no, dear boy. I never joke; you know that. Our residence together must have taught you that I have very little sense of humor. Defeated men seldom have."

Adam waved this aside; he said, "But why?"

"Oh many *many* reasons," he said negligently. "The years' accumulation, shall we say? But the funeral was the end. It was really the last straw. You remember the funeral, dear boy?"

Adam remembered. It had been little more than a week ago; he had been in the office when Burbank had returned, disconsolate, in slightly frayed morning clothes.

"*Nobody* was there," he had complained. "Not a recognizable soul. All these blubbering strangers who meant absolutely nothing to me. And I, if I may say so, meant nothing to them. In I came, properly dressed, naturally, but with those dreadful cheap flowers in my hand. *They* didn't realize, of course, what cheap flowers they were — quite frankly, dear boy, the family and close friends of the deceased are not the most sophisticated people in the world — but *I* realized, and that was what counted. And all the while those dreadful bastards upstairs were probably chuckling to themselves and chalking up another humiliation for poor old Burbank! Dear boy," he said passionately, "I am praying nightly for your uncle's victory!"

It had begun three days before, with the death of an elderly compositor. He had been in the employ of the paper for fifty years; in the light of the long years of service, it had been felt that the paper should be represented at the funeral. It had also been suggested that some additional gesture might be required. To the first of these points, Amos Force had given immediate consent.

"Of course we will send someone. This man — Joyce, you say his name was? — was a loyal member of our staff; we must show our appreciation. His family will be grateful. Naturally I cannot attend myself; I am far too busy. And with our campaign on against this scoundrel there are very few men I can spare, even for a morning. What I want," he had said, turning to the managing editor, "is someone we can spare easily. Someone whose absence can make no conceivable difference to the paper. That is the man to represent us. Send him."

And so Burbank had been sent.

On the other point, there had been indecision, procrastination. All had agreed that something suitable should be done; the question was, what? A watch? Clearly this was superfluous to the needs of the deceased. Money? This was rejected somewhat more quickly. The decision finally rested in favor of flowers.

"A nice bouquet of flowers," Amos Force had said. "Not too many, I think. Nothing ostentatious. I am told the family is in moderate circumstances; we must not embarrass them. I sometimes feel that on occasions like this all problems would be settled if we were a Catholic organization. I believe the Catholics send what is called a 'spiritual' bouquet. It is a little card. It comes to almost nothing."

"A bit more than that, Mr. Force," the managing editor said. It was the kind of thing about which he knew. "There's the little card all right, but then you have to give a donation, and by the time you're finished it amounts to the same as a regular bouquet. But I think your suggestion is an excellent one, sir. You can get very good flowers for about ten dollars." Quickly calculating, he amended this; he said, "Or five."

"Yes," Mr. Force had said. "I like that. A nice five-dollar bouquet of flowers. Flowers are always appreciated in a time of bereavement. I like to think that they say things that words cannot. But then I am a sentimental man. Send the bouquet." He added, "The five-dollar one."

But this had been resolved upon too late for the flowers to be delivered properly; Burbank had had to take them in his hand. This had been a further source of shame.

"I was the center of all eyes," he said now, remembering. "Have you ever arrived at a funeral with five dollars' worth of flowers in your hand? No. I thought not. Nobody has but Burbank the Grotesque. It was all done, dear boy, in the spirit of purest revenge. I saw it clearly. And I think that it was at that moment that I determined to endure no more. Poor old wormlike Burbank was going to turn at last. And now, dear boy, he *has*. You might congratulate me."

"I do, of course," Adam said. "Except . . . I'm sure you know what you're doing, but are you quite sure you had to do it so abruptly?" For suddenly he had a vision of Burbank, emancipated from the mooring he had despised: it was not a pleasant vision. For without this security, what was this dapper, pathetic, outdated little man, the hatchet man of yesterday, to do? Somewhat hopefully he said, "I don't suppose you've burned all your bridges?"

"Every last one. They are smoldering ruins. Burbank is now looking to the future, dear boy. Thanks, I may add, to you."

"To *me?*"

"Of course. Otherwise," he said, "I might never have thought of your dear uncle. Our little talks together, you know, stirred up memories of the dear dead days. I said to myself, 'Perhaps, Burbank, just perhaps, a little visit to City Hall might be in order.

Just for old times' sake.' And, dear boy, it proved to be quite in order. Your uncle and I immediately established our old rapport, so to speak. So much so that one word led to another, and before you know it he extended a very kind offer of employment. And all at once it dawned on me that this was exactly the out I had been looking for. It was just that no one had ever offered it to me before. And so, I took it. Burbank shifted allegiance, you might say, in midstream. I have just finished informing Mr. Force. *That* was a moment, dear boy. Burbank's hour, you might say."

He smacked his lips juicily, and Adam stared at him. "You mean you're working for my uncle?" he asked incredulously.

"Like a *Trojan*. Is it so hard to believe that poor old Burbank could actually be in demand? I see by your face that it is. But no matter: I must not be Burbank the Waspish with you, must I? Because, in a sense, we're allies now. I am working, humbly but ceaselessly, for your dear uncle. I am a part of his writing team. An integral part, he assures me. I don't suppose it's really so, but how nice it is to hear! I write speeches and news releases, and I plan to begin work soon on a really rather dreadful *attack* on dear Mr. Force and the rest of the supporters of the innocent Mr. McCluskey. Quite unexpectedly, dear boy, I find myself regrinding the edge of my little hatchet. I cannot *begin* to describe the pleasure!"

He left his chair and did a little dance step; he almost fell, and Adam rose to help him, but was stopped with a gesture as Burbank regained his balance.

"I am *not* drunk," he said. "I have been drinking, in celebration, you might say, but I am definitely not drunk. Not with wine, that is. With joy, yes. I have just spent a greal deal of money on some drastically needed clothing. How do you like my ensemble, dear boy? I await comments."

"Very much," Adam said. He was still bewildered; he said, "Look, Burbank, I'm delighted, naturally, but how about the permanency of this new job? I mean, is it just for the duration of the campaign?"

"Oh, come, come! What an opinion you have of poor old Burbank! Naturally, when your uncle is continued in office, a position will be ready and waiting for me. We have an understanding, your dear uncle and I."

Adam said hesitantly, "Not to be disloyal at all, but have you thought of the other possibility? Just as a man who has to make a living?"

Burbank in his eccentric progress had reached the door; he paused and said with peculiar solemnity: "Dear boy, of course I have thought of it. I have thought about it a great *great* deal. Burbank is not without the normal measure of prudence. But for one thing I'm quite sure the possibility is extremely slight. Your uncle, dear boy, is a gifted man and a formidable campaigner, and this time his opponents are nothing more than ciphers. Absolute zeroes. And, as I may have told you, I *like* your uncle. He was always very pleasant to me. He is a dreadful rascal, to be sure, but he is something those horrid sons of bitches upstairs will never be: *he is a human being*. Do you know what he said to me the other day? I'll tell you what he said, word for word; I remember it very well. He put his hand on my shoulder and said, 'Edgar, come on aboard. I can help you, but what's more to the point right now, you can help me. You're an able man and I'd be delighted to have your services. So forget all that's happened in the past, wipe the slate clean, give us a hand now, and we'll give the bastards the beating of their lives. What do you say?' And that was the first time in twenty years," Burbank said, steadying himself once more, "that *anyone* has told me that I was an able man or that he wanted me around. Quite a change, dear boy, for Burbank, the well-known figure of fun. And while I know that your uncle is a *most* adroit politician and really means very little of what he says, nevertheless, do you know, I got the distinct feeling that he *did* mean this, just a little bit? And that little bit was quite enough for me. So I said yes. And now I'll say farewell; doubtless we'll meet again during the campaign. But not," he said, with a glance of triumph at the wastebasket, *"not* over Scrambled Letters. Dear boy, I bid *you* farewell; *them* I bid good-by. And forever!"

And with a jaunty, joyous wave of the hand, Burbank was gone. Adam sat still, not entirely certain of his thoughts. There was no doubt that Burbank at all times was deeply moved by the subject of himself; there was no doubt that today drink had enriched this feeling. Yet it was not as simple as that, for in spite of himself, Adam had found the farewell speech of his former office mate strangely affecting. Poor Burbank, he thought, and then, on an impulse, he decided to telephone to City Hall. He was put through to his uncle immediately.

"You must be clairvoyant," Skeffington said. "I was just about to give you a ring. What have you got on for this evening?"

It was not for this he had called, but he said, "I'd planned to stay in town to catch up on some work; so far it doesn't seem to be working out too well. Why?"

"I thought that if you had nothing better to do you might take a little trip with me to the other side of the city. You could call it your formal indoctrination into the campaign. Actually, what you'll see isn't a part of the campaign at all, properly speaking, but it's the kind of background I think might interest you. It shouldn't take too long. What do you say?"

This, then, was the moment of invitation, that much-postponed moment which Adam had resolved to postpone still further. It was now that, skillfully, he could begin to extricate himself from the promise rashly made. Instead, he found himself saying, "All right. I'd like to very much. What time?"

"Oh, say seven-thirty. Where'll I pick you up: at the house?"

"No, I'll be here at the paper." It was his habit to stay at the paper one night a week, working late: coincidentally — and perhaps providentially, he thought, all things being considered — this was the night.

"Good. At the side entrance to your building, then. I'd pick you up at the front but that would be conspicuous; evil minds might think I was paying a social call on your employer. Nothing can tear a man down quicker than the rumor of disreputable associations. Besides," he said, "the side door is on our direct route."

"I'll be there. By the way, I watched your opening rally on television last night." With what he hoped was a certain pointedness he said, "Originally, I had thought of going down to see it."

"Would have been a waste of time." Skeffington said. "You wouldn't have learned a thing. At a big rally like that everything is cut and dried and pure routine. You were much better off in your own home; the only thing you missed was the fireworks. I'm told a roman candle ran amuck and severely injured a slumbering indigent."

Adam laughed. "He must have been the only one in the park able to slumber. It was an enormous crowd."

"A tribute to my personal charm." He chuckled. "And also to the fact that it was a fine night and admission was free. A shoeshine boy playing 'Swanee River' on the Jew's-harp could have drawn a crowd under those conditions. Well, so much for our grand opening. I'll be around tonight to pick you up."

"All right, fine." Just in time he remembered Burbank and the original purpose of his call; he said, "Uncle Frank?"

"Yes?"

"Burbank dropped in a few minutes ago. He told me that he's left the paper and is working for you."

"Burbank?" To Adam's horror his uncle seemed perplexed, but then he said, "Oh. Yes. I'd forgotten about him for a minute. He came in one day last week. He seemed to be unhappy and in need of a change; we could use him, so I put him on."

"I see. Exactly what will he do?"

"What he's told," Skeffington said, with a rather frightening candor. Then he chuckled again. "Don't worry about it; your friend will be all right. I'll see to it. And I'll also see you. At seven-thirty. Good-by."

Adam hung up slowly. About Burbank he now felt to some extent reassured; about himself, he had several rather serious misgivings. In talking to his uncle, the resolutions which had been forming slowly within the past two weeks seemed to have dissolved. He reflected with some discomfort that he had not even bothered to ask their destination, or what they were to do when they arrived. The only known effect of this mysterious errand would be to bind him closer to a political campaign which he had almost decided to disavow. This, quite clearly, was nothing more or less than a case of the melting will, and for it he reproached himself dutifully. Yet, surprisingly enough, he found himself looking forward to the evening with a decidedly unreproachful curiosity and eagerness.

Eight

AT 7:30, Adam was waiting; Skeffington, on the other hand, was not. His unpunctuality inviolable, he was fifteen minutes late, and as the long official car pulled up he said genially, "Hop in. As a taxpayer, you're entitled to. Try the comforts of the vehicle you thoughtfully provided for me."

Adam got in. Determined to remove all mystery from the outset, he said, "By the way, when we were talking this afternoon I completely forgot to ask you where we were going."

"So you did," Skeffington said. "I took it as a rare mark of confidence; now I find it was only a lapse of memory. One more illusion lost." He chuckled and said, "Actually, we're going to a wake. Knocko Minihan's wake."

"A *wake?*"

"Surprised? I had an idea you might be: there was just the possibility that you weren't in the habit of spending your free evenings in visiting deceased strangers. But I felt that tonight it might be useful for you to come along. In its way, a wake can be quite an occasion."

"You may be underestimating me," Adam said. "I've been to a few wakes. Not many, but a few."

"I don't doubt it. Probably not exactly like this one, however. Not that poor Knocko's will be unique, but it might be a little different from those you've been to."

Adam was not prepared to dispute this. The car drove on, and he said, "His name wasn't Knocko, surely?"

"No. It was Aram. The mother was part French, and he was named for an uncle in Quebec. The old gentleman had some money, and the Minihans cherished the fond hope that one happy day it would fall into the lap of little Aram. Unfortunately there was a tragic development. The uncle went crazy and gave away all of his money to a convent outside Montreal; two months later he went to a Canadian lunatic asylum where he subsequently died. The Minihans naturally tried to prove that he'd been a madman before he gave the money to the convent. It seemed a reasonable assumption, especially when you consider that the old man suffered from the delusion that he was an air rifle and went around spitting BB's at squirrels. But as anybody can tell you who's ever tried to recover a bequest from an order of nuns in Quebec, the assumption wasn't quite reasonable enough. So no legacy was forthcoming for the little Aram. Meanwhile, of course, he'd been stuck with the name: I don't think he ever forgave his parents for that. It was a terrible start in life for a boy in this city. That's why he gladly became Knocko."

"And how did he make out after this terrible start?"

"Not too well. Save in one respect, that is. He married a grand woman who was a close friend of my wife's — your aunt's," he said. "In every other way he was a failure. He had a hardware store that he ran into the ground almost before the opening-day sale was over. Then he tried several other businesses, all of which petered out in no time at all. I don't know that people trusted him especially, and they certainly didn't like him. And neither," he said, rather surprisingly, "did I. However, *de mortuis . . .*"

"If nobody liked him," Adam said, "I imagine we'll run into a fairly slim attendance tonight."

"Not at all," said Skeffington. "The place'll be crowded to the doors. A wake isn't quite the same as a popularity contest. There are other factors involved. Ah, here we are."

They had arrived in front of a two-story frame tenement house which was in need of paint; the door on the left held a wreath with a large purple ribbon. Skeffington placed a hand just beneath this ornament and then, before pushing the door open, paused to regard the unlovely premises. He shook his head. "Charming," he said. "Come on, let's go in."

A heavy-set woman, dressed in black, and with the face of some large and extremely suspicious bird, came out of the darkness to greet them.

"Hello, Frank," she said.

"Hello, Agnes. Mrs. Burns, my nephew, Adam Caulfield. Mary's boy." There were nods, an exchange of greetings; Skeffington asked, "How's Gert taking it?"

"Pretty good. She cries a little," said the woman. Adam could not help but observe that she was herself noticeably dry of eye. In explanation she added, "She remembers all the nice things he done."

"She has a remarkable memory," Skeffington said dryly.

Mrs. Burns accepted this with a short nod of agreement, then pointed to a door on the right of the narrow hall. "He's in the parlor," she said. "I think there's no one in there now; it's still a bit early. Go right in, Frank. He looks lovely."

Adam followed Skeffington into the parlor: he saw a tall, glum room which might have been designed specifically with this melancholy event in mind. Heavy dull plush furniture had been pushed back against the walls; stretching from side to side across the room were rows of thin metal chairs, of the kind furnished by catering services. At the moment these were empty; looking at them through the gloom Adam wondered whether this was indeed due to the hour of their arrival, or rather to the simple fact that Knocko Minihan had not been widely loved.

At the far end of the parlor, decorated with wreaths and floral sprays, was a gray coffin; to Adam it seemed huge, a sarcophagus fit for a giant. He advanced upon it with his uncle; they knelt by the side of the coffin and Adam saw Knocko in death. He lay stiffly among billows of white satin, a diminutive man lost in the recesses of his mighty container. Across the top of his head occasional strands of yellowish-white hair had been combed strategically; a taut, grudging smile, which somehow fell short of suggesting an interior peace, had been worked into position. His small hands were folded across his chest, clasping a rosary, and over the coffin a large crucifix, heavily studded with rhinestones, had been suspended. Someone of ingenious mind — undoubtedly the undertaker, thought Adam — had fixed a baby spotlight so that it played full upon the crucifix; high above Knocko's final, alien smile, the rhinestones glittered and danced.

Adam said a prayer for this man he had not known. Skeffington, after a moment, got to his feet slowly, looking about him, at the coffin, at the crucifix. "A lavish display," he said. "And you couldn't get the man near a theater in his life." He put his hand lightly on Adam's shoulder and said, "Will you do me a favor and stay here a moment? I have to go in and say a word to the widow."

Adam looked up, surprised; he rose quickly. "You mean, wait *here?*"

Skeffington smiled slightly. "I'm afraid I do; it seems to be about the only place. You could wait in the car, but I've sent the chauffeur on an errand. In any event, it won't be too bad; I'll be back directly. Why don't you just sit down in one of those chairs in back? People will be coming in shortly, and anyway the whole thing is an experience you ought to have; it's a custom that's dying out. Besides, you can regard it as a meritorious act; you'll be keeping poor Knocko company."

Adam nodded reluctantly. There seemed nothing to do but agree, although he was scarcely happy over the prospect of the solitary vigil. Feeling vaguely that he had once again been outgeneraled all along the line, he moved towards the back of the room, as far as possible from the dead Knocko, the rhinestones, and the baby spotlight. Here in the dim light of the evening, he sat down to await the return of his uncle.

In the first few minutes of his wait, the quiet, as well as the gloom, became increasingly uninviting. All light from the outside seemed to fade; the macabre cruciform dazzle above the coffin dominated the room. From somewhere there came the sound of a banging door; no one entered. Adam had indeed, as he had said earlier to Skeffington, attended a few wakes, but his memory of them was obscure. Now in this silent gloom he had a disquieting recollection of a story of Synge's about a wake in the Aran Islands: the long procession of shawled and sobbing women gathering at the bier, rocking back and forth to the wail of the keen. That such a scene could be duplicated in the parlor of Knocko Minihan tonight was wildly improbable; nevertheless, Adam found himself speculating upon it in some detail. Suddenly, from somewhere to his right, there came a sound. *"Sssst!"* it hissed.

He jumped, startled. He turned and at first saw no one; then, in a corner which was darker than the rest of the room because of the shadow of a partially opened door, he saw a small, puckered woman, peering out at him with lively eyes.

"Did I *scare* you?" she said. The possibility seemed to delight her.

"No," Adam lied stoutly. "You startled me. I didn't see you come in."

"Ah, I *was* in," she said. "I was here in my corner when you come in with Frank. Are you the nephew?"

Adam nodded. It seemed to him that with the discovery of this silent little watcher of the shadows a new dimension of eerieness had entered the room. She had spoken of "*my* corner" with a proud possessiveness, almost as if she had come in with the coffin and would remain in her appointed place, firm, open-eyed and irremovable, until it was taken away.

"I'm Delia Boylan," she said. "I knew your pa and I knew your ma and I knew you when you was a baby." Pepper-and-salt eyebrows rose as she considered him now. "You was homely as spit," she said.

"Ah," said Adam. How did one respond more fully to such frankness? He had no idea. He said, changing the subject hopefully, "I'm surprised there are so few people here to see Mr. Minihan."

"Ah, they'll be in," she said confidently. "They'll all want to get a good last look at old Knocko. There's them that's been waiting for it a long time. We're early. I always like to be a bit early." She raised herself to a half-standing posture and gazed critically at the coffin. "He looks grand with the cheeks all puffed out, don't he?" she asked.

She spoke of the corpse with the nonchalant detachment possible only to those who have had vast experience with death. "He looks very nice," Adam said. He was painfully aware of his own lack of the special vocabulary of compliment appropriate to just such an occasion; he was sure that one existed. "Of course," he added, "I didn't know him when he was alive."

This, too, was maladroit; but Mrs. Boylan did not appear to mind. Her narrow little shoulders shrugged in contempt and she said, "A little runt of a man. Thin as a snake and no color to him at all. He was part French, you know."

"I know."

"That makes all the difference," she said mysteriously. *"Aram.* Ah well, that's small matter now." She spoke as one forgiving him the injury of his ancestry. "God be good to the man," she said. "He was mean as a panther, but good luck to him."

Adam said nothing. Once more, there seemed to be nothing to say. The silence was broken by the entrance of a trio of mourners who came in, looked slowly about the room, nodded to Delia, then filed up to the coffin.

"The Carmichael girls," Delia explained, "with the brother Tim. *They* come early, as a general rule." She moved abruptly in her chair, stretching out to face the door. *"Sssst!"* she hissed.

Adam followed her glance. He saw a stout, balding young man, spruce and smooth in the discreet clothing of his profession, moving with purposeful yet superlatively respectful steps towards the coffin.

"Sssst!" Delia said again. "Johnnie!"

The young man paused and looked in their direction; Adam thought he appeared to be annoyed. In response to Delia's frantically beckoning hand he came over to them with an obvious reluctance.

"Johnnie Degnan," Delia said to Adam, adding unnecessarily, "the undertaker. We always like to have our little talk."

"Good evening, Mrs. Boylan," the undertaker said unenthusiastically.

"Ah, Johnnie," Delia said. She introduced Adam. "Frank Skeffington's nephew, Johnnie. The sister's boy."

The undertaker brightened; he made a short, formal bow. "Very pleased to meet you, sir," he said. "I've always been a great admirer of your uncle, although I've never had the pleasure of making his acquaintance. I hope that will be remedied tonight. Ah . . . was there anything in particular, Mrs. Boylan?"

"He looks grand, Johnnie," she said, waving towards the coffin. "Just grand. Did he take a lot of doing?"

An expression of slight strain appeared on the undertaker's round face; clearly, thought Adam, questions from the laity were not encouraged. "Mr. Minihan was in remarkable condition, Mrs. Boylan, for one of his advanced years," he said. He spoke in a low voice and with extraordinary rapidity, as if in the hope that by a sudden sprint through his words he might bring this interview to a close. It was a forlorn hope; Delia had reached out and grabbed the sleeve of his coat.

"And Johnnie," she said, "you laid him out in the *big* coffin! Ah, you rascal, you!" She rolled her eyes and released a little whoop of laughter; down by the coffin the Carmichael triumverate turned in unison to stare. The undertaker made a swift, imploring pass with his hands, and Delia lowered her voice to a stage whisper. "My God," she said delightedly, "wouldn't it kill the man if he knew!"

The undertaker gave her a look of pain. "Mr. Minihan has a very fine casket," he said, emphasizing the final word. "As I'm sure he would have wished it."

"Ah," Delia said, "but the cost of it all! The cost, Johnnie!"

"Mr. Minihan," said the undertaker swiftly, "was a very prominent figure in the community. Very prominent."

Delia nodded agreeably. "He was the cheapest old devil that ever lived," she said. "And you know it. Well, he's gone now, poor man, and you done an elegant job on him, Johnnie." As a grace note she added, "No matter what you charge."

"Ah ha ha ha," said the undertaker tonelessly, giving Adam a nervous smile, presumably meant to imply that they both were familiar with the irrepressible Mrs. Boylan. "Well, I must go now, Mrs. Boylan. Many duties. A pleasure to have met you sir. I hope to meet your uncle." He bowed again and hurried away on muted feet.

"There's a great rogue," Delia said approvingly. "Only thirty years old and he'd steal the skin off your bones. Just give him the chance and it's the big coffin, ten limousines, and the Holy Name Choir to sing you good-by."

"And is he responsible for the crucifix?" Adam asked, pointing to the dazzling object above the coffin.

"The pride and joy," she assured him. "It all goes on the bill." She shook with a sudden rusty flutter of reminiscent mirth. "I says to him one day, I says, 'Don't you dare to stick that big sparkler over me when I'm gone, Johnnie Degnan! Don't you dare!' And he damn well won't; he knows he won't get a ten-cent piece out of me. Ah, he's a sly one," she said, "but he knows I'm on to him. *Sssst!*"

The sound, while no longer unfamiliar, was unexpected; Adam jumped again. An angular woman of forbidding aspect had come into the room and was now engaged in making hand signals to Delia.

"Aggie Gormley," Delia said. "I wonder has she news about the will? I'd best go see. I'll be back in a minute."

She hustled away with jerky, efficient steps, and Adam was alone once more. He looked at Delia, conversing with her newsy friend; he looked at the Carmichaels, talking quietly to Johnnie Degnan; he looked at the coffin and the jewelry above it. He looked, too, at his watch, and wondered absently when his uncle would return. Rather to his surprise, he did not greatly care, for he discovered to his horror that here in this presepulchral room, reserved for mourning, and in the appalling company of Delia Boylan, he was undoubtedly enjoying himself.

Skeffington, when he had left the parlor, had gone back along the hall until he came to a closed door. He knocked softly, then walked in. He was in the kitchen; on the far side of the small, neat room he saw, dressed in black, the tall, stooped figure of his wife's old friend. She was still, even now, a pretty woman, but faded, very faded; life with Knocko, thought Skeffington, must have been a fading experience. A quick rush of pity came over him as he looked at her; this was succeeded by quite another feeling, unexpected and hardly less painful: *My God,* he thought, *we're the same age almost to the day!* He shook his head quickly and said, "I'm sorry, Gert."

"I know you are, Frank." Obviously she had been weeping; now, however, she had stopped. Skeffington sat down across the kitchen table from her.

"Gert, I'm not going to commiserate with you. That'd be nice, but it wouldn't help much. But I do want to have a little talk with you on practical matters. I know you don't feel much like discussing anything like that now, but I want you to. Will you do that for me?"

There was a faint nod. "I will, Frank," she said.

"That's the girl. Now, first of all, do you have any idea of how you're situated? What did Knocko leave you? Was he able to leave you anything?"

One thin hand rubbed the narrow forehead wearily. "I'm not sure what he did or didn't leave, Frank. I haven't thought much about it at all."

Skeffington gently persisted. "Of course you haven't. But I want you to think about it now. That's why I made you promise you would. Sometimes at a time like this you need to change your thoughts every now and then. And sometimes you have to. You've got to think just a little bit of how you're going to live, Gert." He added, although he felt no confidence in this at all, "Knocko would have wanted you to."

She began to cry again, quietly. "He was a good man, Frank. You had to know him."

He let her cry, and said elusively, "I know he would have provided for you if he could. But we can't always do what we'd like to do. Now, I know he had nothing in the bank; he told me that himself. Was there any insurance?"

"There was some once," she said vaguely, "but I think it's gone. They were charging him too much for the premiums, he said. Ah, I don't know. He told me very little about money, Frank. He had such bad luck."

"Yes." Bad luck, he thought, which had lasted no less than fifty years: a new world's record. "Any other holdings he might have had? War Bonds, for instance?"

She shook her head. "Since the store closed it seemed hard to put anything by. I know he got discouraged at times. You couldn't blame him. There was so much went wrong for the poor man."

"I know, Gert," he said soothingly, but to himself he said savagely: *and all of it of his own making*. It was tragic: this once-lively, once-lovely woman, whom he had known since childhood, who had been his wife's closest friend, now left old and beaten and penniless thanks entirely to her marriage to a dour, improvident boob! And yet she had loved him. It was utterly improbable, utterly irrational, and, he thought ironically, it happened all the time. Yet in this case it had happened to someone of whom he was fond; now it was up to him to do what the loved one had failed to do.

"Well, Gert," he said, "I guess now's as good a time as any to make good on a promise." He reached into an inner pocket of his coat and brought out an envelope. "Just before Kate died, she left me a little present for you. I would have given it to you before but there was a condition attached to it — she said I was to hold onto it until I was sure you really needed it. I guess you could say that time is now."

He handed her the envelope, and she took it silently. Still looking at him, she opened it; it was only when she felt the contents slipping out that she looked down. In her lap were ten one-hundred-dollar bills. She said instantly, "I won't take it, Frank. Thank you, but I won't."

He had anticipated this: the woman was not a fool. He reached over and took the bills in his hand. "All right," he said, "it's up to you, Gert. I'm not going to force you into anything. But I'll tell you this: The money belongs to you. Kate gave it to me to give to you, and if you don't use it, I can promise you nobody else will . . . I mean that, Gert."

She shook her head. "I saw Kate before she died. She said nothing about leaving me any money, and she knew I didn't want it. That money comes from you, Frank, and God bless you for it. But I won't take it."

It was no more than he had expected; the maneuver of the imaginary legacy was ridiculously transparent, especially to this woman who had her pride and who, moreover, knew him so well. But he had had no time; it would have to do. He said briskly, "Listen to me, Gert. I'm not an ungenerous man, but I'm not an idiot, either. I'm not in the habit of going around handing out one thousand dollars, even to old friends; it's a habit I can't afford. You can rest assured that if this were my money, no such sum would have come drifting so easily into your lap. Use your common sense, woman. But the point is that it's not my money; it's yours, that's the truth, and that's the end of it. And I tell you again that if you don't take it, I'll get rid of it, nobody'll get it. It was Kate's gift to you and you alone." He reached out and took her hand; then, extending the money towards her again, said insistently, "Come on, Gert. No false pride. Take it. It's yours. My God, woman, it's a mortal sin if you don't!"

She looked at him steadily, the tired old eyes regarding him for what seemed a very long time; then her hand reached out, touched the money, then drew back. She said, "*Was* it Kate's, Frank? *Is* it mine? Do you swear it?"

"I do, Gert," he said solemnly. And he knew that he had won.

She took the money, holding it awkwardly against her lap. Looking up at Skeffington she smiled with an odd, almost a young, shyness. "God bless you, Frank," she said.

"Why, I hope He will," he said, "but hardly for this. I'm just the messenger boy here. All blessings go to Kate, and I'm sure she doesn't need them by now." He got up and patted her on the hand. "I'm going back out front now," he said. "You ought to come out yourself a little later."

"I will, Frank." She thanked him again: for the money, for coming in to see her husband. As he was leaving she said, "Frank?"

"Yes, Gert?"

She looked at the money in her hand and said, "I still don't believe you."

He smiled. "That's your privilege as an old friend. I find that very few of my old friends ever believe me. Maybe that's how they got to be old friends in the first place." She knew, he thought, but she didn't *quite* know, and that was all right: as long as there was the doubt, her pride was saved. He had reached the door when she stopped him again, and this time there was anxiety in her voice.

"I suppose they'll come tonight?" she said. "There haven't been many up to now." She added defiantly, "He was a difficult man in his way, but he had his friends. He had many friends, Frank."

"He had indeed," Skeffington said reassuringly. "They've just been waiting for the final night, that's all. They'll be here tonight, Gert. You'll see. Your only difficulty will be to fit them all in."

As he walked from the room, he thought: Poor woman. If friendship with Knocko were to be the basis for attendance at his wake, it could have been held in a phone booth. . . . However, because of Gert, he had that afternoon taken steps to increase substantially the number of mourners tonight. He had issued an order to all department heads that delegations were to be sent; as a less compulsory, but possibly even more effective measure, he let it be known that he himself would be on hand. While walking along the hallway back to the parlor he thought of the crowded rooms, in which he would now have to remain at least another half hour; he thought of Gert; he thought, with no particular pity, of the miserable Knocko, whose death, in a sense, gave point to the evening.

To the thousand dollars he had just given away, however, he gave no especial thought, for, as Charlie Hennessey had once pointed out, the opponents of Skeffington who believed him to be an avaricious man, or one even concerned with money as such at all, could hardly have been farther from the truth.

He came in to the parlor to discover that the crowd had begun to arrive. The rows of chairs, empty before, were now rapidly being filled; as he entered the room the heads turned towards him at once. He looked for Adam and signaled to him; Adam approached, only slightly behind Delia Boylan.

"Ah now, Frank," she said eagerly, "how is she taking it back there?"

His reply was brief. "As well as could be expected." He added dryly, "I'm happy to see that you're bearing up under the strain, Delia."

Once more Adam heard the derisive whoop of laughter; it rang through the gloomy room; heads turned; at his position of duty down by the coffin Johnnie Degnan frowned reprovingly and did a plump little dance step of despair. "I'll live," Delia said. "Well, me and the nephew has been having a lovely talk about poor Knocko, the old devil."

"I wish I'd been here to join you," Skeffington said. Turning to Adam he added, "Mrs. Boylan's pious reflections on the faithful departed never fail to uplift the spirit. She has a splendid attendance record at the deathbed of her many friends."

"I go to them all," she said proudly. "I don't miss a one."

"Everybody has to have a hobby," Skeffington said. "Now if

you'll excuse us, Delia, I want to take my nephew into the next room and introduce him to some people. Give my best to Tom and the family."

"I will, Frank." The sharp little eyes glinted maliciously and she said, "And will I tell them you wouldn't mind hearing from them come Election Day?"

"I always treasure the Boylan vote," Skeffington said, "and yours in particular, Delia. Every time I get thinking about the wisdom of giving the women the vote I think of you and my fears become quiet."

She crowed with delight. "Ah, that's all mush, Frank. But you know we're with you every single time. The whole family."

"I do, Delia. I appreciate it. And now," he said, with no change of expression, "we'll leave you to your prayers. Good-by, Delia."

Out in the hall he drew Adam aside and said, "I hope you see how things work out for the best. If I hadn't left you alone in there, you wouldn't have met Mrs. Boylan and had your little devotional chat. Your field of experience has been immeasurably widened in the space of but a few minutes."

"I won't deny it," Adam said. "I've certainly never met anyone quite like her before. She's a fantastic woman."

"I suppose she is," Skeffington said carelessly. "I'm so used to her I don't notice any more. It takes a fresh eye to fully appreciate Delia. I may add that she's a woman it's far better to have with you than against you. She has the tongue of a cobra."

"And does she really spend all of her time going to wakes?"

"Apart from a few hours of sleep each night, I believe she does. As she said, she doesn't miss a one. You must remember that she's a singularly devout woman. Also," he said reflectively, "it's somewhat cheaper than going to the movies."

While they stood in the hall, more people came in; clearly, the wake of Knocko Minihan was expanding. As it did, Adam was struck by the altered deportment of his uncle; it was almost as if, from being one of the visiting mourners, he had suddenly become the host. He nodded and spoke briefly to all the new arrivals; without exception, all responded in identical fashion: a muttered acknowledgment of the pitiful fact of Knocko's death, followed by a perceptibly more fervent statement of good wishes for Skeffington in the coming elections. A short, round woman with a serene face approached them with slow, heavy steps; to her Skeffington spoke at somewhat greater length.

"Glad to see you, Annie," he said. "I gather that everything got here all right?"

"It did, Frank. You wanted no whisky or anything like that?"

"No. What have you got out there?"

"Coffee and tea, sandwiches, and cake. There'll be plenty for everybody, no matter how big it gets."

"Good. Where are you setting it up, in the kitchen?"

"There's a problem there, Frank. God knows there's no place else we can put it, but that's where Gert is, sitting all by herself. I don't like to bother the poor woman."

"Go right ahead and bother her," Skeffington said decisively. "That's what she needs right now, someone bustling around, something to take her mind off things for a few minutes. It's not good for her to be sitting out there all alone. See if you can't get her to come in here, just to go through the motions. If she doesn't want to do that, try to get her doing something out there. If you have any difficulty, let me know."

"All right, Frank, I will." The woman went down the hall with her calm, weighty tread, and Skeffington, who had been noting with some amusement his nephew's polite if imperfect attempt to conceal his curiosity, said, "That's a role I occasionally practice: the combination physician, caterer and master of ceremonies. It's something I might have to fall back on one day when I retire from politics."

"I am impressed," Adam said truthfully. "I hadn't realized that all this was a part of your job."

"Well, this is rather a special case. The widow's an old friend, and in her present condition she's in no shape to arrange for the usual civilities. So I just had a few things sent over." It was a detail he had taken care of that afternoon; the food had come from the ample commissariat of the Wadsworth Hospital. As this was a city institution, the food had been provided for by public funds; it was, in a word, a tax-supported wake. And all for Knocko Minihan; the beneficiary, thought Skeffington, was unworthy of the occasion. He said to Adam, "I'm not so sure that all the arrangements would meet with Knocko's approval, but then of course, when you come right down to it, he's not really in much of a position to complain, is he? Come along, I want to go in here."

They entered the next door down the hall; Adam found himself in a room which compared favorably with the parlor in its size and general hideousness, but which contained many more people and a great deal more noise. It was not until he had been in this room for a moment that he realized that there was still another difference: here, the mourners were exclusively male. To his surprise, he recognized some of them as the old familiars of his uncle's outer office. They had disdained the chairs which had been set out for them in a severe row which paralleled the wall; they preferred to stand, talking, smoking, moving, waiting. When Skeffington came in, the waiting was over. They surged around him, the noise grew, and Adam was soon separated from his uncle by a tight, struggling double ring of the self-appointed palace guard. He caught Skeffington's eye; in return he received a quick but unmistakable wink, the meaning of which was quite clear. For the moment at least, he was again on his own; Skeffington had decided that it was time for his field of experience to be widened still further.

But this widening was to be temporarily postponed, for his first encounter was with an old acquaintance who held no surprises. It was Ditto Boland. Just seconds before, Ditto had been valiantly attempting to crash through the impenetrable living barricade to gain his idol's ear; he had failed. Once more, craftier, stronger, more resourceful men had beaten him to the punch; a veteran at rejection, he had accepted defeat, and had settled for the next best thing. He had gone to talk to Adam.

"Good evening, Adam," he said, panting slightly. The heat of the evening and his own obesity had been hard on Ditto; the tiny, ridiculous head streamed with sweat, and the clothes on his huge body were rumpled and awry. "Well, well, and isn't this a grand evening, Adam. A very spirited occasion, as we say. Apart from the unhappy death of poor Knocko, that is."

For not the first time that evening, Adam wondered at this ability, apparently rather widely possessed, to separate sharply the occasion from the melancholy event that had produced it; he thought it unlikely, however, that Ditto could shed much light on the matter. And so he said merely, "Hello, Ditto. Have you been here long?"

"No, no, Adam, not very long at all. The fact of the matter is that there was a slight mixup at the Hall. An unhappy confusion, as we say. I and some of the boys were waiting there for the Governor to ride over here with him, but he got away without us being properly informed. I and the boys had to come in a taxicab," he said in an aggrieved voice. "I make no accusation against anyone in particular, Adam, but it's my personal belief that the Governor was not told I was out there waiting. There are certain confidential secretaries who are getting too big for their britches and are keeping from the Governor valuable information he'd like to hear. That's all I'll say, Adam. I make no definite charges, but all the same, Adam, I wouldn't like to be a certain high-and-mighty secretary when the Governor finds out what's been going on in Denmark, as we say."

As the pre-emptor of Ditto's position in the official car, Adam felt it only prudent to change the subject; he said, "I suppose Mr. Minihan was a friend of yours, Ditto?"

"Knocko? Oh, yes, yes, Adam. Of course he wasn't in politics like the Governor and myself, so I didn't see so much of him through the years. We weren't on the intimately bosom basis, as we say. But we were friendly. Oh yes, Adam. When he had the hardware store I was one of the very first to give him business with a purchase. I purchased a screwdriver. Poor Knocko. Gone but not forgotten. A very lovable man, Adam. Everybody loved him."

"That's curious," Adam said, "because I had the idea that he hadn't been terribly popular."

"Is that so now, Adam? Is that really so?" Circumspection had suddenly descended; it sat upon him oddly, like an ill-fitting hat. "Now isn't that interesting? Yes, that's very interesting indeed, Adam. Yes it is. And from who might you get an idea like that, might I ask?"

Rather unfairly, Adam said, "From my uncle."

"And who would know better?" Ditto said instantly. "Who

would know better than the very same man, Adam? You can't beat the Governor when it comes to sizing a man up. He has a grand knowledge of the human man, as we say. I remember he spotted the mean streak in Knocko the first time he met him. He said to me personally at the time, he said, 'Ditto, the man has a bad eye.' I freely admit to you, Adam, I didn't see it myself at the time, but how right the Governor was as always was proved beyond all doubts when my screwdriver broke not a week after I made the purchase. But," he said largely, "forgive and forget: that's always been the Governor's grand motto, and mine has been as per the same. The Governor held nothing against the man and neither did I, and that's why the two of us are here tonight. Letting bygones go by the boards, as we say."

Death, then, had atoned for the defective ten-cent tool; Adam, not without some guilt remembering that it was he who had introduced the theme of Knocko's unlovelier side, switched to a less personal level. He said, "You must be an old hand at these wakes, Ditto."

"Yes, yes, Adam. I've been to some grand wakes in my time, very nice affairs. I remember the time I went with the Governor over to Danno Herlihy's wake. You remember Danno no doubt, Adam?"

"No, I don't believe I ever knew Danno."

"The Assistant Water Commissioner with the bum ear. He died of a bad appendix which the doctors couldn't find in time; it was later told to me in secret confidence, as we say, that when they took the man apart they found it around in back down by the spine. There was a grand wake, Adam. One and all had a grand time. The Assistant Commissioner was given the send-off in A-Number One par excello style. There was turkey, ham, roast beef, potato salad and some lovely brisket." Ditto smacked his lips *in memoriam*. "And then of course there was the Wenatchee apples that the brandy had been put in. They were a tasty treat to the tongue, as we say. Do you know the Wenatchee apples that they put the brandy in, Adam?

"No."

"They're big hard red apples from out West in California or Iowa or some place like that. They grow them in the apple orchards out there. You take out the cores and that leaves the empty hollow center, which you put the brandy in overnight. It all soaks up into the apple and gives people something nice to munch on the next day. A grand dessert."

"And this was the feature at Danno Herlihy's wake? A brandied apple?"

"*One* of the features, Adam," Ditto said, correcting him. "Oh yes yes, just one of the features. It was all grand otherwise as well, as we say. I remember the Governor came up to me at one point in the evening and said, 'Have you ever seen a grander wake than this, Ditto?' 'No, Governor,' I said, 'I haven't.' And it was the truth, Adam. The only bad spot in the whole entire evening came with the black sheep brother from New York. The family hadn't seen hide and hair of him, as we say, for thirty years, but he turned up the last night of Danno's wake. And what do you think he did? He got *himself* an appendicitis attack just as they were saying the Rosary! The very same identical thing Danno had died of, and he had to get one for himself just as they were saying the prayers for Danno! The family never forgave him."

"And damn well they shouldn't of," Cuke Gillen said. He had come up in time to hear the last of the story. "The bum was a flycatcher, a scene stealer. He tried to cop the act at his own brother's wake. I knew the bum years ago, in vaudeville; he played the small time with me. He used to beat hotel bills. What he'd do, he used to walk around the lobby with his tie pulled up tight around his neck, giving himself the old chokeroo. After a while his face would get all red and he'd look like a country boy. You know, a big honest hick kid. So the manager might be worried as hell about his dough, but one look at that face and he'd figure that no guy with a kisser like that could sneak his way out of the bathroom, let alone a hotel. So he stops worrying, and the first thing you know—*Zing!* The bum puts his cardboard suitcase under his arm, hops out of the window onto the fire escape, and it's good-by Swanee to dear old Peoria!"

"A very low type of a man," Ditto said virtuously. "You could tell it from the way he behaved himself at Danno's wake. But every other way you looked at it, the evening was a grand success for all members present, as we say." The sight of Cuke now seemed to unsettle him, to remind him of something temporarily forgotten; he glanced hastily over his shoulder at the center of the room, where Skeffington stood, still surrounded. "Did you have a chance to say a few words to the Governor tonight, Cuke?" he asked anxiously.

"Sure. I was over there shooting the breeze with him just a few minutes ago."

"Ah," Ditto said. "Aha. Is that a fact, Cuke? You were over there talking with him, were you? I'll have to go over myself in a minute. I know he's been wanting to see me." He looked unhappily at the circling, suppliant guard; there seemed to be more of them than ever. It was hard, very hard. In another moment he would try again; maybe the Governor would see him, would beckon to him, and the terrible protective lines would part. Meanwhile . . . he said wistfully, "And how is he this fine evening? In the best of fettles, I hope."

"In great shape. He was just telling the boys a minute ago about the way it looks in the Second Ward. It's looking very good. Tom Healy is coming around; at least it looks like he is. Anyway, we're putting on the heat over there next week. The Governor tells me we'll be going over there every single night for different meetings. And of course as usual I'll be right on hand with my scintillating assortment of snappy stories for young and old, rich and poor." He winked at Adam, and then, because he was Skeffington's nephew, favored him with a particularly choice specimen bit from the act: with his palms he slapped his thighs to the rhythms of "Glowworm"; he capered about and executed his celebrated off-to-Buffalo break. Adam had witnessed this performance before; he was not now greatly astonished to see that the presence of the deceased Knocko in the adjoining room in no way affected its gymnastic vivacity. "One solid boffola from beginning to end," said Cuke, coming to a sliding stop, "guaranteed to make you split your sides with good clean laughter." Smartly, he spanked his collar with a forefinger.

"There's no doubt I'll be going along with the Governor to all those meetings," Ditto said without conviction. "No, no, there's no doubt of that at all. As per always, Ditto will be ready and waiting for the Governor's beck or call, as we say. The Governor's a great one for sticking by the old and trusty friends, no matter what certain swell-headed secretaries may think. I mention no names. Was there any more news mentioned, Cuke?"

"Camaratta was talked about. Apparently he's getting smart and coming in with the boys. The Governor mentioned him in high terms."

"Oh yes, yes," Ditto said, nodding. "They're very close these days. All together in the one cause. Camaratta's done some very dirty business in the days gone by, as we say, but the Governor's not the type of man who holds onto a grudge. No no, Camaratta is sitting very pretty these days. That I know. I'm so used to the Governor I can tell how he feels towards a man by the way he mentions his name. The rise and fall of the voice. The inflections, as we say. Was there any news about Jimmy Murtagh and the Park Commission, Cuke?"

"A gone goose," Cuke said. "On account of he was caught playing easy-kneesy with Mother Garvey."

"Aha. Well well well. I could have told him that, if he'd come to me and asked me. I knew the Governor's feeling on the matter very well. Jimmy was running around on the thin ice, as we say. Oh yes yes."

Adam could not help marveling at the completeness of Knocko's failure to dominate, or even to intrude upon, his own wake. Here in the antechamber he was playing a bad second fiddle to the swapped vote and the living Skeffington; in the adjoining room, where the women were gathered before the bier, was he equally unfortunate? Presumably so: City Hall undoubtedly possessed its Ladies' Auxiliary. Yet there, perhaps the tactless presence of the casket and its contents might severely hamper political discussion; upon further consideration, however, he was inclined to doubt this. It was evident now that they had come tonight neither to bury Knocko nor to praise him; they had come to ignore him. The more one considered this neglect, Adam thought, the more callous one discovered it to be, and despite his resolutions to be prepared for all possible developments, he was somewhat shocked by this one.

Cuke and Ditto had continued to talk; they were interrupted

by the approach of old John Gorman. He had been standing to the left of the ring surrounding Skeffington, talking to petitioners with more modest or more localized requests. Now he came across the room, a remarkably neat, spare old man, straight as a string; when he reached them he said softly, "Ditto. Run down to the car now and tell Patsy to take you down to Ryan's for a half-dozen boxes of cigars. He'll know the kind. You'd best go along with him, Cuke. The fresh night air will do your lungs a world of good."

The two men obeyed instantly. It was, for both, an errand of pleasure, and besides, an order from Gorman was an order from Skeffington. Gorman turned to Adam, smiling faintly.

"There's no greater turn you could do Ditto," he said. "Up in the back seat of the big black car, just himself and Cuke. Almost as good as if it was just himself. Well now, did the two of them tell you all about politics?"

"Not quite," Adam said. He was slightly abashed by the question, which seemed to place him in the undesirable relation of pupil to two such dubious tutors, and which, moreover, had come from a man for whom he had both liking and respect. He knew the regard in which his uncle held Gorman, and he could only assume, now, that Skeffington had told the old man of his nephew's proposed initiation into the campaign; the consequence had been this gently ironic question. (The assumption, as it happened, was quite incorrect. Skeffington viewed his conversation with his nephew as a peculiarly personal matter, and he was not in the habit of discussing his private affairs with his political associates. Gorman, however, had required no special information. He had known Skeffington intimately for many years, he knew of his fondness for this nephew, of his bitter disappointment in his son, of his loneliness since his wife had died. The old man could put two and two together. The answer he had arrived at now pleased him. He's a good lad, he thought, and it's a good thing for Frank.) Adam added, "Although the subject did manage to come up, Mr. Gorman. As a matter of fact, it was just about the only subject that did come up."

"Ah well, that's natural enough," the old man said mildly. "If you met the Pope you'd talk about religion."

Adam smiled. "I suppose so. Still, wouldn't we also talk just a bit about Knocko Minihan? Particularly if we happened to meet at his wake?"

"It would be the pious thing to do, no doubt," Gorman agreed. "But then if you both knew Knocko, you might damn well want to talk about almost anything else in a hurry. Out of respect for the dead, you might say."

"Yes, I see. But what I don't see is this: if Knocko was such a generally disliked man, why are so many people here tonight? They didn't come to gloat, obviously; they're not ghouls. But then why did they come?"

"That I'm not sure about. Still," the old man said thoughtfully, "I wouldn't think you'd be far wrong if you said they came as you did yourself. For the very same reason, that is."

Adam stared at him. "But I came only because of my uncle."

"So you did," Gorman said. "So you did, indeed."

"Then you mean that all these other people came because of Uncle Frank, too?"

"Ah well, I wouldn't say all; that'd be a bit of an exaggeration. You had a little chat with Delia Boylan, I hear" — suddenly and irrelevantly, it occurred to Adam that there seemed to be very little that this old man did *not* hear — "and there's some that came like Delia: they just enjoy themselves going to a wake. It's like little boys and girls going to birthday parties. Then there's some that came on the widow's account: Gert's a fine woman, and she has her friends. And there may be a few no doubt came for Knocko himself; they say," he said wryly, "there's saints amongst us even today. I don't run into many myself. But most of them that are here tonight stopped by for the one reason: they knew your Uncle Frank was to come. And that's the long and the short of it." He saw no point in mentioning the delegations from the different city departments who were here in compulsory attendance; it would only complicate the issue. The boy, he reflected, was a good boy, but young; naturally, he could have no idea of the way things were done. To tell him would be to serve no purpose save perhaps an educational one, and John Gorman was really not wildly interested in telling the young the facts of life.

"And so," Adam said, "while it's Knocko's wake, it's really my uncle who's the main attraction?"

Gorman nodded. "It is."

Adam said, "And naturally business goes on as usual? Only here instead of at the Hall?" His feeling of shock had increased; the whole business, he decided, was a really appalling mixture of hypocrisy and hardness.

"You have things a little twisty," the old man said softly, "if you don't mind me saying so." A little rap across the knuckles was in order, he decided; not a hard rap, to be sure, for he was a good lad and he was Skeffington's nephew, but a rap all the same. It was for the lad's own good; it would help to keep him from leaping about like a salmon to the wrong conclusions. He said, "You're a bit hard on your uncle, I think. The man has no need to go to wakes if he wants to collect a crowd about him; he can do that anywhere. All he has to do is stop on a street corner to light his cigar and fifty people come out of the cement to say, 'Hello Frank, and what can you do for me today?' And when he showed up here tonight it wasn't to talk politics. He can do that any minute of the day, any place he likes; he needs no dead man in the next room to help him tell Tommy Mulcahy that the polls are open from eight to eight on Election Day, and only one vote to a customer this year. What he came here for tonight is simple as simple can be: he came to bring a crowd to Knocko's wake so the widow would feel a little better. Knocko's been lying here all day yesterday, all last night, and all day today: how many people d'ye s'pose came in to see him in all that time? Maybe thirty-five, and ten of those came in to get out of the rain. Tonight there'll be hundreds here, and the widow'll think it's all Knocko's pals, waiting till the last moment to bid him good-by. But with all those people in here, and your uncle here to bring them, what in the name of Heaven are they to talk about but what they like and what they know? God knows they can't talk about Knocko. Half of them never knew the man, and the other half that knew him didn't like him. That's not the kind of thing that makes for easy conversation. And you can't keep a roomful of men talking in soft voices about what a terrible thing death is, and will he go to Heaven, and maybe is he up there this very minute looking down on us all? Those are grand thoughts, but somehow nobody is able to keep thinking them for two hours whilst waiting for the priest to get here to say the Rosary. So they have a little food and they talk a little politics, and I don't know that they do a great amount of harm with either. And then when the priest does get in at last and they all kneel down to pray for Knocko, you might put your mind to this: there'll be ten times the people here praying for him as would be here without your uncle and all the chatter about politics. I don't s'pose they'll all be praying away as holy as St. Francis, but you never know about a thing like that; maybe some of them will mean it, and maybe it'll do Knocko a bit of good. I have the suspicion that he's in no mood at the moment to throw away any prayers from friend or foe; he's likely to be needing anything in that line that comes his way." He paused; it had been a speech of fantastic length for this ordinarily taciturn old man. Still, he reflected, sometimes a bit of gab was needed to drive a point home. He wondered: had it done the trick? He hoped so; looking at the boy, he thought so. In any case, it was all he had to say on the subject. "So that being the way it is," he concluded, his mild blue eyes resting on Adam's face, and his thin old lips twisted once more into the just perceptible smile, "don't be too hard on us, boy. I don't doubt but that it's a bit different from what you're used to here tonight, but it's no terrible thing that's being done."

During the first part of this speech Adam had been surprised, then uncomfortable; during the latter part he had felt his face growing redder by the word. He could not know that his embarrassment and evident sincerity had touched the old man. It was the kind of reproof he had never before experienced as an adult; it was the admonition customarily reserved for the world of the refractory child: quiet, paternal, expressed in such simple terms that even the most backward little boy could somehow grasp the fact that he had been impertinent. It had been humiliating, but what had been far worse, it had been justified. For he had come here tonight as the alien guest; once ashore, he had lost no time in the uninformed criticism of the customs of the land in which he found himself. He had been rude, and he had been told about it: it was as simple as that. Apologetically he said, "I'm sorry, Mr. Gorman. I'm afraid I'll have to plead stupidity and some pretty bad manners."

"Not at all," the old man said courteously. "You said nothing that was so bad; just a small mistake you couldn't help but make unless somebody told you different. And who was to tell you? Ditto? You might as well go to poor Knocko for the news. And your uncle couldn't very well tell you. You could hardly expect the man to grab you by the arm and whisper, 'Come along, now, we're off to a wake. There's two main attractions, the corpse and me, but just between the both of us, the corpse ain't in it with me!' So the only one to tell you the way things stood was myself and so I did." He looked appraisingly at Adam and said dryly, "I don't think the damage was too permanent. You look like you might be able to sit up and take a bit of soup in a day or so."

Ruefully, Adam said, "Just about." But the old man's softening of the blow had left him feeling a good deal better; he said, "Anyway, I am sorry, Mr. Gorman. And thanks."

The old man moved a hand slightly. "Ah," he said mysteriously, "it's all a lot of nothing." He added briefly, "You'll do, right enough." It was a compliment, an astonishing one from the old man. But he was pleased by the way the boy had reacted; respectful, he thought, but not a slaverer. Not a sorehead, but not a ninny either. A decent lad, and good for Frank; too bad, he reflected, it couldn't have been the son. A damn shame. But that was the way it went, and a man could waste his whole life away wishing, wanting, and wondering why; John Gorman was far too busy for such waste. He considered the subject of Adam's instruction now closed. With his lips slightly pursed, he began to look slowly about the room, watching for developments that might have taken place while he had been talking. One of these was in the doorway even now. He said to Adam, "Now there's your man for you, over by the door. D'ye know him?"

Adam saw a short, stout man with oddly protuberant eyes who had paused to regard the room before entering; he was middle-aged, and dressed in a rumpled gray suit; under his right arm he carried what looked to be a small shoebox. Although he stood motionless in the doorway, there was something about him which suggested perpetual and hectic movement; one felt that to see him thus at a standstill was like seeing a hummingbird forcibly immobilized: it was somehow unfair. Or at least so Adam felt; it was the first time he had set eyes on Charlie Hennessey.

Evidently Charlie had chosen Gorman and Adam as his immediate goal. He came towards them with his curious little skating steps, and was on them even before Gorman had an opportunity to identify him for Adam. In any case, such indentification would have been unnecessary, for Charlie identified himself.

"Hello, my dear man," he said to Gorman. "You're looking very well, John: a nice, even, healthy color. That speaks of a good circulation. Marvelous! The blood's the thing. And this must be Frank's nephew, Adam Caulfield by name. I'm Charles Hennessey, my dear man. I read you daily in the funny papers. Nice drawing, a good sense of humor. Marvelous! I read all the papers and everything that's in them. Well, my dear man," he said, turning again to Gorman, "I see the boss still has the touch. Oh, the grand touch! You have to hand it to the man. The most unpopular man in the ward dies and almost before he's cool there's a mob scene round the casket shouting, 'Three cheers for Skeffington for mayor!' Marvelous! Shrewd! Getting votes out of Knocko, like getting blood out of the turnip. They call it alchemy, a kind of old-time magic. And Frank's the master magician. Imagination! Foresight! The only man among us to realize that you could get a good turn out of Knocko after all: you only had to wait until the man was dead. Oh, clever! My hat's off to the man!"

Adam looked up sharply as this extraordinary man voiced what was substantially the charge he himself had made only minutes before; would he, too, suffer the Gorman rebuke? But the old man merely seemed amused; he said simply, "Ah, that's all moonshine, Charlie. All gas." To Adam he said significantly, "Charlie here is running against your uncle for mayor."

"Yes, yes, fighting him tooth and nail," Charlie said briskly. "All in the interests of decent government. And of course what I'm saying is the very reverse of gas, my dear man. All truth! It's a matter of public record that Frank Skeffington has been campaigning at wakes for fifty years. Big wakes or small ones, it made no difference. If nobody died for the six months before an election he wouldn't know where to go. He's spent half a century with one eye on the coffin! A Skeffington maxim: Never neglect the relatives, friends or enemies of the deceased. I've studied the man all my life and I'm very familiar with his methods of operation, my dear man."

Gorman said, "Charlie — "

Charlie held up a warning finger, he bounced up and down for emphasis. "Which is not to say the man does no good," he said. "Far from it. Oh no no no, my dear man! In his way he does a world of good: I freely give him credit. He comes to a wake, he draws a crowd, and he keeps everybody in the house that should be crying so busy carting sandwiches they forget to cry. Occupational therapy, my dear man! The touch of a master psychologist! Another Skeffington maxim: Stampede them! Give them no time to think! And on top of that the man is charitable. A heart of gold, you can't take that away from him. If the widow here tonight should need a little cash, she'll get it without asking. If she needs a job, there'll be one waiting for her at City Hall tomorrow morning; she can sit around all day stuffing empty papers into envelopes and mailing them to herself. Nice light work and one of the best-paying jobs in the city. Marvelous! A likable trait in the man. Not good government, but likable. Generous! But by the same token, my dear man, it's not a one-way street. Oh, by no means! *Quid pro quo,* as Julius Caesar used to say. Which means, 'I'll do fine by the wake, but it'll do twice as fine by me!' Oh yes yes! Marvelous! Shrewd!"

Altogether, thought Adam, an amazing performance; however, its primary effect had been to leave him increasingly doubtful about the necessity for his own apology. Once more he looked at Gorman, anticipating some sign of rebuttal, but apparently the old man was done with argument. He said, "Charlie. Where's your cap? The one that's made out of tar or lumps of coal or whatever it is. Did you leave it home out of respect? Could you not get a nice little one made out of black sateen you could bring to funerals and wakes?"

"Dacron," Charlie said promptly. "The cap's made out of Dacron, my dear man: the wonder material of the age. Not one head cold since the beginning of the year! You ought to wear one yourself at all times, my dear man, because of your advanced years. At your time of life even the head cold can be fatal. I'm supported in that opinion by the best of competent medical authority. Oh yes yes! Precautions, they're the thing!"

"I'll try one more year without it," Gorman said, "and see will I live." He pointed to the oblong box under Charlie's right arm and said curiously, "What's that you've got there with you? Did you bring a little present for the deceased, Charlie?"

"Better than a present, my dear man," Charlie said, whipping out the box and opening it. "A camera! A self-developer, my dear man!" He pointed it at Gorman; there was a clicking sound. "In sixty seconds exactly," he announced, "you'll have a full-fledged picture of yourself as you stand at this moment, my dear man! All done within the camera itself! An automatic process! Marvelous!"

The old man shook his head. In spite of his long experience with both Charlie and most of the varieties of abnormal behavior, he had found this demonstration slightly staggering. "And why would you bring a thing like that here tonight?" he said. "Were you out to snap a picture of Knocko in the box?"

"No, no nothing like that. I have it with me at all times these days, my dear man. A universal benefit to modern man. Grand for use in checking up on the sick and dying, for instance. Oh, marvelous! Knocko might still be among those present tonight if they'd had the good sense to use it on him. I know what I'm talking about, my dear man!" He patted the camera affectionately and said, "Grand, grand! It gives you a permanent picture record of how the patients are doing from day to day. Marvelous! Great for people visiting their sick relatives in the hospitals. Annie McCaffrey's husband Bill is over in the Simmons Memorial. I went to her the other day and said, 'Tell me, my dear woman, how does he look?' She said, 'He looks about the same from one day to the next. He doesn't change.' I said, 'That's where you're 100 per cent wrong, my dear woman. All patients change, for better or for worse. Disease isn't constant. Oh no!

Your trouble is that you're relying on what the doctors tell you and your own memory. Dangerous! Don't trust the memory! You go in to see him on Monday morning and you've already forgotten just how he looked on Sunday. Does he look better or is he slipping? You don't know, you can't remember. Foolish! Take this camera along with you, my dear woman. Snap a picture of him in bed at the same time every day for a week. At the end of the week compare the pictures. Marvelous! Right before your eyes you have the day-by-day pictorial record of whether the man is picking up or whether he's slowly wasting away to nothing at all! Regular check-ups in pictures, that's the thing! Take the camera now, my dear woman, I implore you! Get over to the hospital and start snapping away before it's too late! That's the only thing to do!' Oh, marvelous!" he cried, lifting the camera high above his head, and waving it about. "Here's the thing, my dear man, the very latest thing! The greatest single development in medicine since the invention of the bandage!"

Adam was fascinated. The matter of his apology had been forgotten, at least for the moment; he was dazzled by the ghastly anecdote he had just heard and by the turbulent little raconteur who had now begun to move about rapidly, circling them as he talked. Was he serious, Adam wondered? There seemed little doubt of it. Gorman sighed and said, "Charlie, Charlie. By God, you're a wonderful comfort to a worrying woman. And did she take you up on it?"

"No no," Charlie said. "You could hardly expect her to. A simple woman of the type you can do nothing for. Backward! Retrogressive! A childish faith in the attending physician. Sad, sad! I had to let her go her way. I said, 'Very well, my dear woman, I don't want to push you into anything. Only don't come around for the camera a couple of weeks from now when he's all skin and bones and his head's all shrunk up to no bigger than a walnut! I'd let you have it, yes, yes, of course, but it'll be too late, much too late! Oh yes!' Sixty seconds!" he said, breaking off suddenly. He halted his circling movements, brought down the camera from over his head, flipped open the back of it, and tore off a small rectangular piece of glossy paper. "Sixty seconds later and there you are!" he announced triumphantly, handing the paper to Gorman. "A picture record of John Gorman as he stood in this very room not a minute ago! All taken and developed within the camera itself! A sixty-second miracle! Visualize the possibilities in all fields, my dear man! It defies the scope of the imagination!"

Adam studied the small sepia photograph which Gorman held gingerly in his hand. It was not a flattering likeness. Cloudy, out of focus, with the head remarkably attenuated to approximately the length of the trunk, it offered striking evidence that the photographer had imperfectly mastered his instrument. "By God!" the old man said, in an awed voice.

"I haven't quite got the complete hang of it yet," Charlie said, "but you see the idea. Marvelous. And only the beginning! Modern science is on the march, my dear man! We're living in a wonderful age. Another generation and everybody'll live to be a hundred and they'll all have teeth like Eskimos! The dentist is all done, my dear man. He'll go out of the picture like the bison — "

"That's the kind of talk that's sure to gain you the unanimous support of the Dental Association," Skeffington said. He had been moving unhurriedly towards them for the past few moments, stopping to talk to newcomers to the room, picking up an attendant here and there to add to his bustling retinue. "It can't miss. There's nothing people enjoy quite so much as being told they're doomed to extinction. I'm surprised at an old campaigner like you, Charlie, antagonizing the dentists like that. To say nothing of the bison."

"Facts, facts!" Charlie said. "You can't hide facts, votes or no votes. How are you, my dear man? You're looking well, very well. Better than I've seen you in a long time. No slumping of the posture, nice and firm under the chin, clear eyes: grand! Grand in a man of your years. They tell me you're on the low-salt diet. Don't put too much faith in it, my dear man. No no no! That's what Billy McGrath was on and he perspired himself to death. *The system needs salt;* that's important to remember!"

"I'd almost forgotten poor Billy," Skeffington said thoughtfully. "The only man who ever literally sweated away. He used to move about accompanied by drip pans and sponges to collect the excess moisture. I'll try to avoid that fate if possible, Charlie. How's your campaign coming along, by the way? I hear you've got the sound truck out."

"Yes, yes, telling the public the facts, day and night. I'm telling them the facts about you, my dear man, as well as about your nut-boy opponent McCluskey. I watched you on television last night, my dear man; I took down every word you said on the tape recorder. Marvelous! Verbatim! Every last word! It doesn't stand up, my dear man. A grand first impression, but when you play it all back a second or third time on the tape recorder you realize the lack of substance there. Oh, inadequate, my dear man! Grand delivery, but poverty of thought. I played it back three times on the tape recorder and realized it more each time. Yes, yes!"

"Charlie, that's unfair," Skeffington said reproachfully. "You listened. I don't know that I like these radical departures from fine old traditions. I only hope it doesn't start a trend. Suppose everybody got the bug and suddenly began to listen to what was being said in political speeches? You're playing with fire, Charlie. You may be even tampering with the health and well-being of the nation. I listened to a political speech only once in my life and I nearly died as a result. It was twenty-five years ago. Cal Coolidge was President. I was in the hospital, recovering nicely from a minor operation, when some enemy turned the radio on in my room so that I could hear a presidential address. Well, I was weak and didn't realize what I was doing. I listened to him. I listened to every word he said for nearly five minutes and then I began to sink fast. They got me just in time. They slapped me in an oxygen tent, and while it was touch-and-go for the next few days, eventually I pulled through. A good many Republicans never forgave Cal for not talking a little faster that day. But I hope you see now how dangerous your little experiment is, Charlie, and what it might lead to: the possibility of a national breakdown. Still," he said, "it may not catch on altogether. There must be a few mossbacks in the electorate who don't bother to tape-record every political speech they hear."

There had been visible and audible signs of amusement from the crowd all through this speech; there was loud, shouting laughter at its conclusion. From the periphery of the crowd came a high-pitched laugh which carried above all other sounds. Ditto had returned with the cigars.

"Tape-record every political speech they hear!" he cried. "Oh, that's a good one, Governor! Yes, indeed!"

"Marvelous!" Charlie cried happily. "A great performance, my dear man! The born raconteur in action! Marvelous! Not a word of sense or truth in the whole performance from beginning to end, but they loved it! Oh, marvelous! A great example of crowd psychology, my dear man! I give credit where credit it due! I take nothing away from you, my dear man. I give you your due every night in the wards while I'm campaigning against you. Oh yes! I stand on the sound truck and say, 'Dear folks, don't underestimate the mayor. Don't think he has no capacity merely because the city is going to rack and ruin around us, our fine civic buildings are all held together with Scotch tape and library paste, our nice residential streets look like back alleys in South Timbuctoo, and every man among us who owns property is taxed like the Aga Khan. But dear folks, don't condemn the mayor totally for this! Be just, dear folks! Remember that while he may be a bum administrator, we have to admit two things about him. One, he has a grand heart, and two, he's the greatest orator and crowd psychologist that this part of the world has ever produced! These are facts I'm telling you, dear folks! There's no one to touch him in that department! Oh yes,' " he cried, crouching, and weaving back and forth, his hand clutching an invisible microphone, the floor beneath his feet miraculously transformed into the platform atop his sound truck, " 'there's no one to touch him at all! The last surviving member of his species! Only last week I wrote letters to the sociologists down at Yale, Harvard, and Princeton, telling them to get their best men over here to watch Frank Skeffington in action before it's too late! Oh yes! Important! I told them to get them over here and watch him set the buffoons on fire, all laughing and jumping and cheering and stamping their feet, while he stands up there nodding his head and in the big air-conditioned voice telling them fifteen lies and a bedtime story to send them home happy! Marvelous! The talent is inborn, dear folks! A terrible mayor but a great entertainer! And what's the lesson in that, dear folks? Simply this: I say to you tonight that you have to make up your minds whether or not you want an entertainer in the mayor's seat. And if you do, dear folks, if you want a good laugh while the buildings of your city are falling to the ground one by one all around you, then by all means return Frank Skeffington to office!' "

This sustained performance won more laughter and applause; Skeffington had listened, greatly amused. He liked Charlie Hennessey, and while the liking was comfortably buttressed by the knowledge that, as a rival, Charlie could do him no serious damage, still, the feeling had more genuine roots. Skeffington knew that he had much common ground with this exuberant little pepperpot. They shared the same background, the same traditions, and even, to a considerable extent, the same gifts; it was just that in one of them, Skeffington reflected, somewhere along the line someone had forgotten to tighten a necessary wire, and the result was Charlie. Charlie, with all his volcanic but essentially purposeless eloquence, his thousand and one unrelated interests, his wild undisciplined quixotic pursuit of impossible ends! Looking at Charlie in full flight was for Skeffington a little like looking into a mirror in a fun house: through the lunatic distortions, he could always manage to discern just a little bit of himself.

However scattered his shots, though, Charlie was almost always hugely diverting in process; at least Skeffington found him to be so, and he was now pleased to note that apparently his nephew did, too. He had been watching Adam with some care during the progress of Charlie's monologue; he was satisfied with the results. The boy was clearly fascinated by this extraordinary orator; now he was laughing like the rest; his earlier reticence seemed gone, he was caught up in the atmosphere of the room. Still, while that was all desirable, Skeffington reminded himself that this atmosphere must now be controlled; otherwise it could get out of hand. And, after all, it *was* a wake, Knocko was in the parlor, and, more important, Gert was in the kitchen. He looked at Gorman, who had gone over to the door and who had been talking to the stout woman who was in charge of arrangements in the kitchen. The old man now nodded at Skeffington, and he put up his hand, slowly quieting the crowd.

"Charlie," he said, "you put me to shame. When I hear those complimentary words you've been directing to the electorate on my behalf, I deeply regret that I haven't shown the same generous spirit towards you. Maybe I can repair that deficiency in the weeks to come. Meanwhile, I hope you haven't been favoring me exclusively. I hope you've been fair enough to extend the same courtesies to friend McCluskey!"

"Never fear, my dear man!" Charlie said. "Absolute impartiality! I'm after the nut-boy hammer and tongs, yet at the same time I say a good word for him. 'Oh, dear folks,' I say, 'it's grand to see a nice, clean-living young man want to make his way into public life today! Nice! I've got respect for him. Dear folks, I don't hold it against him for a minute that the poor boy's nothing but a decoy duck for Mother Garvey as well as the power-trust gang! A duck in a double-breasted suit! It's not his fault, dear folks. Oh no! Innocent! Innocent as the day he was born! Doesn't belong in the dirty business of city politics at all; it's a shame to drag him in! A marvelous candidate for the presidency of the senior class in high school! Great at planting bushes in the school lawn on Arbor Day! Grand! Marvelous! But dear folks, a mere pawn in the hands of those that run him today! A clean-living pawn, but still a pawn! The boy's — "

"Fine, Charlie, fine," Skeffington said, interrupting. He was enjoying what was being said, but it would have to wait for another time. "Glad to see you're giving everybody the same treatment. At the moment, however, I think we're all going to have to quiet down a bit. Knocko's widow'll be in here any moment. Naturally she's distressed, and she won't want to linger, so I suggest that you extend your sympathies briefly, and then move out to the kitchen where there are refreshments. I also suggest," he said meaningfully, "that after the refreshments you stay around for the Rosary. I know that most of you intended to, but there may be a few who suddenly remembered more pressing errands. If so, I think those errands had better be postponed. A few prayers won't kill you, and some of you may actually enjoy the sensation of being on your knees for a change. The priest should be here shortly."

"Marvelous!" Charlie said. "The swiftness and dispatch of it! Marching orders! I hand it to you, my dear man. Marvelous!"

It was the entrance of the widow that returned Adam to a sense of the occasion. Guiltily he realized that he had succumbed completely to the mood against which he had protested; before the caperings of Charlie Hennessey, he had found no trouble at all in forgetting Knocko Minihan. This feeling of guilt was heightened when his uncle, a moment later, steered him towards the widow. She was a tall, somber woman with a gentle, grief-drawn face; clearly, she had not forgotten. Contrite, Adam tried hastily to summon up some last-minute emotion more or less appropriate to death; in this he was regrettably not successful. Skeffington presented him to the widow; he muttered what he hoped was an acceptable phrase of condolence; she nodded and gazed at him with a polite, dulled curiosity. He left the room quickly and joined the men in the kitchen. Skeffington remained behind while the others in the room paid their respects, quickly and quietly; then he took the woman by the arm and directed her down the hall and into the parlor itself. To Adam, it all seemed very hard indeed on the widow, and he could not imagine why his uncle appeared so determined that she should go through with it, as though it were some form of compulsory ritual. Doubtless it had its value; Adam did not know what this might be. To him, it merely seemed an unnecessary and, very probably, a peculiarly painful procedure.

He did not wait long in the kitchen. He stood by the table, talking with some of the men whom he had seen in his uncle's office; Ditto had deserted him for the moment. Soon he saw his uncle come back down the hall with the widow. She disappeared, and Skeffington came into the kitchen.

"I think we might move along up to the parlor," he said to Adam. "I saw a priest come in as I was coming back down here: I imagine they'll be saying the Rosary any moment now. We'll join them, and then we'll go."

Led by Skeffington, the men left the kitchen and trooped up to the parlor; there, at the door they were met by a priest. Or, more accurately, by a Monsignor; it was the Cardinal's secretary.

"Good evening, Governor," he said pleasantly.

"Well, well," Skeffington said, some slight surprise in his voice. "Monsignor. This is an unexpected pleasure. Nice to see you again. Are you here as an emissary of His Eminence?"

"No, no," the Monsignor said. "I'm on my own tonight. Mrs. Minihan is something of an old friend. When I was a boy in this part of town I used to drop in to see her fairly often. Most of the children of the neighborhood did, I think."

"Yes," Skeffington said thoughtfully. "So they did. I'd almost forgotten. Poor Gert." Then, speaking less to himself and more to the Monsignor, he said, "Well, it's very good of you to remember and drop in now. Tell me, how's your boss these days?"

"Very well. I'll tell him I saw you, Governor."

"Do that," Skeffington said. "He'll be overjoyed."

The Monsignor smiled. "You may be misjudging His Eminence, Governor. It's a case of the bark being a good deal worse than the bite."

"I wouldn't know," Skeffington said. "I've never been bitten. There were a few quick snaps in my direction, but I managed to avoid them. However, that's neither here nor there at the moment, I suppose; there's no reason why you should be bothered with these old-time vendettas, Monsignor. By the way, have you met my nephew, Adam Caulfield?"

The Monsignor, who would have given rather a lot to be bothered about the old-time vendettas, greeted Adam with an automatic affability, but his mind was on Skeffington. The old politician captivated his imagination; he saw him a unique, a rich, extraordinary personality who contained within himself a part of local history which soon would be no more and which never again would reappear. It was a vein that called out to be tapped before it disappeared, first, from view, then even from memory; for just a moment the Monsignor thought of suggesting to Skeffington the possibility of a luncheon, a meeting, a talk. Then he thought of the Cardinal, and of the old, tough, knobby face darkening with rage and disappointment when he learned — as he surely would — of the deliberate encounter, planned by his own subordinate. It would be imprudent; worse, it would be unfair. For the time being, at least, any such meeting was impracticable; a little later, perhaps . . . And so the Monsignor, nodding towards the parlor, merely said, "I suppose we'd better go in now."

They went in, they knelt, and the Monsignor led them in the Rosary. They recited in unison the five decades of the beads which commemorate the Sorrowful Mysteries of the Church; they prayed for the immortal soul of Aram Minihan. And as they prayed, their responses low, rhythmic, and at times not quite distinct, riding high over all other voices came one which to Adam was familiar, clear, unhesitating, and infinitely fervent. It was the voice of Delia Boylan.

The Rosary over, it was time to go. Skeffington swiftly and efficiently made the rounds, saying the necessary good-bys; then he signaled to Adam, and uncle and nephew walked towards the front door together. They had almost reached the door when Skeffington, suddenly halting, said, "Hold on a minute. I want a word with that undertaker before we go."

They both turned and saw the head of Johnnie Degnan, poking out of the kitchen at the far end of the hall; obviously he had been watching their departure. Skeffington beckoned, and he came running quietly to them.

"Ah, good evening, Governor," he said, in his swift hushed tones. "A very sad occasion. I wanted to see you before this evening, to make your acquaintance, but the pressure of my duties didn't quite allow. I'm John Degnan, Governor."

"Glad to know you, Mr. Degnan," Skeffington said. "As you say, it's a sad occasion. I'm happy to see you've done your best by it, however. I've been admiring your handiwork with the deceased."

"Thank you, Governor. Thank you very much. That's nice to hear. I did my best," the undertaker said modestly. "I don't mind telling you, Governor, that Mr. Minihan presented a very difficult case. Because of the age and the sunken cheeks and the wrinkles. I'm sure you can appreciate the difficulty of the task, Governor. Everything had to be smoothed out delicately, the youthful contours restored, and so forth."

"Yes. Now, Mr. Degnan, only one feature of your work disturbs me and that is the probable cost. You don't mind if I say that I was rather struck by the fact that the coffin, and what might be called the general deathroom décor, seem a trifle splendid for someone who was in decidedly modest circumstances?"

The undertaker smiled; it was, Adam thought, a nervous smile. "I see what you mean, Governor," he said swiftly. "I appreciate that point of view. And yet I always think the family is more satisfied if the final homage, as I like to think of it, is really nice in its every aspect. Something that the deceased would have been proud of if he could have seen it."

"Why, those are the feelings of an artist," Skeffington said. "They do you credit, Mr. Degnan. I presume, incidentally, that you've discussed all this with Mrs. Minihan?"

"Well, no. Not exactly, that is, Governor. I thought it best not to in her distraught condition. Just a few words here and there. I think you could say, more or less, that it was left to my discretion, as it so often is. I always believe in taking as many worries as possible from the shoulders of the family."

"That's very thoughtful of you. Now then, you're a young man, Mr. Degnan, but I understand you've had quite a bit of professional experience. As you might put it, you've been in charge of a good many final homages. Or as I might put it, you've buried a good many people. What would you say was the lowest price you've ever buried anyone for?"

"The lowest *price,* Governor?" The smile remained; it wavered uncertainly. "I don't quite understand. . . . What I mean to say is, Governor, I don't believe that's anything I've ever quite figured out."

"Try," Skeffington urged him. "Make a rough estimate. Would it be . . . oh, say thirty-five dollars?"

"Thirty-five dollars!" The gasp of astonishment and pain broke through the modulated occupational tones; the undertaker looked wildly at Skeffington and said, "You couldn't *begin* to bury anyone for that price today, Governor!"

"I'll bet you could if you really tried," Skeffington said pleasantly. "I'll bet you could both begin and end. And just to prove my confidence in your resourcefulness, Mr. Degnan, why don't you do that very thing with Mr. Minihan? Let's give it a real try. I think you can do it. I'm sure the final bill won't read over thirty-five dollars. Matter of fact, I'll instruct the widow to that effect immediately."

"But Governor, you can't be serious!" Degnan cried. The smooth round face had become agonized; the soft hands were united in front of him in a tight, beseeching clasp. He looked as if he were about to hurl himself at his persecutor's feet, and Adam, who had not until a moment ago realized just what it was that his uncle was doing, now felt a sudden pity as well as disgust for this abject little profiteer. "The costs alone, Governor," Degnan moaned. "They're going up every day. I couldn't possibly do it. It's all *arranged* — "

"Fine," Skeffington said. "Then let it go through as arranged. But for thirty-five dollars."

"But, *Governor* . . . "

Skeffington pulled his watch from a vest pocket and examined it with apparent surprise. "It's later than I thought," he said. "Well, then, Mr. Degnan, it's all settled. I'll leave the details to you. A suitable funeral conducted for thirty-five dollars, with no cutting of corners. All the normal courtesies extended, the usual paraphernalia available. I'll have a few men on hand just to see that everything goes along well. I know you'll do a grand job. In any event, I'll be sure to hear about it: my observers will give me a full report."

The undertaker's face, which for some moments had been the color of putty, now had turned a vivid red. "But Governor! I hope you know how eager I am to co-operate in anything you suggest. How eager I *always* am. But what you're asking is *impossible. . . .* "

"Why, that's one of the words that doesn't belong to the bright lexicon of youth," Skeffington said reprovingly. "I've always believed that nothing is impossible when one has youth and ambition. I hope you won't be the one to shake this treasured belief. Because if you do," he said, regarding Degnan with a stare which its recipient suddenly found to be as unpleasant as anything he had ever experienced, "you might shake my confidence in you. What's worse, you might even begin to shake public confidence in you. That is a bad thing to have happen to a young undertaker with dreams, Mr. Degnan. You never can tell how far it might reach. It might even reach the members of the licensing board for your profession. You never know. But we mustn't keep you from your labors any longer. I suppose you have many things to do at a time like this. Possibly even more than you'd anticipated. Good night, Mr. Degnan. Glad you introduced yourself."

They went out the door and down the steps; Degnan's anguished voice trailed them to their car. "Thirty-five dollars!" it wailed. "Governor, I *appeal* to you . . ."

When they were under way, Skeffington said: "I hadn't planned on rounding your evening off in just that way. I hope you weren't too shocked by my treatment of the widow's helper."

Adam shook his head. "It seemed to me that the widow's helper rather had it coming. And will he do it for thirty-five dollars, do you think?"

Skeffington chuckled. "I wouldn't be surprised," he said dryly.

"And the sum? That puzzled me. Why exactly thirty-five dollars?"

"No particular reason. It seemed a nice round humiliating figure. I'm not very fond of these deathbed bandits." Especially, he reflected, when they propose to enrich themselves at his expense; for rather early in the evening it had occurred to him that the funeral would necessarily be paid for from the thousand dollars he had given to the widow. "I'd heard about this Degnan, but I'd never happened to run into him before tonight. After tonight I imagine he'll see to it that I don't run into him again. Well," he said, shifting his position and facing his nephew more directly, "I didn't think we'd be in there quite so long. I apologize to you. I only hope you weren't bored."

"No, no. Far from it." Adam thought for a moment, looking back over the evening. There were a number of questions he wanted very much to ask his uncle; the difficulty was that some of them were not so easily put. He began with one that was; he said: "Uncle Frank, what about a man like Charlie Hennessey? I mean, what is he? What does he do?"

"He runs for office, mostly. Against me or against anybody; Charlie plays no favorites. He hasn't been very successful lately, but back about twenty years ago, Charlie was considered quite a comer. He was always a great talker and he started off with a bang. He was on the City Council, a member of the Governor's Council — not under me, I might add — and he even served a term in Congress. In those days Charlie seemed to be looking into a rosy tomorrow."

"And the roses faded?"

"They did indeed. You see," Skeffington said, "they suddenly discovered two things about Charlie. First, that he was honest, and second, that he was crazy. It was the combination that killed him. Theoretically at least, an honest man can succeed in politics; and there's a considerable body of evidence to prove that a crazy man can. But a man who's both honest and crazy might just as well be a Chinese midget for all the good he'll do himself at the polls."

Adam protested. "But he's not a madman, surely?"

Skeffington shrugged. "It's a nice question of definition. He's not a certifiable lunatic, if that's what you mean, but he's certainly at that stage where a man's friends begin to call him 'eccentric.' What his enemies call him is apt to be something else again. Politically speaking, it's my opinion that Charlie is harmless except on those rare occasions when for some mysterious reason he decides to support me; then I want to run for cover. He's a dangerous man to have in your corner. He's great on the platform, but he has a crack right down the middle, and you never know when or where he's going to take off. I remember that when he first entered the City Council we were having a big to-do about a new municipal sewage system. Danny Leary was Council President, and he had Charlie all lined up to make the big speech in favor of it. Well, it was a big speech, all right. It lasted an hour and a half; the only trouble was that somewhere in the middle of it Charlie got sidetracked into talking about the marvelous advantages of having universal, compulsory fingerprinting introduced into the city, with the FBI coming in to take the prints of everybody who was still breathing. 'Not even the nuns in their convents should be exempt!' said Charlie. Naturally that made a tremendous hit with the good Sisters; poor Leary spent the next two weeks crying in convent vestibules, explaining to Mother Superiors that his own daughter was a nun, and that he himself often went to daily Mass when the weather was good. Some of us wondered, however, what all this had to do with the problem of municipal sewage, and it was just about this time I began to suspect that Charlie's political value had its limitations. It's too bad, in a way, because he's a good fellow — smart enough, and knows the local political situation from A to Z. And, as I say, he won't take a dime from anybody. Charlie's trouble is that he's not content with asking the voters to lend him their ears; halfway through the speech he starts wanting to take their pulse as well. The result is that he's the kiss of death. What was that he had with him tonight, by the way — a camera?"

Adam told him of Charlie and the self-developing camera. Skeffington listened attentively, chuckling from time to time as he heard of the photographing of John Gorman, and of the grisly potential of the camera as an instrument in the sickroom. When Adam finished the story, which seemed to him in the retelling even more improbable than when he had witnessed it in actual development, he looked questioningly at his uncle; both men broke into laughter.

"You see how it is," Skeffington said. "The authentic Hennessey touch: I'd recognize it anywhere. I wonder how the patient is supposed to react when the photographer asks him for 'just one more'? Sounds a little final, as if he were soon to be among the souvenirs. What else did Charlie have to say for himself?"

Adam hesitated. Then, because there was much he was still curious about, and because a note of comradeship, almost of complicity, seemed to have been established between them on this ride home, he decided to move into more doubtful waters. He said, "Actually, he didn't talk much about himself at all. He talked mostly about you, Uncle Frank. About you and the wake."

"Reasonable enough, under the circumstances. The wake was there, and so was I."

"Yes. The thing was that he seemed to be saying that the conjunction had a rather peculiar effect on the wake, that it changed its character pretty drastically."

Skeffington nodded. "From the funereal to the political," he said. "And what did you think of that?" Adam hesitated again, and Skeffington gave him a look of pleasant inquiry. "Go ahead," he invited. "I'll probably be able to bear it."

"Well," Adam said reluctantly, "to be honest, I had something of the same thought myself a little earlier, before Charlie arrived. I had quite a talk with Mr. Gorman about it." Now that he had gone this far, further frankness seemed unavoidable; somewhat uneasily he gave his uncle the full account of what had passed between Gorman and himself. Was it a mistake? he wondered. Probably not; it occurred to him that Gorman would himself unquestionably have mentioned it in due course.

As he talked, he kept his eyes on his uncle's face: the scrutiny proved remarkably unfruitful. The heavy features registered nothing more than a polite, unchanging interest; it was impossible for Adam to tell whether his uncle was indignant, whether he was outraged, whether he was totally unaffected. Or — in a sense, even worse — whether he was simply amused. It was most disquieting . . .

He completed his explanation. Skeffington said, "I've seldom heard of John's being so eloquent; it stands as a great tribute to your qualities as a listener. I must say he put the case for me rather well; I couldn't have done better myself. Charlie's approach, on the other hand, must have been considerably different. I imagine he probably said something to this effect." And then, while Adam stared at him, he proceeded to duplicate Charlie's speech in astonishing detail; it seemed to Adam, remembering the original, that the reproduction was virtually word for word. Finishing, Skeffington said, "Close enough?"

"Close enough," Adam agreed, bewildered. "The question is: How? You couldn't have heard it from where you were."

"Extrasensory perception," Skeffington said gravely. "A man can't go far without it today." Once again, Adam heard the familiar deep chuckle. "Of course, there is the additional fact that Charlie's principal addresses don't change very much over the years. He has the unwillingness of the artist to tamper with the perfect production. This is one of his best, a regular party piece. Or wake piece, if you prefer. I must have heard it a hundred times. It's extremely entertaining. In addition to which," he said casually, "it contains more than a little truth."

Adam looked up sharply, but his uncle seemed preoccupied in withdrawing a cigar from his vest pocket. It was long, fat, dull-greenish in color. It did not appear to be at all the same grade of cigar that had been provided in quantities for the wake.

"One over the limit," he said cheerfully, lighting it. "A happy shortcut to the Dark Encounter. Well, you see me refusing to be less than candid with you. I don't want to give you a misleading impression. I should add that while Charlie was telling the truth, up to a point, so was John Gorman. Actually, they were both right: Knocko's wake was and it wasn't a political rally. Given the circumstances, and," he added, with a faintly deprecatory wave of the cigar, "given myself, it could hardly have been anything else. You see, what you're up against here is the special local situation. To understand what happened tonight, you have to understand a little bit about that situation, and just a little bit more about my own rather peculiar position in it."

He leaned back, relaxing against the cushions; simply, detachedly, without boast or embellishment, he began to talk about himself. It was an extraordinary procedure; just how extraordinary, Adam did not realize. For while Skeffington had long studied his city and his own relation to it, the results of these studies he had been careful to keep to himself. From the beginning of his career, he had sharply divided the private from the public side of his life. Of the many friends he had made in politics over the years, none — not Gorman, even — had been admitted to the isolated preserve of the private thought, the personal concern. His wife had been his single, ideal confidant; with her death had come a void. Because Skeffington was, literally, a family man, he had tried one day, somewhat against his better judgment, to fill this void with his son. He had talked of himself, his work, his problems and his plans, and as he talked he had gradually become aware of the look upon his son's face: that characteristic, pleasant, glazed half-smile which indicated that somewhere beneath the surface inattention struggled with incomprehension. There had been more than the look; there had been the dancing feet: they had begun an abstracted, rather complicated tapping on the floor of the study, doubtless in anticipation of their evening's work ahead. *I should have been*

Vernon Castle, Skeffington had thought bitterly. He had left the room abruptly and the experiment had never been repeated.

And now, as he had one afternoon three weeks before, he talked to his nephew.

"You see," he said, "my position is slightly complicated because I'm not just an elected official of the city; I'm a tribal chieftain as well. It's a necessary kind of dual officeholding, you might say; without the second, I wouldn't be the first."

"The tribe," said Adam, "being the Irish?"

"Exactly. I have heard them called by less winning names: minority pressure group (even though they've been the majority for half a century), immigrant voting bloc (even though many of the said immigrants have been over here for three generations). Still, I don't suppose it makes much difference what you call them; the net result's the same. I won't insult your intelligence by explaining that they're the people who put me in the mayor's chair and keep me there; I think you realize that the body of my support doesn't come from the American Indian. But as a member — at least by birth — of the tribe, you might give a thought to some of the tribal customs. They don't chew betel nut, and as far as I know the women don't beautify themselves by placing saucers in their lower lips. Although now that I come to think of it," he said, "that might not be a bad idea. It might reduce the potential for conversation. However, they do other things, and among them they go to wakes. And so do I."

"Which are and are not political rallies?" Adam asked. "Or was Knocko's case a special one?"

"Not at all special, except that the guest of honor was somewhat less popular than many of his predecessors. But of course when you speak about wakes as being political rallies, that's a little strong. You have to remember something about the history of the wake around here. When I was a boy in this city, a wake was a big occasion, and by no means a sad one. Unless, of course, it was a member of your own family that had died. Otherwise it was a social event. Some of my most vivid memories are of wakes. I remember my poor mother taking me to old Nappy Coughlin's wake. We went into the tenement, and there was Nappy, all laid out in a little coffin which was kept on ice. Embalming was a rather uncertain science in those days. It was a hot day in July and there were no screens on the parlor windows; there were flies in the room. I can still hear the ice dripping into the pans underneath the coffin, and I can still see Nappy. He had one of the old-fashioned shrouds on, and he lay stretched out stiff as a ramrod. And on his head he wore a greasy black cap, which his good wife had lovingly adjusted so that the peak was pulled down over one eye. It gave him a rather challenging look; you had the feeling that at any moment he might spring out of the coffin and offer to go four fast rounds with you. My mother was horrified at the sight, and I remember that she went directly over to the widow and told her she ought to be ashamed of herself, putting her husband in the coffin with his hat on. Whereupon the widow simply said that he'd never had it off; he'd worn it for thirty years, day and night, in bed and out. So naturally she left it on, not wanting to say good-by to a stranger. However, when Father Conroy came in, the hat was whisked off fast enough. I can remember — it was my first wake, by the way — going into the kitchen, where somebody gave me a glass of milk and a piece of cake. And while my mother was in the parlor talking with the other women, I was out there with the men, just sitting around, eating cake, and listening to them talk. I hadn't the faintest notion of what they were talking about, but it didn't matter much. I was in seventh heaven. Everybody seemed to be enjoying themselves, and I knew I was. When my mother came to get me and take me home, I left with the greatest regret; I decided I'd never had a better time. Well," he said, "so much for memories of happy days. I wouldn't imagine it would sound like very much to anyone who'd been brought up today."

Adam smiled. "It sounded like a little boy having a wonderful time for himself. Although I must say that it didn't sound very much like death. Or even a political rally, for that matter."

"Matter of fact, it was the first political rally I'd ever been to," Skeffington said. "I was just too young to know it. You see, that's what all the men were talking about: politics. There was even a moment, just before I left, when Charlie McCooey himself came in: a fat man with a red face and handlebar mustache. He was the ward boss. I didn't know what that was, at the time, but

I did know that the name of Charlie McCooey commanded respect and awe. I thought he must have been some kind of god. Twenty years later this childhood illusion was blasted. I gave him the beating of his life in a fight for the leadership of the ward; the vote was four to one. In the process of doing so I discovered that the god was nothing more than a dull bully-boy with no imagination and just enough intelligence to read his way through the daily adventures of Happy Hooligan. No offense intended, incidentally, by the reference to a rival comic strip."

"No offense received," Adam said. "I lack the artist's pride. Besides, I think that Happy is defunct these days." But he spoke absently, for he was not thinking of comic strips. He had suddenly remembered, while Skeffington was talking, that once, years ago, and from a source he could not now place, he had heard a series of quite different stories about the old wakes; in these, the cake-and-milk had not figured largely. He said, "But I had the idea from somewhere, Uncle Frank, that many of these wakes got to be pretty violent affairs. I know there was always a certain amount of drinking, but didn't some of them actually become brawls?"

Skeffington's heavy face assumed a mildly shocked expression. "Why, I hardly know what to say," he murmured. "I have heard that drinking men occasionally forced their way into these gatherings, but I like to believe that they were instantly sobered by the sight of decent men and women shrinking from them in revulsion." He glanced at his nephew, and his lips twitched just slightly. "No," he said, "of course you're right. There was drinking and sometimes things got a little rough. You might not have enjoyed it very much. But it's all gone by the boards long ago, and it was the exception rather than the rule; while it may seem terrible enough from your point of view today, you might reflect on the fact that there just might have been some excuse for it. I think what you have to do," he said, "is to see the wakes and everything that happened at them in the light of the times. I mentioned to you the other afternoon that life wasn't exactly a picnic for our people in those days. They were a sociable people but they didn't get much chance for sociability. They were poor, they worked hard, and they didn't have much in the way of diversion. Actually, the only place people got together was at the wake. Everybody knew everybody else; when somebody died, the others went to pay their respects and also to see and talk to each other. It was all part of the pattern. They were sorry for the family of the deceased, to be sure, but while they were being sorry they took advantage of the opportunity to have a drink and a chat with the others who were being sorry, too. It was a change, an outlet for people who led back-breaking, dreary, and monotonous lives. And if, once in a while, someone took a few too many and wanted to set fire to the widow or play steamroller in the kitchen, it was possibly deplorable but it was also slightly understandable. All in all, I've always thought the wake was a grand custom, and I still do."

"Yes," Adam said slowly. "I hadn't thought of it in that light — I mean, I hadn't thought of the wake as being a kind of *relief* from grimness. And yet I guess it must have been, all right. But what about *now,* Uncle Frank? Those same conditions don't exist, do they?"

"No," said Skeffington, "and neither does the wake. Not in the same way, that is. It's a disappearing phenomenon, like the derby hat. As the younger people grow up, the wakes are more and more changing their character: for example, they're being held now in funeral parlors rather than in the homes. The wake will still continue in some form; after all, it takes a long time to get rid of old tribal customs. And Knocko's was a bit like some of the old wakes; that's why I wanted you to see it. And as for the political discussion, that was in the grand tradition, too. By the way, did you happen to wonder why they might have been talking politics tonight?"

"Well, I naturally thought it was because you were there. But — "

"But," Skeffington said, interrupting with a look of some amusement, "was I there because they were going to talk politics? Right?" It was all too remarkably right; Adam flushed and began to protest, but Skeffington said, "A perfectly natural question. I'd be astonished if it hadn't occurred to you. The answer, by the way, is a little bit of both. I suppose I went at least partly because it was one more opportunity to keep the ball rolling. It's almost impossible for an old campaigner to avoid the occasions of sin. But whether I'd been there or not, they would have talked politics anyway. It's what interests them most. It ought to: it gave most of them everything they have. I mentioned to you the other day that the main reason I went into politics was because it was the quickest way out of the cellar and up the ladder. A good many others felt the same way. A lot of the younger men wanted a nice new dark serge suit that didn't necessarily come equipped with a chauffeur's cap. And the only way out was through politics; it was only when we gained a measure of political control that our people were able to come up for a little fresh air. They know that; they think of it as the big salvation for them; that's why they talk about it when they all get together. It's a very serious part of the business of living. And when I'm around, naturally I'm expected to talk it with them. And I do. I may add," he said, "that I don't find it a hardship."

Adam thought of one more question. "And the family?" he said. "The family of the deceased, I mean. Like Mrs. Minihan tonight. How do they feel while all this is going on? Don't they sometimes mind, Uncle Frank?"

"I know what you mean," Skeffington said, "but I think you're a bit wrong there. I don't think they mind a bit. There is a contrary opinion, however. Every once in a while I see where some advanced young public servant, who still had the ring of the pot on his seat while all this was going on, publicly applauds the passing of 'that cruel and barbarous custom, the wake.' Whenever I see that I take down my little book and chalk up a new name in the boob section. The man who said it obviously hasn't the faintest notion of what he's talking about. He hasn't the remotest understanding of the times, the circumstances, of our people, the way they feel and the way they regard death. I've seen a good many people die around here and I'll probably see a good many more. Unless, of course," he added, in another of those detached and faintly chilling parentheses which never failed to jolt Adam, "I beat them to it; there's always that possibility. But I've never seen the family that thought the wake was cruel and barbarous. They expected it. They wanted it. More than that, it was good for them: it was a useful distraction, it kept them occupied, and it gave them the feeling that they weren't alone, that they had a few neighbors who cared enough to come in and see them through a bad time. And you could say, too, it was a mark of respect for the deceased: rest assured that *he* wanted his wake. I remember what happened when the Honorable Hugh Archer died. The Honorable Hugh was considerably before your time; I don't imagine you'd have heard much about him."

"No, nothing."

"He was a prominent Republican attorney who once refused ten thousand dollars offered to him if he'd defend a notorious criminal. The noble gesture was unprecedented in Republican circles, and immediately he became known as the Honorable. It wasn't until much later that it was discovered he had asked for twenty thousand. Well, eventually he died. He was a huge man: six foot four and weighing nearly three hundred pounds. At that time, cremation was just coming into fashion, following closely upon Mah-jongg, and they whipped the Honorable Hugh out to the incinerator on the very day he died. Old Martin Canady went to the ceremony, out of a curiosity to see how the other half died, and when he came running back to me he was literally popeyed with shock. 'By God, Frank!' he said. 'They took the big elephant before he stopped breathin' almost and what the hell d'ye think they did with him? They put him in the oven and burned him up with the Sunday papers! When the poor man finished cookin' ye could have buried him in an ash tray! By God, Frank, I wouldn't want nothin' like that to happen to me! When I go I'm damned sure I mean to stay around the house a few days and nights so's some of the old pals can come in and have a drink and the last look! What the hell's wrong with that, now?' And," Skeffington said, "to save my soul, I couldn't think of a blessed thing wrong with it. It's the way I want to go myself. . . . Well, here I am talking away, it's late at night, and you're probably eager to get back in your house."

For the first time Adam noticed that the car had stopped and that they were in front of his house; they had been there, in fact, for some minutes. He said, "Uncle Frank, thanks loads for the evening. I've had a fine time, really." Then, because he felt that somewhere along the line his comments, however courteously they had been received by the older man, had been fairly presumptuous, he added, "And forgive the side-line observations on wakes. I guess the trouble was that I really didn't understand very much about them."

"Nothing wrong with your observations at all," Skeffington said. "To tell you the truth, I was glad you were interested enough to make them. From one point of view, they were perfectly correct. All I was concerned with doing was to show you another point of view. And I'm glad you enjoyed yourself; I was hoping you would and I thought you might. Knocko's wake is the kind of thing you might not have come across in the ordinary run of events, yet in a way I think it's far more valuable to you in understanding the whys and wherefores of the campaign and the city than attendance at any number of rallies would be. I may add that it's been pleasant for me, too: it was good to have you along. When something else comes up that I think you should take a look at, I'll give you a ring. That is, of course," he said courteously, "if you'd like me to."

"Please do, Uncle Frank. And again, thanks for tonight."

"A pleasure," Skeffington said. "Good night, my boy. Remember me to your wife."

The car sped off and Adam, going up the walk, realized with a start that, until Skeffington's final words, he had not once thought of Maeve during the evening. There was nothing unforgivable in the negligence itself; yet all the same, this evening, when he was in the company of her enemy and surrounded by activities of which she would have so disapproved, she had somehow eluded his thoughts. It was odd. He looked up at the house; with the exception of the single front hall light, it was in darkness. He knew that Maeve, as was sometimes her custom when he remained late at the paper, had already gone to bed.

He thought again of the evening behind him. It was as he had told his uncle: he had had a good time, and more, a singularly interesting one. He thought again of Charlie Hennessey and Ditto Boland and Delia Boylan, and even the wretched Johnnie

Degnan; he thought of the outrageously inapposite behavior of one and all in the house where Aram Minihan lay in wake. Except that now, he thought, he was by no means so sure of its inappositeness, for Skeffington's words had not been without their effect, and on the theme of the wake, Adam's previous judgments had been drained of much of their certainty.

Maeve returned to his thoughts, disturbingly. He opened the door, and entered the house; as he did so he reflected that, finally, she would have to be told. It was ridiculous to postpone it any longer; as he mounted the stairs to their room, he determined to tell her the following morning.

Skeffington went home and directly upstairs; he was satisfied with the evening's work. On his way past his son's room he saw, with some surprise, that a thin crack of light shone under the closed door. He pushed the door open; his son was lying on the bed reading a picture magazine; by his side, a phonograph played Latin-American melodies.

"Well well," Skeffington said. "Doing your homework?"

Francis Jr. looked up and said pleasantly, "Hello, Dad. What's new?"

"I'm thinking of running for mayor," said Skeffington.

An expression of mild bewilderment touched the smiling depthless face. "Sure," he said. "I know that. I've been talking you up all over the place. Like crazy."

"Like crazy," Skeffington said. "Fine. Splendid. You're home early, aren't you?"

"A funny thing happened. Well, not funny, exactly, but peculiar, you know? We were at the Club, and I was with this girl and we were doing the mambo and all of a sudden she turned her ankle for no reason at all. The thing is, she's a very good dancer, almost a professional. So I took her home, and then I came home myself."

"Lost the use of her ankle," Skeffington said. "I suppose it means more to a girl like that than to most people. Your ankles are perfectly sound, I trust?"

"Oh sure. In great shape. The best." He flexed them in demonstration.

"Fine. Well, good night."

"Good night, Dad. Sleep tight."

"Yes. By the way, you don't happen to be acquainted with Norman Cass Jr., do you?"

"No, I don't think so. Why?"

"No particular reason. Only it occurred to me that you and he have something in common. Just as his father and I have. As I say, the resemblance hadn't occurred to me until now."

He left the room and went to his own room where he undressed, washed, knelt by his bed for a moment, and then got in. It was not until he was stretched out in bed that he realized how tired he was. It was something to think about, but he was asleep before he had time to think.

Nine

IT was the next night that Adam, at last, told Maeve his news. They had spent the evening quietly at home, and now, in bed, as she lay close against him, relaxed and warm and fragrant in his arms, he decided reluctantly that it was the time for revelation. He said, "Maeve?"

"Mmmm?" she said drowsily.

"I just remembered: I didn't tell you what happened to me last night."

Half asleep, she murmured, "What did happen to you last night?"

"Well, nothing terribly exciting, but it was interesting, and pretty odd. I went to a wake. A huge wake on the other side of the city. It was completely unexpected: all of a sudden I found myself there."

"That was funny," she said, still sleepy. "Whose wake?"

"Nobody you'd know, actually: a man named Minihan. But the point wasn't that so much; it was how I happened to go, and who with."

He waited; she said dutifully, "Who?"

"None other than the great man himself. By name, Uncle Frank." It was an attempt to establish the proper tone of light mockery; once delivered, he was confident of its failure. He felt her body stir at the name, and he knew that instantly she had become wide awake; Skeffington, like Macbeth, he thought, both murder sleep. He began to talk with greater speed.

"He called me at the paper last night, saying that he was coming by, and that he'd stop to say hello. He added that he was on his way to a wake, and thought that I might like to come along. More than that, he thought I should: the grounds being, apparently, that the old-style wake was on its way out, and that

I owed it to myself as a citizen of the place to see one in operation while the seeing was still available. I wasn't quite so sure of that myself, but off we went, anyway, and it turned out that he was absolutely right. It was amazing, Maeve. It wasn't at all like any other wake I've ever been to; it was like going back to what it must have been like about fifty years ago. I wish you'd been there to see it!"

He went on to tell her about Knocko's wake in some detail. He took care to play down the name of Skeffington, and to emphasize the strange and comic aspects of the evening; here the memory of Charlie Hennessey was of great assistance. Adam was a good raconteur and a fair mimic, and as he talked the evening came back to him vividly, strengthening his performance. After a while he was rewarded with a small, subdued giggle. It was the first hint of encouragement; heartened, he continued. There were further and louder signs of enjoyment and when, a few minutes later, he finished his story, he knew that this part of his task, at least, had been completed successfully. Now then, for the graceful elision into Part Two of his peculiar apologia; about this he felt more apprehension. . . .

"All the same," Maeve said, suddenly remorseful, "it doesn't seem quite right to be laughing at it like this, does it? I mean, really? I know it all *sounds* funny about that Hennessey man and that awful Mrs. Boland, and it *is* funny, but then all of a sudden you start thinking about poor Mrs. Minihan. It can't have been so funny for her."

"Well, she certainly wasn't laughing out loud. But actually, I don't think that anything that happened made it any worse for her. No one was very boisterous when she was around, and as for the rest of the time, while she must have heard the noise all right, I don't think she was distressed by it. She must have expected it and no doubt she wanted it; I'd guess that she took all the fireworks pretty much as one last tribute to Knocko from his friends. Besides, all the people milling around were good for her in another way: they kept her busy, and kept her from thinking too much about what had happened. It really worked out very well, Maeve."

It was a fluent and persuasive statement; not until he had

finished it did he realize, with a start, its complete dependence on the dialectic supplied to him the night before by his uncle and old John Gorman.

"Maybe," she said doubtfully. "Anyway, I hope so, for her sake. It's just that it all sounds so . . . *circusy.*" Then, with no pause at all, she said, "How did it happen that your uncle was there? Is that part of the mayor's job, too?"

"A friend of the family," Adam said quickly. "He's known them for years. The visit wasn't an official one. Why?"

"Well, what I really wondered about," she said slowly, "was why he should have suddenly thought that you'd be so interested in the wake. *You* weren't an old friend of the family. I mean, it never would have occurred to me, for example, that you'd want to make a trip across the city to the wake of someone you didn't know."

They had left laughter and returned to Skeffington; it was time to get on with the case. Adam said, "The fact that it was a wake wasn't too important; it could have been any one of a number of things. You see, all this started a few weeks ago when Uncle Frank suggested one day that I might like to see some of the old customs and habits before they disappeared entirely."

He elaborated upon this theme, stressing the fascination and value of the ancient, evanescent rites. It was a method of exposition which did not, strictly speaking, accurately reproduce the spirit of the interview in Skeffington's office; nevertheless, it had the advantage of allowing Adam to present his uncle not as a campaigning politician, but as an avuncular and knowledgable cicerone, familially revealing to his nephew the mysterious folkways of his antecedents. He continued with this partial explanation rather skillfully. Maeve, still resting in his arms, listened quietly. He was alert for any betraying sound or movement which would signal the beginning of debate; none came. She lay motionless and silent; as he talked he could hear and feel only her light breathing. So far, he thought, so good; he began to drive for a forceful summation when, quite unexpectedly, he felt a sharp distaste for the whole evasive business. This voluble pouring of half-truths into his wife's ear suddenly seemed to him a fearful, ridiculous and shabby procedure; he felt both impatient and ashamed. He stopped talking abruptly; he freed one arm, brought his hand up under his wife's chin, and gently lifted, tilting her head backwards so that the large, clear eyes, open wide, looked directly into his own.

"Well, no," he said, with a wry smile, "it wasn't quite like that. Something like it, but not just like it." And then, omitting nothing, he told her in full and exact detail of his talk, three weeks before, with his uncle. He told her everything, from the story of Skeffington's mother in Amos Force's house, down to the final, actual proposal that, under Skeffington's guidance, he should periodically observe the progress of the campaign. Concluding, he said, "So that's about it, Maeve. The whole truth and nothing but, Scout's honor. Nothing up my sleeve. What it all amounts to is that I've been offered a free ride in the Campaign Special's observation car. If I take it, it's true that I won't be mixed up in the campaign in any active sense, but it's just as true that even sitting in on a few things occasionally will mean that I'll have to spend a fair amount of time with Uncle Frank during the next couple of months. I know that's not exactly your idea of how the growing young husband should pass his days. Or nights. But the thing is, Maeve, that I think I'd rather like to. For one thing, I am interested in what went on around here, and what's left of it today: the kind of thing, for example, that turned up at Knocko's wake. I'd like to know something about it, and it seems that during a big campaign is the best time to find out, and also that Uncle Frank's about the best one to find out with. But really and honestly, when you come right down to it, I guess the big reason is Uncle Frank himself. I keep on remembering — or at least, I have been lately — that he is my uncle, after all, that he's a strange and I suppose even a historical figure, and that I really don't know very much about him, or what he's done, or how he's done it. . . . Well," he said slowly, "this may be a chance to make up for a little lost time. It's probably his last big push — or so *he* says, at any rate — and I think I'd like to see him in action as he makes it. And for some strange reason, I think he'd like to have me. Exactly why I don't know. But I think maybe I should. So," he said, looking down at her, and moving his hand gently to the side of her face, lightly brushing against her cheek, and smoothing back her hair, "what do you say? What would you say to that, Maeve?"

"Well," she said, "why not?"

He was astonished; after a moment he said, "Do you mean that?"

She nodded resolutely. "If you really want to, I don't see why you shouldn't. Do you?"

Her voice was perhaps not quite certain; Adam did not notice this. He was startled and almost incredulous before the unexpected assent, the objections which had vanished before they had appeared. He held her close and said softly, "Ah, you're a good girl, Maeve. It's only for a few weeks, and you'll see: it'll all turn out fine."

She nodded, responding to his embrace; she did not respond so readily to his assurance. For she was not altogether convinced that this quick capitulation, this ready agreement was indeed the wisest course; nevertheless, upon advice, it was the course she was pursuing. It would have astonished Adam even further had he known that he owed this victory chiefly to the ready counsel of his old opponent, his father-in-law.

It had happened in this way.

Although Maeve was young, she was neither stupid nor unobservant, and during the recent weeks she had seen, almost from its beginning, her husband's rising — if surreptitious — interest in the Skeffington campaign. Words had not been necessary; the signs were many. There was the heightened preoccupation with the local news in the morning paper; there was the attention given certain television commentators, hitherto ignored; there was the skillful avoidance of even the usual teasing mention of his uncle in their table talk. These were minor but ominous deviations in behavior, and to Maeve they had represented steps along the road that led, finally, to Skeffington. She did not know quite what her husband planned. She was hurt a little by the sustained secrecy, but thought it probable that Adam did not himself yet know exactly what he wished to do; when he knew, she was trustingly sure that she would be told. But — and this was her problem — when told, what was she to do? When the situation arose — a situation which could only suggest some sort of affiliation between her husband and Skeffington — how was she to handle it?

She had thought this over solemnly, and decided that the difficulty was in part due to her own inexperience — not with husbands, but with men in general. She concluded that she really did not know much about them. It was only after her marriage that she had realized — with something of a shock, at first — that by the standards of some of her husband's more emancipated friends her upbringing had been an astonishingly sheltered one. In both academy and college there had been an almost conventual discipline, and while there had been dances and social functions and while she had never gone unescorted, the partners of these rigorously supervised evenings had been just that and no more. There had been no question of the "steady" beau, and indeed only two of this company of transients — friends of the family, brothers of girls at school, and so on — had impressed her more than casually. It had been only Adam whom she had met and loved; she had married him, and that had been that.

She did not regret her background for an instant, but she felt that in a sense it had left her unprepared for certain crises; now, uncertain of her exact course, she had consulted experience. She had gone first to Nancy Mangan, whom she liked, and behind whose vague and placid surface she sometimes found a helpful practicality.

"But sweetie, it's wonderful!" Nancy had breathed. She had been relaxing, her full body collapsed lazily along the length of a divan, her eyes half-closed against the afternoon sun. Her voice, however, had been rapturous as ever. "Adam in politics! Well, not exactly *in* politics, maybe, but *interested* in, which is just as good. You'll love it: he'll be *completely* changed!"

"But what if I don't want that? What if I happen to like him the way he is?"

"*I* like him the way he is too, sweetie. Adam is an old dear. When I say he'll change I don't mean he'll *really* change. Just in little ways. He'll be more preoccupied. You know, with big issues. I don't know anything that men like more than big issues. To play with, I mean. Look at Jack. He's just about the perfect husband, but before he got interested in politics he was always fussing about little things: the food, or why the laundry put starch in his shirts. *I* didn't know. About the shirts, I mean; I knew about the food, but I couldn't *do* anything about it. I just haven't got a green thumb, or whatever it is that cooks are supposed to have that's like a green thumb. Anyway, I haven't got it and I don't want it. It's all so *silly,* except that I couldn't get Jack to see that it was. Then all of a sudden along came politics, and the first thing I knew he was eating his dinner without making all those horrible faces. Or anyway, not nearly so many of them. And he began talking about the governor and the lieutenant-governor instead of his shirts: it was *much* better. Oh, sweetie, politics make all the difference. You ought to *push* Adam in!"

"I don't know," Maeve had said doubtfully. "Adam doesn't fuss much about food or anything like that. He just doesn't fuss much, so maybe he doesn't need to be preoccupied with big issues. Besides, in his case there wouldn't be any issues at all: it would just be his uncle. And that's what I don't like. At least with Jack you never had to worry about Frank Skeffington."

"That sweet old man with the beautiful voice," Maeve said dreamily. "Sweetie, he's a charmer, I don't care what they say about him. Even Jack likes him, really. I'd *much* rather settle for him than some of the people Jack brings home. They're *so* honest! I mean, they're so *serious* about being honest. And they're always so *right.* About everything, not just politics. There's this one little professor with a funny head: he's right *all* the time. About politics, and television comedians, and movies and the right way to feed babies. Jack says he's very bright. But he's just so serious and so right and so *angry* about being right. No, sweetie, I don't think Uncle Frank's so bad. And I don't think it would be so bad for Adam. I mean, there's nothing so tragic about it, after all, is there? Besides," she said, her speech suddenly less vague and drifting, "if he really wants to do it, he's going to do it. You could make a fuss about it, but that wouldn't be so good, would it? Even if you won. And if you lost it would be *much* worse. No, sweetie, it's just not worth it. You just go home and give Adam a great big kiss and tell him to go out and become President. That's the way to do things."

It had been practical advice, but it had not been the advice Maeve wanted, and so she had gone to her father. He had listened to her, nodding wisely from time to time, and when she had finished her story, he had immediately responded with somewhat surprising counsel.

"I thought something like this might happen," he had said. "I don't say much about these things, but I manage to keep my eyes open. Now, if Adam has the idea that he wants to get a little closer to his uncle, my advice is to let him. It would be a mistake to try to stop it. No, no, that wouldn't be at all the intelligent way to handle a situation like this, my dear. Don't put obstacles in his path. In fact, you might even encourage him if he suggests it."

Maeve had been thoroughly perplexed. "But I don't see . . . "

"Trust me," he had said, with a confident little smile. "Trust your old father, Maeve: he hasn't gotten where he is today without a pretty fair knowledge of human nature. I think I understand what's behind this very well; I'm not a bad psychologist. You see I know Skeffington. I know him from A to Z. And because I know him so well I can understand why it is that he sometimes appeals to people who don't know him so well, or who haven't had my experience in dealing with the type. Skeffington has a certain superficial attractiveness which can even sometimes fool intelligent young fellows like Adam. That's nothing against Adam, mind you. He's a fine young fellow and I like him. But he hasn't had enough experience with Skeffington to know him, and besides that, there's also the family relationship. That could blind him to certain defects until he had a chance to see for himself at first hand just what these defects were. No, the proper way to handle this is to let him get to know Skeffington better. That's really all that's needed. It's been my experience that as soon as all really intelligent people come to grips with Skeffington they realize exactly what he is, and soon refuse to have anything more to do with him. That was true in my own case, and it will be the same with Adam. It can't fail. I *know*. Oh, I may make a little mistake now and then, but not on a thing like this, especially when my little girl's happiness is at stake. No, Maeve," he had concluded, "trust your old dad: that's not a bad policy to stick to. I think you'll agree it's always worked out pretty well in the past."

He had patted her hand encouragingly; she had gone away somewhat comforted, vaguely dissatisfied, and yet feeling that on the whole it was as her father had said: his words were not to be taken lightly. In the end she had decided to follow his advice and the result had been tonight's bedroom scene of soft acceptance. Now, cradled in Adam's arms, she was happy but not entirely so: she looked to the future with love for her husband, faith in her father, and — faint but persistent — a few small whispering doubts of her own.

Ten

AND now the campaign moved from the shadows into full public view. Skeffington was busy, busier, indeed, than he had been at any time in the past four years, for the burden of electioneering was now added to the routine of each day. This burden included problems and difficulties of a kind unsuspected by Adam; it included, for example, the case of Johnnie Byrne, which Skeffington decided to settle abruptly one afternoon. He summoned Byrne to his office for a private talk.

"Good afternoon, Governor," Byrne said jauntily, so jauntily that Skeffington immediately said to himself: He's nervous. . . . Byrne was a City Councilman: a slight, pleasant-looking man in his forties with a small, pale-pink mouth and gentle eyes. "Tom said you wanted to see me?"

"I do," Skeffington said. "You've been out of the city for two weeks, Johnnie. I hear you went to Baltimore."

Byrne was nodding eagerly even before the sentence was completed. "Yes, that's right," he said quickly. "I spent a few days there. A fine city, very much like our own in most ways, Frank. That's really why I went."

"I see. Pleasure trip?"

"No no, business," Byrne said, answering as rapidly as before. "I'll tell you what I wanted to do, Frank: I wanted to take a look at their port facilities. You know the trouble we've been having around here on the waterfront. Well, I'd heard that they had their waterfront problems pretty well licked, and since they're so much like us, and have the same problems, I thought maybe I could pick up a few tips from the way they handled things. And I did, too. I came back encouraged, definitely encouraged." The small mouth formed a frank, open smile. "Too encouraged, I guess, Frank. I felt so good about it, you know what I forgot to do? I forgot to bill the city for the trip. I'll have to do that the first thing tomorrow morning."

Skeffington looked at him bleakly. "No soap," he said. "It won't wash, Johnnie."

This time the reply did not come quite so quickly. "Hah?" Byrne said. A new expression came into the gentle eyes for just an instant; it disappeared and the frank smile popped into place once more. "What's the matter, Frank?" he said. "What's the hitch? It was official business; I'm entitled to reimbursement."

"Stop it," Skeffington said wearily. "When did you ever hear me haggle about reimbursement? We're not talking about reimbursement and you know it. You're lying to me, Johnnie. You went to Baltimore all right, but not on any trip connected with port facilities. In the first place, it would have been pointless: Baltimore's port situation isn't remotely like our own. They have an entirely different set of problems. You know that. In the second place, you'd never have gone on any such trip without getting an O.K. from me before you started. You know that, too. And in the third place," he said, "your wife has been in to see me. I know all about it, Johnnie, and so does she. You went to Baltimore to chase a girl. I knew that even before your wife came in. I can tell you who the girl was, where you stayed, and what you did. So we're all in on the little secret, Johnnie, and you can stop all this nonsense about port facilities. I don't like being lied to."

Byrne's soft, pleasant face seemed to retreat before each blunt word; panic now started in the gentle eyes. "I swear to God," he began, and then stopped, as if realizing that the rushing words of denial would serve no purpose. He was a trapped man with no defense but a last desperate show of bluster and indignation. "A fine thing!" he burst out bitterly. "Oh, a fine thing, Frank! A nice reward for loyalty! A man breaks his neck working day in and day out for you and the first time he leaves the city on a private matter of his own, you put your watchdogs on him!"

Skeffington shook his head. "Don't credit me with any fine feelings. I didn't wait that long. I put them on you right here in the city as soon as the campaign began." He gestured impatiently. "Of course I had you watched. What the hell do you think I'm running here: a political campaign or a protective association for wayward husbands? I know all about these 'private matters' of yours, Johnnie; I've warned you about them before. I don't know what's wrong with you. You've got a good wife and a fine family, yet you go chasing around after every stray skirt that passes through town. What are you after, a title? The Tomcat of the Year?"

Bluster and indignation had disappeared; Byrne said despairingly, "Ah, lay off the lecture, will you, Frank? It's all I get day and night from her."

Skeffington nodded grimly. "This is a different kind of lecture," he said. "I'm afraid you'll have to listen; it won't take long. You see, I don't like what you've done to your wife, but that's none of my business. What is my business is what you've done to me."

"What I did to *you?*" Byrne cried. Panic was crossed with bewilderment; the pale pink mouth remained open, and he looked at his accuser with a stupid agony. "May God strike me dead if I did anything to you, Frank!" he cried. "All right, it was a dirty trick on Irene, I admit it. I don't know why I did it. I don't know what comes over me, Frank." He was becoming increasingly abject; it was a turn which Skeffington did not find attractive. Byrne said weakly, "It seemed like I couldn't help myself, somehow."

"Good," Skeffington said. "Then you'll have had some experience in not being able to help yourself. Because that's just what you can't do now."

"But I swear to God the whole thing has nothing to do with you, Frank!" he cried. "Nothing! It was a private matter, a family affair. . . . "

"Cut it out," Skeffington said curtly. "I don't enjoy having people play the boob with me. You know what I'm talking about. You put me in a bad spot because of your stupidity. Everybody in your ward knows you're one of my men. Thanks to you, I find myself right over a barrel in the middle of a close election. The man who's been running up and down the ward acting as my right hand suddenly winds up in the middle of a first-class scandal right before election day; how many votes do you think I'll lose just because people want to turn against you? How many people do you think will vote for McCluskey just because they know if he gets in it's curtains for you? All this, Johnnie, because of your little 'private matter.' "

"But my God, Frank, they won't turn! Why would they turn on me? I've got the ward in the palm of my hand, you know that! I— "

"They'll turn on you," Skeffington said inexorably, "because you've done the one thing you can't do with our people and get away with it. You're a married man who's been fooling around with another woman, Johnnie, and it's all going to come out. Your wife is going to divorce you. And don't deny it," he said sharply, as the pale pink lips started to move. "She's been in here twice to see me. I know she's moved out and is living with her mother. I know she's been to see Father Casey, and I know that no matter what he or anybody else says — least of all you, Johnnie — she's fed up and she's going to sue for a civil divorce. And you know what'll happen when the word gets out. They'll repudiate you so fast you won't be able to catch your breath. Which leaves only one course open to me, Johnnie. I'm going to repudiate you first. I'm cutting you off, Johnnie."

"For the love of God!" Byrne cried. "You wouldn't, Frank . . ."

"I would," Skeffington said simply. "I just did. Now. You're through, Johnnie. I mean it."

Byrne's little puffy white hands tugged pathetically at each other; he made a curious whimpering sound. "You *don't* mean it!" he cried. "Say you don't, Frank! You've got to give me another chance, for the love of God! Anyone can make a mistake, can't he? We're all human, aren't we? Aren't we, Frank? We all have our little faults. Listen," he said, desperately shifting his approach, "listen, Frank: you've got it all wrong about Irene and me. I mean, it's not as bad as you say. I'm going to fix it up with her. You'll see, Frank. Everything will be all right. I'm fixing it up with her right away, maybe tomorrow . . . "

"You're fixing it up with nobody," Skeffington said wearily. "Stop trying to kid me, Johnnie. And stop trying to kid yourself. You're not a man who's made a mistake; you're a man who's made the same mistake over and over again, and now at last it's caught up with you. This is a long story. I warned you half a dozen times, and each time I got your promise. Well, it's too late for the promise now; I'm not buying it any more. The simple truth is this: you've become a luxury I can't afford. You're not a mean man, you're not envious, and you're not a double-crosser, but in a tight political campaign you're something just as dangerous. You're a weak sister, Johnnie, and I can't trust you any more. I'm even tired of thinking about trusting you. And so you've got to go."

He stopped, for the soft face confronting him had gone into boneless collapse, and Byrne had begun to sob. Skeffington watched him, more in distaste than in pity. He had witnessed the performance before; tears, he thought, came as readily as promises from the cornered Byrne. He could not bring himself to feel any great sympathy for him; he did not feel kindly towards either offender or offense. Like the voters who would now turn sharply against the guilty Byrne, Skeffington took a poor view of marital infidelity. Like most of his people, he did not regard it as one of the genial sins. It was perhaps the single offense with which he had never been charged, not even by opponents who were surely aware that it was the one charge which, if substantiated, could ruin him with the local electorate. But the charge had been impossible to introduce; domestically, Skeffington was unassailable. It was, he thought, another of his sources of strength. This had not been true of poor Byrne. When, some years before, Skeffington had first discovered the weakness of his subordinate, he had taken him to task sharply for it; at the same time, however, because he was above all a practical politician, he did not dream of cutting him loose. Politically speaking, there was no cause; the dismissal could only damage, however slightly, the organization, and although he thoroughly disapproved of what Byrne had done, he considered it as something quite apart from the main issue. Now, however, it was no longer apart; now Byrne's "private matter" had become public enough to threaten not only his own home but the campaign, and Skeffington himself. And so Skeffington had acted, swiftly and necessarily. The man, he reflected, had been a boob, and a boob engaged in what was essentially dirty business. As he watched the tears fall, he found that he was not deeply moved.

"All right, Johnnie," he said finally. "Stop it now. The lecture's over. That's all I want to say to you. You can go now."

Byrne stood, automatically obedient even in his anguish. "Frank," he said, and sniffled. "Frank, for the love of God. I *promise* — "

"No," Skeffington said. "I told you I meant it, Johnnie. Run along, now."

Byrne went, shuffling slowly, without another word. Skeffington sat looking at the door which had closed noiselessly behind him. He did not look long; he had work to do. It was late in the afternoon when John Gorman entered and said, "Johnnie Byrne dropped in to see me."

Skeffington nodded. "I thought he might. That's where I'd go if I were in trouble, John. And Johnnie's in trouble."

"It's a damn shame this had to happen," Gorman said. "He's a popular lad in the ward."

"He *was* a popular lad in the ward," Skeffington corrected. "Three weeks from now a gypsy could beat him. He's done. You know that, surely?"

"I do," Gorman said. "I do indeed. You did what you had to do and nothing else. Still, I hate to see a thing like this happen so soon before election. It always means a bit of trouble, no matter how you grease the ways."

"It does," Skeffington agreed. "But not too much in this case. There may be a few who'll stick with him, but Johnnie's hardly the type to breed a schism. Besides, all the sympathy will be with the wife, once the news about the divorce gets out."

"Ah, it's hard on the woman," Gorman said reflectively. "She's a good sort who deserved better than Johnnie. Now she'll be alone, she'll have the kids, and she can't marry again. Will she squeeze enough out of Johnnie to get along on, d'ye think?"

"I sincerely hope the good judge'll see to that," Skeffington said. "Meanwhile, we'd better keep an eye on her. See that she doesn't want for anything. If she needs any money or clothing or anything like that, see that she gets it. As for Johnnie," he said, "I don't know what he'll do. He's able-bodied; I presume he can go to work. It'll be a change, but he can do it."

Gorman considered for a moment. "Johnnie's a bit of a little rat, right enough," he said. "A weakling, ye know, from the very first word. And yet, in a way, likable. He was very popular in the ward. By God, Frank, I don't know where a man like that belongs unless it's locked up tight in a monastery for the rest of his days."

"Or locked up tight with a good veterinary for a couple of hours," Skeffington said, remembering his remark about the Tomcat of the Year. "I have a feeling that might work wonders with Johnnie. But enough about our former playboy; let's get down to work. We have a lot to get done before tonight."

And so the case of Johnnie Byrne had been disposed of. It was perhaps the most serious of a group of problems that had arisen, and although Skeffington had expected the usual hazards of the campaign, he nevertheless had to confront them when they arose; this made his day a long one. He rose, as always, early, but now, more often than not, he retired late. Too late, he thought grimly, as he noted that on several nights his arrival home had coincided roughly with that of his son.

"I almost feel I should apologize," he said one night, when he came in to discover that his son, for the second time that week, had beaten him home. "I hope I'm not damaging you in the eyes of your friends?"

"Damaging, Dad?" his son said, with a puzzled smile. "I don't get it. What's the scoop?"

"Well, the word might get around that you were getting in before your father. I can't believe that a whispering campaign of that kind would do an ambitious young night owl any good. I presume your crowd must have a certain set of standards about such matters."

His son laughed pleasantly, "Oh, they wouldn't care, Dad," he said.

Skeffington nodded. "Fine. They must be a tolerant group. Still, I won't push my luck too far; I'll try to get in earlier from now on. It may be a bit difficult because I'm a little busy these nights. You see, there's talk that we're going to have an election in November. If we are, I want to be prepared. I wouldn't want it to sneak up on me. I know you can appreciate my position."

Faint lines of perplexity, the blemishes characteristic of these baffling interviews with his father, now touched the boyish face. "Sure we're having an election in November," the son said. "The first Tuesday. Teddy Thornton was talking about it only tonight."

"You can't keep a secret from Teddy," Skeffington said. "Well, if that's the case, I guess I might just as well get some sleep and try to rest up for it. Good night."

"Good night, Dad."

Skeffington went to bed; once there, lying motionless under the single blanket, his bones seemed to expand and contract within his aching flesh; he felt the spasms of fatigue. He was doing too much; he knew it, but he knew too that at this point any reduction in activity was impossible. The most prudent of men where his health was concerned, he had suspended this prudence for the final weeks of the campaign. And, he thought, necessarily so, for although he had no great opinion of McCluskey as an opponent, he respected the strength of those behind him, and he had seen overconfidence obliterate the dreams of far too many of his fellows to feel at all complacent. He campaigned hard, therefore, as he always had, and reflected ironically that, thanks to such modern technological advances as radio and television, the going was immeasurably tougher than it had been twenty-five years before, when he had been twenty-five years younger.

Skeffington used radio and television and used them exhaustively, yet he considered both to be essentially secondary approaches; he did not believe in shortcuts to the electorate. He thoroughly enjoyed, but was not converted by, the spectacular success of his own recent television appearances. The rich voice, the full photogenic face, the presence of the natural actor: all these had combined to evoke an extraordinary response, far beyond political circles. To his surprise and amusement, the television professionals had been alerted; he had received several suavely worded letters from advertising executives, delicately suggesting that, in the event of unexpected political reverses, a career in television awaited. One communication, more urgent and less tactful than the rest, had come from the president of a company engaged in the maufacture of nasal ointments; it had offered him immediate and unconditional employment as the firm's television spokesman. Skeffington had been grateful for this letter; it had furnished him with useful material for further speeches.

"You see the alternative I face if you fail to return me to office," he said, addressing the television audience, and waving the letter before him. "I'll become a television announcer, the oldest television announcer in the world. Very possibly I'll wind up between the waltzing cigar and the talking beer can. That's an unhappy fate for a man of my years. I beg your assistance in preserving me from it!"

But, satisfying as he found this experience on television, and valuable though he conceded it to be, he did not for an instant consider it a substitute for the technique of personal contact which had served him so well for decades. The indirect penetration of the home via the television screen was all very well; to his mind, it did not begin to compare in effectiveness with the direct and personal visit — with the sign of recognition, the extended hand, the solicitous inquiry into family affairs, the donation of favor or promise of favor. It was this procedure, painstakingly accomplished, that had always been the heart of Skeffington's campaign; he did not change now. Instead, he added to it the newer techniques and thus acquired a schedule heavier than any he had attempted before. He felt that he was weathering it well. While, day after day and night after night, he whirled his way through the swelling, unremitting series of speeches, visits, receptions and official appointments, he found it hard but nevertheless enjoyable, a tough routine in which he somehow discovered stimulation. It was only at night, when the halt came and there was, finally, pause instead of motion, that he became fully conscious of his own exhaustion. Here, in bed, he achieved the low point of his day, and in the interval — mercifully brief — of dull, bone-aching wakefulness which preceded the regular relief of sleep, he was apt to look forward with longing to that date in November, now just a few weeks away. It was the blessed terminus, the point of time at which all would be finished.

"Probably including myself," he said aloud. It was the last sardonic tribute to the day; he fell asleep immediately afterwards. The night could be counted upon for recuperation; he awoke refreshed and began the routine all over again, not aware of weariness until, once more, he reached the late, lonely, helpless hour. In the past few weeks he had become accustomed to this ebb and flow of fatigue; it was mildly bothersome, it did not concern him greatly, and it did not interfere in the least with the progress of his campaign.

As the days went by, Adam came to spend progressively more time in his uncle's company. These meetings were, for the most part, unscheduled, and often occurred at odd hours and at a moment's notice. Skeffington would telephone and suggest that Adam, if he were interested, might meet him in fifteen minutes: there was to be some piece of campaign activity which he might find rewarding. Sometimes more warning was given, and several hours would elapse between the call and the event; more rarely, there were meetings between the two which were arranged as much as a day or so in advance. Whatever the notice, Adam responded without fail; the flexibility of his own day eliminated conflicts at the paper, and when the invitations interfered with his evenings at home — as they came more and more to do, with the acceleration of the campaign — he was troubled in his conscience by the small woeful shadow that was briefly visible on his wife's face (for in spite of her brave resolution, Maeve was imperfect at dissimulation); but then, determinedly recalling her permission, and reminding himself that in any event it would all be over in a matter of a few weeks, he felt better, kissed her, and went off to join his uncle.

Behind the swift and apparently random crisscrossing of the old and sprawling city, there was in fact a carefully worked-out plan. Skeffington, in this as in all else, had left nothing to chance. These were routes he had traveled for half a century; like a veteran guide, he knew the opportune moment for retracing old trails. The districts and quarters which were as strange to Adam as the ruins of Angkor Wat were, to Skeffington, as familiar as his own living room. Physically the city had not changed greatly since his boyhood, and the changes that had been made were largely of his own inspiring. He knew it block by block, almost building by building, and while there had been population shifts, he had noted each one in detail. As the Yankees had moved in indignant retreat before the Irish, as the Irish had done likewise before the Italians, as the succeeding if much smaller invasions of Greek, Syrian and Chinese had worked their minor dislocations, Skeffington had marked them all with sustained care, losing interest only when the migrants passed beyond the city limits, and so beyond the local vote. Adam, fascinated, watched his uncle in his tireless, accomplished conduct of these bewildering expeditions; he followed him up narrow, crooked, ill-surfaced streets into musty lodge halls, into dark little basements where a solemn Chinese shook hands with Skeffington over a partially ironed shirt, into long, narrow stores with hanging rows of salamis and herbs and cheeses, into tall, dirty, dangerous tenement buildings, bursting with families. As they left one of these one night, Skeffington said to Adam, "A place of refreshment and light, you might say. Did you enjoy it?"

Adam shook his head emphatically. "It was right out of a sociologist's casebook. Hardly the ideal place for the casual visit."

"No. Even more than that, perhaps, hardly the sort of place in which you'd like to grow up. I speak," he said, "from some personal experience. There are a good many buildings like this still around, but I particularly wanted you to see this one. Have you any idea who owns it?"

"No, none."

"Your employer," Skeffington said. "Part of the family inheritance, passed on to him by his diminutive Dad. Naturally, as a man of strong family feeling, Amos wants to keep the old place exactly as it was when it was handed down to him. He does this by eschewing the use of paint or modern conveniences. I like to see sentiment combining so happily with thrift."

Adam looked around at the whole unlovely area. "But surely something could be done about it?" he said. "Hasn't the city the right of seizure if it wants to exercise it? As a matter of fact," he said, remembering something he had recently read, "you did that, didn't you, somewhere in the city? Started a slum clearance project, I mean?"

"I did," Skeffington said. "I did it in a couple of places, years ago. I suppose I should have had the bulldozers in and cleared up the whole mess while I was at it. There's the unhappy fact, however, that things aren't done quite that easily. Rest assured that such a move wouldn't have been unopposed. And while I don't mind opposition, you have to decide whether you're ready to declare all-out war on one front, with the knowledge that if you do, there's always the possibility that you'll be murdered on another. Reformers never have any trouble with decisions of that sort. They declare war right away; they even mow down half their own side in fighting it. And that, by the way, is why the mortality rate among reformers is so high. Still," he said, more slowly, as he turned to look up and down the filthy, littered street, "I've sometimes thought that they might have had something, at that. However," he added, more briskly, "thoughts of that kind don't exactly further the present campaign effort. Come along, I want to make another visit or two before we call it a day."

In these few short weeks, Adam's knowledge of the city grew rapidly. The trips with his uncle were not limited to slum visitations; in search for the vote Skeffington penetrated all levels, revisiting old strongholds, cultivating the friendly pockets in the land of the enemy. In this way virtually every sector of the city was covered, including parts that Adam knew fairly well; even these, however, he saw now under a different aspect, as his uncle's rich stream of anecdote and information poured over buildings, statuary, landmarks and memorials which Adam may have noticed casually in passing, but which hitherto had held no meaning for him.

"Everything has a history around here," Skeffington said one night, as they were riding back through a prosperous residential area. "For example, this street we're on was once part of a battleground in the Indian wars. And over there on that corner there's an interesting plaque set into that big oak. Did you ever take a look at it, by any chance?"

"Not too close a look, I'm afraid. It's in memory of some army officer, isn't it?"

Skeffington nodded. "A major. Major George Sumner Willoughby. The story has it that back in the early days he was the saviour of the city, personally leading his troops in courageous battle against marauding Indian bands. Then early one summer he got together with a few of the Indian chieftains who, according to the story, were so awed by his fearless behavior that they dubbed him 'Big Chief Bear-Who-Thunders.' At this meeting they concluded what came to be known as 'Willoughby's Peace,' and now every year, on the second Sunday in June, we have a little commemorative ceremony, sponsored by the Descendants of the Colonial Men. They meet right in front of that plaque. I usually attend, bringing the greetings of the mayor's office and an inexpensive wreath. A delegation from the Colonial Men shows up, wearing blue flannel coats and ice-cream pants, slightly yellow with age. The pants, that is; the Colonial Men are rather nicely preserved. To make it official, they even have a genuine Indian. He's a captive Navajo they keep locked up down in the southern part of the state. Strictly speaking, he's the wrong kind of Indian — there were never any Navajos around this part of the world — but he's the best they could find; they keep him locked up, eating frugal meals and playing solitaire. Once a year they spring him; he comes to town, they give him a new deck of cards, and then they all come over to the oak tree for the ceremony. I place the wreath below the plaque and say a few words, the Colonial Men doff their hats and give the Navajo a few symbolic kernels of corn, and we all sing, 'Oh, Beautiful for Spacious Skies'! All in memory of 'Willoughby's Peace.' You ought to drop around next June and see us in action."

"I will," Adam promised. "I wouldn't miss it for worlds. Is it true, by the way? About Willoughby, I mean?"

"Up to a point," Skeffington said "I have a few small doubts about the Major's reputed fearlessness. You see, I got interested enough to investigate the situation a few years back, and I found out that among his troops George Sumner Willoughby had been known as 'Arsey' Willoughby. It was an irreverent nickname, derived from the wounds he had received in combat. It seems that he had been wounded three times, each time in the behind. Apparently Big Chief Bear-Who-Thunders did most of his thundering in rapid retreat; I gained the impression that his orderly did very little else but pluck arrows from the Willoughby bottom. I imagine it's possible to believe that 'Willoughby's Peace' came about because the Indians simply got bored with shooting at the same old target. It's only fair to say, however, that the Descendants of the Colonial Men adopt no such cynical point of view. And I'm sure they're right; it doesn't do to go poking too deeply into our most valuable traditions."

Right or wrong, the story, like so many others of Skeffington's, fixed a point of local history firm in Adam's memory; never again would he pass by the familiar corner without glancing at the plaque and thinking of the long-dead Big Chief Bear-Who-Thunders, scrambling back towards his own lines in the heat of battle, his rear bristling with the feathered mementoes of the enemy.

As Adam's knowledge of the city increased, so too did his appreciation of his uncle's task. Accompanying Skeffington on these varied expeditions across the city, he soon saw that campaigning, even for one of his uncle's great experience, was far from being an automatic or an easy matter. From each separate trip Adam gained some small idea of the labor involved, but it was not until he accepted Skeffington's sudden invitation to spend an entire day with him on the campaign trail that he began to realize its extent.

On this day, he went to Skeffington's house shortly after an early breakfast; he arrived in time to see the front door opening to admit the line of supplicants. From a chair in a corner of the library, Adam watched with wonder as his uncle, seated at the long table with two secretaries, handled the petitioners as they filed up to him, one by one; he seemed to listen to them with patience, attention and courtesy; more remarkable still, he seemed to satisfy their wants. Adam carefully observed this queer parade of the aged and the middle-aged — there were, he noticed, few young people among them — as they approached his uncle and as they left; without exception, they left with lighter step. The placation and encouragement of so many people could not have been a simple job, Adam thought; his uncle had accomplished it without apparently turning a hair.

These interviews over, the two secretaries went directly to City Hall. Skeffington did not; in these final weeks he had interrupted his habit of swooping down on the city each morning; he went, instead, to a radio station. Here, every day, he delivered a midmorning broadcast to the housewives; it had been a valued tactic for years. Entering the studio from which the broadcast was to originate, Adam saw that his uncle's chief secretary had arrived before them; he was arranging a series of papers across the table on which the microphone rested.

"The script?" Adam asked his uncle.

"No, no," Skeffington said. He pulled from his pocket a couple of newspaper clippings, torn from the morning's papers. "These'll do for a script. We don't want to get too formal. Those are just official papers I have to sign; it seems that the city has to conduct its business even during a campaign."

The radio studio, then, had become a temporary adjunct to the mayor's office; Adam watched while his uncle seated himself and began to read and sign the papers rapidly. One he lifted and gave back to the secretary, saying cryptically, "Not a chance." He then resumed his work. Adam looked at the clock. The broadcast was to begin at 11:00; it was now 10:58, and there were no signs of preparation. He heard a tapping sound on a large studio window which faced into an anteroom for spectators; looking around, he saw Ditto Boland waving anxiously. Ditto, at least, was ready. With him had come three more members of Skeffington's unofficial entourage; somehow, framed by the studio window, their devoted and slightly grotesque duplication of their idol seemed slightly more emphatic. Skeffington nodded briefly at them and continued to work; promptly at one minute before broadcast time, he passed the last paper over.

"All right," he said. "Now: we go to the docks after this?"

"That's right, Governor. Then lunch at 12:30 at the Abington Park with the Audubon Society."

"It's a shame that robins haven't got the vote," Skeffington said. "I'd be in in a walk. Did Sam get back from Washington?"

"Just about an hour ago, Governor."

"Did he see McArdle?"

"Yes, apparently everything went very well. I've tentatively arranged for both Sam and John Gorman to come in at 2:30 this afternoon. Will that be all right?"

"Yes, fine." He glanced at the clock for the first time. "Well," he said, standing, "we'll let everything else go until after lunch.

I guess we're just about set to say a few words to the good ladies." He walked over to a microphone in the center of the studio, and placed the two ragged newspaper clippings on the reading stand which was next to it. Pointing to them, he said to Adam, "You see there a mark of distinction: I'm the only politician in the country whose broadcast addresses have weather reports and necktie advertisements printed on the reverse side."

An announcer hurried in and greeted Skeffington; Adam slipped out of the studio and into the anteroom, so that he might better hear his uncle. Ditto and the others welcomed him hastily and then fell into silence; clearly, they did not want to run the risk of missing a word. The announcer made his brief introduction; Skeffington was on. He stood easily at the microphone, his hands in his pockets. He spoke without written assistance of any kind; for the moment, even the newspaper clippings were ignored.

"Good morning, ladies," he said. "I almost hesitate to interrupt you; I know how busy you are with your household chores. But I thought that perhaps you might welcome a few moments rest from your labors before the children come in from school, and your good husbands come home for lunch. I thought you might like to hear just a few words on the progress of the current political campaign. I like to talk to you on this matter because I know you're deeply interested. Some people seem surprised that the womenfolk have such concern over political affairs; I notice that a young opponent of mine only the other evening expressed his astonishment over the large number of women at the last meeting of the Women's Democratic League. I must say that I myself wasn't a bit astonished. I might even go so far as to say that I was a little shocked that any man — especially a young man — *would* be astonished by the fact that a great many of our wives and mothers cared enough about the civic problems that affect them and their families to go to a meeting and discuss those problems. A man who's astonished at that, in this day and age — particularly if he's a young man — is something of an anachronism: he has a nineteenth-century mind in a twentieth-century body. He probably thinks that a woman's place is standing barefooted and subservient in a basement, breaking her back over a washtub. He probably thinks, to use that terrible phrase of Kipling's, that a woman is no more than 'a rag, a bone, and a hank of hair.' Now, I don't say that my young opponent, if he believes this, is at all malicious about it. I'm sure he's a fine young man who doesn't mean any harm. I think it's rather that, being so young, he hasn't had a great deal of opportunity to see for himself the magnificent things that women have been doing in the world of public affairs. Matter of fact, I think he probably relies a good bit on what his older advisers tell him. I'd like to remind you in this connection of something I mentioned the other morning: that two of his most prominent advisers were years ago the leading opponents of woman suffrage. I suppose it's a bad thing for an impressionable young man to fall into hands like that; I suppose he can hardly avoid picking up some of that evil philosophy." He paused to pick up one of the newspaper clippings. "And speaking of my young opponent," he said, "I saw on the front page of a newspaper of small circulation this morning that he had addressed an 'overflow gathering' last night in the Jewel Room of the Kilgore Hotel. Well now, that sounds impressive. Everybody in public life enjoys speaking to overflow gatherings. However, in this particular case, what the newspaper neglected to mention — and I'm sure it was an oversight: I can't believe that it intended to deliberately delude the public — was that an overflow gathering in the Jewel Room of the Kilgore doesn't necessarily mean very much. I know the Jewel Room well. It's the smallest hotel assembly room, not only in the city, but also in the state. Legend has it that it's the only hotel assembly room in the world that was once a closet. I would guess that the total capacity of this mighty chamber is three adult males and a puppy dog. And it's not at all difficult for me to believe that my young opponent addressed an overflow gathering there last night, for the reason that if he took the simple precaution of bringing only the members of his own immediate family, he was assured of one."

In the anteroom there was delayed laughter: a giggle exploded from the small head of Ditto Boland. "Oh by God!" he said admiringly. "That was a good one, one of the Governor's very best. Three adult grownups and a puppy dog!"

There was hasty assent to this from the others; they then sank back into their attitude of undeviating audition. Yet despite the apparently rapt attention, Adam had a curious feeling that he had experienced more than once in the company of these followers of his uncle: he felt that he was being watched. He looked around quickly; four pairs of eyes seemed to shift slightly. Once again he realized that as his uncle's emissary, his reaction was being observed. His reaction, that is, to *their* reaction: he knew that it was hoped that he might carry back the report of dutiful behavior. Once again he was baffled and slightly awed by this relentless compulsion to demonstrate fidelity.

Skeffington continued to talk. He read the other newspaper clipping; he recited from Wordsworth:

> A perfect woman, nobly planned,
> To warn, to comfort, and command!

As the fifteen-minute period was nearing its close, he cast one eye at the clock, and finished precisely on time. The broadcast over, the retainers flooded from the anteroom to congratulate him. Skeffington welcomed them briefly, nodded to Adam, and uncle and nephew walked out of the studio together, down the corridor which led to the street door. Skeffington's secretary was already waiting in the car; Ditto and the others crowded close behind.

"We're off to the waterfront," Skeffington said to Adam. "Here you'll notice that I have to use a slightly different approach. The fishermen and stevedores prefer a somewhat more robust delivery than do the ladies of the radio audience."

"I think the ladies must have enjoyed especially your reference to the 'perfect woman, nobly planned,'" Adam said.

"Yes, it gave them the feeling I was talking about them as well as to them, you see. I always like to use a little poetry in talking to the ladies, although sometimes there's the temptation to use the wrong kind. The thought crossed my mind as I was talking to them just a moment ago that there's a charming verse by Tom Moore about women:

Ask a woman's advice, and whate'er she advise,
Do the very reverse and you're sure to be wise.

"Now that more or less sums up my own sentiments rather neatly," he said, getting into the car, "but I'm a little doubtful about its value as a vote-getter. Just suppose some of the good ladies took it the right way?"

The car started off; the addition of Ditto and friends made for cramped space, but Skeffington did not appear to mind. He talked briefly to his secretary; the car stopped at City Hall and the secretary got out. Then they were on the way to the waterfront. Ditto said, "The boys and I were wondering, Governor: when we get down to the docks will you be giving a speech to Camaratta's longshoremen?"

"Among others," Skeffington said. "We'll do that later. First I want to stop at Fleet Pier and say a few words to the fishermen."

"A very loyal group, the fishermen," Ditto said approvingly. "Right behind you every solid inch of the way, Governor. I always said there was nobody like the fishermen," he said, turning to the others, "for sticking to the Governor through thick or thin, as the case may be. Many's the night I stopped by Fleet Pier on the way home of an evening and got myself a nice piece of swordfish or a little bit of haddock. And all of it free for nothing, as we say. Absolutely positively on the house. Jumbo Jim Kilcullen would see me coming and he'd hand me the fish right off the boat. 'Here Ditto,' he'd say, 'take this home to the missus with my compliments.' Oh it was very tasty fish. A grand man, Jumbo Jim. A heart as big as the State House. You remember Jumbo Jim, Governor? The big man with the one lung and the cock eye?"

"I remember him well," Skeffington said. "I have every reason to: he double-crossed me three times in a single year. However, I admit that I look at him in a rather peculiar way: I keep on forgetting to measure his loyalty by the number of free flounders he passed out."

"Oh, you're right there, Governor!" Ditto said quickly. "One hundred and ten per cent on the bull's-eye target, as we say.

You couldn't *trust* Jumbo Jim. What I meant was, he was a great hand with the free-for-nothing fish, but you wouldn't trust him with a ten-cent dime! Oh, you're right enough there, Governor! Yes, yes, yes!"

They had reached Fleet Pier; the car turned in through the gates and they rode to the very end of the pier. All along both sides were strung the vessels of the fishing fleet. Adam had seen this fleet only once before. It had been on a holiday: a Sunday in summer by tradition reserved for the official Blessing of the Fleet by a prelate. Then the vessels, newly painted and gay with flags, had presented a colorful sight as they sailed around the harbor in long parade; now, on a rather forbidding day in late October, stripped of their gaiety and in their workaday surroundings, the aspect was decidedly different. The ships seemed small, soiled and dingy; the men who came from them, one or two at a time, seemed suspicious and resentful. The outlook, thought Adam, was surely not promising, but Skeffington reassured him.

"Believe it or not," he said in a low voice, getting out of the car, "we're among friends. Just sit tight and see what happens."

Adam sat tight, as did Ditto and his friends. Skeffington walked alone out onto the pier, making towards a squat, dark man who sat on a piling near one of the boats. The two men shook hands; fishermen from the other boats began to gather around slowly. Skeffington moved among them, shaking hands, exchanging greetings. The atmosphere seemed cordial enough, yet there was a curious reserve; there was, certainly, none of the rapid dissolve into high spirits, into the boisterous good fellowship which Adam had seen on display at meetings where Skeffington was greeted by his own. Adam knew nothing of the fishermen; clearly they constituted a group of substantially lower volatility. Skeffington continued to talk to the men one by one; finally some one placed a small box next to him, and he stood on it and began to talk more generally. The men converged upon him in a grave, attentive circle; Skeffington spoke with increasing emphasis, repeatedly pounding a fist into an open palm. Adam heard very little of what was being said, for although his uncle spoke loudly, the damp wind which now came in steadily off the harbor carried most of his words away. It was, apparently, a serious talk; no one at any time laughed; there seemed to be no jokes. Occasionally the wind slackened and Adam caught an isolated phrase: " . . . meet the rising menace of cutthroat Canadian competition . . . ," " . . . experienced man to protect your interests, one who can go to Washington in your behalf . . . " ; twice, unless he were mistaken, he heard mysterious and laudatory references to Portugal. Skeffington talked for perhaps ten minutes; it was a most unusual talk for him in that at no time had he been interrupted by cheers, applause, or laughter. He finished abruptly; rather to Adam's surprise, the silent men now burst into applause; they clambered about Skeffington, shaking his hand. Obviously, thought Adam, the talk had been a hit after all.

Skeffington came back to the car. "Take her around to the Morgan docks," he said to the chauffeur. To Adam he said, "A good few minutes' work. Could you hear anything at all?"

"Very little," Adam said. "The wind took most of it away. But did I hear you mention Portugal a couple of times?"

Skeffington nodded. "Foreign policy," he said gravely.

"Foreign policy?"

"Very important. A man can't run for mayor on the domestic issues alone. Not in this day and age. We all have to cultivate the wider vision."

"You mean that in a local election you have to talk about, say, Russia?"

"No. That's one of the great handicaps for the local politician: he can't call his opponent a Communist. It's a shame, but there you are. Of course you can *call* your opponent a Communist if you really want to, but it won't do you any good; nobody'll believe you. They all know he goes to Mass on Sunday, so he can't be a Communist; you might just as well say that the Cardinal and the Kremlin exchange pen-pal letters. No, Russia and Communism never have been much of an issue around here. We're under the disadvantage of having to evolve a foreign policy that meets local requirements."

"Which includes what?" Adam asked. "Portugal?"

"You'd be surprised how important Portugal becomes," Skeffington said, "when you're speaking to the Portuguese. These fishermen, almost all, came originally from the Portuguese mainland or the Azores. I find they appreciate an occasional reference to the glorious country of Henry the Navigator. I've been trying to find a more contemporary figure than Henry, but with Portugal that's not so easy. However, it isn't a major point. There aren't enough Portuguese. When you come right down to it, there are only two points that really count."

"Such as . . . ?"

Skeffington held up two fingers. "One," he said, ticking the first, *"All Ireland must be free.* Two," he said, ticking the second, *"Trieste belongs to Italy.* They count. At the moment the first counts more than the second, but that's only because the Italians were a little slow in getting to the boats. They're coming along fast now, though; in twenty years the Irish issue will be about as burning as that of Unhappy Ethiopia. Fortunately, I don't expect to be among those present at the time."

The car drove back through the gates and turned right; after a moment Adam said, "But is that sort of thing really so important today? I had an idea that the old emotional appeal to the homeland was dying out. You know, as the younger generation came along."

"That's what the books say," Skeffington said. "I must say, however, that I haven't noticed it myself. Maybe the books are all written by the younger generation. All I know is that just before midnight in Hibernian Hall, when the tenor starts to sing, 'I'll Take You Home Again, Kathleen,' young tears fall as freely as old. So if it's dying out, at least it's dying out moistly. Meanwhile, no matter what its state of health, I intend to see that it's not neglected."

They had reached their destination: a long pier, larger than the first. Here there were no fishing boats; a large ocean liner was berthed alongside. There were no signs of activity, either on the ship or the pier, and as the men got out of the car, Adam saw that this was not, apparently, to be another open-air address; they were going inside to talk to the dockers. Led by Skeffington, they marched into a large and barren hall. Here, burly men stood around in groups of three and four; *in toto,* thought Adam, they looked like some extravagant sub-species, an unacknowledged breed of giants. While Adam, Ditto, and the others remained in the back of the hall, Skeffington went directly through the suddenly silent groups of men, nodding to left and right, and stopped before a large, swarthy, smiling man.

"Hello, Camaratta," he said. "Good to see you again."

"Sure," Camaratta said. He winked one eye and laughed loudly. "Camaratta's a real nice fella. Everybody likes Camaratta around election time, huh?" He laughed again and said, nudging Skeffington, "Only a joke, boss. Camaratta likes his little joke. It's good to see you, too. Real good." He laughed again.

The poor fool, thought Skeffington without compassion; *he'd better laugh before the bomb goes off.* For the method of disposing of Camaratta had now been worked out; all that remained was its proper execution. It was towards the furtherance of this end, rather than that of securing the longshoremen's vote, that he had really come to the pier today. He said aloud, "I'm glad you're fond of jokes, Camaratta. A sense of humor's a blessing from above. 'Given to jest, yet ever in earnest': that's what they used to say of Lincoln. I'm happy to be able to point out the parallel between yourself and the Great Emancipator. By the way, speaking of jokes and laughter, how is Johnny Nucatolla these days? Is he laughing much?"

"Poor Johnny," Camaratta said regretfully. "A sweetheart of a kid. A real nice fella. He wanted to be mayor real bad. But I guess he just couldn't get the dough up. I hear some guys he figured he had in his pocket backed out on him. Too bad. I hear it broke the kid's heart."

"I see. Then I don't imagine he's laughing too much, after all."

"Nah. It's a shame," Camaratta said. "A real shame. A nice kid like that. Well," he said, looking around the room, "you wanta chew the fat with the boys, huh? Okay, come on over here. I'll interduce you myself, real pretty." Again he laughed.

They walked over to the small platform at the far end of the hall; jumping up on it, Camaratta yelled for attention, and then embarked upon a long, illiterate and — to Skeffington — decidedly unpleasant introduction. He heard the note of insolence in it; there was at least the firm yoking of his name with that of Camaratta, somewhat to the latter's advantage. During this introduction, Skeffington derived considerable comfort from the thought that, all unsuspected, this was one of the orator's final public performances.

At last Skeffington began to talk; he did so vigorously but simply, confining himself to the usual remarks about backbreaking toil being unaccompanied either by sufficient safeguards or appropriate reward. It was a speech he had given many times before on the waterfront, and he did not change it now, for he felt that even the slightest alteration in the anticipated pattern would arouse only suspicion in the slow bosoms of these hulking men. (As a group, he did not hold the stevedores in high regard; once, in a moment of irritation, he had expressed himself on the subject to John Gorman. "Pinheads and troublemakers," he had growled. "The only difference between them and a bunch of orangutans is that orangutans don't spend all of their time out on strike!")

As he talked, he did not give his entire attention to his words; his eye scanned the audience, from his nephew and Ditto in the rear of the hall down to those longshoremen who were stolidly bunched a few feet from him. He was looking for someone; at last he found him. He was standing by himself in front of the large bulletin-board, his huge hands folded across his belt buckle. He was a tall, big-boned, angular Scot with a harsh, watchful face; his name was Macpherson. Skeffington knew him slightly: he was a person of consequence among the stevedores, and after some weeks of careful preliminary investigation, Weinberg had reported that here was the instrument for the destruction of Camaratta. Weinberg had talked to him, at first circumspectly, then more boldly; he had discovered that here, indeed, was a spirit ripe for revolt. And so Skeffington had come down to the pier to see for himself, to carry proceedings one step further. He watched Macpherson while he talked; he would have to speak to him alone for just a moment before he left the pier. The problem was to do this without awakening the suspicions of Camaratta. It was only during the last few seconds of his talk that Skeffington discovered the perfect way out. It was so perfect, indeed, that he almost smiled at the very moment he was reciting, in tones of some passion, the melancholy catalogue of miseries that were the unfair lot of men who worked the waterfront.

Finishing his speech, he was applauded. He left the platform, Camaratta glued to his side; he did not stop to talk to the longshoremen, but walked quickly to the back of the hall. It was one of those extraordinary moments when he was grateful for the presence of Ditto Boland. He introduced Camaratta to Adam, then said easily, "Everybody else you know. As a matter of fact, Camaratta, it's a happy coincidence that we're all here together today. I want to discuss something with you, and Ditto can be of some help. I've been thinking lately that perhaps the city should pay some sort of municipal tribute to these longshoremen of yours. Possibly an annual ceremony, honoring those hardy men who have died in the performance of their arduous duties. How does that strike you?"

Camaratta nodded languidly. "Great," he said. "Real great. And about time. There's men died like rats down in them holds. Loadin' patriotic stuff for their country, like dynamite and bombs, and — *whoom!* Like rats."

"Exactly. It's high time the city recognized these dedicated men officially. I suppose we might annually honor an anonymous longshoreman, as the nation does its soldiers each year at Arlington Cemetery. We could pay our respects to the Unknown Stevedore. Or," he said, "we could honor a different one each year. I suppose he might be subject to your designation."

"Yeh," Camaratta said instantly. "I like that. I'll designate."

"Splendid. Now we have a little ceremony we perform each year in memory of the heroic Pilsudski. A wreath is cast upon the waters, and so forth. I thought something similar might be done for the longshoremen. And as Ditto, who's our authority on the Pilsudski ceremony, is right here, I think I'll have him fill you in on the details and see what you think about it. Maybe you'll have some suggestions for improvement. Meanwhile," he said, backing away slightly, "I can make my farewells to your men."

Camaratta's eyes narrowed. "Hey," he said, moving forward a step. Then he hesitated, momentarily irresolute, halted both by the eager, confronting mass of Ditto Boland and by his own cupidity. From the words of this fat man could come profit; he shrugged and said, "O.K. . . . What's the pitch?"

"What the Governor and I do every spring for the memory of that grand Polish hero Pilsudski is a lovely thing. It warms the cockles of the soul, as we say," Ditto began enthusiastically. Skeffington moved off, pleasantly aware that the swarthy deceiver, caught in the web of Ditto's intricate narrative style, would be held fast for some time to come.

He greeted the stevedores singly and in small groups, pausing to say a few words to each. As he had expected, Macpherson had arranged it so that he would be standing alone. Skeffington spoke to him no longer than he had spoken to the others; only the content of his message was slightly different.

"Glad to see you again, Mr. Macpherson," he said. "Sorry it has to be so briefly. I understand you have some interesting ideas about the waterfront. I wonder if you'd care to discuss them at some future date?"

Macpherson looked at him with light, almost colorless, gray eyes which blinked slowly in the harsh face. "Aye," he said.

"Good," Skeffington said crisply. "Tomorrow night at ten, at my home. You know where I live."

Macpherson smiled tightly. "I'll find ye," he promised.

"Splendid. Until then, Mr. Macpherson."

And he continued on his rounds, satisfied. Weinberg had been right; Macpherson was his man. Tomorrow night would mark officially the beginning of the end of Camaratta's unsavory parochial regime; the thought heartened him immeasurably.

Adam had made very little out of all this. He had disliked Camaratta on sight; he had disliked him more as the moments progressed. In the car, leaving the pier, he said to his uncle, "Who is he, anyway? Does he really control things so absolutely down here on the pier?"

"Camaratta? One of Nature's noblemen," Skeffington said. "I believe his friends like to think of him as a diamond in the rough." The rest of his nephew's question he answered as truthfully as caution would allow; he said, "He's controlled things down here for many years. Did you find him at all engaging?"

"Not very, no. Is he generally regarded as such?"

"He's irresistible," Skeffington said dryly. "Obviously. Ask Ditto." Turning in his seat he said, "Was he an attentive audience, Ditto? Did he listen with interest to the tale of Pilsudski?"

"He was all ears and eyes, as we say, Governor," Ditto said promptly. "You never saw a man more interested in the facts and the figures and the et ceteras and so forths. I informed him to the fullest on all the details. He even wanted to know what happened to the beautiful wreath after we threw it out on the river. I told him it got all bashed up by the stones down by the dam, or maybe it got water-logged and sunk to the bottom of the river like a heavy stone, as we say. And he had a great idea as per this respect, Governor. He said why didn't we use a rubber wreath or a plastic one? He said that's what he'd use: a nice big wreath with maybe nice rubber roses and ferns. That way it wouldn't sink to the bottom and you could fish it out and use it over again."

"The ideal memorial to the Unknown Longshoreman," Skeffington said. "The floating, waterproof, retrievable wreath. Camaratta must be among the most sentimental of living men."

"A very nice man," Ditto said. "Oh, you're right there, Governor. I remember the time I didn't used to think so, but that was before he got smartened up, and learned that you had to take the bittersweet, as we say, and made up his mind to join up on the right side of the fence. You wouldn't find a nicer man today. And he's happy as a singing bird about the nice ceremony you're arranging for the longshoremen, Governor. He can hardly hold his horses till we throw the wreath out. Oh, that'll be the day for him!"

Skeffington agreed. "Yes," he said, "that'll be the day."

They returned to City Hall. Adam went with Skeffington up to his office; somewhere in the tangle of corridors they disengaged themselves from Ditto and his friends.

"We'll only be up here a minute," Skeffington said. "We have to hurry along to this luncheon with the Audubon Society."

Adam demurred. "Do you think I should go? I thought that was more or less a private affair. I mean, I didn't think it was political, as the other things I've been to were."

His uncle corrected him. "Everything's political," he said. "At this time of year, when I blow my nose it's political. I'm very probably appealing to the victims of hay fever. Come along, you'll enjoy yourself. You can chat about the speckled grackle to your nearest neighbor."

They entered his office, not through the private door, but through the more public access of the reception room. It was, as always, crowded; Skeffington moved slowly through it, nodding, bowing, responding by name, but never quite pausing. It was a remarkable technique, Adam thought, as he trailed his uncle; apparently the problem was to be seen by all yet stopped by none. Skeffington seemed to have solved it admirably.

His uncle disappeared; Adam sat down to wait for him. He did not wait long; in a remarkably short time he was summoned into the private office; Skeffington was ready for departure. "Come along," he said, smiling, "I think we're about a half-hour late as it is. I never like to keep a bird fancier waiting too long for his fruit cup; it's apt to make him snappish."

They went to the luncheon. It was a small gathering; protocol demanded that uncle and nephew be separated. Skeffington was given a central spot at the head table; Adam sat at a small table in the center of the room, feeling some doubt of his ability to maintain suitable conversation: he had no bird-talk. As things turned out, he need not have worried. The seat to his left was empty and remained so throughout the meal; that to his right was occupied by a frail old man with a very large hearing aid. Adam spoke pleasantly to him; as there was no sign that he had been heard, he concluded that the enormous instrument was nonfunctional. All during the meal the old man ate voraciously, keeping his eyes fixed on the head table and, in particular, on Skeffington. Three times he spoke aloud.

First he said, "That man is a disgrace!"

Later he said, "He has *two million dollars* secreted in vaults in Mexico City! It is a matter of public knowledge!"

Still later he said, "A man like that does *not* like birds!"

Each statement was firmly delivered in clear, cavernous tones. It was evident that no response was required, none was desired, and—more to the point, thought Adam—none was possible. His companion enjoyed the immunity of the totally deaf.

When the luncheon was over, Skeffington spoke briefly. He gave what seemed to Adam an extremely curious talk, establishing a parallel between the commuting businessman and the migratory fowl. It was the ornithomorphic view of man; although Adam had never before heard it expressed, there was no doubting that to Skeffington's present audience it was a most welcome one. Only the old man with the hearing aid remained unmoved; sitting in motionless, mute inaudition, he said suddenly and loudly, *"Mexico City!"*

Adam went to join his uncle at the door; he heard him saying to an elderly lady, "Madam, I agree with you wholeheartedly. And not alone to the birds: sometimes I even think that *Felis domestica* is an enemy to us all."

In the car, Adam told Skeffington of the table talk of his companion. Skeffington listened with amusement and said, "Your friend took the southern route that leads to Mexico City. There's an alternative, you know; it's permissible to hold that the money's in Montreal. For some reason, however, the sum seems to be fixed; it's usually two million dollars. Exactly why that should be, I haven't the slightest idea. By the way," he said, "I was thinking that this has been a pretty heavy schedule for you; you deserve a bit of a respite. As a matter of fact, now might be as good a time as any. I have to go back to the Hall to straighten out a few details. It's nothing that would interest you at all, but it'll probably take me an hour and a half or two. Do you suppose you could occupy yourself for that length of time without inconvenience?"

"Yes, easily." The return to City Hall, he knew, was for the meeting, earlier mentioned, between his uncle and Gorman and Weinberg. Adam was by no means sure that this would be of no interest to him; he was altogether sure, however, that it would be considered none of his business. And so he said, "Actually, it fits in very well. I have a few things to do at the paper."

"Fine. I'll drop you there." He consulted his watch. "It's a quarter of three now; supposing you come by the Hall at about 4:30 or quarter of five? By then I'll have all the underbrush cleared away, and we can get moving again."

Adam agreed. In a few moments, the car pulled up in front of the newspaper building; Skeffington said, "My compliments to the management. Tell them I think they're doing a grand job. You can also tell them I just noticed that their side door opens contrary to the fire laws. In other words, it's not an accredited egress. I wouldn't be surprised if they had a little trouble with the building inspectors shortly." And, with a cheery wave of the hand, he was gone, the long car speeding towards City Hall and the rendezvous with his two chief lieutenants. Adam watched the departure with regret. He knew that the role of the observer was a limited one; he reminded himself that he had been eager for his uncle's promise that he should in no way be implicated in the campaign. All the same, he found himself wishing that his uncle's attention to this promise might be somewhat less scrupulous; he would have given much, for example, to be allowed within earshot of this particular council of war this afternoon. And then, even as he thought this, there came the more sensible reflection that it was not a matter of the promise at all. For, promise or no promise, he believed it extremely unlikely that Skeffington would have admitted any outsider — even though that outsider might be a favored nephew — into such an important and secret deliberation.

In this belief, Adam could not have been more right.

He went to his office and began to work on his comic strip. Little Simp had been neglected of late. While Burbank no longer shared the office to serve as a distraction, there had been the disruptive force of the campaign. For the past two weeks Adam had done his work, but he had done it at odd hours and in fits and starts. He had managed to extricate the little boy and his companions from the Argentine predicament, but now a new adventure was begun; so far, it was not going well. Now, taking advantage of the unexpected hour of grace, Adam resumed where he had left off the day before. He had been working only a few minutes when the door opened and the managing editor came in. He was, these days, a man of altered appearance: he was thinner, appreciably so; his eyes had acquired the habit of blinking with great rapidity. As he entered the office now, he turned to glance nervously over his shoulder; it was as though the old, irascible, merciless voice which trailed him so constantly down the corridors had suddenly become a visible thing. He had expected to live a life of terror in these weeks of pre-election; his expectation had been more than realized. Adam pitied him; he knew that he came into this office, not to see its occupant, but merely because it was a place where Amos Force was not.

Adam went on working. The managing editor stood silently behind him, looking over his shoulder; after a moment he said dully, "Where's the chipmunk?"

He was observant in his misery; the companionable rodent was no longer perched on Little Simp's shoulder. "He's in the hospital," Adam said. "I've put him there until his fur grows back."

"Is that what eating the cornflakes did to him?"

Adam nodded. Recently, Daddy the Chipmunk had performed with heroism. An agent of Big Boris, aware of the dietary habits of Little Simp, had cunningly secured employment in a neighborhood supermarket; there, one afternoon, he had sold the little boy a carton of poisoned breakfast food. The next morning, at the breakfast table, wise Daddy, scenting danger, had sprung from his little master's shoulder and had devoured several of the lethal flakes, subsequently collapsing in agony. Fortunately the poison, while fatal to humans, was less effective against the rodent; it acted merely as a particularly painful depilatory. And so Daddy, alive but hairless, had been necessarily confined.

The managing editor made conversation. "I should think you'd draw him in anyway. Even without the fur."

Adam objected. "It wouldn't be especially appealing, would it? He'd look rather thin and shiny, like a young rat. I couldn't have anything like that on Simp's shoulder. The readers would object."

"I suppose so," the managing editor said gloomily. After a while, he said, "Where are you sending the kid this time? Abroad somewhere?"

"Yes. Rotterdam, I think."

"Rotterdam, hey?"

"Yes, Ralph, Rotterdam."

"Well well," he said hollowly. Then, suddenly, the name of this faraway city recalled a vivid memory, and for a moment he spoke with some animation. "We sent a reporter to Rotterdam once. Seven years ago. The whole thing was a hell of a mistake. The paper got an awful sticking on the deal. It was a two-week junket, run by an air line; our understanding was that they would take care of all expenses. Well, they didn't. They weaseled out of it. They claimed they promised to take care of only the *basic* expenses. So the paper was stuck with the rest. It cost us roughly $7.25 a day. Multiply that by two weeks and you get some idea of the total cost to the paper. We laid out a cool $101.50 just to let this fellow have a close-up view of a couple of dikes. Never again!"

"Once bitten, twice shy," Adam said. He went on working.

"You said it," the managing editor said feelingly. Then, as suddenly as it had come, emotion waned. His shoulders slumped, he gazed about him dejectedly, he looked with glum, unseeing eyes at the comic strip in progress. In a slow, grudging voice, he asked, "How's your uncle?"

Adam recognized it as a question torn from him by the demands of duty. Reluctant to introduce a subject which caused him daily pain, he was compelled to do so by loyalty.

"He's very well, thanks, Ralph."

The managing editor went on gamely. "That's good. Because he'll need his health. It's all he'll have left after the election. You can tell him that for me."

"Which reminds me," Adam said, "I have a message from him to you." He told what Skeffington had said about the side door of the building in relation to the fire laws. "He mentioned some potential trouble with the building inspectors," he concluded. "Is that a possibility, would you say?"

"Oh my God," said the managing editor, sagging further. "How the hell do I know? Don't I have troubles enough as it is?" He thought of the defective side door; he thought of Skeffington; he thought of expense; he thought, finally and inevitably, of Amos Force, even now waiting for him in his office. With a little moan he disappeared through the doorway.

Adam worked for another hour, then left the building for City Hall. The conference was over; Weinberg and John Gorman had gone. Skeffington joined him without delay, and together uncle and nephew once more took to the campaign trail. Here, in these hours of late afternoon and evening, Adam saw his uncle shift gears: perceptibly, the pace quickened, the routine became more complex, the burden heavier. In between the hours of five and midnight, when Skeffington decided to call it a day, they passed, almost without pause, through a swift, bewildering succession of widely scattered appearances, speeches, and presentations. And when, the night over, the two men at last were on their way home, Adam dazedly looked back over the day, and found that he was hopelessly confused. There had been too much of everything; it was only with difficulty that he could separate one event from the other; succeeding in the separation, he could not be at all sure of the sequence, especially during the later hours. There had been an open-air meeting in the West End; Skeffington had talked of a reduced tax rate, cheaper public transportation, and a proposed statue to honor the memory of Christopher Columbus. Across the city, they had gone indoors; there had been a tea party; over the teacups, and to the exclusively feminine audience, Skeffington had talked quietly of home, poetry, and the necessity of the experienced hand in guiding the body politic. They had visited a hospital; Skeffington had toured the wards, stopping by the bedsides of patients to tell a joke, to murmur encouragement; here he did not ostensibly electioneer. They had gone to not one dinner, but two. Both had been huge affairs at which Skeffington had been the principal speaker; Adam could not remember what he had said. He could remember vividly, however, that at these banquets he himself had eaten little, upon Skeffington's recommendation.

"The best advice I ever received as a young politician came from old Martin Sullivan," his uncle had said. "He said, 'Go to all the dinners, but eat none of the food. That's the stuff that kills a man!' He was right, too. Occasionally I've forgotten myself long enough to experiment with the food; always regretted it. I'm not sure where they get the meat for these ceremonial dinners, but I've suspected it comes from a kind of inedible beast especially bred for the occasion. Probably a banquet variety of yak. Anyway," he had concluded, "a word to the wise: *Don't go near it.*"

Adam had not. Hungry, after the banquets — or had it been *between* banquets? — they had gone to a television studio. Here Skeffington had talked for a quarter-hour; as Adam remembered it, it had been the grave and kindly talk of an elder statesman who, rather against his will, has been compelled to dwell at some length upon the appalling deficiencies of his opponent. Then there had been the house parties. There had been two of these: the houses of old friends had been thrown open for Skeffington's purposes; here, in the living room and library, over opulent buffet spreads, Skeffington had welcomed those of the neighborhood who had come trooping in. Here he had been among his own people, and Adam had again noticed the change of approach, the hearty camaraderie with which he greeted those who, regarding him as in some manner uniquely theirs, proudly employed his Christian name as a badge of confraternity.

Of these parties Adam remembered chiefly hilarity: his uncle standing there, telling anecdote after anecdote, mostly about politics and politicians who seemed to be familiar to them all. He recalled few details; now, weary, he did recall that he had enjoyed himself completely.

Throughout these later hours, Ditto and the rest of the entourage had made their mysterious entrances and exits; once or twice they traveled from place to place with Skeffington and Adam. Then, suddenly, they would fade away, to reappear in half an hour in quite another locale: Adam, in the course of the evening, had seen Ditto on at least six different occasions. It was apparent that although this ridiculous cordon sometimes slipped from visibility, they were never far from their protector.

In the car now, riding home, he said to Skeffington, "I don't see how you stand it. Is it like this every day?"

"Pretty much. Sometimes more, sometimes less. You have to remember that we're coming to the end of the trail now; things naturally bunch up at a time like this. As a consequence, I manage to keep busy."

"Conceded," said Adam. He glanced wonderingly at this septuagenarian, relaxed so casually on the seat beside him; he looked considerably fresher than Adam felt. Curiously he said, "What about the effect of all this on you, Uncle Frank? Doesn't it tire you, really? I'm exhausted, but you look as though you were good for a few hours more of the same thing."

Skeffington regarded him with amusement. "I have to," he said simply. "In politics, only a young man can afford to look tired. He doesn't have to prove he's young enough for the job, you see. On the other hand, if a man well along in years still wants to be elected to office, he has to demonstrate that despite the actuarial tables, he's in the prime of life. It's very important; some men go to rather extreme lengths in their demonstrations. I remember that when Arthur Grigsby Powell first ran for the United States Senate, he had his picture taken chopping wood. He won, and that became his trademark; every election thereafter he had to swing the axe. The last time he ran he was close to eighty, and he hadn't lifted anything heavier than a soup spoon for five years, but he didn't dare give up the demonstration. They taped the axe in his hands, and they held up his arms with guy-wires while a friendly photographer snapped the picture. He won, too. And to give you a more recent example, just a couple of years ago, one of our respected elders who wanted to be President went out to the Convention in Chicago, jumped off the train at the station, and raced the reporters on foot to his hotel. The hotel was two miles away, but he was out to prove something, you see. He had to. And," he said, "so do I. Except that I don't chop wood, or wear a wig, or trot along the streets at Scout's pace. I merely concentrate on not looking tired."

All of which, thought Adam, did not really answer the question of whether or not he was tired. He looked at his uncle again and concluded that, incredibly enough, it was quite probable that he was not, that somehow the long years of campaigning had left him conditioned for the effort, that the habit had in fact provided a sheath against fatigue. It was a conclusion which, though quite inaccurate, paid tribute to Skeffington's powers of concentration.

The car drove on, and Adam was silent as he reflected upon still another aspect of the day. He had realized, for the first time, something of the tactical skill of his uncle at handling the voting public. In traveling back and forth across the city, he had observed that no two of Skeffington's expeditions corresponded exactly; each had its distinct object, each was aimed at a special group of the electorate. What had astonished Adam was not that such special groups existed, but that they existed in such numbers. They were divided not only along the broad lines one might have anticipated: race, religion, national background, sex, capital and labor; inside whichever category one chose, it seemed that there were limitless special cells, each of whose concerns appeared to be in direct opposition to those of every other cell. Adam was staggered by this multiplicity of minority interests. For the first time he was witnessing directly the chaotic diversity of the democratic process in action, and he was amazed that his uncle could move so confidently and unwaveringly among the warring elements. He mentioned this to Skeffington now, and added, "It's all too complex for me. As near as I can figure it, what you really have to do is be all things to all people."

"Not a bit of it," Skeffington said imperturbably. "I only want to be one thing to them. I want to be their mayor. This involves a little juggling here and there, of course, and sometimes you have to keep half a dozen balls in the air at the same time, but it's no great trick once you're used to it. It's mostly a matter of practice. That, and of knowing what each group really wants. There's a considerable difference between what they *say* they want, and what they'll really settle for. You can promise them the first, but you only have to deliver the second."

"Yes, but they all seem to want so many things! And sometimes one group wants exactly the opposite of what the other group wants. How do you keep everybody happy in *that* situation?"

"Why, that brings us to man's best friend," Skeffington said. "The compromise. I'll give you a small illustration based on something you saw only this afternoon. You remember we were in Ward 5: it's an Italian district all the way through. You may remember that I spoke to a crowd of people in that little plaza opposite the Vocational High School. I spoke about a statue soon to be erected on the plaza."

"Yes. A statue of Columbus."

"His name was mentioned," Skeffington said dryly. "I think I should explain to you, however, that this afternoon's audience consisted exclusively of members of the local council of the

Knights of Columbus. But there are certain practical objections to putting up a statue of Columbus. In the first place, the city is already loaded with statues of Columbus; he's vulgarly known as the Pigeons' Friend. Secondly, there's a good deal of opposition to it within the ward; other groups want other statues in the plaza. The Sons of Italy have been shouting for a statue to Charlie di Mascolo, who was their head man around here for years. They'd really like it chiseled out of the side of Mount Rushmore, but failing that, they'll take the plaza. A small band of lunatics wants a statue to Roosevelt. A substantial group, headed by the venerable Monsignor Tancredi, is rather partial to a statue of Monsignor Tancredi. Feelings on the matter run high, and the erection of the statue can't be postponed much longer. As the plaza's city property, it's pretty much up to me to decide. And to decide without making enemies forever. That's where the compromise comes in: I'll announce it right after the election."

"And what is the compromise?" Adam asked, curious. "Who is it to be?"

Skeffington chuckled. "Mother Cabrini," he said.

"Mother Cabrini?"

Skeffington nodded. "Italian born, and the first American saint. Let's see them get out of that. The first man, woman, child or monsignor who objects will be stoned out of town. That's what I mean by compromise. Well," he said, as the car slowed, then stopped, "here we are, safe and sound. It's been a long day; did you enjoy it at all?"

"Very much," Adam said truthfully. "Many thanks, Uncle Frank."

"I hoped you might; I'm glad. I'll give you a ring as soon as something else breaks. Good night, my boy."

"Good night, Uncle Frank."

The car pulled off again for the last time that day. Adam went slowly up the front walk, thinking of his uncle. Mother Cabrini! The compromise was cynical, outrageous, reprehensible; nevertheless, as Adam let himself into the house, he found himself laughing. He thought again that his uncle was a most extraordinary man.

PART III

Eleven

IT was the final week of the campaign. It was the time for the big push. . . .

Skeffington now pulled out all the stops. Now he was exclusively the campaigner; even the token attention he had paid the routine duties of the mayor's office of late ceased entirely as every waking hour was given to the far more urgent business of returning himself to that office. He had every expectation of doing just that. In this next-to-final hour, such old and careful hands as Weinberg and Gorman had expressed themselves as satisfied; more important, so had Skeffington himself. With a cold, experienced eye, he had assessed his position and found it good. As he had predicted, the campaign had been expensive, even for one who had never hesitated to spend freely. It had been made the more so because of the formidable pooled resources of the opposition: in the past fortnight the big money had begun to pour into the McCluskey campaign. Skeffington had expected this; it did not worry him. He thought it probable that, dollar for dollar, he could not match the strength of his opponents; he thought it somewhat more than probable that he would not have to. For his own purse was not slim; it was entirely adequate to his needs, and moreover he knew — quite objectively and without any vanity — that he had one great advantage that the other side had not. He had himself; the others had McCluskey. There was, he thought dryly, a difference.

Upon this difference, of course, ultimately rested everything. Whether or not it would carry the day was the question; of the answer, Skeffington had little doubt. Looking back over the weeks of the campaign, he was content with what he saw. All anticipated support had come through, his organization had worked smoothly and without hitch, the opposition had been able to spring no disquieting surprises, and he himself had been at the top of his form. In short, there had been no setbacks of any consequence. Defections had occurred, it was true, but they were inevitable in any campaign, and they had been few in number and negligible in effect. Only the case of Johnnie Byrne had even threatened to be the exception, but this too had been resolved without damage for, as Skeffington had foreseen, the news of the divorce action had left Byrne a sadly discredited figure, suddenly without influence in his own domain.

And so, in this final week of the campaign, satisfied and confident, Skeffington acted characteristically. He began to work harder than ever. He knew that this was the fatal period, the crucial hour in which only the unwary would relax. He proceeded to step up the schedule of his personal appearances; his newspaper ads became larger, more frequent, more prominently positioned; his name, face, and the words AN EXPERIENCED LEADER blossomed on huge new billboards; he doubled the city-wide distribution of posters, leaflets, and handbills; he purchased more radio and television time. He was on television every night now, delivering a series of direct and stinging attacks against McCluskey. Following the custom of his political lifetime, he did not once mention his opponent's name, the principle being that in the demolishing of one's victim, it was hardly necessary to advertise him. From every front, then, he attacked and attacked hard; it was his customary home-stretch drive for victory.

In this week, McCluskey too picked up the pace, chiefly by increasing the number of his television appearances. Indeed, from the beginning of the campaign, this had been his chosen route to the public. Skeffington, before all else, favored the direct and personal contact with the voter; this approach had left McCluskey cold. He wanted television, and — more significant — so did his principal supporters. These improbable allies, who had met in mutual detestation to down the common foe, were political veterans who had been to the wars before; as such, they had few illusions about their candidate. For all their backing of him, their private opinion of him was similar to that held by Skeffington. They saw him as a young man of, at most, moderate ability, and this did not displease them. They had not chosen him because of his gifts; they had chosen him because, conceivably, he might win. He had been selected, quite simply, because he was the best available combination of the necessary if negative virtues. He was their joint offering for public leadership, and as they came to know him better they came more and more to feel that their hope of success lay in preserving a decent distance between him and the public. A certain amount of direct contact was, of course, unavoidable; any more than that would be, they felt, suicidal. They had not the slightest desire to see this pleasant, inexperienced man, of somewhat suspect capacities, compete with Skeffington in that dangerous arena where the latter was so thoroughly at home: the place where there were hands to be shaken, heads to be patted, solicitous familial inquiries to be advanced, and sudden, embarrassing questions to be answered on the spur of the moment. It was far better, they felt, to preserve their candidate from such strain; they saw no point in multiplying the possible occasions of awkward comparison. The solution, then, was television. Here the candidate could address the electorate effectively, but at a safe remove; it was a costly procedure, but a prudent one. And so McCluskey had gone on television, often; now, in this last week, he was on more than ever before.

For this television campaign, experts had been consulted; the results were programs which were staged and handled with imagination and skill. Most of them originated, not in a television studio, but in the living room of McCluskey's home. Here, night after night and day after day, with camera and microphone tastefully concealed, the candidate was revealed to the voters: a tall, plumply handsome, well-turned-out young man, with neat sandy hair, large earnest eyes, and a boyish smile. The series of programs was called "At Home with Kevin McCluskey." Usually the candidate sat on a long divan, facing the camera, smiling slightly; at his side sat an associate who was to interview him; before the divan stood a coffee table; behind the divan were the appurtenances of Home: the bookcases, the comfortable easy chair, the large Irish setter stretched out sleepily in front of the fireplace (this docile beast of aristocratic appearance had, in fact, been rented for the duration of the campaign: the authentic McCluskey dog had proved to be a snappish, untelegenic cur), the spinet piano in the corner. On the rear wall, prominently visible, hung a single large painting. It was a portrait of Pope Pius XII.

This, too, was a recent acquisition. It had been the gift of Norman Cass Senior, as the campaign had begun. He had presented it to McCluskey with the quiet suggestion that perhaps it might be hung immediately. The candidate had not been entirely certain of the propriety of this.

"It's a lovely painting, Mr. Cass, and Margaret and I both thank you for it. There's just the question of when to hang it, and I feel that it might not be quite appropriate to hang it just as the campaign is beginning. It might look to some people as if we were doing it merely for campaign purposes. You understand what I mean: they might feel that we were trying to capitalize on something that . . . well, that shouldn't be capitalized upon."

"I see what you mean, of course," Cass had said politely. "Still, I'm sure that you're being overly scrupulous. Surely you're not capitalizing on anything. I agree with you that the portrait is a good one. I hoped that you might be proud enough of it to make it a permanent feature of your home."

"Yes, we will indeed. We have every intention of doing so, Mr. Cass. And once again, I want you to know how much Margaret and I appreciate it. But about hanging it just at this time: I feel instinctively that it might be a mistake, that it might be misinterpreted. . . . "

"You may be right," Cass had said judiciously. "Yet it would seem to me that it might be a mistake *not* to hang it at this time simply because you fear that a few people might misinterpret your motives. In fact, if you did fail to hang it now, don't you think that, in a sense, your motives might be misinterpreted even more seriously?"

"That hadn't occurred to me. I don't see how . . . "

"I seldom discuss religion," Cass had said thoughtfully. "I imagine that most people would say that I am not a religious man. They may be right. Be that as it may, I don't mind admitting to you that in a way I envy you your splendid faith. And I think what impresses me most is the evident pride with which you and your co-religionists bear witness to that faith."

McCluskey had been moved by this unexpected tribute. "I'm delighted to hear you feel that way, Mr. Cass. Naturally, I am proud of my religion, although at the same time I believe that other men may be honestly convinced of — "

"Yes," Cass had said. "Now I hope you won't misunderstand what I'm about to say — I hope I can speak to you as a friend rather than as a purely political associate — but I would think that at a time when you are presenting yourself and what you stand for to the public, you would wish to have continually by your side some symbol, some evidence, if you like, of that in which you believe most deeply. It would seem to me that this might legitimately be expected of you. In fact, if such a symbol were not present, the misinterpretation of which I spoke might easily arise. Undoubtedly there would be some who would say that although you were ready enough to proclaim your belief in ordinary times, you appeared rather reluctant to do so in the heat of a political campaign."

And so the portrait had been hung, immediately. It now dominated the room as, night and day, McCluskey and the associate by his side played the television game of question-and-answer.

ASSOCIATE: Well, Mr. McCluskey, how do you feel now that you're nearing the end of the campaign?

MCCLUSKEY (resonantly): I feel fine, Dick. And I feel especially fine because I honestly believe it's been a great campaign for us — for myself, that is, and for the hundreds of good, unselfish people who've worked with me — and I think we've managed to get through a few home truths that badly needed telling to the people of the city.

ASSOCIATE: Is it too early to ask for a prediction on the outcome? Or would you rather hold off on that for a while?

MCCLUSKEY: No, Dick, it's not too early. I'll be perfectly honest with you, as I've tried to be with everybody throughout this campaign. I honestly believe that we're going to win, and win by a substantial majority. You see, Dick, I think that for the first time in many years the people have been awakened to what's really been going on around them, to the deplorable situation that exists here in our city. I think that if we've done nothing else in this campaign we've at least revealed to everybody for the first time the terrible extent to which this fine city has been riddled by graft and corruption and mismanagement by a cynical administration. And we haven't done this by any guesswork. We've had the facts and figures and we've laid them right out here in the open for everyone to see. I think they constitute an appalling indictment of my opponent and his administration, and I honestly believe, Dick, that now that the people have seen for themselves the frightening record in black and white, there'll be a public revolt against the man who is chiefly responsible for it. I think that the people now, as never before, are ripe for a change to good, efficient, responsible, moral government, and moreover I think they know — at least I hope they do — that we can give it to them.

ASSOCIATE: There's some talk, Mr. McCluskey, to the effect that if you do win next Tuesday, it will be largely as a result of the "protest" vote. I was wondering if you'd care to comment on that?

McCLUSKEY: Yes, Dick, indeed I would. We anticipate a large protest vote. As a matter of fact, when it comes to protest, I suppose no one has protested more vigorously against my opponent's wasteful and scandalous administration than I have myself. But I'd like to add in this connection that I don't think the people of this city will vote merely *against* something. I think they'll also vote *for* something. I honestly believe they'll turn out to vote for an administration that will *get things done*. In other words, Dick, an administration that will operate at all times for the best interests of the people. I'm not interested in protecting special, privileged groups. I'm not at all interested in the welfare of that small number of City Hall hangers-on who have been enriching themselves year after year at the expense of the city. I'm only interested in the ordinary, honest, tax-paying, God-fearing citizen, who works hard day in and day out to support himself and his family, and to try to give them a little better life. Those are the people I'm interested in, Dick. They're the very same people that the great Al Smith was interested in, that Franklin Delano Roosevelt was interested in, that Harry Truman was interested in. In other words, I'm interested in seeing that those people get exactly what my opponent never even bothers to mention in his speeches. He seems to be interested chiefly in jokes and sarcasm. Well, I happen to be interested in something else. I happen to be interested in such things as better low-cost housing, a decent minimum wage, a reasonable tax rate, better pay for our splendid schoolteachers, better pay for our policemen and firemen who risk their lives daily for us. Those are a few of the things I'm interested in, and I honestly believe that they're the very same things that the vast majority of our people are interested in. That's why I'm sure, Dick, that on next Tuesday the voters will speak up, and act in the interests of themselves and their families by turning against this old and decadent regime, and sending a young, fresh, honest administration into City Hall!

ASSOCIATE: Well, if one can judge by talking to the different reporters and political analysts around the city, men whose job it is to evaluate the trends, that's the way things undoubtedly seem to be pointing. (*A change of pace*) By the way, Mr. McCluskey, I suppose this hasn't actually anything to do with the election itself, but I suspect that a good many of the women watching us tonight would like to know how Mrs. McCluskey is bearing up under the strain. Would you say that the life of a candidate's wife is a happy one?

MCCLUSKEY: Ha ha ha. Well, Dick, it's certainly a busy one. As to how happy it is, perhaps you'd better ask her about that. I think I heard her coming downstairs just a moment ago. (*He turns on the divan and calls out in a mellow voice*) Dear! (*Mrs. McCluskey appears before the camera, entering from the right: blond, slightly buxom, maternal, bearing a tray on which are a glass of milk and some cookies*) Ah, here you are! Dear, you know Dick Bulger, of course. He has a question to ask you.

MRS. MCCL. (*Acknowledging Bulger by smiling, not at him, but at the camera*): Yes, of course. Mr. Bulger and I are old friends by now. But I'm afraid before I answer any questions, Mr. Bulger, I have to remind my husband that a candidate is supposed to eat as well as work! (*She places the milk and cookies on the coffee table before McCluskey, smiling at him in gentle reproof*) He hasn't eaten a thing since breakfast, he's been so busy!

ASSOCIATE (*laughing*): I can appreciate that, Mrs. McCluskey. And I can also appreciate how you must feel about that. All of which ties in with the question I wanted to ask you: How does it feel to be the wife of a candidate for mayor?

MRS. McCL. (*glowingly*): It feels absolutely wonderful, Mr. Bulger! It really does. Of course I've never been so busy in my life, with the children to take care of, and the phone ringing day and night, and Kevin working so hard and at all hours, but it's all been terribly exciting, every moment of it. And it's been so *rewarding:* both Kevin and myself have met so many wonderfully generous people who wanted to help out that we're just a little bit overwhelmed by it all. And then of course I have to admit that I've been very proud of my husband and of what he's trying to accomplish, and of the wonderful way the people have been responding to him. It's been a perfectly thrilling experience for me, Mr. Bulger!

ASSOCIATE: I'm sure all the women watching us tonight can understand that, Mrs. McCluskey. By the way, speaking of your children, I imagine they're getting quite a kick out of all the excitement?

McCLUSKEY (*whose milk and cookies are as yet untasted*): Of course the children present a bit of a problem at a time like this, Dick. Both Margaret and myself have quite a job making sure that they don't get too much excitement. Of course, Kevin Jr. is away at school — he's at Saint Ignatius's, a fine school run by the Jesuit Fathers — but the others — Tom, the twins, and little Valerie — are here with us, and we try to see to it that the campaign doesn't interfere with their schedules. But it's pretty hard at times, Dick. You know, they see all this excitement around, and they want to be part of it.

MRS. McCL.: As a matter of fact, dear, they came downstairs with me just now. They said they wanted to see you go on television. I was just putting Valerie to bed, but nothing would do but that she come too!

McCluskey (*shrugging in mock helplessness*): You see how it is, Dick. They know something's going on; just try to keep them away from it!

Associate (*eagerly*): As long as they're down here, do you suppose we could get them to come over before the camera? Just for a moment? I know the television audience would love to see them.

McCluskey (*exchanging humorous glances with his wife*): Well, dear, it seems as if we'll have to produce the stars of the family. (*Turns and calls*) Come over here, children, and say hello to Mr. Bulger. (*Four children — Tom, age ten; the twins, age six; little Valerie, age two — come trooping into camera range, approaching the divan dutifully and arranging themselves promptly about their parents. Only little Valerie is without self-consciousness. She toddles over to her father and, in the process of hauling herself up onto her father's knee, seems to get stuck midway. She struggles to pull herself up, her little dress shoots up in back, and the camera is focused for a long, dominant moment on the cunning sight of the little backside, encased in little rubber pants. It is a touching and comic sight; parents, the older children, and Mr. Bulger break into laughter. . . .*)

"Oh by God that's good!" Festus Garvey cried in admiration. Seated in front of a television set in a vacant store which served as a temporary political headquarters, he had been watching with interest this latest performance of his candidate. He snickered now in delighted appreciation. "The cute little baby bottom shootin' right up into the camera so's every woman in the audience feels she can reach right out and give it a lovin' pat! Ah, that's grand stuff! By God, the little behind is worth a thousand votes in the pocket. What decent mother could vote against the lovin' father of that little behind? He's a good lad, that McCluskey! A grand family man from the word Go!"

"Don't kid me," said Camaratta. He had come in, unbidden, shortly after the beginning of the program; he had watched it with dull, disinterested eyes. He had a mission of his own; he was, in fact, now fighting for his political life. He wanted to see Mother Garvey and he did not want to see Kevin McCluskey, even indirectly. Yet even though he was absorbed in his own desperate concerns, the favorable mention of another stirred him now, as always, to smoldering disgust. He removed the sodden cigar butt from his thick lips, and spat largely into a cuspidor. "Don't kid me," he said. "This is Camaratta, pal. I know this McCluskey kid. He couldn't figure out no sharp gimmick like that."

"Who the hell cares who figured it out?" Garvey cried. "It might of been him or it might of been the smart Jewboy we got from New York City to handle all the television stuff. Or it might of been the Man in the Moon, for all I give a sweet damn. The point is, 'twas done, slick as a whistle and neat as you please, by nobody else but the lad himself. And no ifs, buts, or what-the-hells about it. He held her right up there, right in the spot, so's the little behind was pokin' into the bull's-eye. Oh, I tell you he's a grand lad! A pleasure to work with, and a credit to us all!"

The program had had a remarkably tonic effect on him; he was in that state of phenomenal good humor into which he could be lifted only by the ingeniously reprehensible behavior of an ally. His quarrelsome little features had softened, and were now set in a grotesque pattern of intended benignity; his normal truculence, while not entirely shed, had been made less manifest. It was a time of satisfaction for Festus Garvey; he felt that now, for the first time in years, there was truly a chance of defeating Skeffington. He was satisfied by the progress of the campaign. He was satisfied by the coalition of which he was a part, satisfied by the funds it had collected, satisfied by the fact that none of its members, with whom he worked day after day, appeared to suspect his duplicitous intentions towards them all, the minute the election was over. But most of all, he was satisfied by his candidate. Not by his ability, but by his remarkable, unlooked-for plasticity. In the beginning, Garvey had had some fears that McCluskey might prove intractable. As an old politician he had more than once observed, in otherwise promising young politicians, a fatal obstinacy: a reluctance to jettison promises and ideals, a refusal to respond to the little suggestions of older, wiser, and more flexible men, men who understood the ways of indirection. (He himself, for example, over the span of many years, had had a little trick he liked to use on his political broadcasts, when he was all alone in the radio studio, and nobody could see what he was doing. He would stop, all of a sudden, in the midst of a sentence, maybe, and drop his penknife or a few coins on the floor, just to make a little clatter that the radio audience could hear. Then, after a bit, he would start up the old gab again, saying, "Excuse me, ladies and gentlemen of the radio audience. I beg your pardon for breakin' off so sudden in our little chat together, but my rosary beads slipped out of my fingers and dropped to the floor and I had to stop and pick them up. I know you'll understand my feelin's!" Oh, it had been a grand trick and one that had worked like a charm; it had been all the better because it had been thought up by his own lovely mother. May God have mercy on the Ma, he murmured with silent piety, as he reflected upon all that he owed to her training. Until the very day she died, he went to her for advice: you could always get some good out of a few minutes gab with the Ma.)

McCluskey, unlike so many of the others, had not been stubborn. He had listened; he had responded. It was true that sometimes he frowned, and sometimes he balked, and sometimes he even got up on his high horse, but, thought Garvey comfortably, he comes round nice as Nelly in the end. You just had to talk to him a bit, put things in the right way, show him that there was nothing really wrong, that 'twas all the very same thing as he'd wanted to do all the while but a little different way of doing it, that was all. And he came round. It was the kind of ready adaptability Garvey liked to see in a young man; he thought it augured well for his own prosperity in the months to come after the election. "Oh, a grand lad!" he chortled. "By God, between the both of us — him and me — we'll kick the stuffin's out o' that big baboon with the air-conditioned Amos 'n' Andy voice! Oh, I'll teach the bastard to lock out o' City Hall the man who put in the Phil J. Rooney Memorial Macadam Parkway! By God I will!"

"Yeah," Camaratta said approvingly. "Sure. That's the stuff. Kill the bastard." He spoke with swelling emotion, for it was only that morning that he had learned of his deposition and ruin. There had been a secret convocation of the longshoremen; he had heard about it, but too late. Rushing there in a rage, he had been met by a united front, and from the dour and suddenly commanding Macpherson he had learned the fact of Skeffington's coup and his own betrayal. He said now, savagely, "I'll give it to him good. I'll chop him down and carve him up a little. I'll cut his heart out with a meat axe." He went on to describe in blunt, precise and obscene terms his further proposals for retribution.

Garvey heard him with annoyance. The pleasant feelings which had been produced by McCluskey's performance were, like most emotions alien to his bosom, swift in passing; his habitual combativeness was now returning in waves. Quite suddenly he became aware that the man who was sitting in this room with him and to whom, indeed, he had been talking in almost congenial terms, was, after all, Camaratta. With considerably less sociability he growled, "What the hell d'ye want, Camaratta?"

"Look," Camaratta said. "Look, Garvey." He spat again into the cuspidor. "I come here on business. You and me can talk. I'm gonna ditch Skeffington. That punk don't get my boys in this one. You wanna make a deal for your kid, O.K. Maybe we do business. You do me some good, I do you some good. What about it?"

"For the love o' God!" Garvey cried irritably. "You do *who* some good? With what?" He felt fine now. His ill nature completely restored, he was in the midst of a disagreeable situation in which he held all the cards. "By God," he said, "a man like you has got a hell of a nerve, Camaratta! Comin' in here with nothin' in your pockets but the dirty paws you were born with, and sayin' you feel like doin' me some good!"

"Listen, Garvey," Camaratta grunted. "Don't kid around with

Camaratta. You wanna win an election. O.K. I got votes. And I can deliver."

"You got nothin'," Garvey said contemptuously. "Nothin' at all. And after what happened on the docks this mornin', the most you'll deliver'll be a pound and a half o' dog meat from the butcher shop! By God, he fixed you good, Camaratta! I hate the sight o' the murderin' scoundrel, but I give three cheers for the man when he knocked you arse over teakettle off of your perch! He done a grand thing there. I only wisht I done it my-self! So get along with you, back to your little outhouse or wherever the hell it is that you'll be hangin' your hat now that those lummoxes down there got some sense in their skulls and pitched you off of the waterfront. Good-by and good riddance to you!"

The broad olive face before him had been darkening with each word. Camaratta stood still, squat, saurian, and rooted in rage, his hands opening and closing by his sides. He began to speak: the words rushed out in a thick, demented stream of primitive abuse. He made as if to rush towards Garvey, but the latter leaped spryly from his chair and hustled across the room, over to a jumble of objects that were piled in a corner. He turned, then, to face his adversary: a gnarled, red-faced, fearless little old man, jumping up and down, a poker in his hands.

"Come along here now, Camaratta!" he howled. "Come along, my fine big bully-boy! Two steps closer and ye'll get this poker smash in your fat Eyetalian mush! Come on now! By God, they'll be blottin' you off of the walls with pieces o' cotton! Where's my big brave Camaratta without all his fine big lads from the waterfront to stand in the back of him? Come on now! Why don't the big bully-boy step up here all by his lonesome?"

Camaratta remained fixed in one position, breathing heavily; his little opponent waited for him almost joyously, still jump-ing up and down, waving the poker. Camaratta looked at him for what seemed a long time; then, suddenly, spat on the floor, turned abruptly, and walked out of the office, slamming the door viciously as he left. For a few seconds after he had gone, Garvey continued to leap and to brandish his weapon; it was as if he were some elderly, gnomelike, mechanical toy which, once set in motion, could not be stilled until it had run down. Finally he stopped. The poker slipped from his fingers, and he came slowly back to his chair, and slumped down into it, gasping for breath. He was exhausted but exultant. Oh by God, he thought, as he fought for respiration, but didn't that take the biscuit? Wasn't it a grand thing? A little bit of a tangle every now and again: that was the thing to keep a man lively!

He was happy: the near encounter had taken him back to the campaigns of the good old days. He sat for a while, slowly catching his breath; when, at last, he began to breathe more regularly, he fixed himself more comfortably in his chair, and kicked a stool around so that it formed a support for his outstretched legs. He removed his teeth, both upper and lower plates, and placed them carefully on an inverted box next to his chair. The exercise had left him sleepy; he had decided to rest. His eyes closed; soon his breathing became heavier, noisier; in another few moments, a smile began to creep over his tough, unlovely little features. Festus Garvey was dreaming. In his dream, he stood in the corner of this very room, the poker in his hand. Camaratta was coming towards him, his huge fists raised. He was coming faster and faster; now he was within striking distance. Garvey swung the poker, there was a loud *squunch;* the face of Camaratta disappeared, to be replaced, miraculously and immediately, by that of Skeffington. This too came closer; Garvey, yelling his defiance, swung the poker and hit him again and again and again and again. And on the tough little sleeping countenance, the smile grew ever broader; Festus Garvey was having a lovely dream. . . .

Some distance away, Norman Cass Senior and Amos Force had been watching the television program of their candidate together. They watched, with careful attention, every gesture; they listened to every word. They heard him impassively as he spoke with enthusiasm of Smith, Roosevelt, Truman. At the mention of low-cost housing, Amos Force shook his head angrily; when the heightened minimum wage was suggested, he came down hard on the table with the flat of his hand. His thin, irritated whine bit into the voice of the candidate and overrode it.

"No!" he said. "I say, no! This is too much. You're listening, I presume, to what he is saying? To what he's been saying, week after week? And now it gets worse than ever! And on our money!"

"What would you suggest that he say?" Cass asked calmly. "Would you prefer that he advocate a return to the seven-day week? Or the abolition of the trade-union? Is that your idea of the expedient campaign platform?" His cold, steady eyes regarded his colleague with impatience and curiosity. He found him, at times, a decided trial; but he wondered, too, if he were not becoming more than a little lunatic. Still, he was indispensable. Cass said: "We've covered this ground before, Amos. You know that this is necessary. He's saying what we agreed he should say. He's saying precisely what he must say."

"And do you enjoy it?"

"Do I enjoy what?"

"Paying for it, of course. Paying for the privilege of cutting your own throat. And mine as well. I am in favor of expediency, but I tell you we are going too far: I feel it more and more each day. I have a sixth sense in such matters. I am rarely wrong. I don't trust him. I have never trusted any of them. They are all shabby, tricky, ungrateful people. And I do not trust him. Listen to him mouthing that nonsense! Listen to the *way* he does it! There is *enthusiasm* there! I tell you he means it!"

Cass remained calm. "Very possibly he does. What is that to either of us? He can mean whatever he needs to mean in order to get elected. After that," he said quietly, "we can change the meaning."

"You seem extremely sure of this. I am not. That is because I refuse to trust him. Do you mean to tell me that *you* trust him?"

"Naturally not. But what does that matter? I don't need to trust him. I know him. So do you. And I think we both have sufficient evidence that he is amenable to the proper handling." The portrait of Pius XII came to mind; with a certain grim satisfaction he noted, in looking at the television screen, that it was in its position of prominence directly behind the candidate. No, he had no doubt of McCluskey's malleability. Moreover, there was the fact of Mrs. McCluskey. She had appeared now on the program: she was smiling at the audience. Cass did not smile back. He regarded her with his chill, unchanging stare; he was not attracted by this brightly smiling, overly eager young woman who, in his presence, never failed to mention and inquire after his cousin Althea with whom, apparently, she had once served on a civic committee during the war years. Yet she had her value: this socially aggressive woman, so ambitious for herself, her husband, and her children, would surely respond to occasional invitations to the Country Club or to a few decorous musicales. He might even see Althea and prevail upon her to renew this frail and forced alliance of long ago. Much could come, he was sure, of small courtesies extended in this direction, and in any event, the acceptance would have the advantage of being both partial and transient. He said brusquely, "Stop worrying. I tell you this will be perfectly all right."

"Then you think he's a complete fool?"

"Of course I do," said Norman Cass. "And so do you." Then, to secure the point with finality, he added, "Moreover, he is also the one alternative to Skeffington."

It was an effective reminder; Amos Force watched the remaining portion of the television program without protest. He was even partly mollified by the canny display of little Valerie at the conclusion. Cass rose, and turned off the television set. The two men left the building together; they had an important appointment with Nathaniel Gardiner at the latter's club.

Gardiner received them in the reading room. He greeted them cordially, his light gray eyes beaming pleasantly behind the rimless glasses that were slightly too small for him. The three men were all members of the club; they had all known one another for a very long time; now they sat together over their drinks, talking generally and to no particular purpose. Some minutes went by before Cass said abruptly, "Well. Now to business. Nathaniel, Amos and I have something to suggest to you."

"Yes? Somehow, I thought you might have. You see how shrewd we lawyers are?" He smiled and said cheerfully, "Well, suggest away."

Cass began to talk. He talked for perhaps five minutes, forcefully and well. He wasted no words; such was the power of his economic delivery that Amos Force interrupted him only twice.

Cass deftly surmounted these roadblocks; he went on smoothly to an effective finish. Gardiner listened politely; when it was all over, he said, pleasantly but firmly, "No."

"No?"

"No."

Amos Force became agitated. "But do you understand what we are asking? We want no contribution. We're not asking you for a penny. Did Norman make that quite clear to you? I thought, in passing, that he might not have. The point is this: *We are asking for no money at all.*"

"I should hope not," Gardiner said. "Just for my own amusement, I did a little checking yesterday afternoon with some of the boys downtown about the amount of money you fellows have raised in this campaign. I congratulate you. You must have raised enough to elect a President."

"We have enough," Cass said briefly. "I thought I'd made our position quite clear. But just for Amos's benefit, I take it you did understand what I was asking for?"

"Oh yes. I never have the slightest difficulty understanding you, Norman. You're the most lucid man I know. What you want is a simple statement from me, saying that I support your candidate. In short, you want my endorsement for McCluskey."

Cass nodded; Amos Force said, "Yes. That's it. Now you have it, Nathaniel. We want nothing more than that. The endorsement, and that is all. I cannot emphasize too strongly that no money is needed. Just your friendly support."

"Well," said Gardiner, "you're not going to get it."

Amos Force began the series of curious, rapid spitting sounds which served him as a form of protest in moments of extreme stress; Cass cut him short with a gesture. "I see," he said calmly. "You don't mind telling us why, I suppose?"

"I don't mind at all," Gardiner said genially. He pointed to a corner of the reading room; there, on a table, stood a very small television set. "You ought to come around more often to keep up with our latest improvements," he said. "That's one of them. It works quite well from time to time. I've been watching your young man on it. I watched him only tonight, in fact. I don't like him very much."

"Yes. Of course," Cass said dryly, "you're not being asked to adopt him."

"I think I'd rather do that than vote for him. I have nothing against him personally. I would have a great deal against him as mayor."

"Possibly so. Although if he doesn't become mayor, there's only one other choice, isn't there? I suppose you would grant us the point that at least he's the lesser of two evils?"

"Well, you know, I'm not so sure about that," Gardiner said. "I haven't the slightest intention of becoming a Skeffington enthusiast in my old age, and I admit that I would freely support anyone who would represent an improvement. Even a slight one. The trouble is that I don't think your young man would. In fact, I feel sure he wouldn't."

"Nevertheless," Cass said, "we're fairly certain that he's going to become the mayor. We'd like to be even more certain, which is why we've come to you. Apparently we don't see eye to eye; apparently there's not much chance of our doing so. All right, Nathaniel. Just one more question: You seem convinced that he would be no improvement. Why?"

"Well, for one thing, he's not a very able man. I should think that was rather obvious. And for another," he said gently, "I'm really not sure that I like what he represents."

With no change at all in his voice Cass said, "Then you are sure you know what he does represent?"

"Oh yes. I know very well. Both what and whom." The light gray eyes held Cass's; Gardiner said quietly, "And you know that I know, of course. We're neither of us children, Norman. Let's just say that I don't want to play."

"All right," Cass said. He rose to his feet; looking down at the still-seated figure of his host, he said, "You can do what you want, naturally. But you're making a mistake: we're going to win."

"Possibly. Although I have a few doubts about that, too."

Amos Force had risen also; he cried accusingly: "It's perfectly clear what is happening! You've decided to vote for Skeffington!"

"No. Although I'll admit that in many ways he appeals to me more than your young man does. But I'm not going to vote for him, Amos. Nor for your young man either, I'm afraid."

For the first time bitterness crept into Norman Cass's voice. "Or, in other words, a plague on both your houses," he said. "Good night, Nathaniel."

"Good night, Norman. Good night, Amos."

The two men left; as soon as they reached the outer hall Amos Force said furiously, "You bungled it! You bungled it badly! I knew you would! You made no fight at all! Why didn't you apply pressure? Why didn't you argue the point?"

"Because I'm not a fool," Cass said contemptuously. "I don't talk for the sake of wasting time. And I don't argue when there's nothing to argue about. His mind was made up. You know Nathaniel, or at least you should. And about pressure: don't be ridiculous! Exactly what kind of pressure would you suggest? Do you think he can be bullied? Have you ever thought of him as being in any way helpless? Stop talking nonsense!"

They had quit the club and were on the sidewalk before Amos Force said, "I am not exactly helpless myself. Nathaniel is entirely too high-handed. I resent his attitude extremely. I am seriously tempted to attack him in the paper!"

Cass laughed unpleasantly. "Try it," he said. "Go ahead and try it. I give you one month before you're back in the club on your knees, begging for mercy. If you have any sense at all, you'll let well enough alone. We'll win without him." He hailed a taxi and said, "Where do you go now? Home?"

"No," Amos Force said viciously, "back to the paper!" For, if Nathaniel Gardiner was unhappily immune to his wrath, there were others who were not. He would return to the paper. He would write an editorial, far more blistering than any so far produced, on the subject of Skeffington. He would call his subordinates to his office. He would whip them into action. He would *really* make them jump!

It proved to be one of the worst nights in the managing editor's career.

In the Cardinal's study, only the Cardinal himself was watching the television screen with full attention; the young Monsignor was watching both the screen and his superior. For two weeks now, the Cardinal had taken to following these nightly programs of McCluskey's; through them he had come to a fair estimate of the ideas, the taste, and the style of the young candidate. So it was, then, that even before the program had begun that evening, distaste had settled in anticipation upon the prelate's round, veined face. The Monsignor had seen this distaste grow by the minute and when, finally, little Valerie was displayed in her controlled filial acrobatics, there was a loud grunt of exasperation, and one large, still-powerful hand motioned violently towards the television set. The Monsignor turned it off.

"The hope of the future!" the Cardinal said bitterly. "A mealy-mouthed, maneuverable piece of dough!" He threw a fretful glance at his secretary. "I imagine that to a young man who has the typically romantic conception of Skeffington, all this must seem most amusing. You must find great comfort in witnessing these nightly performances of the candidate and the Cardinal."

It was the kind of flicking little jab which the Monsignor was proof against, for he understood the disappointment of the old man. "No amusement, and certainly no comfort, *Eminenza,*" he said, smiling slightly. "And I'm really not so completely sold on the incumbent. Still, I have to say that his opponent seems a fairly feeble proposition."

"Dreadful," the Cardinal sighed. "Simply dreadful." He closed his eyes as if in pain. "Worse, even, than I was prepared for, and," he added grimly, "I was prepared for a great deal. A lifetime of experience with our local politicians has not left me optimistic. But I had hardly expected this parade of banalities. And above all, not this cheapness, this vulgarity! That hideous billboard of the Holy Father! Why doesn't the man put an altar in the room while he's at it? And invite me in to bless it, preferably during one of his broadcasts?"

"Possibly because he hasn't thought of it," suggested the Monsignor.

"Yes. Although I very much doubt," the Cardinal said shrewdly, "that he thought of the painting, either. That has the mark of the conniver, not the dunce. It's obvious by now that he's no more than a pawn. I'm told that Cass is calling the turn;

I'm disposed to believe it. The painting could be his touch. Then again, it could be Festus Garvey's. That man is a perennial reservoir of trashy pietism. Anyway, it makes no difference. Whoever's doing the persuading has found a ready pupil. McCluskey must be responding beyond his fondest expectations." He shook his head, and then, suddenly opening his eyes, he shot an unexpected question at his secretary. He said abruptly, "Is that the best we can do?"

The Monsignor, unprepared, said, "Pardon, *Eminenza?*"

The old man waved irritably at the television set. "That," he said. "Is he representative of what we have to offer? I have spent my life in establishing a system of diocesan schools, in encouraging our people to send their children to them, to our Catholic colleges and universities. Is this the result? A McCluskey? Is he typical of this young educated laity I keep hearing so much about, but which, by the way, I never seem to encounter? What is our contribution? Are we mass-producing McCluskeys? You should know: it's your generation."

The Monsignor said slowly, "It's a complicated question. . . ."

"Very well then, give me a complicated answer. Or better still, simplify it by not telling me that we're still young, that there's a 'time lag,' that it will be some years yet before our colleges can catch up to the others. I know all that. At least it's another of the things I keep hearing, and I suppose to some extent it's true. But I want to know about right now. Today. Is this spineless clown a fair specimen of what we're turning out?"

"He's a fair specimen of some of them," the Monsignor said slowly, "but by no means of the best. It's pretty hard to say just how well we're doing; in some departments — and in a few schools — I think very well indeed. Of course everywhere we're producing McCluskeys, *Eminenza,* but we're also producing much better than that."

"Very well. Then where are they?"

"They're not in politics, that's sure," the Monsignor said. "Mostly they go into the traditional professions, but they want no part of politics. And for obvious reasons, I think. There are more fields open to them now; it's no longer the best way up.

And lots of them just don't want to get mixed up with the mud. They feel that it's just inviting trouble to get involved in a business that everyone seems to regard as being fairly shady."

"Another victory for Skeffington and his breed," the Cardinal said savagely. "They can be thanked for this reputation. And the upshot of it all is . . . what?" He pointed to the television set. "That!" he said with disgust. "A McCluskey!"

The Monsignor became daring. "But still," he asked, "better than Skeffington?"

The Cardinal shifted about in his chair swiftly, the beginning of anger in the old, moist, faded eyes; then, as he looked at his secretary's face, anger slowly disappeared, and he gave a short, mocking laugh. "It isn't really necessary to point out that my position has its ridiculous side," he said sardonically. "That has occurred to me. However — yes, still better than Skeffington."

The Monsignor became consoling. "There is this," he said. "As you say, he's maneuverable; that may not be entirely a curse. There are other people behind him besides Garvey and Cass, and pretty decent people at that. If he should get in, it's conceivable that they could exert a certain influence. Don't you think it's just possible that he might respond to a push in the right direction?"

The old man groaned. "These silver linings!" he said. "No, I don't think it's just possible. I'm hardly in a position to disavow the possibility of miracles, but I can't believe in the likelihood of one here. And as for the better people in back of him: maybe. I'm by no means so sure of that; they seem a mixed and peculiar bag to me. No, there is only one thing to be said for McCluskey. He is awful, but he is inept. He is so inept that even with Cass and Garvey to show him the way, he can't possibly drive us to further disaster as swiftly and certainly as an expert marauder like Skeffington can. That, as I see it, is the brightest possible view that can be taken of this situation." He rose, and moved slowly and with some arthritic difficulty towards the door of the study. "Good night, Michael," he said.

"Good night, *Eminenza*. . . . "

It was one of the rare, pre-election evenings when Jack and Nancy Mangan had been able to dine together, without company, and at home. Even here, however, Jack was at work: he was watching the progress of his candidate on television. Nancy watched with him. She watched in silence, and when the program was over, she yawned and said, "You know what, sweetie? I've decided I like Adam's dear old crooked uncle much, *much* better than that man of yours."

"So do I," Jack said promptly. "Right at the moment there are very few people I don't like better than that man of mine. But I'm made of stern stuff, sport. Like him or not, it's Little Sir Chump for me, all the way to the mayor's chair. Or so we hope."

"*You* hope," she said. "Not me. I'm all for that nice corrupt old man who hasn't got a fat happy little wife to bring him milk and cookies on television."

"And bear him children," Jack said. "Don't forget the kids. They're very important, sport. Especially Flying Valerie. And all served up with you girls in mind. This is the big pitch for the discriminating housewife vote. Mumsy-Daddy at home, et cetera. The paterfamilias who breeds prolifically, eats cookies, drinks milk, and operates at all times under the protective Papal eye. An irresistible parlay for the homemakers."

"Aren't you the big bad cynic?" Nancy said lazily. "And what does your little professor say to all this? Don't those big, old, common-man brown eyes cry just a wee bit? I mean, he's always talking to me about ethics. He's always talking to me about *everything,* really, but mostly about ethics. Ethics in politics. Didn't he write some kind of book about it?"

"Sure," Jack said. "Shortly after he wrote the New Testament. He's written most of the really big stuff. You find that out when you talk to him for a while. But he approves of the campaign. He's actually suggested a few little tricks of his own. You see, he isn't much concerned about our ethics; it's the other side that worries him. He worries mainly about the fact that they don't agree with him. That's because they're reactionaries, hence of doubtful ethical standards. You have to worry about what people like that will do, obviously. Especially if they disagree with you. Whereas what we do, even if it may not look quite aboveboard at times, is really all right, because we're on the side of the angels. Or even better: we're on the side of the professor."

"And you can't make an omelet without scrambling eggs," Nancy said.

"Misquotation," Jack said. "It's always dangerous when you venture into the idiom of the kitchen, sport. *Terra incognita.* The eggs are broken, not scrambled: old Communist maxim. Therefore not in favor in our camp. We're all rather sensitive on that point. Spare your husband's sensitivity."

"Anyway," she said, "why even *bother* to break an egg for McCluskey! Sweetie, he's such a *cluck!*"

"Check," Jack said. "One of the cluckiest. And we're not too happy about that. But you see our predicament: we have no place else to go."

"I don't care what you say, I'd a *thousand* times rather take Skeffington."

"Derisive laughter all around," Jack said. "You don't take Skeffington; he takes you. He's been doing it for years. Besides, we couldn't work with him. Because, all kidding and the professor aside, all we want are a few simple changes for a little better government. And we haven't a ghost of a chance of getting them while Uncle Frank is driving the car. So it's the cluck for us, sport. At least he's a new cluck. And you never can tell: maybe we can do something with him."

"Sweetie," Nancy said, reaching over and stroking his cheek, "you're absolutely marvelous and I love you dearly and I can't *stand* your little professor *or* your pet cluck and I'm *still* for that darling evil old man. So there! Besides," she added irrelevantly, "Adam seems to be having a wonderful time with him."

"The time of his life," Jack agreed. "But then it's different with him. He doesn't really give a hoot about the political situation around here." He shook his head in some disapproval and said, "Adam's a queer bird on things like that. Anyway, the whole thing's personal, not political, with him. It's a six weeks' tour of the funhouse. How about Maeve? How's she holding up under the Bold Experiment?"

"She doesn't talk much about it. I don't think it's working out exactly the way she planned. And I mean, how *could* it? Here's

Adam obviously enjoying himself more every minute, and the whole idea was that after a while he wouldn't be enjoying himself at *all*."

"Another bum idea from her maniac of a father," Jack said. "The Girdle King. Why doesn't he mind his own business? They ought to coop that old menace up. The man cries out for vengeance. Listen, we could take matters into our own hands and deal out a little punishment. How about inviting him over for dinner some night? You could give him one of your casseroles, sport."

"Ha ha ha," she said. She lit a cigarette and said, "Jack?"

"Hello?"

"No fooling. Who *is* going to win?"

He hesitated, then said, "Honest Injun?"

She nodded. "Honest Injun."

"Probably Skeffington. We'll give him a good go, but I think he may be too tough and too smart. He can be knocked off, all right, but probably not just yet. And probably not by McCluskey. No, it'll be close, sport, but I'm afraid your darling evil old man may take it by a nose."

Nancy blew a thin drift of smoke across the room; after a moment she said softly, "Poor old Jack. I'm really on your side."

"No commiseration, sport. We're in no hurry. We'll catch up with him," he said, a trifle grimly. "Maybe not yet, but it's purely a question of time. And we might even get him on this one. Only," he said, getting to his feet, "a word to the wise: Don't put any of the egg money on it. . . . "

At a busy corner in the heart of the city, Charlie Hennessey had parked his sound truck. It was a warm night for the first of November, the stores were open to accommodate the late shoppers, and Charlie, climbing to the small platform fixed to the top of his truck, had no difficulty in collecting an audience. In his campaign he had been scrupulously fair; playing no favorites, he had picturesquely, vigorously, and equally attacked both Skeffington and McCluskey. Tonight, it was McCluskey's turn.

"Well, dear folks," he began, his powerful platform voice reinforced by the public address system, "I only hope you had the good luck to be tuned in on young McCluskey on the television tonight. Marvelous! The greatest entertainment of our age, dear folks, and positively no charge to any of us! All we have to do is turn the little knob of the television set, any hour of day or night, and the next thing you know, there he is, big as life, saying his prayers right there in the room with you! Oh, marvelous! It's a modern miracle, dear folks! If it wasn't for television there wouldn't be a one of us who'd see him at all, for the simple reason that his keepers don't let him out! Here's a big strong boy who wears Size 11 shoes, a 44 suit, a 17 collar and a 7½ hat, and they don't let him out in the back yard even to play! Isn't that cruel, dear folks? A great big boy who finally got through college and the university, who had three fine years of shore duty in the Navy during the war, and they don't let him come out on the public platform and talk directly to you people as I'm doing here tonight! There's a lack of confidence there, dear folks! Sad! Disturbing! They don't want him to come out in the damp night air where he might be asked a few questions! Dangerous! Very dangerous! They like to keep him away from people. They like to keep him in his own house where the only question he'll be asked is whether he wants a lamb chop or a pork chop for his dinner! Oh, I tell you, dear folks, if it wasn't for the miracle of television, we'd hardly catch a glimpse of him at all! The keepers might put him in some kind of portable hen coop and trail him around the streets behind a horse, so's you could see what you were voting for but you couldn't catch up with him to ask him what about putting rest rooms in the public parks! Oh, evasive, dear folks! But now that there's television we see him at all hours, right in the bosom of his family. We're given the good, safe, long-distance peek at what goes on around the McCluskey house when Dad's at home! Oh dear folks, it's nice! Heart-warming! Grand to see a father playing patty-cake, patty-cake with his little children! Grand to see a man who's running for the highest office in the city sitting nice and easy in his home while his wife comes galloping in from the kitchen with a big tall glass of milk and a plateful of Uneeda biscuits smeared all over with Skippy peanut butter! Nice! Nourishing! And dear folks, it's grand and homey to see a candidate for mayor in his own living room, answering nice little questions put to him by his pet parrot, with a picture of the Pope put up there like wallpaper, and a grand big rented dog in front of the fireplace! It all goes to show you how times have changed, dear folks! Back in the old days, when a man wanted to make a speech, he rented a tuxedo! Now he's got a tuxedo but he has to rent a dog! Think of that! The man who wants to be mayor of our great city and who talks night after night about practising economy in government is actually paying out fifty cents an hour to hire a hound to sit in front of his fireplace! Isn't that unbelievable, dear folks? Isn't it amazing what I'm telling you? Would you call that economy? Would you call those the tactics of a sane man, fit to be the head official of this great city? Oh no, dear folks!" he roared. "I'll tell you what they are: THEY ARE THE TACTICS OF A NUT-BOY!"

A short distance away, on a side street within sight and hearing of the sound truck, the long, official car of the mayor of the city had halted. In the darkness, and off the main thoroughfare, it was for the moment unobserved; inside, Skeffington sat listening to Charlie Hennessey. He listened with obvious amusement; after a few minutes he said to Adam, "This appears to be my night off; McCluskey's getting the benefit of all the little courtesies. I must say Charlie's in great form. I wonder how he found out about the rented dog? I intended to have a little fun with that one myself."

"Is it true, then?" Adam asked. It seemed absurd, and yet not so absurd as it would have seemed a month ago. His political education had progressed rapidly. "Did he actually hire that big setter?"

"That big IRISH setter," Skeffington corrected him. "There's a difference. A significant difference. Yes, indeed, he did hire it. Apparently it was felt to be a necessary domestic touch and as the authentic, or noncampaign, McCluskey dog looks a little like a dwarf goat, they thought they'd better pick up something a bit more presentable. So they rented this handsome, well-behaved animal. I'm surprised they didn't rent an additional child while they were at it."

"Little Valerie seemed adequate to the occasion," Adam said.

"Little Valerie's useful," Skeffington agreed, "but a girl is under a handicap in a situation like that. You can't very well call her Franklin D. Whereas think what they could have done with a bright-eyed little boy, procured by the week from some friendly orphanage. Little Franklin Delano McCluskey. And best of all, *this* Franklin Delano could be given back the day after the election. Unhappily, you couldn't do that with the original."

They drove off; Skeffington said: "We have about an hour to kill before the rally at the Auditorium. I have a suggestion: I'll drop you at your house now, and then pick you up on my way back. That is," he amended, "if you really want to go. I suppose there's no reason why you should, actually. We have only three days left, and there'll be several of these wind-up rallies, every one pretty much like the other. There doesn't seem to be much sense in subjecting yourself to all of them."

"I don't imagine the subjection will be unbearable," Adam said, smiling, "and I think I'd rather like to go along tonight. If you have no objection, that is."

"Not an objection in the world. Always a pleasure to have you." It was, for Skeffington, that rather rare thing: the compliment which was no more than the simple truth. Over the past few weeks he had been deeply pleased by his nephew. He reflected, now, that the boy had behaved well under circumstances where suitable behavior was by no means inevitable: it was all too easy for the amateur to become the nuisance in a busy political campaign. But Adam had not been a nuisance. He had been observant but unobtrusive; he had asked no purposeless questions; he had followed along the complicated, alien trails with an alert, intelligent interest. Moreover, he had obviously found pleasure in his uncle's company, and from this Skeffington had derived an unexpected satisfaction. Yet at the same time, he was occasionally aware that this sudden, close association must have created a domestic problem for his nephew. It was not a consideration that occurred to him with any persistence, but it did so now, and he said casually, "By the way, I've been remiss. I haven't asked you about your good wife in some time. How's she getting along? I don't suppose she looks with much favor upon your choice of companion these evenings?"

The supposition was a reasonably accurate one, but Adam said loyally, "You know, she's never raised any objection to my doing this, Uncle Frank. In fact, it was quite the contrary."

Skeffington nodded. "Then in addition to her other good qualities, she's a remarkably considerate young woman, with a great regard for the wishes of her husband. Because I've gathered that personally she's not exactly one of the more impassioned Skeffington supporters. I must admit I can understand her position."

"I'm glad you can," Adam said, "because of course it's a peculiar position. She doesn't know you at all — I'm sure the only time you've met was at our wedding — but she's gone through a fairly formidable indoctrination on the subject. And you know the stumbling block there."

"Indeed I do. I know him well. One of our leaders in that respect: a stumbling block of many parts. You should give thanks, by the way, that your wife takes after her mother rather than the stumbling block. The mother was a grand girl who died much too young. Well," he said, "be that as it may, and as generous as your wife has proved to be, I don't imagine she'll be exactly unhappy when the campaign is over."

"Well, no," Adam admitted. "I don't imagine she will."

They fell silent; the car continued down the parkway for several minutes, then swung down one of the parallel residential streets, pulling to a stop before Adam's house. The house was well lighted; Maeve was at home. Adam was preparing to leave the car when he felt his uncle's hand on his arm.

"I tell you what," Skeffington said thoughtfully, "I think I might like to come calling for a few minutes. On you. Do you think that might be arranged?"

The request was completely unexpected, and Adam, taken by surprise, hesitated just an instant before he said: "Yes. Certainly. Of course it could. Please come in, Uncle Frank." Clearly, there was nothing else that could have been said, yet having said it, Adam felt decidedly uneasy. With sinking heart, he thought of Maeve and the encounter to come.

"A pause in the day's occupation," Skeffington said, getting out of the car. "Possibly a pause for refreshment. I hadn't realized until now that it's been such a long day. I think it's almost time to stoke the fires a bit. Do you suppose I could impose upon you for a glass of milk and any old thing in the way of a snack? I hate to duplicate my opponent's television fare, but something of the sort would do nicely."

"No imposition at all," Adam said automatically. "And I'm sure we can do better for you than that." He was still uneasy, but the saving thought had occurred to him that the situation was not without its comic side. Somewhat wryly, he pictured his father-in-law's face when he learned of this visit.

"Anything at all will do," Skeffington said, following his nephew up the walk. He added urbanely, "We'll surprise your good wife."

"Yes," said Adam. "Yes, we will."

He opened the front door and the two men walked into the house, Skeffington for the first time. Adam heard the light footsteps coming across the kitchen; a moment later Maeve appeared in the hall. She was wearing a small blue apron and her face was slightly flushed. She saw Skeffington and halted abruptly; the flush deepened and she said, simply, "Oh!"

Adam said hastily, "You remember Uncle Frank, dear." Presumably there were more felicitous ways of breaking the ice; he could not think of them.

"Yes," she said. There was a small pause before she added, with an awkward, compulsory politeness, "It's nice to see you again."

It was an uncomfortable moment; only Skeffington appeared perfectly composed. "And it's very nice to see you, my dear," he said, walking forward and taking her hand. His manner was courtly, so courtly that for one startled instant Adam suspected that the hand was about to be lifted and kissed. The suspicion was unfounded. Skeffington merely held it lightly; Maeve stood still, smiling uncertainly, clearly in troubled doubt as to what was to happen next. She looked quickly at Adam; in the clear, lovely eyes he saw both hurt and accusation, and he hastened to explain.

"We're hungry men," he said. "Especially Uncle Frank; I'd be surprised if he's had anything to eat since this morning. What we need is something to tide us over until after the rally tonight. I thought maybe something in the soup, sandwiches and milk department might hit the spot. What do you think? Is the icebox up to it?"

It was an appeal to Maeve's good manners and hospitable instincts; it was an appeal which momentarily diminished even the fact of Skeffington. She nodded and said, "Yes, of course. We have loads of things: I've just finished shopping. Let me go out and see what there is that might be good; I won't be a minute." She began to edge towards the kitchen; the movement was both an expedition for food and a retreat from an embarrassing presence. She found, however, that she did not move far. Skeffington had not dropped her hand; he continued to hold it, gently but firmly.

"Why, I couldn't think of rushing you like this," he said genially. "Besides, the first time I saw you, at your wedding reception, I did little else but drink your champagne. Now the second time we meet, I'm about to eat your food. I can't have you thinking of me as some kind of elderly sponger." He saw the fresh young face color again and knew that she was on the point of dutiful protest; he added smoothly, "In addition to which, I glanced through the door of your living room just now, and saw something I'd like to examine at closer range. Do you suppose we could delay our meal a few minutes while you show it to me?"

He had begun to walk towards the living room even before he had finished talking; Maeve, her hand still in his, necessarily walked with him. It was a maneuver accomplished with such fluidity and ease that they were out of the hallway before Maeve realized with sudden indignation that she was actually being steered into her own living room by the intruder. But indignation had no chance to mount; Skeffington choked it all off by pointing to a large photograph on the piano.

"Your father and mother," he said, stating a fact. "That's

what I thought it was. Your father and I are old acquaintances, my dear. I hesitate to use the word 'friends'; I'm afraid it wouldn't be entirely true. You may have occasionally heard that slight differences of opinion divide your father and myself."

She had heard the case stated in considerably stronger terms; nevertheless, she found its direct introduction, by Skeffington and at this time, disquieting. She flushed again and said, "Yes. I mean, I've heard, of course. But . . . "

"But," said Skeffington, smiling, "why not? Why not differ, I mean? It always astonishes me that there aren't more differences. Your father's a man of strong opinions, he's been extremely successful, and he naturally prefers his way of doing things, as I do mine. This doesn't lead to perfect unanimity of opinion. I don't suppose your father and I agree on much of anything, yet I don't mind admitting to you that I have a very healthy respect for him all the same. He's a courageous antagonist and a man of singular achievement; I can think of very few men who can boast of an equivalent career." So much, he thought, for Roger Sugrue. Far too much, in fact; but here, as in most social encounters, he knew that the truth would have been calamitous. He passed on to a more congenial subject. "And your mother," he said, looking once more at the photograph. "I don't suppose you can remember her at all, can you?"

"No. Not really, that is." From her father to her mother: the numberless thundering warnings of her father came rising to her memory, and she wondered uneasily what devious plan these questions were preliminary to. But Skeffington was facing her, smiling pleasantly, waiting for the rest of her answer; she said, "She died very soon after I was born."

"I know," Skeffington said. "I knew your mother — not as well as I knew some of the older members of the family — but I knew her quite well." He pointed to the piano and said, "Do you play, by the way?"

The tangential question caught her by surprise: was she to be asked to perform? She said hastily, "Not very well, I'm afraid. . . ."

"I'll bet you do play well," Skeffington said. But there was no request; instead he said, "Your mother did. She was a fine pianist, even as a little girl. Matter of fact, I once gave her a medal for it." It would have been, he wondered, how long ago? Thirty years? Thirty-five, more likely. No matter; it was far enough back in time to be in that region where the famous memory was still reliable, where he had, in fact, almost total recall. He said, "It was when she was a school girl in the old Saint Xavier's on Grover Street. There was a musical competition for all the school children of the city; as mayor I presided and distributed the awards. I remember your mother won a silver medal; she must have been about twelve at the time." He chuckled. "A shy, nervous little girl with great big eyes and a little yellow frock: I remember they gave her a push to get her out on the stage; she made her curtsy, announced that she was going to play a piece by Mozart, then ran to the piano and played like mad. When she finished everybody clapped and so did I. Not exactly the behaviour expected from an impartial authority, but I did anyway. To tell you the truth, my dear, quite a few people felt like applauding your mother all along the way. She was a remarkable and a lovable woman."

Maeve had listened, absorbed, caught up in the deep, soft musical tones as they eulogized the mother she had not known. Adam, too, had listened, and now, looking at his wife, he had an inspiration; he made a sudden decision. "If you two will excuse me for a minute," he said, backing off slightly, "I'll run upstairs and clean up a bit before we eat. I'll be right back."

The announcement met with a nod from Skeffington, an acknowledging and rather abstracted smile from Maeve. Then, almost immediately, the sense of what he had said penetrated the echo of the anecdote. The smile vanished, to be replaced by an expression at first startled, then perturbed, then imploring. Adam firmly ignored the appeal; he said merely, "Back in a minute;" then he was gone. Before he reached the bend in the stairs he heard the gratifying sound of the deep, rhythmic rumble, picking up where it had left off. It was upon the success of this resumption that Adam depended.

He remained upstairs for some minutes. He washed; he smoked a cigarette; he fingered through a magazine; absent-mindedly, he washed again. Then, quietly, he went down stairs. Near the bottom he was able to stand unobserved; he looked into the living room. At least they had seated themselves: it was a good sign. He could see his uncle, talking easily to a silent audience. Adam shifted his position and saw his wife: seated opposite Skeffington, she was leaning slightly forward in her chair, and as Adam watched, her lips parted in a little smile at something that had just been said. Adam relaxed. Clearly, this was not the mark of the hostess still hostile. The experiment had been, therefore, at least a partial success; antagonism, if not obliterated, had unquestionably been modified. He felt a good deal easier.

Skeffington saw him and lifted a hand. "Spick and span, you return," he said. "Come in and join us as we explore the family tree. I'm giving your wife the benefit — or the curse — of a talkative old man's reminiscences."

"No, it's not like that at all," Maeve said quickly. She turned to Adam and said excitedly, "Adam, it was wonderful! Your uncle knew everybody in mother's family: grandmother, grandfather, even my great-grandmother!" She caught her husband's eye upon her and suddenly felt herself reddening absurdly again. It was all most confusing; she rose hurriedly to her feet. "Anyway," she said resolutely, "if you're going to have anything at all to eat, I'd better go out and get it now. Otherwise you won't have time."

Once again she was attempting retreat; once again she was balked, for Skeffington rose, too. "We'll go along with you," he said. This expert tactician, having secured an advantage, had no intention of abandoning it. He fell into step beside her. "We can't have you working away out there while we sit in here talking away and waiting to be fed. The very least we can do is take the conversation to the kitchen. Besides, I'm always at home in the kitchen; it's a mark left on me from my youth. When I was a little boy, I always thought the kitchen was the happiest room in the house. I'll have to admit that the rest of the house wasn't much, but even so, the kitchen was a welcome spot. It was always warm and full of good smells. I think I spent at least half my young life one arm's length from the coal stove; I've been partial to the kitchen ever since. It's a pleasure to accompany you to yours."

It was not at all what Maeve had had in mind; nevertheless,

they went into the kitchen together. There, in the small, bright, spotless room, Skeffington and Adam sat facing each other across the gleaming enameled surface of the kitchen table, and while Maeve busied herself about cupboards, cans, pans, and stove, Skeffington began to talk once more, returning now to an earlier subject.

"Just before you came down," he said to Adam, "we were talking about your wife's great-grandmother. Ellen O'Donohue. You couldn't have known her, naturally, but do you know anything about her?"

Adam shook his head. "No. Just the name, that's all."

"She was a little more than a name," Skeffington said. "She was an extraordinary woman. Not many people remember her now, and you rarely hear her name mentioned, but in her time she was a woman of great consequence in these parts. She was an old woman when I was a small boy, but I remember her very well. She'd come over from Ireland as a young woman with a family of six children; her husband had died on the boat coming over. She arrived with almost no money; somehow she scraped together enough to start a small store where she sold penny candy, assorted knickknacks, and various little odds and ends for the household. It was quite a store." He looked at Adam and said, "Matter of fact, you were in it not a week ago."

Adam looked blank. "I don't remember it," he said slowly.

"Well, there have been a few minor changes," Skeffington said. "It's a Chinese laundry now." It was an insert which did not fit the tone of the discussion; he returned quickly to graver discourse. "She was a hard worker and a thrifty and intelligent woman; somehow she raised all six children and, moreover, sent all of them through school. I don't know how she did it; try it sometime when your basic capital is an assortment of nigger-eyes, gumdrops and jelly beans. But she did. And more to the point, in the process of doing so, her own stature in the community increased considerably. I've said she was intelligent, but apparently she was much more than that: she was sensible. I don't suppose she'd had any education to speak of, but every once in a great while you run across someone who seems to be naturally wise and level-headed, and she was one of those. People used to drop into the store for one thing or another; they got into the habit of asking for her opinions, then for her advice. In a situation like that, when the advice is good, the whole thing has a tendency to snowball, and in Ellen O'Donohue's case, the advice must have been very good. She was always a well-liked woman; in addition, and in a rather surprisingly short time, she became an extremely influential one."

He paused, and Maeve, catching the ominous word, said hesitantly, "Influential? You mean she . . . Well, was she . . ."

"In politics?" Skeffington said, with a smile. It was not difficult to complete the question; he had often observed that polite people approached the mention of his chosen profession with a certain tentativeness. "No, my dear, she wasn't. She wasn't even interested. If she had been, she could easily have become one of the most powerful political figures in the state. And this, mind you, in a day when women didn't have the vote. Even as it was, when she got to be an old woman, the mayor and the governor both used to pay annual courtesy calls on her. Just in case, I imagine. But it didn't do them or anyone else any good. She kept out of politics all the way. And probably it was just as well. The people loved her and believed her and trusted her completely, maybe because she was what she was and nothing else. No, her influence was enormous, but it was entirely personal. You never hear her mentioned today, yet when I was a young man, I spent a good deal of time trying to find out all I could about her. As I say, she was an extraordinary and a fascinating woman, in her way extremely important in the history of the city. I remember one time . . ."

He went on, telling story after story of the wonderful old woman, now all but forgotten. A supper was produced; Maeve joined the two men; and as the three sat at the table in the kitchen Skeffington continued to talk, not, now, exclusively of Ellen O'Donohue, but leading gradually into other stories of other people of a bygone age. They were stories which Adam had not heard before, stories of a kind not altogether characteristic of his uncle. They were curiously lacking in the sardonic, irreverent current which flashed through the usual Skeffington narration; they were quiet stories, quietly told: warm and affectionate memoirs, ideally recounted in the rich and softly rolling tones. And as they rolled on, Adam realized that they were special stories, meant for a special audience; he looked at his wife and saw their success. Maeve was captivated by the elderly raconteur; of this he was certain, and the certainty delighted him.

When, sometime later, the two men prepared to leave the house, Skeffington said to Maeve: "Good-by, my dear. And thank you very much. Not just for that extremely agreeable supper, but for the pleasure of talking with you. I mean it when I say I enjoyed it very much."

"I enjoyed it too," Maeve said. "I'm so glad you came." She held out her hand to him and said shyly, "Will you come again?"

He nodded. "I will indeed. We haven't seen nearly enough of each other, my dear. If I may, I propose to remedy that in the future."

It was a promise which strangely pleased her. She kissed her husband good-by; as he was leaving the house, following Skeffington down the walk, she called him back. "Adam?" she said.

He returned and said lightly, "One final word of warning?"

She shook her head; she kissed him again, warmly. He was surprised but elated, for he understood. The debates between husband and wife on the subject of Skeffington were over.

The car pulled away. Back in the house, as she cleared away the dishes, Maeve was thoughtful. What had long been feared had now come to pass, and in the light of the consequences, the fears seemed to have been baseless and even a little absurd. The monstrous relative by marriage, the ogre who had walked so dreadfully through her imagination, had come to call in person; she had found him to be a courteous, charming, and completely engrossing old man. She realized that undoubtedly he had put his best foot forward, and that just as undoubtedly there was another Skeffington of whom her father spoke and whom she had not seen. But she could not reconcile the two, the welcome guest and the unspeakable villain, and while she did not now, because of one short hour, jettison the warnings of a lifetime, she did feel, once again, the faint and unfamiliar throb of doubt.

In the car, Adam said simply, "Thanks, Uncle Frank."

"I always enjoy being thanked," Skeffington said, "but in this case, for what?"

"Just for the visit. I think it was a good idea. I also think that it may have worked wonders."

"I doubt it," Skeffington said. "I haven't worked a wonder since 1945, when I got Sam Delaney to stop drinking for three weeks. That was a pretty fair country wonder; people have been beatified for less. But all wonders apart, I must say that I thoroughly enjoyed myself in your house. So you see the thanks really go the other way around. I'm indebted to you and your lovely wife. Incidentally, she does take after her mother, far more than I'd realized. You're a lucky boy."

"Yes, I think so," Adam said. "And she liked you very much, Uncle Frank: I guess that was fairly obvious."

"I hope she did. Because I liked her. And," he said frankly, "I'll admit I did what little I could to offset certain impressions given her by her lovable Dad. I thought it might ease the situation a little all around."

"Yes, I know. That's why I thanked you."

"Don't thank me too much," Skeffington said. "I'll let you in on a secret: It's just possible that a little session like that might benefit me more than anyone else. Or hadn't you thought of it in that way? You see, I don't exactly find it a hardship to talk about the old days, and the city as it used to be, and some of the people who made the city what it was. In its way, it was a wonderful place, and they were wonderful people; God knows they had to be, in order to survive. But it's a way of life that's virtually disappeared; most of the people are gone, and confidentially I'm not getting any nearer the cradle myself. So it's not too unpleasant to sit back every once in a while and reminisce a bit. Especially when your audience is a new one that hasn't heard the old stories before. And especially when that audience is young, and interested, and, in a certain sense, connected to you. I find that counts." He flashed Adam a swift and correctively derisive glance. "I'm blessed if you don't catch me in a sentimental mood," he said. "It's a privilege of the superannuated man: like wearing carpet slippers with a tuxedo. In any case,

I didn't intend to stake out a special familial claim at this late date. I merely wanted to indicate that no special thanks were due; if any payment were necessary, it's already been made."

They rode on. Adam had found this short speech of his uncle's unexpectedly moving; he did not, however, entirely believe it. He thought he knew well enough the motive behind Skeffington's visit; it was not a selfish one. At the same time, he felt that his uncle had, as he had said, enjoyed himself; it was possible, indeed probable, that the visit had been beneficial to both sides. In the past several weeks Adam had observed his uncle closely; in this short but crowded space of time there had been moments when a word, a phrase, had flashed through the pattern of the old man's conversation and swiftly disappeared, leaving behind it the hint of loneliness. Like many other people in the city, Adam knew something of the history of Francis Skeffington Jr.; he regarded it as a measure of his uncle's pride and disappointment that in their time together he had not once mentioned even the name of his son. And so, perhaps, a conversation over a kitchen table, in the home of young people who were, in a sense, his own, was not without its value to him. For the first time, Adam, looking at this calm, confident, masterful figure who sat beside him, who alone had ruled this huge city for the better part of half a century, sensed in him something curiously pathetic.

It was a fleeting impression, one which did not persist. For they had arrived at the Auditorium; they had gone in; and there, in this arena jammed to the doors with a noisy, enthusiastic crowd, Skeffington made his way to the platform. He began to talk; and here, now, even the suspicion of pathos was impossible.

" . . . I understand my opponent's supporters refer to him as 'a young man of promise,' " he said. "How right they are! I've never heard so many promises from one man in my life. So far, he's promised to eliminate graft and corruption, to reduce the tax rate, to lower the cost of municipal transportation, to settle the city's traffic problem, to give the firemen and policemen more money, to enlarge municipal housing projects, and to put a new wing on the Public Library. And I understand there are still more promises to come. Why, it's enough to frighten a man like myself! Just between ourselves, I continually wonder at my own effrontery in opposing this young man who's going to do so much for us all. But then, of course, I console myself with the thought that we really haven't any assurance that he actually will do anything. All we've seen so far are the promises: we haven't seen any performance. And that's understandable too; it's a well-known fact that you can't see what there isn't any of. It's also understandable why my young opponent has to talk about what he intends to do in the future. It's all he can talk about: he hasn't any past. That makes me wonder a bit. I find myself saying, 'Where has this miracle man been up to now? What did he ever do? Why haven't we heard of him? Where's he been hiding all these remarkable talents?' It all reminds me somewhat of a book I once read by one of the Irish writers. It was about a man who was born at the age of thirty-five with a full set of teeth. My opponent, I believe, is thirty-five, and while I haven't his dental record at hand, I'm sure that it's somewhat more remarkable than his record of accomplishment, although I must say that if you take a look at the latter, you become convinced that he might well have been delivered just the day before yesterday. But that doesn't seem to bother him much. He has his promises. 'Have faith!' is what he says. 'I'll do it! I've never given you the slightest evidence I can do it, but have faith! I will!'

"I must say I admire faith of that kind. Although blind, it's inspiring. It's the kind of faith the followers of Jemima Wilkinson had, many years ago. Matter of fact, my young opponent reminds me in many ways of the good Jemima. As you probably remember, she was a Quaker lady who lived in this country back in the days of the Revolution. It was Jemima's claim that she had died in 1776 and had come back to earth as a reincarnation of Our Lord. There were a few unkind people who were somewhat skeptical about this, but she managed to collect a substantial group of followers who had faith. One day she announced that she was about to give a demonstration of her divine powers: she was going to walk upon the waters. The faithful assembled on the banks; the good Jemima appeared, clad in a flowing robe of white. She put one foot out towards the river, then suddenly stopped and asked the people if they really had faith. They said they did. She asked them if they truly believed that she could walk on water. They said they did indeed. Well then, said Jemima, if that was the case there was no point in going through with it; any demonstration would be superfluous. So she tucked up her robe and went home. Via the northern, or dry land, route. Naturally, this left some of the faithful a bit discontented. They began to feel that they'd been had. They'd heard the promise and they'd come to witness the performance, but the good Jemima just hadn't delivered. And while they had faith, it now began to be a trifle less secure: some of them even began to suspect that if the promised exhibition of water-walking had been carried out, it might have necessarily resolved itself into a demonstration of the Australian crawl. And that, I regret to say, was the beginning of the end of Jemima. Now, naturally I dislike suggesting that this story has a modern parallel right here in our own city, but sometimes it's a little hard to avoid the obvious. The familiar promissory note is once more extended; the cry of 'Have faith!' is heard once more from our own local water-walker. The question is, I think, how many of us are willing to believe that a miracle will be passed, and the note redeemed. For my own part, I must confess to having exceedingly grave doubts. . . . "

He went on in this vein, supplying adroit and telling variations on the theme. It was the kind of talk in which he took particular pleasure, for, effective as he was sure it would be, it would both place a seal upon the long campaign and usher him gracefully into victory.

Twelve

IT was election night. . . .

Adam had neither seen nor heard from his uncle all that day. He had not expected to; his own short experience with the campaign had given him some idea of the last-minute tangle of problems with which Skeffington must now be occupied. The meeting would wait until the night when, at his uncle's downtown campaign headquarters, the candidate and all his workers would gather to wait for the returns to come in.

Late that morning, Adam had gone to the polls with Maeve. They had voted; Adam strongly suspected that they had voted differently. The recent rapprochement between his uncle and his wife had undoubtedly been effective, but that it had been so effective as to nullify the old parental pull he thought unlikely. Under the circumstances, and at this time, sympathy was one thing and support was quite another; he felt reasonably sure that his wife had — although possibly with some hesitation and even a touch of regret — cast her vote for McCluskey. As it happened, in this supposition he was entirely correct.

After voting, he had gone to the paper; on this day of excitement, he nevertheless hoped to get in some badly needed work. In these last two weeks of the campaign, Little Simp had been woefully neglected. Not only was Adam behind in his working schedule; also there had been a falling off in the quality of the strip. Adam had plunged his little boy into a pedestrian and altogether unworthy adventure; in creative desperation, he had sent Little Simp and Daddy the Chipmunk to Hollywood.

Adam had worked on this episode doggedly, but without inspiration; taken all in all, he felt it to be definitely substandard. In the interest of gingering up the plot, he had permitted conflict between Daddy and his little master: he had permitted the chipmunk to go Hollywood. Daddy wearing a beret, Daddy with a monocle, Daddy wearing a tartan tuxedo, Daddy smoking a filter-tip cigarette: all these departures from the chipmunk norm Simp watched with sorrowing eyes. He was sad but helpless; he could not argue against the ego of the diminutive rodent.

This, then, was the conflict, and Adam, working on it, knew it was no good. It was pale stuff, minus the inventive violence and derring-do his readers had come to expect; he knew that there would be complaints.

He worked that afternoon; he read a book; he did a crossword puzzle; he talked to friends on the paper. In this way he effectively killed the day. Evening came at last; he ate an early dinner in a small restaurant near the paper, and then, as though the completion of the meal marked the formal end of the wasted, unimportant day, he set off with a sudden sense of excitement for the business of the evening. He began to walk briskly across town towards his uncle's campaign headquarters.

Arriving, he saw that he was early, but not too early; already, although the polls would not close for another hour, the Skeffington supporters, well-wishers, and hangers-on had begun to gather in the lofty, barnlike room. It was a setting which had about it the marks of the makeshift and the impermanent: unrentable for months, the premises had been commandeered by Skeffington for use during the campaign; within the week, they would be abandoned once more. Now, tonight, the desks and chairs had been pushed back, creating a central floor space; a pair of huge blackboards stood against the left-hand wall; stretched in a row before them were long tables on which rested telephones, long sheets of heavily ruled paper, innumerable black crayons. On another, and smaller, table, to the right of the blackboards, were two large coffee urns. Everything had been made ready. It was a scene which, unfamiliar to Adam, nevertheless stood as an obvious and vivid promise of the spirited activity to come.

Ditto had arrived. He was dressed in anticipation of victory: a tiny new hat sat atop his tiny head. It was a pearl-gray homburg, a faithful if much reduced duplication of that habitually worn by Skeffington. His blue serge suit had been pressed with care;

on the right lapel of the coat the green-and-white Skeffington button, large as a saucer, was proudly displayed. Ditto was smiling broadly; he saw Adam and waddled ponderously towards him.

"Well, Adam," he said. "Well well well, well. The night of nights, as we say. A grand occasion for one and all. Yes yes." He looked all around the room, beaming indiscriminately at people, furniture, anything. He had waited for this night like a child for Christmas Eve; the mountainous body swayed back and forth with joy; the little head smiled happily. He stopped suddenly and pointed to the small cubicle at the end of the room which Skeffington sometimes used for private talks. "He's not here?" he said, in some alarm. "The Governor's not amongst us yet, I hope, Adam?"

"I don't think so, Ditto. I just got here myself, but I'm sure he hasn't come in."

The smile reappeared. "That's all to the goods, as we say. The Governor always likes me to be here a little before him. So's I can keep tabs on people. The Governor's a great man for having the people he really trusts keep tabs, Adam. Yes, yes. It's the men that keep tabs who the Governor really trusts, and not certain high-and-mighty confidential secretaries. I mention no names. Do you get my meaning, Adam?"

"I get your meaning, Ditto."

"There's people would like to make trouble between the Governor and me by slipping him the word I was late," Ditto said darkly. "That I didn't show up as per on schedule. The reason I was a bit late tonight is I had to stop off and say a few cheer-up words to poor Billy Doyle in the sickbed. You know poor Billy of course, Adam."

"No," Adam said. It occurred to him now that, in all his talks with Ditto, never once had he been able to place any of these names which, apparently, were so readily recognizable. "I don't think I've heard of Billy, Ditto."

"A grand man," Ditto said, "and a very loyal worker for the Governor all his life. Aces high, as we say. But the poor man is sickly. There's days and weeks together when poor Billy is covered all over, from the tip to the toe, with boils. You wouldn't find a better man than poor Billy, Adam. He lives like a holy saint, he carries the heavy bass drum for the K. of C. Marching Band, and he's a great worker for the Governor. And yet—boils!" His tiny head shook before the unfairness, the *mystery*, of it all; he added in explanation, "His skin is too weak, they say. He's got very strong blood and the skin is too weak, so there you are. He's been to the very best doctors in the whole entire city and they all tell him the same thing. 'Billy,' they say, 'your blood is too strong for your skin.' But they can do nothing for him. When poor Billy comes in the door the doctors pull in the shingle, as we say. They know when they're licked. There's nothing poor Billy can do but take the bus back home and lie down in his bed and get more boils. That's where I was tonight, over to see him. There he was in bed, all propped up on a couple of old inner-tubes so's he'd be comfortable, reading the funny papers. And hurting with pain all over like he was, Adam, his first words were about the Governor. 'How is the Governor, Ditto?' he said. He knew I'd be in the know, as we say, being so close to the Governor, day in and out. So that's why I was a bit late, Adam," he concluded. "On a merciful errand, as we say. For poor Billy Doyle in the sickbed. Would you remember that, if the matter should happen to come up before the Governor? In his presence, as we say?"

"I'll remember, Ditto." The time had come, he felt, to abandon this subject of poor Billy Doyle and his afflictions; he said, "What about today, Ditto? You must have been a busy man with all your duties."

"Yes yes, Adam, very busy. I and some of the boys were riding around town the whole A.M. and the P.M., as we say. Getting out the vote from one and all. Sick old ladies, shut-ins, crippled-up people with no cars: we took them down to the polls, as per the Governor's wishes. The Governor's very strict about that, Adam. He likes everybody to be a first class A Number 1 American when it comes to voting. Even the blind and the halted, as we say. So I and the boys round them up. Oh yes, Adam, if a man's alive and breathing and he's not nuts, we get him down to the polls. Many's the time I've carried little old men and humpbacks on my own two shoulders up two flights of steps, just so's they could vote for the Governor."

"I see." He wondered if, under such benign circumstances, it was conceivable that the one so benefited might *not* vote for the Governor? He concluded that while it was conceivable, it was not likely; such duplicity could not be the reward for a piggyback ride to the polls.

While he had been talking to Ditto, the room had begun to fill; now there were familiar faces. While none of the leaders had as yet appeared, the subordinates had begun to swarm. Adam saw Cuke Gillen come in; he was leading a long-faced man with an accordion, and a young girl. The girl was perhaps fourteen; she was a squat blonde, and wore a pink party dress that seemed to be made of spun sugar. It was also slightly too small for her. Cuke stopped in front of Adam and Ditto; the long-faced man said, "Hello, Ditto."

"Hello, Tansy," Ditto said. "And this is the little songbird? The pride and joy, as we say?"

"Yeah," the long-faced man said. "Rose." He poked the little girl sharply and said, "Say hello to Mr. Boland, Rose."

On the command, the little girl smiled, immediately and widely; Cuke said crisply, "Okay, Tansy. Go along up there by the coffee jugs and get set up. I'll be with you in a flash."

Obediently, father and daughter went off; Ditto, following them with his eyes, said disapprovingly, "Well well well. I don't know about this, Cuke. Little kids singing songs in the very heart of headquarters on the night of nights! The Governor won't care for that a single solitary iota, as we say. Nobody knows better than me how the Governor feels as per a thing like that!"

"I already asked him," Cuke said. "He said it's O.K., she can sing till she drops as long as she's out of here by the time he gets here."

"Ah well," Ditto said instantly, "a little bit of music never did anyone any harm. The Governor's right — a nice bit of song to cheer up the hearts while we wait for the big news, as we say."

"Tansy Cullen and his kid," Cuke explained to Adam. "Tansy's a bum from way back, but you got to say this for him: he's right down the line for the Governor. Anyway, he thinks the kid can sing, so he comes to me during the campaign and wants to know can she sing at the rallies. Well, she don't sing any better than she looks, so I say nix. Then he goes home and breaks the news to the kid and she falls down on the bathroom floor and starts to foam and bubble at the mouth. A fit, you know? This happens a couple of times more, and the old lady begins to get worried, so Tansy comes to me again and wants to know can't I squeeze the kid in somewhere, just to get him off the hook at home. Well, I figure we can stick her on early tonight, after everybody's voted, and she can't do any harm in front of the boys anyway." He looked at the young entertainer, smiling before the coffee urns. "We might as well get started," he said. In his master-of-ceremonies voice, he added, "Tonight's entertainment, my friends, may not be sweet, but it will be short. I guarantee you that!"

He conferred briefly with the entertainer and her father, then turned again to face the growing crowd. He put up his hands, requesting silence; the request was ignored. He placed two fingers in his mouth and uttered a piercing whistle. This was more effective; heads turned towards him, and the hubbub subsided into a low, mumbling undercurrent of noise.

"Let's have your kind attention, folks!" Cuke said. "Thank you very much. Tonight we have an unexpected treat in store for us. By special request of the Governor, little Rose Cullen of the Twelfth Ward is going to favor us with a song or two. Her program will be very short, but we all know the best things come in small packages, so I'm sure we can all look forward to a grand few minutes of song and give it our very best attention for the very short time it is to be heard." He paused, as if to allow the fact of the program's brief duration to sink in; then he proceeded to list, one by one, the qualifications of the little musician. "Little Rose is only fourteen years of age, is in her last year at the Blessed Sacrament Junior High School, is a member of the Girl Scouts, and is the daughter of our own Tansy Cullen, who will accompany her on the accordion tonight. Let's have a great big hand for the little lady! Let's make her feel happy she came here tonight to entertain us with her short program of songs! Here she is, folks: Little Rose Cullen — in person!"

There was dutiful applause; the accordion sounded; the singer stepped forward and began to entertain. She sang "Trees"; she sang "Oh Danny Boy"; she sang "Roses in Picardy." She sang in a loud, toneless baritone; after the first moments of startled audition, Adam realized that it was the voice of a strangely unmusical middle-aged man. She sang under difficulties, for the noise of the room, which had diminished at Cuke's whistle, had rapidly and inhospitably swelled at the first few notes of song. Cuke, true to the demands of his profession, leaped out before the singer at the end of each selection, summoning reluctant applause; when at last the final song had ended, he hastened to make an additional announcement.

"All right now, folks!" he cried. "Hold your horses for just a minute. Thank you for your generous reception of this little lady with the glorious voice, and now, by way of saying a fond good night to you all, little Rose Cullen is going to sing that fine fighting song we all heard so much of during the last few weeks. Yes folks, in tribute to the finest of them all, to your favorite, my favorite, everybody's favorite, she's going to sing 'The Frank Skeffington Song'!"

It was a song Adam was familiar with; he had heard it often during the campaign. He had observed that it was not a song which left his uncle deeply moved. Only the lyric was original; the melody was that of "Pony Boy." Little Rose Cullen sang it now with fervor:

Skeffington!
Skeffington!
Cast your vote for Skeffington!

He's the man
With the plan
The one for you and me!

He's true blue!
He's for you!
He's the only one!

Hurry up, hurry up, hurry up, and vote
FOR SKEFFINGTON!

During the song, Cuke had rejoined Adam and Ditto. He listened to the deep, inflexible monotone as it pounded its way through song; when it finished he muttered a simple, incredulous blasphemy.

"Well well well," said Ditto comfortably. "A lovely little voice."

"Like water running out of a bathtub," Cuke said, with surprising bitterness. "That's the only sound I've heard could compare with it. The little bitch stepped all over the lyrics!"

This answered a question that had been in Adam's mind for some time; he said, "You wrote the words, Cuke?"

"Yeah," Cuke said. "You mean you couldn't tell?"

Creative pride had been wounded unwittingly; Adam said quickly, "I guessed it, of course. From the professional quality."

"Sure," Cuke said complacently. "I used to do it all the time for the old act. Take an old tune, come up with some snappy new lyrics, and bango! We'd lay 'em in the aisles from coast to coast." More gloomily he added, "There's no use giving anything classy to little crumbs like this and her old man. . . . Aha!" he said, breaking off, his master-of-ceremonies smile appearing magically. "The little lady herself!" For Tansy and his daughter, making ready to leave, had stopped before him to say good-by. "Well well," he said. "Not all ready to say au reservoir so soon, Tansy?"

Tansy nodded. "I got to get the kiddo home, Cuke. She might catch a cold dressed up like this in the night air. She's gotta be careful with her throat, on account of the singin'. Her voice could get all hoarsed up."

"Right you are, Tansy!" said Cuke, snapping his fingers smartly against his collar. "Don't let anything happen to the little lady's voice. Everybody loved her here tonight as you could see."

"A beautiful performance," Ditto said. "I couldn't help but thinking of how sorry the Governor will be when he learns he missed out on it."

"Yeah," said Cuke, more briskly. "Well, so long, Tansy. Abyssinia."

"So long," Tansy said. "And thanks again, Cuke. I sure appreciate it and so does the kiddo. Sorry we have to miss the Governor, but you know how it is. We have to get home on account of the kiddo's throat. Tell the Governor we're with him all the way, Cuke. Tell him I hope he wins by a million, so help me God!"

"Sure, sure," Cuke said. "So long, Tansy."

Father and daughter left the premises. It was not a departure made with ease, for the crowd had continued to grow in the last few minutes, and was now clogging the doorway. Apparently the higher echelon had begun to arrive; Adam saw old John Gorman just inside the door. Characteristically, he was doing no talking; he was listening calmly to the small and intensely voluble group which surrounded him. Men in their shirt sleeves had now slid into position behind the long table; arranging papers and crayons, they were preparing for tabulation. The telephones had begun to ring: first one, then another, then several; then all began to ring together. Someone came over and dragged Cuke off to the far side of the room; Ditto, sighting old pals among new arrivals, drifted away; Adam was alone. He did not mind. He found himself excited; in the last few minutes, the atmosphere had changed. The noise had increased; there was a sensation of mobility: it was as though everyone in the room, no matter how silent or motionless, had become a part of one great whirling activity. Whatever it was that he had come here tonight to see, he realized that it was now beginning.

Skeffington arrived. With Weinberg by his side he came into the room; Adam heard Cuke, ever alert, cry out, "Three cheers for the Governor! The mayor, and still mayor for the next four years to come! Hip-hip-hooray!"

The familiar exuberant cry went up, its double echo following. Skeffington waved in acknowledgment, and waited for silence before he began to speak.

"Good to see you all here tonight," he said. "I want to thank you for your enthusiasm, your confidence, your support. Especially your support at the polls today. I know that some of you couldn't give me all the support you'd have liked to, but we're up against a peculiarly restrictive system: only one vote to a customer this year!"

There were cheers and shouts of laughter; Skeffington continued.

"I know what this must mean to some of you," he said gravely. "We all have our pride; we don't like to be curbed in our work. I see, for example, that Footsie McEntee is here tonight. Limiting Footsie to a single vote on Election Day is like telling a cannibal chief that from now on he can eat only two missionaries a week. Any way you look at it, it works a hardship. I sympathize with you, Footsie!"

He bowed to someone in the crowd; Adam saw a small, elderly man with a wizened monkey face being lifted up in the air by his cheering neighbors. The small man was grinning with delight; he joined his hands together over his head in the traditional gesture of victory.

"One vote or twenty," he crowed, "they're all for you, Frank!"

"Glad to hear it, Footsie," Skeffington said. Addressing himself to the crowd once more, he said, "Footsie's our greatest living proof that the race is to the swift. He could get from one voting booth to another faster than any man in my experience. Twenty-five years ago this fleet and public-spirited citizen won the repeating championship of the city by voting for me seventeen times in one election. He might have done even better but on the eighteenth try he attempted to pass himself off as a Presbyterian divine whose name he'd happened upon on a nearby tombstone. Unfortunately, there's something about Footsie that doesn't suggest the ordained Presbyterian, and he was apprehended by unfriendly elements. But I was always grateful to him for the noble effort, and I'm grateful to him today, as indeed I am to you all. Again, thank you very much. We'll all get together after the returns are in and have a real celebration!"

This met a roar of enthusiasm; Skeffington waved again and began to move through the crowd, slowly, making for his private office in the rear. The short trip took some time; the benign tangle of good wishes, congratulations and handshakes was thicker than usual. He saw his nephew; altering his path to pass by him, he nodded and said, "See you in a few minutes." He kept moving, steadily but without hurry, until he reached the office and was inside.

Here he was joined by Weinberg and Gorman. The office was not a sumptuous one. The thin walls muffled only imperfectly the noise from the outside; the furnishings were few and inexpensive: three folding chairs, grouped around an old wooden desk. On the desk there was a single telephone. This was all: it was not luxury, but it served the purpose.

The three men seated themselves at the desk, and Skeffington lit a cigar. "Well, gentlemen," he said, releasing a slow cloud of smoke, "here we are again. Four years later but still doing business at the same old stand. I find that a comforting thought. Now I suppose we should look into the future a bit." He leaned forward and looked hard at his colleagues. "All right," he said crisply, "let's have it. How are you calling it?"

It was Weinberg who answered first; he did so with no hesitation. "We're in," he said bluntly. "And in bigger than I figured. No landslide, but a good solid plurality. I talked to all the boys, I checked all the figures. It all comes out the same way. The Rover Boy made a hell of a start, but he ran outa gas in the stretch. Just when you come along fast. So it's O.K. And with some to spare." He was moved, now, from flat unemotional speech, to a rare revelation of his admiration for his superior. "You did a hell of a job these last two weeks," he said. "You finished him off, but good. I never seen it done better."

Gorman nodded. "You did, Frank. You did indeed. 'Twas a sight to see, and there's no doubt at all it turned the trick. The little laddo can take down the Pope's picture now and send the dog back to the kennel. He's all done. I hand it to you, Frank. I don't doubt but we'll do better than last time, even."

Skeffington raised his eyebrows. "Well, well," he said slowly. "All the chickens have already been counted before we've even got the eggs. I hardly expected such concerted optimism. If I didn't know you were such prudent, experienced men, I might even accuse you of doing a little wishful thinking."

Weinberg shrugged and regarded Skeffington with expressionless eyes. "O.K.," he said. "So how do you see it?"

"Why," Skeffington said slowly, "I hope I'm a gentleman: I wouldn't dream of disagreeing with you." He chuckled suddenly, and leaned back in his chair, smiling. "Matter of fact, I couldn't agree with you more. I'm delighted to announce that at the present moment, it looks very much as though we're going to have to endure the burden of another four years of public service. A return engagement by popular demand."

Gorman smiled slightly. "It's a terrible task," he said. "D'ye think you might accept, Frank?"

"I'll force myself," Skeffington said. He shifted in his chair, and came forward once more. "However, it does seem as though we've won. As you say, Sam, the boy ran out of gas. He had none of his own to begin with, but they gave him an awful lot to work with. Which made it a bit tough for a while. But I think we've done it all right. And if all the signs mean anything at all, we've done it by a rather comfortable margin. If it turns out we haven't, I suppose I'll have to get out of the prophecy business." He chuckled again and added: "To say nothing of the mayor business. Sam, at this point I'm interested in a few facts and figures. That good solid plurality you spoke of: let's translate it into less general terms. How much?"

Weinberg shrugged again and said, "Eighty, ninety thousand. Maybe more."

"I see. John?"

Gorman said thoughtfully, "I'd say that'd be about right, Frank. Depending on what happens in the Fifteenth Ward. Festus is still damn strong up there. It's a thing you can't tell about at all. Could you sweep half the precincts there, it'd be a sign you might well go over a hundred thousand."

Skeffington shook his head. "Too big," he said. "We're going to do well, but not that well. With things as they are today, God the Father couldn't carry this city with a plurality of a hundred thousand. Or ninety. Possibly eighty, but even that I doubt. Think what it means: it means taking nearly 300 out of 385 precincts. That's a mighty tall order."

"Ah well," Gorman objected, "I wonder is it so impossible after all, Frank! I must say I have very little information about what God the Father might do, but I mind the time we ourselves took more than the 300, and not so long ago at that."

"Longer ago than you might think," Skeffington said. "Time slips by us, John. Unfortunate, but true. It was actually twenty-five years ago, and under rather special circumstances. For one thing, Roosevelt hadn't as yet come along to do his celebrated impersonation of the Great White Father. For another, I ran practically unopposed. The others were hopelessly split up, and the best of them was Silly Jim Casey; I might just as well have been running against Ditto. There were other slight advantages: Footsie McEntee was at the peak of his agile powers, and so were several of his friends. No," he said, smiling, "I mourn the loss of those ideal conditions, but they're gone. Facts are facts. It's my guess that we'll go in, and handily, but with a plurality of about fifty thousand. Or sixty thousand at the outside. Which, I may add, is quite satisfactory. We mustn't be greedy."

"I still say eighty minimum," Weinberg said. "The kid didn't hold up; he faded fast. Down to nothing. So you lose the First Ward, you lose the Seventh, you maybe lose the Fifteenth — and maybe he nibbles away a few precincts along the road. Where else?"

"I hope you're right," Skeffington said, "and I know you're wrong. Although in any case it doesn't matter. If you're in, you're in well: the size of the plurality is like the color of a raincoat in a typhoon. What difference does it make? But we'll soon see who's right." He looked at his watch and said, "The returns will start coming in in about fifteen minutes. Meanwhile, let's do a little work. We have a few rather important details to clear away before the festivities begin."

The three men slid smoothly into organizational matters. Their discussion was brisk, extremely private, and altogether essential to their future well-being. For the next quarter-hour they were very busy indeed.

In the outer room, Adam was moving about, wandering with no particular purpose through the jam of people. The polls had now closed; everyone, like Skeffington, was waiting for the first trickle of results. Adam passed through a hundred different snatches of conversation in his passage; all turned about Skeffington, the campaign, or the memorable campaigns of other years. Occasionally he was halted by a hand reaching out and grabbing him by the sleeve: someone had recognized him as his uncle's nephew; that fact, on this night and in this place, was sufficient basis for congratulation. Occasionally he paused of his own accord to listen to what was being said, or to greet some of the men he had met during recent weeks. He soon discovered that the prevailing mood was one of unqualified optimism: that Skeffington might lose was not a possibility entertained in this room. He continued to wander; in the center of the crowd he came suddenly upon Footsie McEntee. This spry little oldster, raised to an unexpected eminence by Skeffington's direct reference to him, was surrounded by a knot of admirers; in a delirium of joy, he was recalling the great day of infamy at the polls.

"Seventeen times, by gee Joe!" he cried, winking rapidly at the crowd, and beating the air with an emphatic finger. "The Governor had it right on the button: seventeen times it was! And no trolley cars or pushcarts or fancy limousines to lug me around from place to place! All done on me own two leggos! Seventeen times at the polls in the one day, and here's the most marvelous part of it all: *'twas only three o'clock in the afternoon by the time I done it!* Damned if I didn't have the whole blessed day before me still! Oh boys oh boys!" More rapid winks were complemented by a startling sequence of triumphant grimaces. "Well now," he said, "get ready for the sad part, lads. Here it comes. Over I go to Firehouse Number Three, where they was votin' in the Seventh Ward in them days. I'm out to make it *eighteen,* d'ye see, and in the country of the enemy! Well, I slide in, bold as brass, and call out me new name to the man at the books. The Presbretrerian minister name, like the Governor said. 'The Reverend Arthur Barker,' says I. 'What?' says he, lookin' up and givin' me the fish-eye. 'You ain't the Reverend Arthur Barker. You ain't no minister at all!' I give him as good as he sent. 'The hell I ain't!' says I. 'I'm a Presbretrerian minister, that's what I am! And don't call me no liar, you bastard, or you'll get a hell of a smash in your ugly mush!' Well," Footsie said, shaking his head in regretful remembrance, "that's where I made the mistake, d'ye see. I lost me head. They suspicioned it wasn't proper Presbretrerian talk. So the long and the short of it was, lads, I came to a stop at seventeen! But by gee Joe!" he cried. "It was a grand day all the same! Oh, them was the great times for us all. . . ."

Adam moved away from nostalgia up to the coffee urns. He took a cup and filled it; drinking, he began to overhear still another fond evocation of the past. It was not entirely dissimilar to Footsie's. . . .

"All very tame today," one man was saying. "Oh, very tame indeed. I was thinking not so long ago of the time Frank had Father Fahey working the wards for him. Do you remember Father Fahey, I wonder?"

A second man chuckled. "Father Fahey," he said. "Oh, indeed I do. I remember the Father well."

"Father Fahey . . . ?" a third man said, more doubtfully. "I know the name, but I can't place the man. A priest, was he?"

"You might say he was a priest part-time," the first man said. "Frank ordained him for the campaign only; the rest of the year he worked hauling sacks in the post office. He was a chubby little lad with round red cheeks and a big smile. It was one time when Frank was running against Festus he got the idea. He put fat little Fahey in the collar and the black suit and sent him around ringing Protestant doorbells. He'd ask to see the lady of the house. He'd be let in half the time, and then he'd go into the speech. 'Good morning, madam,' he'd say. 'I'm Father Francis Xavier Fahey, of the Jesuit Fathers, up on the hill. I'm calling on you in the interests of good government. The Jesuit Fathers are highly interested in the candidacy of Festus Garvey and we're trying to drum up a little support for him.' Then he'd give her a sneaky smile and a little wink. 'He's a good man for the office,' he'd say. 'By that I mean, madam, that you can depend upon him not to forget who his friends were.' Then he'd wink again and say, 'I think you know what I mean.' Generally, that was all that was needed. After that you could chill a side of beef in the room, and Father Fahey was out on the sidewalk in a minute and a half, flat. But he'd done the job."

The third man whistled in appreciation of this bold, ingenious arrangement. "By God!" he said. "That was a good one. And would she vote for Frank after that, do you think?"

"Maybe not," said the first man. "But you can be sure of one thing: she wouldn't vote for Garvey."

"There was the Reverend Mr. Payne, too," the second man

said reminiscently. "Do you remember him? He was the other end of the stick from Fahey. I don't remember rightly what his real name was; he was a stranger. Anyway, in he'd come, just as the campaign got started: a skinny bald feller with a frozen puss. Frank would stick him in a gray suit and turn him loose on the Irish. He'd rap on the door with his stick, and when herself 'd finally come, red-faced and mad from the kitchen and the kids, he'd tell her he was the Reverend Mr. Payne from the Methodist Church. 'We Methodists are all for Mr. Garvey, madam,' he'd say. 'He's promised to give us the many rights we've been deprived of by Skeffington. We hope to be able to count on your vote and that of your husband in our behalf.' Slammo! would go the door, and the Reverend Mr. Payne would be out in the cold again, and damn lucky he hadn't got a skillet across his skull. And of course Frank would be in two more votes."

"By God!" said the third man admiringly. "That was another good one, all right." Then, considering, he seemed to find it less admirable; he said deprecatingly, "Ah, but sure he would have had them two votes in the first place."

"Maybe he would," said the second man. "Maybe he would indeed. I don't doubt it. But what a lovely bit of insurance!" Turning to the first man, he asked, "Whatever happened to Father Fahey in the end, Dan?"

"He died of the distemper," the first man said. "A mad dog bit him in the post office and he caught the distemper and died. Poor Fahey! Roman collar to dog collar." He chuckled heartlessly and said, "Ah, those were the days, though. It's very tame today. Very tame indeed. . . ."

Footsie the false Presbyterian, Father Fahey, the Reverend Mr. Payne — how much of it, Adam wondered, was true? In the past few weeks he had discovered with what surprising ease legend surrounded Skeffington; it was virtually impossible to disentangle the thin hard fact from the elaborate embroidery of the years. Certainly in his own association with his uncle he had seen no evidence of any such essentially shameless manipulations, yet at the same time, there was a cockeyed, hilarious quality to their shamelessness that suggested rather strongly the presence of a familiar hand. Someday, he resolved, when the right moment presented itself, he would ask his uncle about Father Fahey. . . .

A light and playful hand tapped his shoulder; a light and artificial voice sounded in his ear. "Dear boy," it said, "how *good* to see you! Will you recognize an old associate, I wonder?"

"Burbank!" Adam said. He was surprised and pleased by the encounter; he had not seen his former officemate since the day of his leaving the paper. Apparently the change had been a happy one, for Burbank, in middle age, had acquired a new radiance. His brittle little body was gay in an ensemble of chocolate brown; he wore a Kelly green waistcoat, a dashing Tyrolean hat. From the breast pocket of his jacket drooped the voluminous and vivid folds of a matching green handkerchief; a light cane, held with an air of negligent elegance, completed his equipment. He was smiling; it was clear that the euphoria of departure day had persisted. Adam said warmly, "It's very good to see you, Burbank. You look fine."

"Not too bad, I think," Burbank said, surveying himself with some complacency. "A trifle flamboyant, perhaps, but then one must keep the nature of the evening in mind. And you look fine, dear boy, but then you always do, don't you? You are *resistant* to care. I, on the other hand, am not. I was decaying visibly in that dreadful journalistic swamp until your dear uncle stepped in and rescued me. How is my former employer, by the way? Prostrate, I trust."

"With grief, Burbank. Ever since you went away. How's the new job? All expectations met, I hope?"

"Oh, much more than merely 'met,' dear boy. 'Exceeded' is the word. Your dear uncle is among the most generous of living men. And then of course you must remember that I find it a labor of love. You may have noticed the series of recent broadsides against our dear Mr. Force? Although 'broadsides' is hardly the correct word — I like to think of them as something just a bit more subtle. A touch of the poniard, the delicate, poisonous traceries. You've noticed them?"

"Yes." He remembered having seen, somewhere among the vast accumulation of campaign literature, a series of attacks on Amos Force which had dripped with venom; he had suspected the authorship of this at the time. He said, "Yes, I've noticed them, Burbank."

"All my work," said Burbank modestly. "Oh, I *have* done other good things to earn my keep — rather neat and effective little jabs at Mother Garvey, and, of course, at our dear Candidate McCluskey himself — but none, I think, had quite the *feeling* of the Force series, if you know what I mean. *That* was Burbank writing at the top of his form. And that is really why I am here tonight. Here," he said, looking about him with obvious distaste, "among these cigar-smoking, anecdotal yahoos. I am here purely in the spirit of revenge. In short, dear boy, you see before you Burbank the Tiger, positively *thirsting* for the kill!"

Then Burbank, too, was convinced of victory; it was unanimous. Adam said suddenly, "Burbank, you're an old hand at these election-night affairs. Explain something to me."

"Gladly, dear boy," Burbank said promptly. "The appeal to Burbank the Authority — I find myself completely disarmed. Proceed."

"It's about this universal optimism. Now, quite naturally, I think my uncle's going to win. That doesn't mean much because, first, he is my uncle, second, I'm partisan, and third, I don't really know much of anything about local elections. But I know I want him to win, I know he feels he's going to win, and I know that most of the pre-election polls and the commentators seem to agree with him. What puzzles me, though, is that everyone here tonight seems to take it for granted that he's going to win; nobody seems even aware that anything else could happen."

"Including, of course, Burbank," Burbank said. "Is this a reproof, dear boy, of Burbank the Sanguine?"

"No, I'm still working on Burbank the Authority. And what I want to know from him is whether this pervasive confidence is really the genuine article, or whether it's just something that has to be worn for the occasion. In other words, is everyone really so sure my uncle's going to win, or is it simply that in a candidate's headquarters on election night all the boys come in with compulsory high spirits? For example, what's happening over at McCluskey's headquarters just about now? Are they confident too, would you say?"

"Dear boy, your uncle *has* made a convert, hasn't he? No matter. I should say that the optimism is *entirely* genuine. As you suggest, there is always a certain assumed buoyancy of spirit at these little gatherings. But the experienced observer — and here, dear boy, I must modestly point to myself — can quite easily detect the false note, and I can assure you there are no false notes here tonight. Everyone is completely convinced that your uncle is to be re-elected. I can tell you that if there were the slightest doubt of the outcome tonight, this room and the sidewalk outside would not be *crawling* with people. Oh, the faithful would report, to be sure: they always do. But the scavengers — and they are rather more numerous, dear boy, than you might think — would not. They take no chances, you see. They report *en masse* only when the sure thing is at hand. They do not begin to circle until the footsteps stagger and the body starts to sink upon the sand. They are rarely wrong, and, dear boy, they are here in force tonight. And as for your final question: No, I do *not* think that hearts are high in the McCluskey camp. Because, dear boy, they have been reading the signs for the last week or so: they know which way they point. And now, tonight, the scavengers are here, not there; rest assured, dear boy, that their absence has been duly noted. Well!" he said brightly, "so much for instruction. Were you enlightened? Perhaps not: Burbank the Didactic is not necessarily Burbank at his best."

"No, no, it was quite enlightening." Surprisingly enough, he felt easier in his mind after listening to the words which the little former contest editor had spoken so knowledgeably. There was comfort to be found, he reflected, in the notion of the inerrant scavenger; he supposed it made some sense. "You have a talent for instruction, Burbank," he said. "You should do something with it; it may be your true vocation."

"Thank you, but no. I have discovered my niche, dear boy. It is with your uncle. I am satisfied with that. I look forward to a *most* rewarding association in the months to come. I break no confidence, dear boy, when I tell you that I am definitely included among your uncle's plans for the future. We had, in fact, a most satisfactory little talk about it only the other day."

"Good. I'm glad, Burbank." He recalled his own fears of some weeks ago when his old officemate had decided to cut the ties that bound him alike to humiliation and security; he recalled too Skeffington's brief and casual promise that all would go well with this friend of his nephew. Apparently the promise had been observed, and he added, "I'm glad that everything's worked out this way for you."

"Thank you, dear boy. I know you are. Even when you teased poor old Burbank most, I always somehow felt that at bottom you wished him well. In the dark days, you were Burbank's friend." He inclined his head towards Adam: it was a grave, almost ducal gesture, somehow implying that this old and isolated friendship would one day bring its own reward. He glanced at his watch, a golden baguette on his left wrist. "And now," he said, "at any moment your uncle should emerge. The moment, dear boy, is at hand. The polls have closed; the returns will be coming in. Just *listen* to those telephones ring! A sound to annoy at times, dear boy, but tonight sweet music to Burbank's ears!"

The telephones were ringing in concert; Skeffington had not appeared. Adam said, "How long will it be, do you think, before anything definite is known?"

"Now that," Burbank said, "is the poser. It is difficult to say, dear boy. Of course it is infinitely faster now than it was in the old days, thanks to the voting machines, but theoretically it could take hours. If it should be a very close race, that is. If, on the other hand, there should be a landslide, we should know in less than an hour. But those are the extremes. Speaking practically, I should say that for a nice, neat, *substantial* victory, of the kind we may expect for your uncle this evening, it should be somewhere between two and three hours. After which, dear boy, we are free to go home to beddy-bye. I shall fall straight to sleep and dream *blissfully* of dear Mr. Force. And you, on the other hand — Ah!" he said, breaking off — "Here is your uncle now, at precisely the strategic moment. The conquering hero, in a word, comes. Flanked, inevitably, by the ever-faithful two. Has it ever occurred to you, dear boy, that there are times when the good Messrs. Weinberg and Gorman seem just a wee bit *too* adhesive? I see by your face that it has not, but then of course you are infinitely more charitable than Burbank the Waspish. No matter; let us watch the procession to the post, as it were."

Skeffington, with Gorman and Weinberg, had come out of the private office, and was walking towards the long table, the blackboard, and the telephones. As he advanced, two men seated behind the table, rose, turned to the blackboard, and began to chalk in the first reported figures. It was at this moment that Adam, for the first time since he had entered the room, became aware of tension. It was impossible to ignore; despite the general optimism, the atmosphere of the room had changed appreciably and quickly. All noise had subsided; the shuffling, aimless crowd-movements had ceased.

At the top of the room Skeffington, seemingly unaffected by the shift of mood, continued his steady progress to the head of the table. He reached it, and just as he did so, one of the men at the blackboard pulled his chalk carelessly across the slate; there was a piercing, scraping squeal. The whole room winced; Skeffington turned to the offender and said casually, "You're disturbing the class, Danny. I guess you'll have to stay after school and clap erasers."

It was a mild enough pleasantry, but it did the job. There was a loud laugh; the tautness, which had flashed out swiftly when the formal business of reckoning began, now just as swiftly retreated and disappeared. The mumble of conversation picked up once more; if it was not as insistent as before, this was perhaps because now everyone, Skeffington included, gave the major part of his attention to the all-important blackboard.

Adam watched the board at first with interest, then with some concern. He realized that any such early tabulation was surely inconclusive, that from it nothing of significance could be deduced. Still, it had produced two developments for which he had not been prepared and which he found disconcerting. The first was that McCluskey, not Skeffington, had jumped into an early lead. The second was that this lead, far from diminishing, was increasing and increasing rather rapidly. Adam eyed the mounting score: with more than two thousand votes reported, his uncle was behind at least five to one. He wondered uneasily if this was the way victory began: had this early sweep been altogether anticipated? He glanced at his uncle. Skeffington was regarding the blackboard, his face as imperturbable as ever; he turned and with a slight smile said something to those directly around him; there was another burst of laughter. Clearly, this was not a sound born of alarm.

It was Burbank who provided the explanation.

"Dear boy," he said, "history repeats itself. The Ward Seven votes lead all the rest: they are so *punctual* up there. And so consistent. They are always solidly against your uncle, they are always the first to report. These first few moments after the polls close is always a delicious time for them; they savor every second of it. Because, you see, in just a *very* few minutes more, the returns will be coming in from those nasty, unruly, unwashed wards — and then, dear boy, the pendulum will swing, never to return. That is why, at this very moment, and underneath that oh-so-majestic calm, your dear uncle is positively bubbling with joy!"

It was not too far from accuracy: Skeffington, watching the vote pile steadily against him, was amused. In all his years of campaigning, he had never succeeded in denting the hard shell of the Seventh Ward; fortunately, the failure had not been serious. The ward was the smallest in the city; he had usually been able to win handily without it. Now, while he continued to campaign within its borders, he did so largely out of a mischievous desire to infuriate the natives; he had not seriously included it in his plans for many years. And so, as the adverse total continued to soar, he watched, untroubled; with considerable satisfaction he anticipated the pleasant turn which the next quarter-hour would bring.

In his watching he was interrupted by a not entirely unexpected visitor. On these election nights his son could be counted upon to make a brief appearance; he did so now.

"Hello, Dad," he said pleasantly. "Well, this is the big night, right?"

"Right," Skeffington said. These rare public father-and-son meetings were not easy for him. He knew that, among politicians, the boy was regarded as something of a figure of fun; he was conscious now that neighboring eyes and ears were alert and curious.

He said agreeably, "Glad you could get down. Will you be staying awhile?"

"No," his son said. "No, I don't think so, Dad. You see, I have some friends waiting outside for me now, and we have to drive along and pick up some other people. You see, the Bop Room is re-opening tonight, and I promised to be there."

The Bop Room? thought Skeffington; aloud he said, "I see. Nice place?"

"Oh, sure. Or at least it used to be before it closed. One of the best places in town. You remember the old Nut Room, Dad?"

"Only vaguely," Skeffington said. "Well, have a nice time. Glad you dropped by."

"O.K., Dad. I just wanted to come and see that everything was O.K., and to wish you good luck." He paused to gaze around the room; he looked up at the blackboard, his happy, incurious eye passing swiftly over the total massed against his father. "Well," he said cheerfully, "everything seems to be shaping up fine, right?"

"Right. Come in a little later if you have time."

"Sure," his son said blithely. "Sure, Dad. Well, so long."

"So long."

Francis Jr. went off through the crowd; Skeffington returned to the blackboard. After a few moments he was able to so discipline his thoughts as to be able to attend to it properly. What he saw was encouraging: even in the short interval provided by his son's visit, the columns of figures had begun to shift slightly. The Ward Seven vote was now slowing down; the first edges of the swell from John Gorman's big ward were creeping in. Skeffington noted the development immediately: others in the room, hardy veterans at these election nights, saw it almost as soon: this gradual alteration of balance, always so difficult to perceive in these first transitional minutes. Still others, less experienced or less acute, saw it too, as the weight on the Skeffington side grew more conspicuous, and in a very short time the trend was obvious to all. The room became livelier, more boisterous; the shift had been expected, yes, but its actual arrival, confirming all faith and banishing the small doubt, was the signal for rejoicing. The swing was on: what was happening was recognized by everyone.

What happened next was not recognized by everyone. Characteristically, it was Skeffington himself who caught the first sign. The Ward Seven tabulation had stopped; the vote from Gorman's ward continued to yield its comforting harvest; one by one, the other wards had begun to declare themselves. Now the blank spaces on the blackboard — one for each precinct of each ward — received their first chalked markings; Skeffington examined them swiftly with a sharp, professional eye. He had hardly begun the examination when he stopped short. Like an engineer, powering at full speed down a long-familiar stretch of track, he was jolted from routine by the faint, half-hidden gleam of an unexpected light. Instantly he retraced his steps; he saw at once that he had not been wrong. The light was there, tiny but unmistakable; exactly what it meant — if indeed it meant anything — Skeffington could not as yet tell. It was nothing more than a small return from a single precinct, so small as to be almost negligible — yet it had stopped him. It had flashed out to catch his experienced eye; immediately he had seen that something was wrong. The precinct from which the return had come had never been a doubtful one; as far back as Skeffington could remember, he had always carried it comfortably. And, moreover, he was carrying it now, although — and this was what had brought him up so sharply — the margin of comfort was lacking. In this small, reliable precinct, the race was proving to be surprisingly close; he was barely squeezing by. In itself, this was not disturbing. The small, erratic fluctuation, isolated and unexplainable, was not a rarity in municipal elections, and furnished no cause for alarm. Nevertheless, it was there; it had not been expected; it was unwelcome, and it might — just possibly — be dangerous. Only a novice or a fool would have overlooked the possibility, and Skeffington was neither. His eye ran down the length of the board, taking in each new figure; it was a swift but complete survey to determine whether the fluctuation was part of a pattern, or whether it was in fact a freak. But it was still too early to tell. No adverse trend had been established, that much was clear; on the other hand, the returns from two of the precincts, while not bad, had left him far from reassured. He turned from the board and glanced casually around the room; the look told him that what he had seen had not been seen by others. There was universal cheer, spirits ran high; therefore, Skeffington thought, they see only the clear horizon. He had a thorough understanding of the minor politicians, the workers, the officeseekers, who surrounded him; he knew that they were loyal but apprehensive. Their total dependence upon favors from above had not left them with any great courage. He knew what would happen if, suddenly, through the room, there should drift the first faint scent of possible defeat; he could see the clouded, worried eyes as laughter died. Undoubtedly good men and true but, he thought sardonically, their spirits a little bit lacked staying power: ebullience could be counted upon to wither at the first whisper of disaster.

But had disaster whispered here? He doubted it; still, it was hardly the time for doubts: he had to be sure. He looked out into the room again, and this time he looked specifically at Gorman and Weinberg; he saw that they were looking at him. He knew that, as he had expected, they too had noted the flaw. He gave a short, barely observable nod, and turned back to the board; the two men moved slowly and unobtrusively from their positions, and soon were at his side.

"Sam," he said in a low voice, "go into the office and get on the phone. Talk to Teddy, Charlie Ferrino, and Mike Gallaher. Don't talk to anybody else; stay there till you get them but get them fast. Find out what's going on. If anything."

Weinberg went off, wordlessly. In the same low voice Skeffington said, "What's your guess?"

"I don't know, Frank. I don't like it much," Gorman said candidly, "I'm not a great man for the little surprises. Though I don't know is this one anything at all." His old blue eyes passed up and down the board thoughtfully; he said in his mild voice, "It could be just the one precinct. Still, I don't like the soft look of those two spots in 3 and 13. You've noticed them, of course?"

Skeffington nodded. "I have. I've also noticed," he said, "that they seem to be getting softer. Again, that doesn't necessarily mean much: the one in 3 is a wobbler anyway; the other's in Patsy Tiernan's territory. It wouldn't be the first time Patsy'd fallen down; he's getting too old. Nevertheless, I agree it could be trouble; we won't know until Sam gets back. Meanwhile — "

But he was interrupted. "Well well well, Governor," said a voice. Skeffington looked up from the urgent, private discussion into the beaming, tiny moon of Ditto's face. He controlled his exasperation; it was important that Ditto, above all, should be unaware of concern in high places: the fat man's capacity for dissolving into a boneless and peculiarly communicable alarm was all too well known to him.

"Why, Ditto," he said pleasantly, "the evening's now official. I always look upon your appearance as a symbol of good luck on these election nights."

The fat man radiated his happiness. "I do my very best, Governor," he said. "Yes yes yes. I and the boys want to give you all the happy felicitations on this night of nights, Governor. We're all looking forward to that grand and gorgeous victory when you slip McCluskey the mitten, as per the people's choice, as we say. Oh yes yes! I and the boys are over there by the door there, and I'll go back there on the double time, and get the boys so they can come over here and tell you how they feel in their own identical words, as we say. Oh yes, I'll — "

"Ditto," said Skeffington. "I'll tell you what I want you to do. I want you to go back to the door, to stay there, and to keep the boys with you. Tell them I said so. I have an important job for you. I want you all to keep your eyes peeled for the radio and television people, who'll be arriving sometime this evening; I want you and the boys to be a kind of reception committee, to clear the way for them and for their equipment when they get here. You'll be in charge. Is that clear?"

"Oh yes yes, Governor. Clear as clear can be, as we say. I'll take the matter into my own two personal hands, Governor, and I — "

"Good," Skeffington said. "You'd better get along now and get started. It's a big job, and an important one."

Ditto hurried back to the door. It was at the other end of the room, far distant from Skeffington and the blackboard; the useless assignment would keep Ditto and the others from making nuisances of themselves. He looked towards the door of the private office: the reappearance of Weinberg was what mattered now. Even as he looked the door opened: Weinberg emerged and came towards him. He came along at his normal, half-shambling pace: a slumping figure with a weary face. From his movements and his appearance it was possible to deduce absolutely nothing. He joined Skeffington and Gorman at the head of the long table; in this position they were slightly apart from the others and were permitted a measure of privacy. The meeting could arouse no suspicion; it was Skeffington's habit, on these occasions, to confer frequently and alone with his two chief aides. He said now, quietly, "Well, Sam?"

"I dunno," Weinberg said. "Something's up, and it ain't good. I don't figure it yet, but I tell you this: I think we got trouble."

"All right," Skeffington said impatiently. "We've got trouble. Where? What kind of trouble? Come on, Sam, out with it. Fast."

In swift, blunt terms, Weinberg told his story; it was not a comforting one. He had talked with the three men; he had discovered that they had been on the point of calling Skeffington — always a bad sign. There was both confusion and concern in some of the ward headquarters. They were some minutes ahead of the main Skeffington headquarters in receiving their own returns, and as the results came off the machines, it was apparent that McCluskey was revealing unexpected strength. He was piling up respectable totals in a number of areas considered inviolable; in several marginal precincts he was actually leading. What it all meant, whether this was or was not the beginning of a turning tide, was not quite clear; the next half-hour would tell. At the moment, however, this much could surely be said: the leak that Skeffington had noted originally was far from being isolated; there had been disquieting break-throughs all along the line.

"I tell you what," Weinberg said, concluding. "I think maybe you oughta talk to them yourself."

"I intend to," Skeffington said grimly. "Right now. Come along."

With Weinberg and Gorman close behind, he walked rapidly to the office. He made no attempt now to disguise the note of urgency, and he knew that the ever-watchful eyes of those about him, observing the haste of his passage, would darken with alarm; inevitably, the wondering would begin, the whispers would rise. He did not care. In the last few moments the preservation of mass morale had become a matter of secondary concern; what was required immediately was a definition of his own position. He had to know exactly where he stood; as he walked, he considered the possibilities quickly and without confusion. His mind was absolutely clear: the thoughts streamed through his head in a cold orderly sequence; he balanced one against the other. In the office, he snatched up the telephone and made a half-dozen calls to key points; in each call he snapped a series of abrupt questions and quickly cut short any sustained reply. He was after the bare bones of information, and by the sixth call he had them.

He put down the phone and said, "All right. Now at least we've got some sort of general picture. It's not a pretty one. We've got trouble: you were right, Sam. I should say reasonably serious trouble. The boy's begun to pull in about thirty precincts, and widely scattered ones at that. In a couple of them he's started to snowball."

"Where's he doing it, Frank?" Gorman said quickly.

Skeffington reeled off the list of defecting precincts. "Now," he said, "if those are all, it's not so bad. Gallaher thinks they are all; he thinks the boy's about played out. I think Gallaher's a fool. From the location of the precincts, it's fairly clear that this whole thing is no mere wave in a chamber pot. It has an excellent chance of spreading; and if it does, we've got one hell of a battle on our hands."

Gorman agreed; he said thoughtfully, "I'd say it'd swell before it shrinks, that's sure. It damn well could hinge on how the East End holds. You've heard nothing from Cavanaugh or Paddy Montgomery?"

Skeffington shook his head. "No. It's too soon." The East End — or a large part of the East End — was the single section of the city where the voting machine had not yet been introduced; as a consequence, the tabulation would be slow and the returns delayed. He said, "We should be safe enough over there, although after what's happened so far, I'd hate to guarantee it. Nothing's running according to the book." He spoke calmly, and this was a tribute to the firmness with which he held himself, for when he had received the news over the telephone, he had been more than surprised; he had literally been stunned. He had wanted his position defined; it had been defined with a brutal clarity. He knew now exactly how desperate it was. And, faced with the fact, he could arrive at no reasonable explanation for it; he had been hit especially hard because he had been completely unprepared for the blow. Too shrewd and too experienced to be guilty of overconfidence, he had come to his headquarters tonight secure in the knowledge that he had kept his guard up, that he had taken every necessary precaution, that no stray sign of danger was to be seen. And yet the cyclone had struck, rushing out of nowhere, preceded by no warning; he knew now, better than anyone else, that in the face of this development his chances of winning comfortably had vanished, and his chances of winning at all were no better than even. If that, he thought grimly; over the years he had had some experience with these sudden, insane, rising winds: he knew their power. And this wind, obviously, was still on the rise; he did not attempt to fool himself into believing that its force had begun to sag. The question was: how, *how* had it started? It was a question to which he had no answer at all; at the moment, it made no difference. He said steadily, "Very well. We may be all right. If the East End holds, we surely will. In any case there's just one thing we can do now and that's to sit tight and see what happens. Not a very aggressive course, but at the moment we haven't a great many alternatives."

John Gorman's tranquil old face was now troubled; one thumb softly and ceaselessly massaged the side of his nose. This serene old man, who had thought that life could hold no fresh surprises, had been surprised tonight. He was faced with something he did not understand, and he had a distrust of mysteries. "It's a very queer sort of business indeed," he muttered. "How does it come we got not so much as a hint of it? Somebody fell down on the job, right enough. And a damned sight more than just the one somebody, it looks like." Baffled, afloat on strange waters, the old man, normally so self-sufficient, now turned to his one authority for the answer; he asked, "D'ye have any idea who, Frank? Or why?"

Skeffington's right hand moved in a slight gesture of impatience. "No. Does it matter? At this point, that is? Obviously there were slip-ups all along the line. All right. We can attend to them later. What matters now — and the only thing that matters now — is what's going to happen in spite of the slip-ups. We can play parlor games and fix responsibilities when this is all over."

Weinberg had risen. Anger over probable betrayals had driven him from slouching immobility; he walked restlessly across the limited floor-space of the small office, his dull, lackluster eyes now bright with fury. "Those bastards!" he said. "O.K. So we fix responsibilities later. So what do we do now? Sit around on our keesters and wait for the moon to come up? Or do we go out and try to fix this mess?"

For just an instant Skeffington's temper flashed through. "Fix it with what?" he said savagely. "What would you suggest? Sticking plaster? Staples? How in hell can you do any fixing at this stage of the game? Everybody's voted. *It's all over.* Do you think we ought to bomb the polls? Assassinate McCluskey? For the love of Christ, wake up to realities!" He exhaled sharply and shook his head; when he spoke again it was in a different tone. "No," he said. "Forget it, Sam; I didn't mean to chew your head off. I know how you feel; I feel the same way myself. But the thing is — and of course you know it, if you'll only stop to think about it — that we're not in a position to fix anything or anybody right now. And it couldn't be of less importance at this moment. First things first, Sam: we have to wait and see what happens. With a decent break, we'll make out all right in spite of everything. Once we do, we'll take care of our defecting friends, whoever they are; I can promise you that. But for the moment," he said, rising, "we wait. Sam, you'd better wait in here. I want someone by that phone every minute. Get in touch with Cavanaugh and Paddy; tell them I want every bit of information they get the second they get it. Call Teddy; tell him I said to get over here. Meanwhile," he said, his hand on the door, "I'll wait outside, along with the faint of heart. I imagine they're already posted by the wailing wall, ready to throw a little dirt on the lowered coffin.

I'd better impress upon them the fact that they're slightly premature; we're not quite ready for the funeral yet. Sam, come out as soon as you have any dope."

Weinberg nodded; long in the service of his employer, he did not harbor injury. Skeffington and Gorman left the office; in the outer room, as Skeffington had predicted, the spirit of the gathering had plunged. The figures on the blackboard had now caught up with those received by Skeffington over the phone; they had had the anticipated effect. Skeffington pushed quickly through the subdued and murmuring throng; roosting upon his coattails, some of them for decades, they now had visions of the disappearance of their perch. All eyes turned to him for reassurance; as he walked along, he spoke briefly, jocularly; it was virtually a chain of brisk, heartening comments all the way to the blackboard. Reaching it, he turned and, addressing the crowd, said: "Gentlemen, it begins to look as though we could have used Footsie to advantage today!" Again, it was the shock tactic, the unexpected admission; there was some laughter, and he said: "However, I've just done a little checking around the city, and I find that our blackboard reports are a bit misleading; I think in a very short time you'll see an improvement in the overall picture. You have to remember that old saw: It's always darkest just before the dawn. Most of you, I think, have been with me to see a good many dawns come in in the past. It's been an agreeable custom; I have no intention of discontinuing it now. And so I invite you all to join me: let's all gather round and watch this latest dawn together! I think I can promise you it's going to be a good one!"

Artificial respiration, he thought, of a rather extreme kind: it was pumping the hearts back into the corpses. Still, he saw at once that it had been effective, that the atmosphere had lightened with the buoyant words. These men of easy vacillation were not confirmed in their despair; they were eager for the note of hope, and once it had been sounded they had responded readily. Something of the former clamor arose; they pressed closer to the blackboard and, with their leader, prepared to watch the sun come up.

The wait — for Skeffington, at least — was not long. It was all too mercilessly brief. Before a quarter of an hour had passed, he knew that he was beaten. With an agonizing vividness he saw exactly what the end would be: the promised sunrise would be bitter.

For now the signs were there for him to read; as he watched the new figures chalked in upon the board, he read their meaning clearly, and once again, in advance of all others in the crowded room, he sensed misfortune — this time, not its possibility, but its confirmation. And while the clamor rose on newfound hope; while Footsie circled, demonstrating unfaded agility to all who would attend; while Cuke, surrounded by confreres, remembered one last-minute anecdote in dialect; while Ditto, with pompous zeal, arranged and rearranged the reception committee which was to meet the television crew; while still more reminiscenses of the great old days of "Father" Fahey gave rise to laughter; while Adam, hard by Burbank, joined with all others in either forthright or surreptitious contemplation of the board — while all this went on, Skeffington stood erect, impassive, and perfectly still: the unique possessor of the knowledge that he was a defeated man.

Out of the corner of his eye he saw Gorman stir suddenly, and he knew that his old associate had read the signs, too. He heard the office door open; he sensed, rather than saw, the swift approach of Weinberg, bringing with him the news that, at worst, would be additionally unpleasant — at best, utterly useless. For the East End, which just a few minutes before was of such vast significance, now no longer mattered at all. With or without it, Skeffington was beaten, for the signs he had read did not point merely to defeat; they pointed to cataclysm. Everywhere, in all precincts, the McCluskey totals were on the move; of all the wards in the city, only John Gorman's held firm in the Skeffington camp. Throughout the room the loyal supporters watched these soaring figures but, mindful of the words of their leader, they were waiting eagerly for the turn to come; only Skeffington — and now Gorman — knew that there would be no turn. For he was not simply to be beaten; he was to be buried, buried under a great, roaring, sliding avalanche of votes which at any moment now would come sliding down for everyone to see. It was the thing of which he had not even dreamed: it was the McCluskey landslide.

It was unthinkable, unimaginable, and yet — it was happening. He closed his eyes. When he opened them, he turned to look at Weinberg and Gorman; now, as earlier that evening, the eyes of the three men met. They shared the secret; in the silent, strong, almost tactile communion, the two aides seemed to be waiting for a direction, a word, a response of any kind. At last, in a low, private voice, Skeffington spoke.

"No comment," he said, simply, slowly. "No comment at all."

The look held for an instant, then the three men turned from each other and returned to the blackboard. It was safe, neutral territory; the figures were accumulating, the chalked digits now pouring in to the McCluskey columns, but the three men paid them no attention. The exact dimensions of the disaster to come was of no importance; each man thought now only of the terrible, unforeseeable fact of the disaster itself, and how it could conceivably have come to be.

It was a mystery to Weinberg, but he saw it primarily as a matter of betrayal. There had been, obviously, sell-outs all along the line: people who had been trusted had been bought by flattery, promises of money, of political advantage. Who they were, how many they might be, why they should have sold out now and never before, were questions as yet unanswered; Weinberg had no doubt that the answers would be found. This ruthless, efficient, dedicated man had a nose for duplicity. Throughout his long association with Skeffington, he had made it his prime concern; he had moved with a tough, skeptical spirit among men of another breed, men whose loyalty he continually suspected because it was not as fierce and hard as his own. As a result he had often uncovered treachery where it had not been thought to exist. But he had not done so now. In this biggest crisis of all he had scented nothing, and now he saw that it had been there, greater and more dangerous than ever before. He had, then, failed: the awareness filled him with pain. For his loyalty to Skeffington was not an impersonal one. Skeffington was not merely his boss, his general; Skeffington was his friend. To Weinberg, forever conscious of his own apartness, of the fact that, although he had worked hand-in-hand and over the years with these people, he was unattractive to and unloved by most of them, this meant much. He knew that Skeffington respected him, trusted him, and — strangest of all — was genuinely fond of him. It was because of this last feeling that the cold little man did not simply respect and admire his leader: he worshiped him. And so the conviction that he had failed him now left him more than pained and disappointed; it left him crushed in miserable self-reproach.

The defeat was a mystery, too, to Gorman. Saddened, he saw it not as a betrayal, but as an organizational breakdown. Somehow, and everywhere, there had been slip-ups; the boys had not done the job, the leaders had not held their wards in hand. It was the infiltration of laziness, coupled with the relaxation of the reins: all along the line, they had not been kept on their toes. Discipline, the very heart of the successful political machine, had somehow been allowed to go to pot — else how account for the penetration by the foe into areas which had been sacred ever since he could remember? Carelessness had been the flaw, and although he could not understand how so much carelessness could have arisen simultaneously on so many fronts, or how the discipline could have dissolved so suddenly and without the slightest warning, he had no doubt that this was the answer. For in his own ward there had been no carelessness, no relaxation — he had seen to that, as always — and the ward had remained faithful, the only one to do so. In fact, it occurred to him now, he alone had emerged unscathed from the chaos; in his own demesne he was still enthroned, McCluskey or no McCluskey. It was a reflection from which he was able to draw singularly little comfort. For while he was in, Skeffington was out, and between this taciturn old ward leader and the gifted man he had chosen to serve, there was a rich and extraordinary bond. Gorman, contemplating the savage defeat of his old friend, was overcome by a rare, deep melancholy. He had seen Skeffington defeated before; he had seen him bound back with an astonishing, unparalleled, flashing vigor; but now he was forced to a sad home truth: Skeffington was no longer young. Like himself, Skeffington was in old age — and could a man in his seventies, even one such as

Skeffington, come driving back hard from what was not just a defeat, but the most devastating defeat of his entire career? Gorman hoped so. He hoped so with a sudden, bursting passion which would have astonished all who thought they knew this withdrawn, silent old man. And as he hoped, he glanced at Skeffington, standing graven-faced and pale just a few feet from him. John Gorman was a realist; with a heavy heart, he concluded that his hope would remain a hope, and nothing more.

But most of all, the defeat was a mystery to Skeffington. Less limited than his colleagues, he could not bring himself to ascribe the catastrophe to the simple, single cause. He had thought immediately of the possibility of betrayal, of a failure in his organization; he had dismissed the thought. He knew that neither singly nor in combination could they have occasioned his defeat. Undoubtedly they had been there, but they had always been there, and what had beaten him now was not something old, but something altogether new. What it might be, he simply did not know. He tried desperately to think it through, but it was no use. His mind would not work properly. It churned away, but its edge had been dulled by the disaster; it bit into nothing, it merely raced by images and impressions, bouncing off them, assimilating nothing and arriving nowhere. In a kind of narcosis, he could grasp solidly only the one fact: he had ridden into the election a confident man, backed by four years of his most effective administration; in the twinkling of an eye, he had been knocked out of office, repudiated overwhelmingly, subjected to humiliation which he had never thought possible. And always the question returned: *Why?* Why the debacle? . . . All through these stunned minutes he came no closer to the solution; he stood staring straight ahead at the board, instinct and habit controlling him, warning him to be still, to do nothing, to make no gesture yet. In a few minutes, he would have to acknowledge publicly, to the room, to the city, to anyone in the world who might care to listen, the fact of his own defeat; meanwhile he stood quietly, looking before him with unseeing eyes, in his mind turning over and over and over again the aching, unanswerable question: *Why?*

By now the secret was a secret no longer; the whole room knew.

For several minutes, after Skeffington, Weinberg, and Gorman saw the truth, most of the others had remained cheerful despite the ominous growth of opposition totals. They were waiting for the break, the sudden, gasping collapse of the foe which would precede the steady, powerful surge of the Skeffington machine as it ground its accustomed way home. But then, suddenly, the figures had begun to cascade from everywhere — and, in a startled moment, all optimism died. There would be no collapse. There would be no surge to victory. Skeffington was beaten. One moment he was standing above them, the carrier of their banner, proud leader of their hopes; the next, he had been blasted from the skies. It was a realization which did not sneak into the room in uneasy whispers; it burst upon them like an explosion. And at once they began to look quickly and with a hurried sympathy at the big man who stood like a statue before the blackboard; then, hastily, they came back to themselves and the frantic consideration of what mattered most: how would the defeat affect *them?* For they had their lives to lead, they had their wives, their children, themselves: this was really the heart of the matter. As they explored it, they had a frightening vision of a future filled with pain, uncushioned toil, economy; a future bereft of sinecure, privilege, protection; a future, in short, without City Hall.

The fretful sounds of defeat rose higher and swarmed around the room; then, curiously, they gradually subsided, to be replaced by an odd silence. It was a silence of awe: the McCluskey figures had continued to come crashing in, and the staggering plurality now began to be revealed. For the first time, those in the room realized the size of the defeat. It was enormous; shocked, they shuffled their feet uneasily and looked at one another. It was beyond their experience and their comprehension; they did not know what to do and so kept still; no one wished to speak, no one knew what to say. Suddenly the silence was broken. One of the men, anticipating pleasantly, had brought along a portable radio to the headquarters; another man now, in turning, accidentally struck it with his elbow, a control was flicked, and the set turned on. On, moreover, to its full volume — a strident, exuberant, professional voice roared through the room:

". . . . long reign ended in a stunning upset!" it shouted. *"While returns are not yet complete by any means, the McCluskey forces are jubilant. In what promises to be the greatest election surprise in many a year, it has become apparent that the career of Frank Skeffington, long the undisputed boss of the city, may at last be over! He — "*

The radio was jammed off; men glared at its owner; he returned their looks guiltily, helplessly, then stole a glance at Skeffington. He was still standing motionless before the blackboard; he gave no sign of having heard. Farther back in the room, Adam had heard. He had heard the radio, the murmurs about him; he had seen the figures on the board. He knew, now, that defeat was certain, but still he turned to Burbank the Authority, seeking contradiction.

"Is it true, Burbank?" he asked. "What does it mean?"

"All true," Burbank said bitterly. "Oh yes, very true indeed. All too true. And the meaning is clear enough, I should think: Just one more kick at poor old Burbank!"

Adam stared at him; he opened his mouth, but before he could say anything there was a commotion at the door. A group of men were attempting entrance; Ditto, near hysteria, was attempting to prevent them. They were the television men; as the head of the television committee, Ditto saw his duty clear in this altered, terrible situation: he was now to protect his chief, to stop these men from getting at him with their instruments, which would expose him in his defeat. For this occasion, and from some unsuspected reservoir, Ditto had summoned up courage; the television men stopped in their tracks at the sight of this shouting, wildly waving, fat man who blocked their path.

"Out!" he was shouting. "Get out of the door to the outside! Get out or I'll give you a punch with my very own fist!"

It was Skeffington who restored order. He had heard the noise and had turned from the board; he saw the jam at the door and recognized it for what it was. His head was clearer now; the first numbness was beginning to wear away. He knew what he had to do, and decided to do it quickly. He called sharply, "Ditto!" The fat man looked around, in instant obedience; with one flip of the hand Skeffington signaled him away from the door, and then motioned the men to come in. The television crew entered, reinforced by additional newspapermen who had been rushed here by the papers; it was a story that demanded extraordinary coverage. Skeffington started to walk across the room to meet them; Gorman touched him on the sleeve. "Frank?" he said.

Skeffington halted. "Yes?"

"What d'ye plan to do?"

Skeffington smiled faintly. "At the moment, I haven't a great many choices. I'm going to concede."

Gorman uttered an automatic protest. "Ah, there's no hurry for that, Frank. There's no need to rush yourself for a while yet. No need at all."

"Well," said Skeffington, "all these people are here and seem to want to see me. I don't think they want my autograph. So I think I'll accommodate them by giving them what they do want." He smiled again and said, "Don't worry, John. It'll be all right."

He walked to the center of the room. Here, earlier in the evening, a space had been cleared and the mobile television equipment set up; it was now being readied for use. Skeffington nodded pleasantly to some of the reporters; he made no comment other than to ask when the cameras would be ready. They were ready now; he was introduced briefly; he nodded again, and he was on the air.

"Ladies and gentlemen," he said slowly. "Just a word about today's election. The results are of course still incomplete. It appears, however, even from these partial returns, that Mr. McCluskey has won, and that he will be your next mayor. I congratulate Mr. McCluskey, and I wish him luck. He doesn't need the congratulations; he may need the luck. I know some of his friends and advisers. Again I congratulate him, and to each and every one of you who were kind enough to cast your vote for me today, I can only say Thank you, and God bless you all."

He stepped back; the camera light went off. Flash-bulbs popped as the photographers went to work in earnest; the reporters began to shoot their questions. Skeffington put up a hand and waited for silence before he spoke.

"Gentlemen," he said, "beyond what I said on television a

moment ago, I have no comment to make at this time. No more pictures, no more questions. I'll be at your service tomorrow morning at eleven in my office. Until then, I have nothing to say. Good night, gentlemen."

There was a flurry of murmuring protests; one reporter, more intrepid than the rest, cried, "Just one, Governor! Just one question! Have you made any plans for the future?"

Skeffington looked at him; then, slowly, he said, "Yes. Yes, I have."

The reporter said quickly, "Mind telling us what they are, Governor?"

A familiar gleam came into Skeffington's eye; for just a second, it was as if something irrepressible was sparking up through the gloom. "I'm going to run for governor of the state," he said, with something of his old urbanity. "Tomorrow morning I'll officially announce my candidacy for the elections next fall. I expect to win. And now, good night, gentlemen."

It was a bold statement, delivered boldly while he was still on his back; he thought grimly that it would startle them. It did; they thronged around him, pressing for additional comment. He would say nothing; slowly, he moved towards the door. Once again, as he made his way through his supporters, he nodded, bowed, murmured acknowledgements; he noticed now an embarrassment; he knew that they were embarrassed because they did not know what to say to him. He saw Ditto before him; he reached over and patted him on the shoulder. "Thanks, Ditto," he said. "I appreciate it. I'll see you around." He saw the tiny, clumsy, loyal face light up with gratitude, and he moved on to the doorway. At the door he stopped, and turned to say a final word to those in the room.

"To all of you who were here with me tonight, thank you," he said. "I'm sorry you had a disappointment; we'll try to make it up the next time. Again, thank you very much for all you've done. Most of you have worked very hard, and for that I'm grateful, as always. Good night; I'll see you tomorrow."

He waved and left the room; he heard behind him Cuke's voice cry out, "Three cheers for the Governor: Hip-hip-hooray!"

He was getting into his car when he heard the rush of footsteps and, turning, he saw his nephew struggling through the crowd. With all that had happened, he had completely forgotten about the boy; he was glad that he was here now. Smiling slightly, he said, "Hello. Sorry we couldn't produce a better show for you. It was just one of those things."

"Uncle Frank," Adam said abruptly, "where are you going now? Home?"

Skeffington nodded. "Yes. I think I'll turn in a little early tonight."

"Well, look," Adam said awkwardly, and then he began to speak very rapidly. "Would you mind if I came along with you? Or better still, would you like to come over to our house for a little while first? There'd be no one there but Maeve and myself and I know she'd love to have you." He added urgently, "Come along, Uncle Frank."

Skeffington smiled again; he put a hand on his nephew's arm. "Thanks," he said, and added, "I seem to be doing nothing but thanking people tonight. Under the circumstances, it's slightly ironic, isn't it? However, I do thank you, my boy — you most especially. And your good wife. But I don't think I'll take advantage of your kind offer. I'm a little tired, and I want to get home. So I think I'll just shoot along by myself. Besides," he said, the familiar gleam coming into his eyes momentarily, "I have a few things I want to do before I go to bed. I may write a few pseudonymous letters to the press, in an attempt to start a new mass movement. A Return-Skeffington-to-Public-Life Movement. In any case, I'll see you. Will you drop in tomorrow?"

"Yes. If you want me to."

"I do," Skeffington said. "Good night, my boy."

"Good night, Uncle Frank."

The car slid quietly away. Skeffington, in defeat, was going home; Adam, deeply moved, thought that he had never before seen anything quite so lonely. He remembered suddenly that he had not even told his uncle, in so many words, how sorry he was. He hoped his uncle knew; he rather thought that he did.

The November air was cold, and it had begun to drizzle; Adam buttoned his coat around his neck. He looked back into the long room; the mob was already dispersing in dejection. Some had left the hall and were walking off glumly into the night. They had all planned to stay out very late, for there was to be the great Victory Party; now, as things had turned out, they would be home very early.

Adam did not go back into the room. He walked away towards the paper and his car. It was time for him, too, to go home, to put an end to the turbulent, unique, and finally unhappy day.

Skeffington's car drove quickly through the city; when he was about a mile from his home he said to the chauffeur, "Pull up here, Patsy. I need a little air; I'll walk the rest of the way."

The car came to a stop, and the chauffeur turned around in protest. "It's a long way yet, Governor. And it's rainin' outside."

"A little moisture never hurt anyone," Skeffington said, getting out, "and we're a hardy people, Patsy. Go home now. Bring the car around the same time tomorrow."

The chauffeur said emotionally, "It's a damn dirty shame, Governor! The crazy lunatics'll get no better than they deserve out of this! I'm sorry as hell, Governor!"

"I know you are, Patsy. And thank you. But don't be sorry. Remember I'm going to run for governor; we'll get that nice, low, license plate back on the car in no time. You'll like that, won't you?" The chauffeur nodded dumbly, and Skeffington said, "Well then, let's count on it. Go along now, Patsy, and get yourself a good night's sleep. Everything's going to be all right. And I'll see you in the morning."

The car went off and Skeffington, at last, was alone. The rain was no more than a mist; adjusting his coat, he began to walk slowly towards his home. He did not walk along the boulevard; he took, instead, an irregular course, walking through the side streets of the handsome residential area. It was a course that more than doubled the length of his homeward walk, but he did not care; he wanted to walk, he wanted to think. His mind was perfectly clear now, and as he walked he began to trace in detail the movements of the campaign, going over them carefully from the first to the last, probing for the soft spot, the place where defeat had begun. He could not find it. It was there, somewhere; obviously it had to be. But it eluded him. Stubbornly, he began again, and as he continued to go over and over the familiar ground, he found concentration becoming increasingly difficult. A train of thought would suddenly come to an end against a wall of emotion which had suddenly arisen; it would be some moments before he realized that he was not attacking the problem at all, but was considering instead the fact of his humiliation, of the enormity of his defeat, of the stunning hopelessness of it all. It was a profoundly depressing consideration and Skeffington came close to nausea. Then, because he knew it was also a useless consideration, a dangerous dead end, he shook his head, walked faster, and forced himself back into deliberate thought. The walls continued to arise, breaking thought; but gradually despair gave way to anger. Skeffington was a proud man: in those moments when he had stood so still and apparently unaware before the blackboard, he had nevertheless realized dimly what was going on around him. He had caught the glances of pity; he had seen even John Gorman's glance of compassion and doubt; he knew what the room was thinking. The awareness that he had, even for that moment, been a pitiable object, that he had been considered as someone *finished,* stirred him to a growing fury. For he was not only proud, he was extraordinarily tough. Over fifty years ago, he had come, as little more than a boy, into an endless battle against the hardest, wiliest, most skillful politicians that this uniquely political arena had produced. He had fought them all, he had beaten them all, he had broken them all. And now the thought that, because he had been beaten by a young simpleton, through some incomprehensible conspiracy of freakish circumstances, he was somehow regarded in the same light as some weak-kneed, lily-livered, spineless beginner, incapable of smashing back and destroying this imbecile boy, spurred fury on. It was an emotion that took over and drove him forward; he went faster and indeed had even passed the walk of his own house before he realized that he had arrived. He turned and, puffing slightly, went up the front walk and let himself in. There was no one at home; he dumped his hat and coat on the hall table, and decided to go directly upstairs. Anger had subsided somewhat, but he felt better, stronger for it. He would make his plans tomorrow, after a night's sleep; still gripped by some of the driving force of emotion, he began to mount the stairs rapidly.

He had gone halfway when he felt the first pain. It was in his chest; it was quick and sharp. He paused abruptly; the pain weakened. He picked up his feet again, cautiously now; and then, all at once, the pain came back, cutting in savage knife strokes across his chest, his left shoulder and down the length of his arm. It was agonizing; he felt that he could not breathe; he reached out, puffing for the support of the bannister as pain came on in still another wave — and he pitched forward on his face, senseless. . . .

PART IV

Thirteen

SKEFFINGTON was ill, seriously so.

Adam, notified the following morning, hurried to his uncle's house; there, from a pale, dazed, and barely coherent Francis Jr., he received a confused and unsatisfactory account of what had happened the night before. It was the doctor who, later, gave him the full and disquieting report. Francis Jr. had come home early, he had discovered his father, he had gone into a panic; nevertheless, he had retained enough command of himself to telephone the doctor. From the first few garbled words, the doctor had realized exactly what had occurred; he had rushed over and, with the uncertain assistance of the son, had placed the still-unconscious Skeffington in bed. The bedroom had now become the sickroom; a nurse had been installed; Skeffington had regained consciousness and, under medication, was sleeping.

"It was his heart, then?" Adam said.

"Yes. A coronary, and a bad one." The doctor lit a cigarette and stared out through the drawing-room window. He was himself well advanced in years, and he had known Skeffington for a long time. He said, "It's not his first, you know. Or did you know?"

Adam shook his head. "No. He never spoke about it; at least not to me. I had no idea that anything at all was wrong."

"Very few people did. Naturally," the doctor said, "your uncle wasn't eager to publicize the fact. But he had an attack just about three years ago. It wasn't too severe, but it was the warning. He's a sensible man, and he's been watching himself pretty carefully ever since: sticking to his diet, cutting down on his activities, and so on. Up until this campaign, that is. I know what he's been doing lately; a month ago I told him to stop it." He shrugged, and said, "In the middle of a campaign, your uncle is not too open to conviction. Especially when he has an idea that it may be his last campaign. . . . So he kept on, and I suppose this is the inevitable result. Whether or not it would have occurred if the election had turned out differently, I don't know. In any case, he's a sick man now; for the present, we'll just have to try to keep him as comfortable as we can."

"Will he stay here?" Adam asked. "I mean, you're not going to move him to a hospital?"

"No. To begin with, he doesn't want to go — he was pretty firm about that when I talked to him earlier this morning — and it would only upset him. And secondly, in his condition, he'll do just as well here. We'll have a nurse with him at all times, and I can always get here in a matter of minutes. Of course there is one problem that's sure to come up as long as he's at home." He looked curiously at Adam, and then said, "I wonder if you could arrange to be over here every day for a while? I mean for a substantial part of each day: say, a couple of hours in the morning, and a couple more in the afternoon?"

"Yes, certainly. Of course."

"Good. I think it would be advisable. Someone in the family will have to take charge, and clearly Francis Jr. isn't up to it." He added charitably, "At the moment, at any rate. You see, the point is that handling your uncle isn't exactly like handling an ordinary patient. He's an important man, and he's tremendously popular; people will want to get at him. Any man in his condition has to have absolute rest; that means no visitors. With your uncle, that won't be easy. There'll be the reporters, the politicians, and then, probably the most dangerous of all, the good and well-intentioned people who have been filing up to the front door here for years. Most of them worship your uncle; they'll come around now just to see how he's getting along, and the worst of it is they'll come every day. If any of them should ever get in to see him they'd exhaust him in two minutes. So they all have to be kept out. Everybody. Including," he said firmly, "all those hangers-on who claim to be 'old pals.' Your uncle has more of those 'old pals' than any man I've ever met. Keep them all out, will you?"

Adam nodded. "Yes." He did not know quite how he was to

do this; he knew, however, that some workable method would have to be found. He added, "I'd like very much to see him myself, if I could. Is that permissible?"

"Yes. When he wakes up, drop in for a minute. He asked for you this morning, as a matter of fact." An old friend of Skeffington's, the doctor had been watching Adam during the campaign with attention; he had seen uncle and nephew together, and he had guessed something of Skeffington's regard for his young relative. He said now, "However, when you do go in to see him, don't stay too long at any one time. And keep the conversation to a minimum. You won't have much trouble there for a while; he's under some sedation, and won't feel much like talking. He asked about Francis Jr., too, and of course it's all right for him to go in. But again, not for long, and I'd appreciate it if you could tactfully suggest to him that he might keep a stiff upper lip while he's in there. Can you do that all right, or would you rather I did?"

"No," Adam said, "I'll do it."

"Good," said the doctor, making ready to go. "Now, let's see if there's anything else. I think you should disconnect the doorbells; they can be a terrible nuisance, especially in this case. It's too bad you can't do the same with the telephones, but at least you can try muffling them a bit. As far as the reporters are concerned, I can give you a lift there. Just send them around to me for all information; I'll work out some kind of daily bulletin arrangement. The main thing is," the doctor said, putting on his coat and walking with Adam to the front door, "to protect him from his friends. That's absolutely essential. Well, if I'm needed at any time, whichever nurse is on duty will know where to get in touch with me. Good-by. I'll be in again this afternoon."

"Good-by, Doctor," Adam said. The doctor was almost out the door before he added, "Doctor?"

"Yes?"

"What do you think? I know he's a very sick man, but . . . how sick is that?" He was floundering; directly, now, he asked the question which he had been putting off. He said, "Will he pull through all right?"

The doctor hesitated, then said, "He has a chance."

"But what kind of chance? A good chance? A slight chance? A better-than-even chance? Or what?" He saw the doctor looking at him, and he was aware that his voice had risen; he said, "I'm sorry. I didn't mean to press you like that."

"That's all right," the doctor said, not unkindly. "He's a good friend of mine, too. The difficulty is that I really can't tell you very much. He's not in good shape now, but if all goes well, he could come through quite nicely. The trouble is — as it always is with a damaged heart — that all may not go well. And when you consider your uncle's age, the fact that he has a history of cardiac trouble, and the severity of this present attack, that isn't just a faint possibility. So you see why I'd just as soon not be too optimistic. Anything could happen. On the other hand, with a little luck — and if we can keep him quiet and undisturbed — he may do it. At least, there's this in his favor: we won't have to inspire him with the will to live. He'll never quit. That can sometimes be a big help. Anyway, we'll wait and see what happens, and hope for the best. The next few days should tell the story."

Adam, left alone with his new responsibilities, went first to see his uncle. Skeffington was awake; the nurse beckoned Adam into the room, and he saw his uncle lying flat and motionless, his head raised slightly by two pillows. His eyes were open; he looked pale and helpless. It was the first time Adam had seen him in a position of absolute disadvantage; it did not seem right. He shut his eyes, feeling a powerful sweep of pity as he thought of the two successive and cruel setbacks that his uncle had suffered in the short space of time since last evening. It was unfair, terribly so, but — it had happened. He stepped quietly towards the bed. Skeffington heard him approach, and turned his head slowly.

"Hello," he said. His voice was cloudy, but surprisingly strong. "Good to see you."

"It's good to see you, Uncle Frank." He blinked rapidly, then stepped forward and touched his uncle's hand. He said, "It'll be better to see you when you get out of there."

"Won't be too long," Skeffington said. "Don't pay any attention to what that elderly interne tells you. He's a professional alarmist." His eyes closed; they opened again and he said, "How's your wife?"

"Fine, thanks, Uncle Frank."

"Good," he said drowsily. "That's good." His eyes closed again, his lips parted, his breathing became more noticeable. He was asleep; the visit was over. Adam left the room quietly, not greatly encouraged by what he had seen.

He went downstairs to talk to the two servants, the cook and the maid. He found them subdued, alarmed, and uncertain of just what was to happen; after first carefully explaining to them that Francis Jr. was naturally too upset at the moment to take charge, he gave them some instructions for the next few days. The women seemed grateful for any direction at this time; they nodded and then asked, simultaneously and with apprehension, about Skeffington. They were clearly devoted to him; Adam passed on the encouragement which he himself did not feel. He then went into the drawing room to meet Gorman and Weinberg, who had arrived while he had been talking with his uncle.

He found, immediately, that here were two sources of strength. Greatly concerned about Skeffington, they were both practical men; they had talked to the doctor, and knew how they could best be of help.

"We'll keep the boys away," Weinberg said. "I already passed the word around; they won't come near the house till it's O.K."

"Fine," Adam said. "Thanks a lot, Sam; that makes it easier to handle. As for the others the doctor was talking about — the ones who'll keep coming from all over just to see how he is — I imagine we can take care of them as they come."

"You'll have no trouble there," Gorman said. "I had a word with Jack FitzGerald not half an hour ago. The Police Commissioner. He'll put a cop on duty, day and night, by the front door. He'll turn them away nicely when they come. There'll be no bother at all."

And so Skeffington's lieutenants had in the crisis become his guardians, moving in swiftly to throw up a quick protective barrier around the man whom they had served for so long. Adam was both touched and grateful; he said, "I wish you could go in and see him. But he's sleeping now, and then the doctor's being pretty firm against all visitors for a while."

"We can wait," Weinberg said. "No hurry. So long as he's O.K.; that's all that counts."

Gorman nodded, and the two men rose to go. Adam said, "I'll tell him you were here."

"He'll know," Gorman said simply. "Frank would know that. But you can tell him all the same, and thank you." With a slight smile he added, "And you might tell him, too, that if he gets well in a hurry I'll get Weinberg into church to make a novena for him."

"Yeah," Weinberg said. "Sure. That's good. Tell him that. You know, to cheer him up. It'll hand him a laff."

It was clearly the continuation of an old joke, one which had weathered the long association of three friends; Adam promised to pass it along. The two men left; they would return later in the day. Adam, once more alone, had now to attend to his remaining responsibility. He went upstairs again, this time to talk with his cousin. It was not a meeting he looked forward to; he did not really know his cousin at all well. Francis Jr. was a few years older than himself; since Adam's boyhood the two had met rarely, and then on a social rather than a family basis: at occasional parties where, among a large group of people, they would exchange a pleasant phrase or two, then part. It was by reputation that Adam knew his cousin best, and that reputation did not cheer him now. To pump courage and good sense into this lightheaded man who had last night gone into collapse would not be easy.

But he received a surprise. Francis Jr. was in his room, but he was by no means prostrate. Autotherapy had begun; he was recovering from his despondency of the night before and the extent to which he had already recovered left Adam flabbergasted. For there on the smooth green carpeting of the bedroom were half a dozen golf balls; standing over them, bending professionally forward, a golf club in his hands, was Junior. He was practising his putting.

"Oh, hi!" he said, as Adam came in. The greeting was pleased and entirely free of embarrassment. "What do you say, Adam?"

"Hello, Junior." Looking around at the golf balls on the floor, he said with some bitterness. "Keeping up with your game?"

"No, just something to do," Francis Jr. said, putting down the club, and sitting on the edge of his bed. He lit a cigarette. "I didn't want to go out or anything, even for a walk, because of Dad. Golly, that was awful, wasn't it, Adam?"

"Pretty bad. You seem to be holding up very well, though."

"Yes, well, maybe *now*. But you should have seen me last night when I found Dad. I guess I made the whole show a lot worse by nearly going to pieces," he said, with great candor. "You know how it is: you never expect anything like that. At least I don't. Not with Dad. I don't know, you just never think about anybody like that getting sick or coming close to . . . well, to *dying*, I guess. You know what I mean: you know how Dad is. And then all of a sudden I came in early last night, just by luck, and there he was on the stairs." He shook his head at the memory. "It was terrible, Adam. No kidding. It was really terrible."

"Yes, I imagine it was." He spoke with more sympathy now; he said curiously, "But didn't you have any idea that something like this might happen someday? After all, he'd had an attack three years ago, the doctor tells me."

Francis Jr. looked vague. "Well, yes, but the trouble is that nobody really was certain it was a heart attack. Do you see what I mean?"

"No. The doctor knew, surely?"

"Well, yes, I guess so. At least he seemed to think it was. He didn't talk much to me about it, but I guess that's what he thought it was, all right. But he's such a Gloomy Gus anyway that I didn't know. You know, he's a very nice fellow, but he's always looking on the dark side of everything. And then Dad said it wasn't anything very much at all. He went away on a cruise for a couple of weeks, and when he came back he was fine and he's been fine ever since. So naturally I forgot all about it. You can see why I would."

Adam nodded. In this astonishing conversation he was discovering what others had discovered before: that it was next to impossible, and seemed somehow unfair, to hold bitterness towards this pleasant, obviously well-intentioned man who, although now approaching forty, revealed in every word the spirit of some growing and peculiarly ingenuous boy. It was Skeffington who, years before, and to his wife, had in a disgruntled moment summed up his son as "a likable featherhead." And it was again Skeffington who, on another and equally exasperated occasion, had spoken to the same audience upon the boy's resemblance to himself.

"It's uncanny," he had growled. 'It's as though Peter Pan had found my body and had come to stay!"

Adam had never heard this; if he had, he would now have understood it and agreed with it.

Francis Jr. continued to talk. "I didn't sleep much last night. You know, thinking about him, and wondering how he was. Then I got up around three, I guess it was, and went over to his room. The doctor and the nurse were in there, but I stayed at the door and I don't think they saw me. Anyway, he was sleeping, and everything seemed to be better, so after a while I came back and went to sleep. Poor Dad. Golly," he said, the fine eyes which were also Skeffington's becoming momentarily anxious, "if anything ever *did* happen to him, I don't know what I'd do. You know, I suppose we don't exactly pal around together much, because he's not very much interested in the kind of things I do, and I've never been able to get interested in politics at all. But just the same . . . you know what I mean, Adam?"

"I know what you mean, Junior."

"Because he's really a wonderful guy." Then, suddenly, the edge of anxiety disappeared; in an instant he was restored to cheerfulness. "Anyway, everything's much better this morning. I talked with the doctor, and it didn't look too bad at all. I mean, Dad had a good night, and if he gets plenty of rest it looks like everything's going to be all right. Anyway, that's more or less what the doctor said, and you know he's a pretty sour old boy usually. So that made me feel pretty good."

Evidently the doctor had decided that a buoyant Junior was to be preferred to a despairing one; therefore he had been optimistic with him. Adam resolved to be the same. By now he had seen enough of his cousin to know that he was a wisp; in a situation such as this he would be up or down according to each shift of the wind. Last night he had been distraught; now, after what had been no doubt a few carefully optimistic words from the doctor, he had made his room a putting green. But better the athlete than the invalid; Adam said encouragingly, "Well, he should know; he's a first-class doctor. I'm glad the news is so good." He decided that it was time to clarify his own position in his cousin's house; he said carefully: "I thought I might slip in during the next few days and give you a lift, Junior. I know it's a bad time for you, and I thought maybe you could use an extra hand around the place." He went on to list some of the arrangements that had been made that morning for Skeffington's protection, and added, "And so, if you'd like me to, I'll drop in from time to time during the next few days, just to check on how things are going."

Junior was grateful. "That would be swell, Adam," he said. "Thanks a million. You know how it is: I'll be here all the time, and all that, but I don't really know much about anything like this. I mean, Dad's always handled all the arrangements around here all by himself. So maybe if you could manage to come in once in a while it would be a big help, Adam. I'd really appreciate it!"

"Good," Adam said. "I'll try to get in at least once every day." That was settled, then; there would be no stepping on delicate toes. He talked with his cousin for a few minutes more; the talk was to no particular purpose, and Francis Jr., clearly restless in his new confinement, soon began to exercise as he talked. He rose from the edge of his bed, rather abstractedly taking the golf club into his hands once more. He got down on one knee and sighted along an imaginary line on the carpet. Still talking, he got to his feet and began to bring the clubhead backward and forward in a series of delicate, rhythmic motions. Francis Jr. was polishing his putting stroke.

Adam did not leave his uncle's house until close to dinnertime. He had been busy, surprisingly so; he found himself in the unfamiliar position of the Authority in the household of an important public man. The reporters came; he shifted them to the doctor, but not before he himself had been thoroughly interviewed. There was the telephone; it rang steadily all day. Many of the calls were routine; the maid was able to take them. A great many, however, demanded more specialized attention. Adam did his best, and was quite confident that the best was not good enough. He realized, somewhere in the middle of the afternoon, that what most of these callers wanted, in spite of everything, was to talk to Skeffington himself; failing that, any substitute, however necessary, was a disappointment.

In the matter of visitors to the house, he was more fortunate. Weinberg and Gorman had been as good as their word: the politicians did not appear, and although, throughout the day, there were people coming to the front door, singly, in pairs, in groups of three and four, they were met by the policeman on duty who told them only that Skeffington was resting comfortably. This presumably satisfied them; they nodded and went away quietly.

"They'll be back," the policeman said knowingly to Adam. "Them and others like them. Every day till the boss gets well. Wait and see."

Then there were the gifts. At least half of those who were turned away by the policeman left behind them small, homely spurs to recovery: a get-well-quick card, a jar of jelly, a pound box of chocolates, a religious medal blessed by a member of the hierarchy. These were welcome gifts: they were well-intentioned, and — more to the point, thought Adam — they were small. They posed no problems of storage or disposal. Something else again were the more imposing gifts from more imposing people. All day the delivery trucks rolled up to the house, bringing intricate and absurd floral arrangements, bulging beribboned baskets of citrus fruit. The donors were many and various: they ranged from a conspicuously successful local gangster to Mayor-elect Kevin McCluskey. As the afternoon wore on and these elaborate offerings continued to arrive, Adam became increasingly puzzled: what was he to do with them? It was John Gorman, arriving late in the day, who solved his difficulty.

"There's a dreadful lot of truck here," he said, his eye roving disapprovingly over the display. "D'ye want me to get rid of it for you?"

"Yes," Adam said fervently. "I certainly don't think Uncle Frank would mind, do you?"

"Why would he?" Gorman asked. "He wears a green carnation on St. Patrick's Day and the rest of the year he never looks at a flower. So what would he want with a whole damn hothouse? We'll just keep who they came from, and then send the whole shebang over to the Sisters at the Mission Hospital. The grapefruit they can eat, and the flowers they can stick on the altar. I'll have a wagon come over tonight and cart it all away."

At the end of the day Adam found himself tired, unexpectedly so. He prepared to leave, and then, before going, he climbed the stairs once more to his uncle's room. This time there was no talk; Skeffington was sleeping, and the nurse, coming quietly across the room, whispered that there had been no change, that the patient seemed to be doing well enough, that the doctor would be in somewhat later that evening. With this information, and with one final look at the pale, familiar, slumbering face on the pillows, Adam left the room. He had finished his first day of responsibility in his uncle's house.

That night he told Maeve of his day. He told her, too, of his brief talk with Skeffington, and of the fact that in this short drifting moment of half-wakeful conversation, his uncle had remembered to ask for her.

"Poor man," she said softly. "What's going to happen, Adam? What do *you* think? Is he going to get better?"

He shrugged. "I just don't know. Apparently the doctor doesn't, either. It seems to be one of those cases where it could turn either way; all you can do is just hope for the best. It's not very encouraging, but there it is."

She said tentatively, "Should I go to see him, do you think? I'd like to, if I could. And if he'd like me to."

He was pleased by the suggestion, but he said, "He'd like you to, all right, and so would I. What the doctor would like, though, is another matter. I should think it would be all right; anyway, I'll ask him tomorrow."

"Even if he says no," she said, "I could come over and help out in some way. Even if it's only answering the telephone. I don't like to think of you having to do everything by yourself. I know I could do *something*."

He smiled. "You might bring along a couple of golf balls and join Francis on the putting green. It must be lonesome for him up there without any competition." He added more seriously, "No, I'd love to have you along, Maeve, and you could probably do a great many things, but I don't think it'll be at all necessary now." Actually, he would have liked precisely this: to have Maeve with him during the next few days at his uncle's house; that afternoon, he had thought of suggesting it to her. But then the figure of her father had arisen in his mind: was it likely that this truculent little meddler would remain silent upon learning that his daughter, for whatever cause, was spending a part of each day in the household of his old enemy? There would surely be complications; there would be the inevitable pompous speeches; and now, with Skeffington so ill, Adam had no tolerance for either. And so it was better to avoid the source of friction; he said, "You see, everything should begin to ease off from now on; there shouldn't be much to do now that we've got things in working order. I'll just drop in now and then to see how everything is. And in any case, Uncle Frank may be a good deal better." He added hopefully, "Let's just wait and see. I have a hunch everything will turn out all right."

But he did not deceive himself. He knew how ill Skeffington was, and his words conveyed an optimism which, try as he might, he could not bring himself to feel.

The next three days passed quietly. Adam, as he had promised, spent a part of each morning and each afternoon at his uncle's house. Each noon he went to the paper and there, for two hours, he worked at Little Simp; the comic strip was given short attention during this busy time. In the city, and particularly on the paper, he heard everywhere the echoes of the two great events of recent days: (1) the surprising defeat of Skeffington at the polls; (2) his equally surprising collapse in his home. Adam heard little else; he joined in conversations on neither theme. His colleagues, not normally the most sensitive of men, now obligingly did not intrude; apart from the natural curious and solicitous questions about his uncle's health, they considerately left him strictly alone. Even the managing editor, a man of celebrated tactlessness, now became aware that this was somehow a time for the exercise of delicacy, and, beyond an occasional crow of triumph over the accuracy of his election predictions, he said nothing. And so Adam went daily to the paper, did his work, and then quickly returned to his uncle's home.

Here, within the house, there had been no great change. For Adam it was easier; he now knew better how to cope with the routine problems that arose from his uncle's illness, and Weinberg and Gorman were invaluable in their assistance. As he had expected, there was no help to be had from Francis Jr. However, his cousin remained in high spirits. Twice each day he went in to see his father; he did not stay long and the words exchanged were few, yet as far as Adam could determine, these visits worked out satisfactorily enough, and their effect on Junior was marked. He seemed to find substantial encouragement in the bare fact of his father's continued consciousness, and each complete sentence uttered by the ailing man was taken as still another harbinger of recovery. He emerged from his room and took to drifting aimlessly about the house, sometimes coming in to talk pleasantly to Adam, then going in to the library and reading a few pages of a novel, then turning the television set on — quietly, so as not to disturb his father — then, other amusements failing, he would be heard faintly from the basement, where he had gone to whistle snatches of popular tunes, occasionally tapping out an accompaniment with his feet. He was like a child, thought Adam, who has been kept in the house on a fine summer's day when all the other children are out playing. It was a remarkably apposite thought; soon afterwards Francis Jr. came in with the announcement that he thought he might go out for a short walk. After that he went out for walks frequently; the walks grew longer, and although he took care always to be in the house at night, during the day, and especially when Adam was on duty, he was often missing for hours at a time. In a way, Adam thought, this was perhaps just as well; it was easier on all concerned. Yet it was dangerous, too; and, because his conscience bothered him on this point, he spoke to his cousin about it one afternoon, just as the latter was preparing to leave the house.

"You know, he still isn't terribly well, Junior," he said. "It's all right to be encouraged and to look at things from the bright side, but you ought to realize that he's not out of the woods yet by a long shot."

His cousin's head bobbed in agreement. "Sure, Adam. I realize that. He's got to take care of himself."

"It's a little more than that, actually. Everything is still pretty much in the critical stage. And while it's certainly no business of mine when you come and go, or how long you stay away, don't you think that under the circumstances it's a little bit risky?"

"Risky?" Plainly, this had not occurred to him; puzzled, he said, "Golly, Adam, I don't see how. I mean, it would be different if I went away on a trip or something. I can see that, sure. But all I do is go out and get a little air now and then, and maybe say hello to a couple of friends. You know, just to kind of break up the day. If I could help Dad any by staying in all the time I would in a minute. But you know Dad, Adam: he's not liable to be asking for me every second. So I don't see what's so risky about it at all!"

Adam did not persist; it seemed purposeless.

On the second day of his stay at Skeffington's house, Jack Mangan dropped in to see Adam.

"Tough break, sport," he said. "A bad one."

Adam nodded. "Bad enough. Still, I suppose it could be worse." He told Jack what the doctor had said; when he finished Jack said, "He's right, sport. The old will to live: at least half the battle. And your uncle's got it to spare. A real hard rock." He looked about the hall, and gestured towards the front door. "I had a hard time getting by the cop. What's he: the buffer against the public?"

"Yes. They've been coming in droves." He added reflectively, "Which doesn't make it any easier to understand."

"To understand what, sport? Why they come?"

"No, I know that all right. What I don't understand is where they were on Election Day. You see," Adam said slowly, "I've been thinking a lot about the election during the last couple of days, trying to figure out why Uncle Frank lost. I haven't been making much progress. And I watch these people come hour after hour, and that makes it more confusing than ever. I'm sure they wouldn't come around like this for anyone else. Certainly not for your man McCluskey."

Jack nodded briskly. "Agreed, sport."

"Well then, what's the explanation? I know it doesn't matter now, but it bothers me because it doesn't seem to fit at all. How could a man as popular as Uncle Frank lose to someone like McCluskey? Come clean, Jack: did *you* think McCluskey would win?"

"No," Jack said promptly. "No, I didn't. To tell you the truth, I thought your uncle had it hands down. I told Nancy so the night before the election."

"There you are," Adam said. "And I know Uncle Frank expected to win; I think he was absolutely sure of it. Yet McCluskey won, and by a huge vote: how do you explain that? You're the political expert, Jack: have you got an explanation?"

"Well, as a matter of fact, sport," Jack said, "I have. Care to hear it?"

"Yes. Yes, I would indeed."

"O.K. Of course you understand this is all wisdom after the event; as I say, I didn't call this thing in advance. I was wrong. But ever since it happened I've been noodling around, trying to figure out why, and I think I've got the answer. In the first place, there were a number of minor factors. I suppose a good many people voted against him simply because they wanted a change. They didn't dislike him, or anything like that: it was just that he'd been in there so long that they just decided they wanted to see someone new in charge of the shop. People do that, sport; they get uneasy. It's the kind of thing that helped Churchill get the boot right after the war."

Adam shook his head. "I don't think much of your answer, Jack."

"Wait. I haven't given it to you yet. That was just one of the things that helped; it wasn't the big thing. Nor was the fact that your uncle faced, for the first time in a long time, a real, concerted opposition with plenty of money behind it. That helped, too, but again, it wasn't the knockout punch. What really did the job, sport, wasn't McCluskey, or Garvey, or Cass or Amos Force, and it certainly wasn't me. You can forget all of us. All you have to remember is one name: Roosevelt."

Adam stared at him. *"Roosevelt?"*

"Sure. F.D.R. Nobody else but. Because he's the man, sport, who really put the skids under your uncle, and he did it years ago. It's just that it took until now to catch up with him."

"I don't get *that* at all," Adam said. "Why Roosevelt?"

"Because," Jack said patiently, "he destroyed the old-time boss. He destroyed him by taking away his source of power. He made the kind of politician your uncle was an anachronism, sport. All over the country the bosses have been dying for the last twenty years, thanks to Roosevelt. Your uncle lasted this long simply because he was who he was: an enormously popular man whose followers were devoted to him. Your uncle wasn't an ordinary boss, sport; the ordinary boss doesn't get that kind of loyalty. But he operated on the old-style principle, and it was just a question of time before what was happening to the rest happened to him, too." He shot a glance at Adam and said, "You sure you want to talk about this now, sport? There's no hurry; why don't we wait awhile?"

"No," Adam said. "Go ahead, Jack."

Jack shrugged. "O.K.," he said. "Well, of course, the old boss was strong simply because he held all the cards. If anybody wanted anything — jobs, favors, cash — he could only go to the boss, the local leader. What Roosevelt did was was to take the handouts out of the local hands. A few little things like Social Security, Unemployment Insurance, and the like — that's what shifted the gears, sport. No need now to depend on the boss for everything; the Federal Government was getting into the act. Otherwise known as a social revolution. So you can see what that would do in the long run. The old-timers would still string along with the boss, of course, because that's the way they always did things. But what about the kids coming along? Did you ever stop to think, sport, about the *age* of the people around your uncle?

I wouldn't mind betting that it didn't exactly look like a Youth Movement."

Adam was silent. He remembered that, for example, at Knocko Minihan's wake, he had been struck by the number of elderly men there; he had put it down, at the time, to the fact that Knocko himself had been old. But then he also remembered his first morning at Skeffington's house, watching his uncle receive the long line of petitioners; there had been no young people among them.

Jack continued. "Your uncle was operating in a diminishing market: that's the long and the short of it. You couldn't pry his old supporters away from him with a crowbar, but their trouble was that they *were* old: they were dying off, sport, and they were being replaced by the kids. And what about the kids and your uncle? To begin with, they were one step further away from the old country; he didn't have the old emotional appeal for them. You know, the racial-spokesman kind of thing. For another, a lot of them had been educated away from home. They didn't know much about Skeffington, and they didn't much care. Think of yourself, sport: if he hadn't been your uncle, how interested would you have been? And finally, most of them had never had the slightest contact with him because it wasn't necessary. When they got out of the army, for example, and needed a little spare cash to tide them over, what did they do? Did they go to the boss? Not on your life; they didn't have to. They joined the 52-20 Club and got twenty bucks a week for the next year, all supplied by good old remote, impersonal Washington. And when they went to work at last, and then got laid off for a while, the same thing happened. No boss; Unemployment Insurance instead. It was a new era, sport, and your uncle belonged to the old. If everybody who voted was middle-aged or over, the election would have been strictly no contest: your uncle would have won by ten to one. But it didn't work that way. A whole group of voters who never had the slightest contact with your uncle, who even considered him as something out of the past, somebody they'd seen in cartoons and read about in books, went to the polls. And I suppose what happened was inevitable. That's hindsight, of course. I thought it would happen one day, but not quite so soon. But it did, sport. And I think that's the answer."

For a moment Adam was silent; then he said slowly, "Then you think, really, that under these circumstances, almost anybody could have beaten my uncle?"

"Almost anybody did, sport. McCluskey did. He's my boy, but I certainly never claimed he was any great shakes. He was strictly a minor leaguer against a big leaguer, but the big leaguer's day was over. All the rules and playing conditions had changed. And so the minor leaguer won."

"And you think that's a good thing?"

"Well, look," Jack said, "I haven't any enthusiasm for McCluskey. You know that. But maybe we can work with him, and we knew we couldn't work with your uncle. There wasn't a chance. He didn't believe in our ways and we didn't believe in his. So we opposed him and backed McCluskey, and now we hope for the best. It may be a faint hope, but at least it's there. With your uncle, it wouldn't have been. It couldn't have been. It's as simple as that."

"Well," said Adam, "I suppose it is. All the same, you can have your faint hope. I think I'll take my uncle."

"I would too," Jack said, "in any way but the political. Because personally there's no comparison. No comparison at all: your uncle is a wonder. There's never been anything like him around here. And I don't mind telling you, sport, that I envied you like hell all through the campaign. You had a seat I would have given my right arm for. It must have been wonderful."

Adam nodded. "It was all of that," he said.

"Sure. It couldn't miss. He's unique, sport. Miles ahead of all the rest. He doesn't even belong to the same species as that bunch that's always on his coattails. And I was thinking last night," Jack said, getting to his feet, "that that must have made it a little tough for him at times. Because, when you come right down to it, out of all that crowd that were with him night and day, who did he have that he could talk to? I mean, *really* talk to?" He looked at Adam and shrugged. "Not many, I'll bet. And probably not even one. Kind of a lonely business, wouldn't you say?"

"Yes," said Adam, "I'd say it was."

"Well," Jack said, more briskly, "he'll be all right, sport. You wait and see. And you were a lucky boy during the campaign. None luckier. Sometime, when this is over, I wish you'd tell me about it. Meanwhile," he said, opening the front door, "stay with it. We'll see you and Maeve soon?"

"Yes, sure. As soon as we get straightened out around here. Thanks for dropping in, Jack. And thanks for the explanation."

"A pleasure and a privilege, sport. So long." And with a wave, he went down the front walk to his car.

Adam went back into the house. The explanation, he believed, was a good one: it was logical, it fitted the facts, it was very probably true. And yet he could not willingly accept it, for he could not bring himself to think of Skeffington as a survivor, as someone who was, quite bluntly, out of date. He shook his head; the conclusion was too harsh. . . .

He did not think about it long, however; a matter of more immediate concern crowded it from his mind. He was worried about his uncle, for Skeffington, in fact, was not improving.

"Although he's not declining, either," the doctor had said that morning. "He rallied just after the attack, and from that time on he's remained just about constant. That's not unusual. This isn't a head cold and he's not a boy; only a lunatic would expect him to bound back quickly. I will admit, however, that I'd be just as happy to see him start picking up a little, any time now." Glancing at Adam, he said in a less impersonal tone: "At any rate, don't worry about it. There's no additional cause for alarm. You're protecting him very well, and he's getting all the rest and quiet he should have; that's important. And you always want to remember that he's a pretty tough customer. I'd say right now the odds were about even. I've known your uncle a long time; at those odds I'd hate to bet against him. In anything."

It was reassurance of a sort, but Adam continued to worry.

As for Skeffington himself . . .

He was lying awake in his bed. He had no pain; the opiates which had been given to him immediately following his attack had been discontinued, save at night. Now, although he dozed occasionally, he was for the greater part of each day fully awake. Or was it a full wakefulness? This was a question he sometimes asked himself when, after lying for what may have been a long time with his eyes wide open, with his brain working smoothly and clearly, with his senses alert, catching all objects, figures, movements and sounds within the room, he suddenly and with a slight start seemed to snap into a state of special awareness of himself and everything about him. He knew that he had not been asleep, that he had been awake, yet it was as if in an instant he had somehow become much *more* awake, with every perception so sharpened that he realized with a new vividness each detail of his surroundings, and with this same heightened intensity, and almost with a sense of fresh discovery, understood exactly what had happened to him, and why it was that he was here, bed-ridden, in the middle of the day, doing nothing more than wondering just how awake he had been the moment before.

He came to the answer: it was the daydream. Somewhat ruefully — for nothing in his vigorous and colorful life had prepared him for these aimless mental drifts — he acknowledged to himself that the majority of his conscious moments were spent in this mood of soft, boneless, not unpleasant reverie. In the intervals of sharper consciousness he would sometimes, with a little shrug of irritation, reproach himself for allowing the hours to slip so lazily by. Then, always, reproach would fade, as he would reflect that in this time of recovery, on these long afternoons spent in this room washed with the subdued, dreamy, golden light of autumn, there was, after all, not much else for him to do, and so slowly, easily, unresistingly he would begin once again the agreeable drift into the past.

For it was the past, now, that held him. In these slow, unbroken hours, he thought scarcely at all of his recent defeat and humiliation, of the long and mounting disasters of election night, or of present facts or future plans, and when, every so often, he did think of them, he did so briefly and with an odd and extremely uncharacteristic impatience. Today and Tomorrow, not Yesterday, had always been first in the thoughts of this most realistic man. But now it was different. He reminisced, and as he traveled back through his own long and richly varied past, it was as if the hazy flood of sunshine which filled the bedroom had somehow penetrated recollection, for it was a benign journey, heavy with warmth and languor and content. Of all the moments, the scenes, the people, the events that had crowded his more than seventy years, he seemed miraculously to come upon only those which had given him happiness. Some of these had been forgotten for years; now they came sliding swiftly and vividly back from memory's exile, and Skeffington remembered. . . .

He remembered, before anything else, the small and shabby tenement in which he had been born. He remembered it better and with more exactness than any place he had ever been since, in all his life. He had remembered it variously, under different lights and in different moods; he remembered it now kindly, because he remembered it under the aspect of love, and of his mother. Memory flashed across seven decades: he saw the small boy, awakening at night, suddenly terrified by reasonless fear, and rushing from his bed into the surprised but ready embrace of his mother; he felt again the gentle, protective cradling as she rocked back and forth; he heard again the single, simple, adaptable verse of lullaby, over and over and over:

Toora loora looral
Toora loora lie,
Toora loora looral —
Frankie, don't you cry . . .

Until suddenly, all fear gone, he had flung both arms up and around her neck, hanging on for dear life, and raining wet kisses on her thin, worried face in an ecstasy of happiness. . . .

Memory skipped about, into the adult years; patiently, Skeffington pulled it back into some sort of sequence. Back to the tenement; then, slipping swiftly over the hard, inconspicuous, and, on the whole, unloved years of boyhood, he came to the summer night when life began. It was in the heart of the old Dabney Street district, not two blocks from where he lived. It was a place of old brick houses which had sadly declined from their genteel beginnings and swarmed with immigrant life; it was a place of livery stables with their huge gray great-beamed horses; it was a place of a hundred small saloons, each with its steady clientele of family men, who converged upon it every night after dinner for the ritual of a quiet drink and conversation. And here, spick and span in his one good Sunday suit, and in his nineteenth year — a tall, slender boy with a head just a shade too large for the still adolescent body — he had stood on an overturned barrel under the gas light in front of Johnnie Mahady's Bar. Through the darkness and the perpetual rich night smell of hay and horses and ale, the men passed by, on their way to or from drink, and as they passed, some of them stopped — and some, although not many, stayed — to give a listen to Rosie Skeffington's boy, who was out on the stump for Big Billy Coughlin. The boy was waving his arms eagerly, and shouting in violent denunciation of Toddy McGahan:

" . . . A viper! Yes, worse than a viper! A scorpion, an *asp!* A reptile in human form whose bite of poison has been felt by every man, woman, and child in the district! Toddy McGahan has the nerve to ask you for your precious vote! Do you know what you can expect in return from him if you give him that vote? I'll tell you what you can expect and all you can expect: *You can expect to be the next to feel his evil sting. . . .* "

A viper. A scorpion. An asp. A reptile in human form. Poor Toddy. His political life had been cut short by the unfortunate fact that his willingness to deceive had not been matched by his capacity to do so. But poor Toddy a viper! At the memory he gave a little chuckle; he saw the nurse, seated by the south window, sit up alertly at the sound. He closed his eyes and pretended sleep, for this day nurse was a talker. She had two topics: the first, her brother, a missionary priest in Japan who uncomplainingly ate raw fish despite a delicate stomach; the second, the insufficient recognition and reward accorded the members of a noble profession — the nursing profession. She spoke of the first with awe and the second with passion; Skeffington had quickly wearied of both. And so he closed his eyes, the nurse relaxed, and he returned to Dabney Street and the enthusiastic, juvenile, inexpert speech of more than fifty years ago. It had been his first political speech. Afterwards, a couple of the men had come up and shaken his hand, one had said, "By God, boy, you got a great bit o' tongue in your head, there! That's Toddy to the life, all right!" And later that night he had been complimented by Big Billy himself — a huge man with great, drooping mustaches, tawny with the stains of tobacco — and he had walked home at midnight in dreams of glory. A whole new world was open, and he was on the way. . . .

Memory jumped forward. He remembered as though it were yesterday one chill night in autumn when the great torchlight parade had swept out from the center of the city, hundreds and hundreds of men and a half a dozen marching bands, all yelling and screaming and singing, swinging along for hours, while at the head of the wild procession strode the young man in his middle thirties, his strong face flushed, his hat jammed to one side of his head, his tie pulled open and his collar ripped almost off, while he waved and rocked and shouted in response and his name went up in one roar after another. It was his first victory parade: he was THE MAYOR. He was the youngest mayor in the long history of the city; by hard work, by intelligence, by the force of personality, by a series of bold and imaginative maneuvers, he had seized the right of organization support from his seniors; he had fought them hard, bitterly, and savagely, and he had won. And now here was the celebration: this great, exuberant surge of men, marching by torchlight through the night, with Skeffington shouting the directions as they marched and sang. He led them down into his home ward where the people, massed on the sidewalks, in the streets, and at the tenement windows, cheered this new young champion in whom they had such hopes; he led them up Cooper's Hill and down the far side to the waterfront, to the very piers where, not so many years before, the boatloads of wondering, impoverished immigrants had docked; then, turning, he led them back into the heart of the city, around City Hall, out onto the Mall, and then, finally, to his goal: that handsome, quiet section where, in prudent elegance, lived the old inhabitants. Into the silent, empty, well-kept streets poured the living torrent; around and through the quarter it circled its boiling, boisterous way; and through the night and early morning hours, the victorious shout of "SKEFFINGTON!" rang out in loud defiance against the decorous window panes. The police were called; they did not come. In the houses there was anger and, on the part of some, a genuine fear: Were these the new Jacobins? Was the Reign of Terror here? . . . But there was no violence, and no damage — except to peaceful sleep. At last, very late, they left, hoarse, tired, and happy, and Skeffington, still leading them, felt a satisfaction that he was never again to know, in quite the same way, in all his long career.

And on the following morning he had met and conferred with several of these same elders whose sleep he had ruined on the riotous night before. They were members of the important Fiscal Committee, with whom, as mayor, he would have to work for the next four years. They had had no direct experience with this young mayor-elect; they came to the meeting, sagging with fatigue and in a cold fury, prepared to do battle with the blatant, disheveled, ruffian who had shaken them from their beds. Instead, they were met by a clear-eyed, urbane young man, immaculate in morning coat, whose first astonishing remark both unsettled them and set the tone of their relationship in all the years to come.

"Gentlemen, you look weary," he said solicitously. "You ought to get more rest at night."

Then, swiftly, before the gasp had died, he passed into a detailed analysis of the city and its problems. He talked seriously, forcefully and without interruption for forty-five minutes; it was a brilliant examination of municipal government, and in spite of their hostility, they were impressed. And remembering, now, he saw in their eyes the growth of the new, wary respect; and then, the hope of the possible rapprochement. The hope had soon died; the respect had endured: it was this that gratified him now. . . .

He remembered so many things: the night of the Governor's Ball, lavish climax to a campaign that had begun when, first defeated as mayor, he had come ripping back in a series of great, joyous, violent, statewide sweeps, through large industrial cities and barren, suspicious, inbred villages, where speech after speech after speech, for months on end, had brought him, exhausted but triumphant, to the Governor's chair; the days and nights of the great, uproarious campaigns against Festus Garvey and that tough, remorseless, venomous ally, his lovely Ma; the morning in May when, temporarily out of office, rumored to be in serious financial trouble, his creditors pressing him, a dangerous lawsuit approaching fast, he had awakened to find the usual line forming outside his front door, but this time much longer than ever before, and this time ready to give, not receive: they had come voluntarily, each with his two dollars or his dollar or his half-dollar, lining up " . . . to give Frank a lift out of the jam"; that one eminently satisfying, if undoubtedly tactless moment when, at a Holy Name banquet, he had, with a single, uncontrollable, irreverent flash of wit, begun what proved to be a never-ending war of nerves with that unforgiving and most formidable man, the Cardinal . . .

He remembered the political masters, cronies, pupils, hangers-on. He remembered the astonishing, unlettered, shrewd old men who had been there when he was beginning, who, from oilcloth-covered tables in their own kitchens, had ruled their wards like czars, and who, on occasion, had passed on valuable lessons in mass psychology to their eager young disciple; he remembered the young men who had grown old with him, who had come to serve him well, who had been good companions through many a campaign, and who now, with the exception of John Gorman, were gone; he remembered the even younger men who had attached themselves to him like happy barnacles in his later political life: he remembered Ditto and Cuke and all the rest, and thought of them now as they had first come to him and he had taken them on, one by one, to make up his comic, preposterous, loyal and likable entourage. . . .

And he remembered Kate. This was the strong memory, the one which had never to be summoned to mind. Since her death, there had not been a day when he had not thought of her, and now, when he was ill and alone, she came back to him more strongly than ever, the one great constant in this pattern of dreams. It seemed to him that he could remember every minute of every day of every one of the thirty years they had been married. It was absurd, of course, and yet, he thought, it seemed that he could, so vividly did a run of laughter, a word, a phrase, an inflection, and the soft muted music of a whisper in the night come floating from the unforgotten years, so clearly did the grace and gentleness and beauty of face and form and every movement now appear before him. He had loved her deeply; his dependence upon her had been great; and when she died, no one knew, and only John Gorman suspected, what Skeffington had lost, and how large a part of his life had now been closed to him forever. Here, in this sickroom, he thought of her as she had been over the long span of their years together, and each distinct recollection melted slowly and dreamily into the next, so that he remembered Kate always with him, Kate listening, rejoicing, consoling, advising, exhorting, tempering, laughing, loving, living; Kate, Kate, Kate . . .

He remembered it all: the warm, glowing flood of golden moments poured over him morning and afternoon as he lay there. And in this tour, so mercifully selective, there were no clouds: the existent shadows were avoided. Skeffington had been a working politician for more than half a century; in that time he had known betrayal, defeat, unhappiness and despair. More, along his road to glory there were those shabby markers which signalized his own dishonor: for he was not a guiltless man. These he had remembered often; he did not remember them now. Partly through will, partly through some kindly co-operation of memory itself, he was able to pass them by, and to think only of the good things of the past. Of the recent years, and of the people and events belonging to them, he thought hardly at all, and when he did, only one figure emerged strongly and persistently. This was his nephew; of him the old politician thought with fondness and contentment and affection; Adam became a part of the sunlit, lingering daydream.

So the reverie — so untypical of Skeffington — continued, and it came to an end one night. It was the night of his third day of convalescence. He had been sleeping; he awakened suddenly to find himself breathing hard, and the flicker of a familiar, dreadful pain shooting from his shoulder down his left arm. He lay perfectly still; the pain flashed faintly again, then again; then it went away. For a moment he felt nausea; he closed his eyes and tried to breathe deeply; after a while, the nausea passed. He felt somewhat better. Cautiously he raised his head, moving his body carefully to one side: there was no recurrence of pain, but his breathing still came hard and too rapidly. He knew that something had happened — very probably another attack, if much less severe than the other — and that as a result he had been weakened still further; his head sank back against the pillow, and, exhausted, he closed his eyes once more. He did not sleep; he simply lay quietly, thinking of nothing at all. In a few minutes, he opened his eyes; through the darkness he saw the white uniform of the night nurse: she was asleep in her chair. For an instant he thought of waking her, and telling her exactly what had happened; then he dismissed the thought. Whatever had happened, the worst stages had passed, and he did not feel like talking. His breathing came easier now, but still not entirely without effort; he felt as if somewhere in his lungs there were constriction. Moving his head slightly he saw the luminous dial of the clock on the bedside table; it was close to three o'clock in the morning. The nurse slept on; from her chair came a series of delicate, ladylike snoring sounds.

Skeffington did not hear them. His eyes wide open now, staring straight ahead, he was thinking of what had just happened, and what it was to mean to him. This was no daydream, no sun-washed reverie; in the stillness of the hour, in a room darkened against even the faint, blue, early-morning light of the first November moon, Skeffington was thinking hard and realistically. He was, at last, and as he had done all through his life, coldly assessing his own position. He thought for a long time, and when he finished, he had come to a conclusion. He lay there quietly. The north window was open just a crack; outside he heard a dog bark. Soon he heard a car: he could hear the motor and the sound of tires against the road, and he knew, from this sound as it gathered, then diminished, that it came from the north and was racing down the Boulevard towards the center of the city. It was the route he himself took — or rather, had taken: with no particular bitterness he reminded himself that such correction now seemed necessary — every morning; and he thought with an unexpected ache of the glistening black limousine, speeding in through the morning streets, the siren clearing all before it, announcing with its hoarse derisive scream that Skeffington was once more arriving in the city: *his* city, the wonderful, old, sprawling chaos of a city, whose ancient tangled streets and rose-red bricks and ugly piles of quarried stone had held his heart forever. And it now suddenly seemed to him that he wanted nothing more than that he should somehow rise, dress, go downstairs and out to the waiting car, and once again — just once again — streak through all the city's streets, every single one, in one last gleaming, jubilant, splendid morning ride. A modest request, he thought, and yet he knew that it would not be granted. For he did not daydream now; he saw clearly the fact which faced him. And at sometime after three o'clock, on this clear chill morning in early November, he knew — sadly, finally, and certainly — that he was going to die.

He lay awake for a long time, thinking; in this dark room, and faced with this new certainty, his thoughts were not now the even, benign thoughts of the long afternoon drifts. At last he went to sleep; surprisingly enough, he slept quite well through the remainder of the night.

It was shortly after nine o'clock when the doctor arrived for his regular morning visit. He exchanged a few words with Skeffington, the casual greeting as always concealing the sharpness of his attention. This morning, almost instantly he glanced quickly at the night nurse, then reached into his bag and produced a stethoscope. He said easily, "I guess we'll do a little listening, Frank. Just to see if you're as well as you look."

"The bedside manner," Skeffington said; he had seen the doctor's glance at the nurse, and he had not been surprised. "The product of that medical charm school you went to. It's very consoling, I must say."

"Don't talk," commanded the doctor. With a long, skillful hand he held the instrument delicately against his patient's chest; he listened for some moments with no change of expression. Then he straightened and, without speaking, replaced the stethoscope in his bag. He turned, as if to say something to the nurse, but it was Skeffington who broke the silence. "Before you begin your little conference, Dan," he said. "I'd like a few words with you. In private."

The doctor looked at him, then nodded briefly at the nurse. She left the room; the doctor said, "Well, Frank? I don't want you talking too much, you know."

"This won't take long," Skeffington said. "I just got to thinking last night. It seems to me that I haven't been allowed many visitors up to now."

"That's right," the doctor said, neutrally.

"Yes. Well, the point is, I think I'd like to have a few. Say, this afternoon. I thought some of the boys might like to come in."

The doctor shook his head. "No. Not a chance, Frank. Now, let's not talk any more about it. You just run the city; leave your health to me."

"Short-term employment for both of us," Skeffington said. He gave a little chuckle. "Come on, Dan. Don't kid me. You're a good doctor. None better. The point is, it doesn't matter much now how good you are, does it? You know it, and I know it. So come clean. You're not talking to one of your little old ladies now."

The doctor looked at the pale face before him; he heard the breathing, more labored now than before; and he saw the old mocking glint in the eyes. He said, "Frank, tell me what happened last night."

"A little spell," Skeffington said. "Nothing much to talk about, but good enough to do the job, apparently. It was all over in a few minutes. But I know now what's going to happen, Dan, so let's not waste any time in comforting small talk. We haven't got much time to waste, have we?" He spoke more urgently. "Dan, I want those boys in here this afternoon. I want to see them."

"Look, Frank," the doctor said. "I'm not going to kid you. You're right: your situation isn't too good at the moment. Now, I'd do almost anything to oblige you, but it so happens that my job is to keep you alive. . . . "

"Stop it," Skeffington said wearily. "I don't want to argue with you, Dan. How much longer will you be able to keep me alive if I don't see these people than if I do? One hour? Two hours? Twenty-four? Don't be silly." He smiled and said, "And have a heart. I just want to say good-by to a few old friends. What's the harm in that?"

"Don't worry about my heart," the doctor said. "What we're interested in is yours. Now be reasonable, Frank. I know what you want to do, and I want to let you do it. But I don't like it. Not just at this time. I'd much rather you'd wait just a little while. . . . "

"No," Skeffington said firmly. "No waiting. In the name of heaven, I don't just want them to see me; I want to be able to see them. So no waiting." Peremptorily he said, "Get them in here, Dan. Tell John and Sam: they'll know who should come. But I want to see them, and today. You say you want to keep me alive a little longer. All right. That's the only way to do it. Because if they're not allowed in," he said slowly, "I'm apt to raise a little hell, and I don't imagine that'd be too good for anyone in my condition, would it?"

The doctor said, with some irritation, "So now I'm getting the treatment. A little moral blackmail: is that the way it is?"

"That's exactly the way it is. You'll have to forgive the habit of a lifetime. But I mean it, and you know I do. So be a good fellow and come across. It's the lesser of two evils, and you know it." He added persuasively, "Come on, Dan. What do you say?"

The doctor looked at him, then shrugged and said, "All right. You win. But just for a few minutes. And just this once."

"The question of a repeat performance isn't too likely to arise," Skeffington said dryly. "But thanks all the same." He gave a sigh and sank back against the pillows, closing his eyes. The doctor looked at him carefully, then quietly left the room.

Downstairs, he told Adam what had happened. "In other words," he said, exasperation mingling with admiration, "it was City Hall right there in the bedroom. He's literally on his deathbed, and he's still pulling squeeze plays. And I was right in the middle. I either let them come in, or else . . . I didn't have much choice. It may have been a bluff, but, knowing your uncle, and even as sick as he is, I wouldn't care to call it. He's perfectly capable of raising the roof, even now, and in his condition that would be the end. So this was the easiest way out. Naturally, he'd figured it that way." He shook his head, and then in a different voice said, "Besides, I suppose there's really no reason why they shouldn't come now. Unfortunately, your uncle is right: it won't make much difference."

Adam said sadly, "It's definite, then?"

"Yes, I'm afraid it is. I'm sorry." After a minute he said: "He's failed considerably in the last twenty-four hours. He seems to have had a slight attack last night. Our friend the nurse didn't notice it; she was very probably asleep. In any case, she couldn't have done much, as it turned out. From what he says, it was all over very quickly. But you see the difficulty is that with his heart there's no such thing as a slight attack. Anything can do the damage, and this one did. Or at least helped to."

Adam hesitated, then said: "Soon? I mean, will it happen quickly? How long does he have?"

"I don't know, really. Not very long. A few days at most, and probably sooner. Actually, it could happen any time. It all depends on the rate of failure." He stopped and lit a cigarette; he offered one to Adam, who shook his head in refusal. "Poor Frank," the doctor said thoughtfully. "In one way or another, he's done a lot for me over the years. And a lot for the hospital. I'd give a good deal to be able to . . . Well," he said abruptly, stubbing out the cigarette he had just lit, "again, I'm sorry. I think you'd better tell young Francis that there's been a change."

"All right," Adam said. He had been prepared for precisely this news for several days; now that it had come, he found that preparation was of no help at all. He felt as if he had been hit, very hard, in the stomach, and as if the pain had worn away, but the shock had remained. Dumbly, to himself, he said only: *Uncle Frank.* He saw the doctor looking at him, and aloud he said, "What about the priest? He should be called, certainly."

"Yes. However, one suggestion: I think you'd better talk to your uncle before you call."

Surprised, Adam said, "You surely don't think he'd object?"

"Oh no. He'll have no objections. But he may have a few ideas." The doctor smiled wryly. "Unless I miss my guess you'll find he'll take charge of that, too. He'll know exactly the priest he'll want; it probably will be some old friend. He won't want any strangers around him now. Anyway, talk to him about it; he'll tell you. Well," he said, "you can get in touch with either Weinberg or Gorman and tell them that it's all right to bring over a few people. The sooner they get here the better, and they're not to stay long. I may be back in time to see them; I have to go along now, but I'll be back as soon as I can."

The doctor left, and Adam, heavy-hearted, began to make what he now knew were his last arrangements for his uncle. He called John Gorman, who immediately understood and promised that the company of visitors would arrive about noon. He then went upstairs to break the news to Francis Jr.; he did not find him. His cousin had already left the house on one of his blithe, unfathomable errands. Now, dutifully in his home each evening, day and night had been reversed for Francis Jr. He retired early and rose early; restless and bored in the quiet house in the strange, post-dawn hours, he sometimes sought refuge in his car and in long and apparently aimless drives. Undoubtedly, this was what had happened this morning; at any rate, it was a postponement for which Adam was not ungrateful: he did not at all relish the bringing of this final bleak word to his insubstantial cousin. He walked out of the room and over to Skeffington's; he looked in the door and saw that his uncle was awake. The failure that the doctor had spoken of now seemed to Adam painfully evident; the full, heavy face was thin and stripped of color, and, looking at his uncle, and knowing what was inevitable, Adam felt a stab of pity so sharp that he almost gasped out loud. He went into the room; Skeffington, shifting his head, said, "Hello. Good to see you." He patted the edge of his bed and said, "Sit down. You know Miss Guilfoyle, of course."

The day nurse said brightly, "Oh yes, we've met several times."

"Good," said Skeffington. He looked at Adam, who saw, with another pang, that the old mischievous light had suddenly flicked up again in his uncle's eyes. He said, "Has Miss Guilfoyle told you of her brother the missionary in Japan?"

"No, Uncle Frank."

"A saga," Skeffington said. "An inspiring story of Father Francis Guilfoyle and his daily diet of uncooked fish." There was still power in the voice, but Adam noticed now, for the first time, that his uncle was speaking with effort. Skeffington said, "You be sure to tell him that grand story, Miss Guilfoyle. In detail."

"Yes, certainly, Mr. Skeffington."

Skeffington nodded; his eyes glinted at Adam once more. Adam said awkwardly, "Uncle Frank, speaking of priests: I was thinking just a while ago that it might not be a bad idea to have one come over. It's up to you, of course."

Skeffington chuckled. "You think it's high time, do you?"

Adam flushed and said quickly, "No, it's not that at all. It's just that making sick calls is a part of their work, and — "

"Sick calls," Skeffington said, interrupting. "When I was a boy we called it Extreme Unction. The penny catechism didn't go in much for euphemisms." He smiled at Adam and said, "However, I agree. I'll tell you what you do. Get in touch with Hugh Burke. That's Monsignor Burke; he's the pastor at the Blessed Sacrament Church. He's the one I want. Just call him up and tell him the situation, and that I want him." Adam rose, and Skeffington added, "No hurry. I'll tell you when."

The doctor had been right, Adam thought: his uncle was still taking charge of his own case. He said, "All right, Uncle Frank. Whenever you say. I'll be right around."

He went to leave the room, Skeffington said, "Adam?"

"Yes, Uncle Frank?"

His uncle was silent for a moment; Adam could hear the heavy breathing. Finally he said, "Did you enjoy it? The campaign, I mean? All that running around through the city?"

"Yes, Uncle Frank. I never enjoyed anything more."

"Good," Skeffington said. "We had some fun, didn't we?"

"We did, Uncle Frank. A great deal of fun."

"I'm glad," Skeffington said simply. He said nothing more. He lay back once again, his eyes closed, and after a moment Adam left. It had been a heartbreaking few moments. He went downstairs and called Maeve to tell her what had happened. In a distressed voice she said, "Oh, Adam, I'm so sorry. The poor man. I'll come right over, shall I?"

"Yes, good." Then, correcting himself, he said, "No, wait a minute. I just remembered. All the politicians will be coming in pretty soon. Why don't you wait until they leave? Maybe it'd be a good idea to come in around two o'clock. That would give him a chance to rest for a while after the others have gone.

Then we could go in. I know he wants to see you very much."

"I'll come whenever you say," she said. "Two o'clock is fine. You're sure there's nothing I can help you with over there before then?"

"No thanks. There's nothing to do. I'm just staying around in case anything should come up. So I'll see you around two."

"All right, darling."

He hung up. As he had said, there was nothing now that needed to be done; he sat for a while by the telephone, thinking of his uncle. He was finding, as the long and rather oppressive minutes went by, that the knowledge of Skeffington's approaching death was affecting him more deeply than he had expected. He had known, of course, that he was fond of his uncle, and that he would miss him, and yet it seemed as if only now were he beginning to realize the extraordinary bond of feeling which his uncle had managed to establish in so short a time. Adam was not an emotional young man, and in his personal relationships he was apt to be detached rather than warm; yet some quality or combination of qualities in Skeffington had penetrated all reserve and had touched him so specially and with such power that he had responded automatically, without really knowing the strength of his own response or why it was so strong.

He now realized, far more clearly than ever before, that his position in relation to Skeffington had been unique; he thought it likely that to no one else had Skeffington spoken, not merely from his vigor, and wit, and charm, and strength of personality, but also from his loneliness and need. Adam knew now what he had felt vaguely and imperfectly before: he knew why Skeffington had wanted him along on the campaign, and why in the first place he had asked him. Adam had accepted the invitation understanding very little of this; in the following months, Skeffington and he had been close, and Skeffington had given him a great deal. What Adam had given in return was something else again: had it been, he wondered, at all adequate? Only Skeffington knew; Adam did not. But he recalled suddenly what his uncle had said just a few minutes ago when he had called Adam back into the bedroom: that they had had fun together. And so it was possible that, in this sudden, surging friendship of a few crowded, swiftly passing weeks, Skeffington too had found something of what he had desired. Adam hoped so; sitting there, waiting and thinking in the silent hall, he knew that never in his life had he hoped for anything more.

It was just after noon when the band of visitors arrived, led by Weinberg and Gorman. There were perhaps a dozen of them: Cuke, Ditto, all the old day-by-day familiars. Without exception they were in low spirits, for they had heard the news, and yet as they mounted the stairs to the second floor, hope rose automatically, for faith in Skeffington was the center of their lives. When they filed into his room, the faith seemed in a measure justified, for Skeffington, propped up by additional pillows into a half-sitting position, seemed to have drawn upon some reserve for the occasion; Adam, watching from the edge of the little gathering, saw at once that his uncle was undeniably fresher and less drawn than he had been earlier that morning. He seemed in excellent spirits.

"The gang's all here," he said. "Good of you to come, gentlemen. I apologize for the lack of refreshments, but I'm at the mercy of an old-fashioned physician who opposes gracious living. Well," he said, looking from one to the other, "how are you all?"

"Tip-top, Governor," Cuke said promptly. "And it's good to see you looking so good. No kidding, you look great. In a couple of weeks you'll be able to kick the world in the old kazzazza."

"The kazzazza kick is a specialty of mine," Skeffington said gravely. "But I do feel better. I'm getting better every day." He spoke with confidence and animation; Adam wondered if only he in the room noticed the effort behind the words: the breathlessness that he had observed earlier had not diminished. Skeffington said, "Matter of fact, I'm progressing by leaps and bounds. Only yesterday I was practically a corpse. I looked so poorly the casual observer might have taken me for a Republican!"

There was laughter; Ditto said delightedly, "Oh, it's very great stuff to hear you talk like that, Governor! Yes, yes! I said to the boys only this morning, I said, 'Wait till you see the Governor in person and you can bet your bottom boots that he'll tell you in his very own speaking voice that he's coming along fine and absolutely dandy, as we say!' Oh, it's grand to hear it with our ears!" In a more aggrieved tone he said: "I and the boys wanted to stop off in the flower store on the way over, Governor, but John and Sam said we should come right over instead. I and the boys wanted to get you a nice bunch of lovely first-class flowers."

"That's the best kind," Skeffington said. "First-class flowers: a grand gift for sick and well alike. It was a nice thought and I appreciate it; but the fact is that so many flowers have been coming in that I understand the downstairs hall has to be licensed as a greenhouse. So it's much better just to see you boys without the flowers. Besides," he said, "I wanted you to come over here for a reason. I want to have a talk with you. I want your advice. It may not look like it right now, but I meant what I said on Election Night: I'm going to run for governor." He noted the stir, the exchange of doubtful glances: he knew that, to convince, a little more would be needed. It was not easy; he felt himself tiring, and the breathing was bad. But he chuckled and said strongly, "Come on, speak up. I'm a long way from being permanently retired. You're supposed to be the experts: let's talk a little politics. Who've we got to beat?"

It was an invitation they could not resist; Ditto said fervently, "You'll win with both hands down, Governor! The only one who would stand in there up against you is old man Potter, the one with the no left arm. And you're just the very man that could beat his two ears off, Governor. Oh yes yes! Right off of the both sides of his head, as easy as floating down a log, as we say!"

"Potter's a cinch," Cuke said. "You got that chump before he even starts, Governor. The bum'll be shaking in his boots before the bell rings for the first round. But the boy to watch out for is Sonny Allen in the primaries. He's strictly n.g. and he bats from the wrong side of the plate, but out in the western part of the state he's a big wheel. He packs quite a wallop with the hay-shakers!"

The others chimed in; Skeffington listened gravely to what they had to say, as gravely as if all the possibilities and probabilities and conclusions were not both elementary and valueless. From time to time he murmured an agreement, a comment, a question, all designed to encourage the flow of absurd opinion and advice. It was his plan to let them talk; besides, it was much easier on him. In the burlesque council of war, Weinberg and Gorman were silent; Skeffington glanced only once at them, and saw that they were looking at him. They knew exactly what was going on, of course. He saw his nephew in the back of the crowd; he wondered if he knew, too.

Adam did know. At first he had found the babel both surprising and reasonless; then, quickly, he saw what his uncle was doing. It was a game: Skeffington had summoned them here today to play the parts they loved the best; now that it no longer mattered, they had become the counsellors to the king. So, freely and eagerly, they chattered on, and Skeffington, playing his part, listened. And Adam understood what the counsellors did not: that it was a farewell present from Skeffington to them.

But it was an exhausting present; Skeffington was finding that even listening was too much for him; he wondered how much longer he could continue. He felt very weak; he wondered if this necessary kindly farce, which now must have been in progress for half an hour, were not literally killing him? He looked towards Adam, hoping for a word, an action that might end the game. Adam caught the glance and read it properly as a signal for help; before he could move, however, the doctor entered the room. Crisply he declared that the visit was at an end.

The men left, one by one, each coming to the bed to shake Skeffington's hand. When, towards the end of the line, Ditto came by, Skeffington held the handshake just a bit longer. "Ditto, Ditto," he murmured, and added slowly, "How in the world do you thank a man for a million laughs?"

"I beg pardon, Governor?" Ditto said. "I didn't quite catch all of that."

"No matter. Good-by, Ditto."

"Good-by, Governor. And I'll be back here every day, Johnny at the spot, as we say." He went downstairs jauntily; at the door, going out, he said to Adam, "The Governor looks grand, doesn't he, Adam?"

"He looks grand, Ditto."

"Well, you can't lick a man like that," Ditto said. The tiny face became serious; the voice became solemn. "Not like the Governor, Adam. He's the greatest man I ever knew in all my whole life. He's the greatest man in all the world, Adam. The greatest man in all the world!"

Upstairs, Skeffington was saying good-by to Weinberg and Gorman. They stood, side by side, at the head of his bed. Alone of all those who had come, they knew what this moment was. Skeffington took both men by the hand; he looked at them and smiled.

"Good times," he said. "A lot of good times."

"Frank," Weinberg said. "You'll do all right. Anywhere."

Gorman nodded. "Ah, Frank," he said softly. "You've done grand things. Grand, grand things."

"Among others," Skeffington said. "But no regrets. No regrets at all. And all my thanks to both of you. For everything."

The two men gripped his hands; Gorman said soothingly, "We'll be back, Frank. This one isn't the good-by."

They heard a faint chuckle. "If it isn't, it's a pretty good facsimile," Skeffington said. His voice was weak now; the nurse hurried over and removed some of the pillows behind him; without the props, he sank gratefully back into the supine position. He closed his eyes; in a moment, one hand was raised in a small farewell salute. The nurse whispered. "He's going to get a little sleep now."

Weinberg and Gorman tiptoed from the room. As they walked down the front stairs, Weinberg began to move faster, and when he reached the bottom he was almost running, hurrying in a direct savage motion across the hall and out the front door. Gorman followed more slowly, looking neither to the right nor to the left, his old mild blue eyes fixed neutrally straight ahead. In their departure, neither man spoke a single word.

Adam watched them go. Looking at his watch, he saw that it was shortly after one o'clock; Maeve would not arrive for another hour. He went into the library; he picked up a magazine, opened it, and closed it again. He walked around the room;

directly over his head he could hear the footsteps of the doctor crossing the bedroom. Adam went over to the bay window; he sat on the window seat staring out at the front lawn. He must have been there for some time — how long he did not know — when the doctor abruptly entered the room and said, "Do you know what priest he wants? Did he say?"

Adam jumped up and said, "Yes, Monsignor Burke. He said he'd let us know when he wanted him."

"Yes, well, we won't wait for that. I think you'd better call him now."

Adam went to the phone; as he did so he asked the question whose answer he knew. "He's worse?"

"Yes. He's failing rapidly now. It's what I was afraid of: Tell the Monsignor that it's urgent, and to come as quickly as he can. I'll be upstairs if there are any hitches." On his way out of the room he stopped and said, "Young Francis — What about him? Is he here?"

"No." Adam realized with a start that he had completely forgotten about his cousin. He said, "I haven't seen him at all. Apparently he went out early this morning and hasn't come back."

The doctor swore, briefly and harshly. "Right up until the end," he said. "See if you can possibly locate him, will you? Call up any place you think he could be. And if you do find him, give him a message from me that even he should be able to understand. Tell him I said that his father's dying, and if he can spare the time, he might come home for the occasion!"

He left, angrily. It was a brutal message, yet the doctor had had long experience with Francis Jr.: possibly only the brutal or the shocking could be counted upon to reach the core of this exasperating phantom. Adam had no idea how to locate his cousin; however, he would make the effort. Meanwhile, there was the priest. He telephoned to the parish rectory, and after some delaying conversation with the housekeeper, was put through to Monsignor Burke. The Monsignor, an experienced man with the deathbed summons, required no explanation; Adam had barely begun to talk when he said quickly, "All right, all right. I'll be over right away."

With Francis Jr. there was no such success. Adam began by calling the hotels; his cousin had been seen in none of them. He called several restaurants; in desperation he even called the city law office where, in theory, Francis Jr. was employed. Nowhere was there any satisfaction. Presumably Francis Jr. had friends who might be called; Adam did not know them. And so there seemed nothing more that could be done, except to hope that through some sudden miraculous dawning of responsibility, his cousin might decide to come home early. It was, Adam realized, a singularly remote hope. He made one more call: it was to his own home, to tell Maeve to come quickly. There was no answer; looking at his watch, he discovered that it was later than he had thought; in all probability, she was already on her way.

Monsignor Burke, as he had promised, arrived swiftly. He was a very tall man with a long, lined, homely face; in age, he was Skeffington's contemporary. In his right hand he carried a small black grip; as he bore with him the Host, there was no conversation. He merely nodded to Adam and, looking towards the staircase, said, "In his room?"

"Yes, Monsignor." They hurried up the stairs together, the old priest leading, his long legs taking three steps at a time. They entered Skeffington's room; Adam saw at once that — doubtless under the doctor's directions — it had been prepared for the priest. At the head of the bed was a small table, covered with a white cloth: on this were two candles, a crucifix, holy water, a spoon, several small balls of cotton. Skeffington was lying perfectly still, his eyes closed, his breathing now was fast and shallow. The Monsignor came over to the bed; to the doctor he nodded and said, "Conscious?"

"Yes. Just barely."

The Monsignor bent over the motionless figure; he touched his arm gently and said, "Frank?"

Skeffington's eyes opened; he whispered, "Hello, Hugh." He mumbled something else; it was not distinct.

"Frank," the Monsignor said. "I want to hear your confession now."

Skeffington nodded; the Monsignor motioned the others away; the nurse, the doctor, and Adam went out into the hall, closing the door behind them. The doctor said, "Well, that's that. Thank God he got here on time. No sign of young Francis, of course?"

"No. I couldn't find a trace of him."

The doctor merely shook his head; he said nothing. For the next few moments there was a complete silence in the hall; all were thinking, in their own way, of the man who was behind the closed door, making his last confession. Adam heard a car pull up in front of the house; he looked out and saw Maeve coming up the front walk. And to his astonishment and intense annoyance, he saw that she was not alone: her father had come with her. How and why this had happened, Adam did not know; presumably, he thought with bitterness, he had come to protect her from the dying giant.

He went downstairs to meet them at the door. Maeve kissed him and said very quickly, "Daddy came in by surprise just as I was leaving the house."

"Yes," her father said. "And so naturally I thought I'd better come along. She didn't want me to, but it's not a very pleasant journey for a young girl to make alone."

"It's not too dangerous now, though." Adam said. "You see, he's dying: even if you hadn't come she probably wouldn't have been harmed at all."

"What's that, Adam?" his father-in-law said, startled. For an instant, he thought he had detected a queer, almost a *hostile* note in Adam's comment. Obviously he was mistaken, yet he was so seldom mistaken that it gave him pause. It was odd . . .

"Adam, *please,*" Maeve said, imploringly. "Please, not now." Shifting, she said, "What about your uncle? Is he really . . . "

Her voice died out, avoiding the final word. Adam nodded and said, "Yes. Yes, he is. The priest's with him now. Come on up."

They went up the stairs slowly, saying no more; behind them trailed the uninvited guest. When they reached the top, Adam saw that the confession was over. The door to the bedroom was open, and the doctor and nurse were just going in. Adam, taking Maeve by the arm, followed; in the room, the last rites of the Church were continuing. They all knelt; the priest, bending over Skeffington, was administering the Communion. Skeffington's eyes were closed, yet now his lips parted slightly to receive the Host, and softly the old Monsignor murmured the grave and final formula, heard only at the hour of death: *"Accipe Viaticum corporis Domini . . . "*

The Monsignor straightened; after a moment, he began the ritual proper of the Sacrament of Extreme Unction. He sprinkled the sick man with a few drops of holy water, reciting the cleansing prayers of the *Asperges.* He prayed for eternal happiness and charity and joy for the man before him; he entreated God to bless all in this house; he recited the Confiteor and a prayer of exorcism. Then began the anointing. With the blessed oil, the Monsignor slowly anointed the five senses of the dying man: his right thumb made a small cross on the eyelids, the ears, the nostrils, the lips and the hands; he prayed forgiveness for the offenses committed with the co-operation of each sense. There followed a short litany; then a longer prayer; and then it was all over.

Skeffington was motionless on his bed; he gave no sign of life.

All in the room had remained kneeling; from the corner of his eye Adam saw, at the door, the cook and the maid, who had come up for the administration of this last sacrament to their master. They were weeping quietly. He felt Maeve's hand gripping his, hard; in her eyes, too, he saw tears. The Monsignor stepped back from the bed, motioning them to rise; he said in a normal tone, "There. It all went very nicely."

The doctor went to the bedside; he said, "Frank?" There was no acknowledgment, and the rapid breathing could now no longer be heard. Yet when the doctor took the wrist in his hand, he felt the pulse beat: it was faint but it was there. Skeffington's eyes remained closed. He did not move, nor did he seem, now, aware of those around him: yet he was still among them. The doctor, with a sign, let them know that this was so.

There was silence in the room. It was an awed, a dreadful silence, the vacant interval when all preliminaries to death had been accomplished, and death itself was yet a moment away. It was a silence which was broken by Maeve's father.

"Well, Monsignor," he said, with a terrible tolerance, "we know now that he's made his peace with God."

There was a stir in the room; the Monsignor gave him a look of unconcealed hostility. "Yes," he said shortly. "Yes, he has."

It was a rebuke, but the little merchant had decided that it was a time for forgiveness; he was going to be generous to his old foe; and he was not to be stopped.

"Well, no matter what some of us may have thought in the past," he said, addressing them all, "it's all different now. And I think we can say this: that knowing what he knows now, if he had it all to do over again, there's not the slightest doubt but that he'd do it all very, very differently!"

It was a statement awful in its smugness. Maeve gasped and said, "Oh, *Daddy!*" The Monsignor turned sharply away; the doctor stepped forward; and Adam, standing beside his wife, felt anger blaze. He wanted to shout this pompous fool out of the house; he felt Maeve holding tightly to him; still, he started to speak, but suddenly there was no need for any of them to answer. For the figure on the bed stirred; they heard the movement before seeing it and, turning, they saw that Skeffington had raised himself slightly. His eyes were now wide open, and in them they saw the old challenging, mocking, gleam. And they heard his voice, as taking charge now for the last time he gave his answer:

"The hell I would!"

The words came out in a hoarse whisper, but they were loud, distinct, confident and undefeated. Adam felt like cheering. He heard the Monsignor exclaim, softly and delightedly, "Oh grand, grand, grand!" And Adam did not even look at his father-in-law. Instead, he watched his uncle: Skeffington was turning his head slowly, looking at them all. After a moment, he said, quite distinctly, "Francis?"

There was no answer. Then, agonized, Adam said, "He just went out for a moment, Uncle Frank. He'll be right back."

"He has a grand sense of timing," Skeffington said. The whisper now was fainter; Skeffington slipped back, and lay flat once more. From this position his head turned, very slowly, to look at them all again. When he came to Maeve, he paused and smiled; his lips parted and moved, as though he were speaking; the words were not audible. His head continued to turn, and he stopped when he came to Adam. Uncle and nephew looked at each other: for one moment, no one else might have been in the room. Then Skeffington smiled again — there was just a faint flicker of his left eyelid, and he spoke his last words to Adam.

"See you around," he whispered.

The whisper was barely audible, but Adam heard. Skeffington's eyes seemed now to snap shut; his head turned back with a queer, abrupt jerk; his body stiffened; and one arm hung rigidly over the side of the bed, pointing to the floor.

Frank Skeffington was dead.

Fourteen

SKEFFINGTON'S FUNERAL was the largest ever held in the city.

It followed a three-day wake which had seen thousands of mourners file into the big house on the Boulevard. Now, this morning, the church was jammed to the doors, more than half an hour before the Mass began; outside, the plaza in front of the church was filled, and the crowd bulged into the street and out along the sidewalks on both sides. It was not a favorable day for the funeral. The sky was dull, and shortly after dawn snow had begun to fall. It was the first snow of the season, and it had come early this year; while the fall had been light, failing to coat the ground, the low, damp-gray clouds held promise of more to come. The wind was sharp and from the sea; the mourners who stood outside the church did so in some discomfort. Yet no one left, and, as the minutes went by, many more continued to arrive.

Just before nine o'clock, the first cars of the long cortege came slowly around the corner, the hearse stopping exactly opposite the main doors of the church. The undertaker's men — the professionals of death — were out of the cars instantly, moving with a kind of solemn speed, opening the back of the hearse, and smoothly transferring the coffin down and out into the awkward hands of the amateurs — the bearers. These six men — Cuke and Ditto were among them — had been friends of Skeffington's; they would carry his body into the church and then, after the Mass, they would carry it out again, replacing it in the hearse. Still later, after the long procession to the cemetery — for the route of the funeral was not to be a direct one: it would proceed from the church along a detour through the heart of the city, along the streets that Skeffington had traveled each morning, out onto the Boulevard past his home, and then back onto the cemetery road — they would complete their sad assignment, and finally place his coffin down on consecrated ground.

Now, carrying their burden, they moved slowly from the hearse across the plaza to the church; the procession to the altar had begun. At the top of the steps they were met by the priest who was to celebrate the Requiem Mass. With the two priests who were to serve as deacon and subdeacon, with the clergy who would be present in the sanctuary, with all the altar boys, he escorted the coffin in slow, solemn progress down the center aisle to the sanctuary itself. Along the way were intoned the psalms of the funeral rite: the *Miserere* following the *De Profundis.* And as the body neared the altar, they sang the anthem *Subvenite Sancti Dei:*

"Come to his assistance, all ye saints of God, meet him all ye angels of God, receiving his soul and offering it in the sight of the Most High. May Christ receive thee, who hath called thee, and may angels conduct thee to Abraham's bosom. Eternal rest grant unto him, O Lord, and let perpetual light shine upon him. . . ."

They had reached the altar rail. The coffin was placed at the entrance to the sanctuary, and the priests went swiftly to the side to vest themselves. Then, in their chasubles of black, they returned to the foot of the altar, and the Mass of the Dead began.

It was not a long service, which was perhaps fortunate, as the church was dangerously overcrowded. In addition to the great number of anonymous mourners, there were the more conspicuous figures, some of whom had come out of curiosity, some out of compulsion, but most out of a desire to pay their last respects to the man with whom they had either worked or fought for so long. The state's senior Senator was there; the Governor had come with all the members of his official family; state and civic officials, justices of the state's various courts, commissioners of public services were squeezed together in the pews flanking the center aisle; uniformed policemen and firemen were several rows deep; the military services had dutifully sent their representatives; there were delegations — some uniformed, some not —

from the innumerable lodges and associations to which Skeffington had belonged: The Knights of Columbus, the Ancient Order of Hibernians, the Sons of Italy, the Eagles, the Elks, the American Legion, the Veterans of Foreign Wars, the Friendly Sons of Saint Patrick — all these and many more. All had come for this last farewell to Frank Skeffington.

Adam knew that they were here; seated as he was, he could not see them. He was in the very front of the church, in the pew reserved for the family of the deceased. Here, alone in the packed congregation, there was no crowding, for Skeffington's family was small. Only Adam and Maeve knelt in the pew beside a nervous, white-faced Francis Jr. As the liturgy unfolded, Adam glanced occasionally at his cousin. Throughout the three days of the wake he had remained in his room, remorseful, distraught, and utterly helpless; Adam and Maeve, together with a few old friends of Skeffington, had attended to the business of receiving the mourners. This morning Adam would not have been greatly surprised to find that his cousin could not firm himself even to attend his father's funeral, but in this he did him an injustice. For Francis Jr. was here and, moreover, was holding himself — so far, at least — under tight control. It was an unexpected turn for which Adam was most grateful.

The Mass continued. Adam followed the three priests as they moved smoothly through the centuries-old ritual which he had often attended, but which only once before — at the death of his father and mother — had he felt deeply and personally involved. And as from the choir loft there arose the portentous chant of the *Dies Irae,* filling the church with its somber, warning echoes, the memory of the double loss of years ago now came back to him strongly, mingling with and reinforcing present sadness. Skeffington was gone: the fact which Adam had known and had accepted for days now, here in this setting of splendid ceremony, seemed to acquire new emphasis, and to be harder than ever to bear. It was a feeling which Adam shared with others; at his side, he saw his wife touch her eyes quickly with her handkerchief, and over across the aisle, in the pew where the bearers sat, he saw the vast body of Ditto Boland, shaking with sobs. For more than all others, the fat man had been inconsolable since Skeffington's death: the end of his idol was the end of everything for Ditto.

On the altar, the Last Gospel was said. The three priests descended and retired to their places at the side of the sanctuary. There was now a pause in the ceremonies; if there was to be a eulogy, Adam thought, it would have to occur here. He knew that the eulogy was not the custom of the Church, yet he knew also that in the case of the exceptional man, one was sometimes given. Surely Skeffington, in the life of this city, had been an exceptional man; at the same time, however, Adam remembered the hostility of the Cardinal. The aged prelate was pointedly absent from these requiem services this morning; was it likely that he would allow this man, whose public conduct he had so long deplored, to be eulogized in a church over which he held dominion? The answer seemed obvious, yet almost at once Adam received another surprise: from the ranks of the clergy seated within the sanctuary rose the tall figure of Monsignor Hugh Burke. Slowly he mounted the steps leading into the pulpit; it was apparent that, whatever his reasons, the Cardinal was permitting Skeffington to be eulogized by the old friend who had attended him at his death. Adam relaxed in relief; it was a good conclusion.

The eulogy was neither long nor elaborate; Monsignor Burke did not belong to the tradition of the great pulpit orator. But it was effective and curiously moving, possibly because it was so unexpectedly personal. Skeffington had all his life been a public man, but it was of a private man that the Monsignor now spoke. From his words one could scarcely have gathered that Skeffington had been in politics at all, let alone the fact that he had dominated the political life of the city for close to half a century. Instead, one caught warm fragments of a story of a boyhood companion, of a man happy throughout his married years, of a friend who might drop in unannounced for dinner at a parish rectory and spend the rest of the evening talking quietly with the priest who had grown old with him. Under the Monsignor's gentle light one saw revealed qualities of wit and warmth and generosity that had gone to make up a most attractive personality. It was a fond reminiscence by a kind man of a valued, lifelong friend, and only at the very end did the Monsignor shift his focus slightly, and for a moment speak of Skeffington against a more accustomed backdrop.

"He was, of course, a politician by profession," he said, "and I find that that is what seems to interest many people. I admit to you that it did not interest me. Although I have lived all my life in this city, I have never known much about its politics. I have been told by those who seem to know a great deal about them that Frank Skeffington did very good things. I have been told by others who seem equally well-informed that he did very bad things. But as, over the years, I listened to all these people, I began to suspect that I was not alone in my political ignorance. It seemed to me that most of these people who talked so knowingly about politics and politicians really didn't *know* that what they were telling me was so; they were merely passing along something that they had heard from someone else who was supposed to know. Well, I imagine we all do that. Everybody likes to be considered a bit of authority, and for some reason most people seem to want to be considered political authorities. Only, you see, that makes it very difficult sometimes to get at the truth about men in public life. As for Frank Skeffington, I suppose there was at least some truth in many of the things, good and bad, that were said about him. Because I suppose, after all, that like most of us, Frank Skeffington did his share of good and bad things. The difference, I think, was that unlike most of us he was a very prominent man and he moved in a world where both praise and blame seem to have a habit of starting out of very little and becoming vastly exaggerated in no time at all. The bigger the man is in public life, the bigger the praise or the blame — and we have to remember that Frank Skeffington was quite a big man. And so I don't know what to say to you about his political career. I really know very little of the truth about it, and I strongly suspect that many who have talked at great length about it actually know almost as little about it as myself. I can only say that, as I look around me, at this city in which I have lived for so long, it seems to me now to be a better city for most of the people than it used to be, and I suspect that Frank Skeffington played at least a part in making it that way. I look around, too, at all the people who have come here this morning for no other reason than to show their respect and affection and love for this man whom they knew and who had served them for so many years. And, if you will forgive just one more personal reflection, I myself think of him as he was just a few short days ago when I went to his home to hear his last confession and to give him the Blessed Sacrament, just before he died. And it seems to me, now, that to have lived a long life, to have left the lot of many of those around you a little bit better than it once was, to have been genuinely loved by a great many people, and to have died in God's good grace, is no small thing to have happened to any man. Yet that is what happened to Frank Skeffington; I hope it may happen as well for all of us."

The church was quiet; so much so that not even the usual shifting and nervous coughing began until the old Monsignor was well out of the pulpit, on his way back to his position in the sanctuary. Swiftly now the ceremonies were concluded. The celebrant approached the coffin, reciting the prayers of absolution; he went slowly around it, continuing with the prayers, and sprinkling each side with holy water. The prayers came to an end; the bearers rose at a signal from the pews and took up their positions beside the coffin. And once again the slow procession began, this time going out of the church, away from the altar, down the steps, back to the hearse which would lead the long cavalcade on its journey to the burial ground.

Many of those who had been in the church accompanied the procession to the cemetery; others did not. . . .

Nathaniel Gardiner did not. It was a busy morning for him; nevertheless, he had taken time off to attend the funeral Mass. It had not occurred to him not to do so. As he left the church, he found that it was beginning to snow again; he turned his coat collar up and started to walk, with short, quick strides, not back to his club, but to his downtown offices. For part of the way the funeral procession crawled along beside him; when he turned off onto a side street, he stopped and peered through his small glasses down the street for a final look at the huge, old-fashioned hearse. And so, he thought, there goes Frank Skeffington. The thought depressed him oddly. He had not agreed with the eulogistic words of the Monsignor; they had been the words of a good friend and a charitable man, but put together, they had not spelled Skeffington. For the good Monsignor had left out too much; as he himself had said, he did not know. But Gardiner did know, and looking back over the almost fifty years of struggle with this adroit and ruthless political maneuverer, he thought that the man's entire career seemed to have been devoted to the contravention of the law. He thought of buildings erected and roads constructed unnecessarily and at three times their normal cost; he thought of contracts skillfully diverted to political friends; he thought of tax rebates handed out in wholesale lots to campaign contributors; he thought of the endless jobs given to old pals, of the time when the entire city payroll seemed to be supporting nothing but a host of indolent comedians; he thought of the gerrymandering, the featherbedding, of the whole, incredible, ridiculous, wasteful tangle, and as he thought he reflected grimly that if he, instead of the Monsignor, had delivered the eulogy, it would have been a far different proposition indeed. Yet even as he thought this, a slight smile appeared on his lips, for in remembering all these items of discredit, he had remembered the other side, too: the astonishing, good-humored audacity of the man which had so often stunned a roomful of opponents; the mischievous gleam in the eye which suddenly appeared as he advanced some particularly outrageous proposal; the extraordinary wit and congeniality which had relieved so many deadly dull committee meetings; the courage, the generosity, the charm, the sheer ability of the man. . . . Gardiner shook his head. Now, he thought, I am back with the Monsignor. Skeffington had always amused him and attracted him, and in a sense, he felt a great sympathy for him. And now he said to himself what he had said, in equal privacy, so often before: *If only he had not been such a rogue* . . . But then he reminded himself, as he had done before, in that case he would not have been Skeffington at all, but someone quite different. And in any case, he was gone now; peering once more, Gardiner could no longer see the hearse: it had turned the corner. Again the feeling of depression settled over him. Skeffington had gone, and it was as if a part of the city itself had gone: a part of the city which Gardiner had both liked and deplored, but most of all a part of the city with which he had grown up, which he knew, and which was as much a part of the city to him as the fine old buildings themselves. And now it was gone, and Gardiner, too, was an old man who would soon be going; the question he asked himself now was: "Who and what is to follow us?" And because he loved this city, he would not have mourned the passing of the old if he could have seen even the promise of improvement in the new. But he could not. Where there had been a Skeffington there was now a McCluskey. The old buccaneer, for all his faults, had at least been a capable, vivid, unforgettable personality; he had been succeeded by the spearhead of a generation of ciphers. The old philanthropist shrugged pessimistically and, pulling his coat more tightly around him, once again struck off briskly in the direction of his offices. . . .

Charlie Hennessey went with the procession to the cemetery. He drove his own car, and by his side was a passenger he had unexpectedly picked up outside the church. It was Festus Garvey, who, at the last minute, had decided he might just as well go along to the grave, to see things safely through to the end.

Charlie was an unsuccessful driver. He made no concessions to the demands of traffic; as he drove he talked continually, sometimes making interesting little experiments, such as driving with one eye closed to test his peripheral vision. His progress was unfailingly hazardous, even in this slow motorcade; several times he bumped, rather hard, the car directly preceding him.

"Easy easy easy!" cried Festus irritably. "For the love o' God, will you watch where you're goin'!" The last bump had jostled him severely, disturbing his train of thought. He had been thinking, not of Skeffington — nor of the funeral, nor of anything of the past or of the present. He was planning for the future: the snow, falling gently but steadily now, had reminded him of the winter months to come. Undoubtedly, with snow this early, it would be a hard winter. There would be snow, lots of snow, and Festus, cemetery bound, could not help but think greedily and happily of the profitable snow-removal contracts that would have to be given out. Oh, he would have his finger in *that* pie, all right; he would see to that! And then, in the midst of such pleasant reflections, had come the hard, disquieting bump. He grumbled again, "Watch out what you're doing. You drive like a damn looney!"

"Be calm at all times, my dear man," Charlie said reprovingly. "No excitement: that's the important thing to remember at your age. The little vessels in the brain are all dried up, my dear man: they could snap and pop like Rice Krispies at any moment. Men younger than you are dropping like flies in the street every day." He switched from helpful counsel to the affairs of the moment. "I saw your tame dunce in church," he said. "Nut-boy McCluskey, wearing the frock coat and the striped pants. And I saw where he sneaked off from the church as soon as the Mass was over. He's not coming to the cemetery."

Surprisingly, this slighting reference to his protégé did not enrage Garvey; now, with the election over, with all danger past, he could afford to be less bellicose and somewhat more candid. "No," he said indifferently. "He's got to go somewheres. With the wife."

"Bad politics, my dear man," Charlie said, clucking with his tongue. "Oh, very bad politics at this stage of the game. The nut-boy should be right out there by the grave with the wife and the kids and the rented dog. He should be right out there where everybody could see him, falling on his knees and boo-hooing into the pit, howling that he'll say a prayer for him to his pal, the Holy Father. That's the real nut-boy style, my dear man. Oh, yes yes!"

Garvey shrugged. "It makes no damn difference. He's in for four years, and four years from now they'll all forget whether he did or he didn't go to the grave. People forget damn fast. Just like," he said, in a suddenly violent voice, "they'll forget that big lummox that had the nerve to lock me out of City Hall and that's ridin' on his arse today in the hearse up there ahead! Inside of six months they'll forget all about him and his fancy manners and his big voice and his hip-hip-hoorays for Skeffington! My lovely Ma, God rest her soul, had it right. She used to say to me, she'd say, 'Festus, me son, ye'll be around to fling dirt on his grave, and ye'll be ridin' around the city in a chariot nine feet tall with people cheerin' for ye when that big bastard is six feet under ground with nobody cheerin' for him but the worms and the snakes!' And oh!" he crowed, "how right she was! The Ma was always right. Here I am, alive and kickin' and full of beans, right up in the driver's seat again, and there *he* is, just like the Ma said, off on the last one-way trip, and the day after tomorrow nobody'll even remember who in hell he was!"

"That big vein is jumping around in your forehead again," Charlie said, looking at him critically. "You'll go up like a jet plane one of these days. And of course that's all nonsense what you're saying, my dear man. All pure nonsense, nothing but hogwash. You could live to be a hundred and twenty-five and put new red, white and blue posters of yourself all around town every day, and still they wouldn't think of you as often as they will of Frank Skeffington when he's been dead fifty years. The difference is that they all loved him and nobody loves you. I say this in no criticism of you, my dear man. It's not your fault that you are what you are. It's all in the genes: you're not responsible. That's the latest up-to-date medical opinion so you needn't blame yourself at all. But facts are facts, my dear man, and the fact here is that Frank Skeffington was a rascal with a heart as big as the state of Kansas and a marvelous way with all kinds of people. Oh, marvelous! There was none like it. Whereas you, my dear man, if you'll look at yourself objectively, in what the college professors call the scientific spirit, you'll see that you're just not in it at all! Oh no no no! It's not your fault, not a bit of it. That's the way Nature is, my dear man. Everything to some, nothing to others. Mysterious! Incomprehensible! Marvelous! But all facts, my dear man, and all explaining why, when it comes to Frank Skeffington, you're simply not in the picture at all!"

Garvey's face had been reddening dangerously; with a little howl of rage he raised his right hand, but at that moment Charlie's car jumped ahead slightly, bumping the car before it once again; Garvey was hurled against the dashboard.

"For the love of God!" he cried desperately. "I tell you, easy, easy, EASY!" The bump had reminded him that he was in a position of hazard; to argue, to remonstrate, to strike, would only distract the driver further and increase the danger. He sank back into his corner, fuming quietly for the rest of the ride, while Charlie drove and continued to talk about Skeffington all the while. . . .

Norman Cass did not go to the cemetery; he had not, in fact, gone to the church. This morning, as usual, he had gone directly from his home to the bank; now, from the windows of his office, he viewed the cortege which had begun to wind its way through the downtown streets. All other traffic had been re-routed; the funeral procession moved slowly along; Norman Cass, looking down upon it, permitted just the faintest of smiles to cross his smooth, brown, expressionless face. There was no need to rejoice extravagantly; he was a man who enjoyed his greatest triumphs quietly. And now he knew that the man who had humiliated him was at last leaving the scene; Norman Cass felt no distress. Even more, he knew that with the man went an era; he was not sorry to see it go. He had done well in it, but in spite of it; had it — and its buccaneer leader — been less aggressive, less obstructive, more tractable, more co-operative, he would have done far better. But the man and the era were going now, to be succeeded by a new man, a new day. And at the thought, the faint smile appeared again; the future was promising. That evening he had arranged a small dinner party for Mayor-elect and Mrs. McCluskey; he did not think that this aspiring young couple would fail to be impressed by their fellow guests. Yes, a new day was unquestionably dawning, and the greatest single threat to that day was even now disappearing down the street. It was a thought to elevate the spirit.

He went abruptly to his desk and flicked a lever on the inter-office communication device; to his secretary he said, "Have my son come in." Then he returned to the window.

Norman Cass Jr. came in almost instantly; he said, "Good morning, Dad. You thent for me?"

Wordlessly, his father beckoned him to the window; he pointed down to the procession in the streets below. The cars inched along, and for a moment father and son watched together.

Then, suddenly, Norman Cass turned to face his son; with a savage derision he said, "*Mr. Commissioner . . .*"

His long and slightly silly face flushing, Norman Cass Jr. retreated from the office; not a week passed that the error of his greatest independent decision was not recalled to him. His father was not a forgiving man.

Norman Cass Sr. resumed his watching by the window. It was not, for him, an unsatisfactory morning. . . .

The young Monsignor who was the Cardinal's secretary did not go to the cemetery. He left the church after Mass and drove back to the Cardinal's palace; there, he reported the events of the morning to his superior. The Cardinal listened, stony-faced; after he had heard the description of the eulogy, he groaned and said, "Poor Hugh. Poor innocent Hugh. And no one laughed, I trust?"

"No, *Eminenza.* Actually, it was quite moving."

"Yes. I have no doubt. And also quite inaccurate." He shook his head and said, "This picture of Skeffington as some sort of kindly old man who went about at night making small talk with parish priests in their rectories! Absurd! That was what he said, you say?"

The sardonic precis had been unfair; the young Monsignor said quickly, "Well, no. Not exactly, *Eminenza. . . .*"

The Cardinal brushed aside all qualifications. "But near enough," he said. "Near enough. I can imagine it all very well: I've known Hugh a long time. He's a good priest, but his fault is that he's too good. Listen to him and you'll find that every scoundrel in the city has a heart of pure gold. Naturally, Skeffington's heart was purer than most. He handed out cold-storage turkeys to the deserving poor at Christmas. And, of course, he stopped in every so often for the famous evening chat at the parish rectory, to talk over boyhood days. Obviously a man who would do that couldn't be a shameless political trickster and a public disgrace. Q. E. D." He added grimly, "I made a mistake years ago. I should have brought Hugh up here with me, so that he could see what trying to run a diocese was like with a schemer in City Hall who would stop at nothing, absolutely *nothing,* to bend and twist the Church to his own purposes. Anything and everything for the vote. My good Monsignor Burke might have formed a slightly different opinion of his old boyhood friend who came a-calling so pleasantly in the evenings. And you, my young friend, might have heard a somewhat different eulogy of this man whom you apparently persist in romanticizing. You might have heard something slightly less naïve!"

The young Monsignor hesitated, then said, "Still — "

"Still," the Cardinal said, flashing in, "I permitted it, eh? And I announced that Hugh was to deliver it, eh? And you'd like to know why: is that it?"

His secretary smiled and said, "More or less, *Eminenza*. Yes."

"Because it was the best way to handle a difficult situation," the Cardinal said simply. "I could have forbidden it. I could merely have said that there would be no eulogy and that would have been the end of it. But you can see the consequences of any such solution as that. At least," he said, with a sudden fierce politeness, "I hope you can. Otherwise we have both wasted a great deal of time during the last few years."

The young Monsignor smiled again and said, "I imagine that no eulogy at all would simply have meant too much fuss and fury."

"Exactly. And pointlessly so. A eulogy was logical, it was expected: Skeffington was undoubtedly the best-known and most popular Catholic layman in the diocese. I have never denied his popularity. Very well. If there had been no eulogy, the people would have grumbled; I am used to that. There would have been the newspaper stories, all the old tales resurrected about Skeffington and the Cardinal; I am used to that, too. But what was far worse, we would have had, once again, this linking in the public mind of Skeffington and the Church. The absence of the eulogy would have started the whirlwind of distasteful discussion once more. All our old enemies would gleefully leap into action with everything from magazine articles to those pitiful little letters to the editor, all talking about Skeffington, the Typical Irish Catholic Politician. I need not add that we could rely upon the controversy's being kept alive by those blustering idiot defenders on our side of the fence. And it would have gone on and on, tragically so, since there would have been no necessity for its arising in the first place. One small, politic gesture, of no significance whatever, was all that was required to forestall it. And so Frank Skeffington got his eulogy. No one, of course, would have realized the implications of all this more completely than Skeffington himself. I'm sure that, in the light of the consequences, he would have greatly preferred no eulogy at all." With a wintry little smile he added, "But he got one."

The young Monsignor nodded. It was all clear enough; he understood his superior. But he came now to the point which was not so clear; he said, "But why Monsignor Burke, *Eminenza?*"

"Also logical enough. He was Skeffington's friend. More to the point, however," the Cardinal said, "I felt that he could be counted upon to give the right *kind* of eulogy. I do not mean that it would be true; I mean that at least it would not be political. And that was the important thing: to see to it that some oaf did not get up in the pulpit and start to bellow about '. . . this splendid fighter who, throughout his political life, never once forgot that he was a representative of his Church and of his People!' " It was a scornful, mortifying imitation of the pulpit delivery of a well-known diocesan orator; the young Monsignor marveled at its exactness. "All pure myth!" the Cardinal went on vehemently. "And whether you realize it or not now, you will later on. This man cheapened us forever at a time when we could have gained stature: I can never forgive him for that!" More calmly, he added, "I knew, however, that any eulogy by Hugh would not be in that vein. It would be purely personal. You say it was moving. Perhaps. I do not think it would have moved me. In any case, it was the testimony of a priest to a friend, and not to a public official, and so it was relatively inoffensive. At least there will be no repercussions. And that, my dear young Monsignor, is exactly why the eulogy was delivered by Hugh Burke!"

The Cardinal looked at his watch; he rose stiffly from his chair. "They are at the cemetery now, are they?" he said.

"Yes, just about, *Eminenza.*"

The Cardinal grunted; he turned and began to walk out of the room. The young Monsignor watched him as he moved slowly along, shuffling slightly. The old prelate was not well, and he had aged greatly in the past year; it was a thought which pained his secretary, for he was very fond of this severe old man who had been kind to him. And he thought of him now in connection with Skeffington: one was gone, and the other, unhappily, was soon to go. The old giants who had shaped an age and a city were now leaving, one by one: soon, they would all be gone. And, as one of their inheritors, the young Monsignor thought of this with sadness, for he realized that they had been unique men who had done much, and he hated to see them go.

At the door the Cardinal stopped, whirling suddenly to face his secretary.

"All right," he said loudly. "He's gone. And may God have mercy on him. I never could; maybe He will. But now the subject is closed. I want no more talk about it. This is one house in the diocese which will not feature endless posthumous discussions of Frank Skeffington. None at all. Ever. Is that quite clear?"

The young Monsignor merely nodded and said, "Yes, *Eminenza*. Quite clear."

"All right," said the Cardinal. He shuffled from the room, and as he did so, he said again, "All right. . . ."

In the newspaper building where Adam worked, Amos Force sat at his desk. Across from him, and at a respectful distance, sat the managing editor. Together, they had been standing at the window, watching the procession go by; it was their contact with the funeral. But now the procession had left the downtown streets; Amos Force was reminiscing.

"A terrible man," he said. "Utterly unprincipled. He cost us money. Twice. I don't know if you remember that."

"Oh yes," the managing editor said fervently. He remembered every significant detail of both libel suits: the amount of the damages awarded, the writing of the checks, the signing of them, the delivering of them to Skeffington, the *cashing* of them. He said, "I remember, Mr. Force."

"A man like that is incapable of governing. At no time did he ever deceive me. I knew him for what he was from the beginning. He comes of bad stock. I am going to tell you something now I have never told you before. His mother was a maid in our house when I was a boy. My father had to dismiss her for stealing food."

"Ah," said the managing editor unhappily. Strictly speaking, it was not quite true that he was about to hear this story for the first time. He had heard it before, all too often: it was one of the little confidences with which his employer regularly harassed him.

"Systematic thievery," Mr. Force began, "conducted over a period of many months by an ungrateful woman. I will tell you about it. You will enjoy it." He told the story at great length, his old voice soaring up and down, caressing each remembered detail. The managing editor listened, feigning attention. Only one particular in the long, dreary account interested him at all: the woman had stolen *food* from the home of Amos Force. Remembering the long succession of ghastly, punitive repasts he had been compelled to endure in this house, he found the crime incomprehensible.

"And so," Mr. Force concluded at last, "like mother, like son. And both punished in the end. And yet there are those who tell us that there is not a Higher Justice! Here is the proof of it right before our eyes this morning." He rose from his desk and walked once more to the window; the funeral had long since gone, but Amos Force let his eye rove pleasurably over the street on which it had passed. "A desperado of the worst kind," he declared. "He tried to get my money. I said I would defeat him with my editorials and I am seldom wrong. You can bear witness to that, of course. I am a kindly man, but I am a bad man to cross. He went down to crushing defeat. And now, to top it off, he is gone." His voice softened, as if in prayer: he might have been thanking the Higher Justice for the unanticipated bonus. "Yes," he said happily, looking up the street and into this distance, "there is a great lesson here for us all. . . ."

The managing editor was silent, but he, too, was glad that Skeffington was gone. Now his employer would go home: the awful, inescapable, summoning voice would no longer be heard whining through the corridors every night and every day. He would come in now only infrequently; the managing editor's hours would once more be his own: he could get back to business. No one knew better than he that during the campaign the paper had slipped. He had seen, once again, the glow of the superfluous electric light; in the sports department the carbon paper supply was diminishing with suspicious rapidity; someone — and he thought he knew who — was wasting the liquid soap in the third-floor men's room; three slugs had been found in a gum machine. No, he did not fool himself: the paper was not what it was a few months ago. But now, with Skeffington gone, Amos Force was going home. The managing editor would be let alone; he would bring the paper back. And so the departure of Skeffington had meant, in another sense, the departure of Amos Force; the managing editor was not by nature an optimist, but now he was forced to admit that everything had worked out very well indeed. . . .

And at the cemetery, the last prayer was said, the last blessing given: Skeffington was lowered into the ground. The crowd who had gathered around the grave slowly began to disperse, making for the main gate of the cemetery, and the cars that were parked outside. Weinberg and Gorman walked off together, silently. At the gate they stopped; they were returning to the city in different cars. After a moment Weinberg said, "A tough day."

"It is," Gorman said. "They'll come no tougher."

"Yeh," Weinberg said. "Yeh. That's for sure. Well . . ." He shrugged and said, "So long. I'll see you. Tomorrow."

Gorman nodded; Weinberg went off to his car. Gorman watched him go. A good man, he thought; there was none better. But the thought was casual, diversionary; he returned to his thoughts of Skeffington. It was hard, even now, to accept the fact that he was gone. Yet it was, of course, a fact, and a fact which left the old politician with a feeling of loneliness which was peculiarly his, which no one else could share. For he had known Skeffington longer than all of them. Although he had been Skeffington's senior by a few years, they had grown up together and worked together for most of their lives; there had been a remarkable communion between them. The variations had of course been there — for one thing, Skeffington's scale had always been much larger — but basically the two men had lived in the same world, understanding instinctively the same things, sharing the same beliefs, the same friends, the same enemies, the same attitude towards the business of life. They spoke — and, more important, could leave unspoken — the same language; for seventy years — and it seemed to Gorman now that it had been no more than five — they and many others had shared a way of life. The others had all gone, one by one — Gorman remembered now the long list of names: Big Tim Donlin, Matthew Healy, Pusher Clancy, Georgie McCabe, Derby Dan Donnelly, Charlie Ryan, Frankie O'Connell, all the others — each one taking with him as he went a little bit of the old ways. And as they went Gorman had missed them, but he had not quite realized exactly what was happening, he had not sensed the slow erosion of the world he knew. For there had always been Skeffington, and now, suddenly, Skeffington too was gone, and for the first time John Gorman realized with a cruel abruptness just how far away the old ways were, and just how completely alone he now was. It was true that in his own ward he was still boss, and that he would be for as long as he cared to be, but there was little joy in that for him now. For, he thought, to be a boss in this new world that seemed to be coming on, a world the nature of which he was just beginning to suspect, a world in which no provision was made for the old ways, the old pals, and — most important of all — a world without Frank Skeffington there to lead the grand big rallies and to whoosh through the city in a great whirlwind of laughter and handshakes and hoorahs — to be a boss in such a world, he thought, was not the same thing. No no, he thought, it was not the same thing at all. . . .

He began to walk from the gate towards the car that was to take him home. On the way he encountered Ditto; the fat man's little face was blotched with recent tears. Gorman said kindly, "Hello, Ditto. Be a good lad, now, and keep the chin high. It's a bad day for all of us."

But Ditto had come to him with a specific problem.

"John," he said, his voice shaking, "one single second, John. Is that all they're going to put up over the Governor's head? Just one single piece of marble stone?"

He pointed with indignation to the headstone, up on the little hill where Skeffington lay buried. Gorman said softly, "Ah well, it's a grand tombstone, Ditto. It's nice and white and big and up high where everybody can see it as they come into the place. Frank would have liked it." With just the faintest of smiles, he said, "What would you want there, Ditto? A castle?"

"I would!" Ditto said fiercely. "Or anyways a huge big tomb made out of big heavy rocks that everybody could see for miles! That's what the Governor should have, John! A huge big tomb with big cloth flags flying all around in the windy breeze, as we say, and big heaps of nice fresh flowers all over it every single day! Like the old-time way-back kings used to have for themselves! Some place," he said, "big and good-looking and *beautiful* where people could drive out to in their cars with the whole entire family to spend the day! That's what a great man like the Governor should have. John! Not that stingy little piece of marble stone!"

Gorman could think only of what Skeffington would have said as, once more, Ditto came through: the grave of his idol to become a combination shrine and sepulchral family picnic ground. But he saw the fat man looking at him anxiously, and so he said simply, "We'll see, Ditto. We'll see. You come around, now, in a day or so, to see me and we'll have a chat about it." He patted Ditto gently on the shoulder and said, "Go along now. Go home and get yourself a little rest."

Ditto went off, and Gorman continued to his car. He had just about reached it when he saw Adam; stopping, he went over to him.

"Well," he said, "everything went as nice as you could wish. No mistakes, and everybody here, just the way he'd have liked it."

"I hope so," Adam said. "And I'm sure he would have. The best thing was that, as Monsignor Burke said, they all seemed to have come because they wanted to. I've never seen a turnout like this before."

"And you never will again," said the old man. He looked towards Adam's car and said, "The son did well enough. Is he with you now in the car?"

"Yes, we're taking him home. I thought it might be better if we took him to our house first, but he seems to want to go directly home."

Gorman nodded absently; he was not thinking of Francis Jr. Even as Adam talked, he had turned back to look at the little hill he had so recently left. Then, after a moment he came back to Adam.

"He was a grand man!" he said, with rare emotion. "Oh, a grand man entirely! Remember that, boy, no matter what you hear, or what they try to tell you. We never had a man like him!"

Adam, for the first time, saw moisture in the old man's eyes; for not the first time that morning his own eyes blinked very rapidly. He said, "I know, Mr. Gorman. I know he was."

The old man inhaled sharply. "Ah well," he said. He put out his hand, and Adam took it. "Good-by now," he said. "You'll come and see me now and again, I hope?"

"I will, Mr. Gorman. I will indeed."

Gorman nodded again, and with a little gesture of farewell, went back to his car. After a minute, Adam turned and walked down the road to his own car, where Maeve and Francis Jr. were waiting for him.

They drove swiftly and in silence out along the road and onto the Boulevard; it was not until they reached Skeffington's house that both Maeve and Adam tried, once more, to persuade Francis Jr. to return with them. But, as before, he refused; although he thanked them profusely, he got out of the car.

"Because," he said, with a wisdom rather odd in him, "I was thinking that even if I did go over to your place, I'd only have to come back here sooner or later, wouldn't I? I mean, even with Dad gone, this is where I live, isn't it? So I thought I might just as well go in right away." He started to turn towards the house and then, with his hand still on the car door, he turned back to look at them, an expression of curious boyish bewilderment on his face. "Golly," he said, "it's going to seem funny in there without Dad. Well, not *funny* at all, of course, but *different* . . . you know what I mean, Adam?"

"I know, Junior." He said, "I'll tell you what: why don't we go in with you for a while?"

"No," Francis Jr. said. "No, I guess not, Adam. I mean, you've got your things to do, and anyway, maybe I should go in by myself. But I want to thank you for everything, both you and Maeve. I guess I wasn't as much help as I should have been, but you know how it was. I mean, I *wanted* to be, but you know how it was, Adam."

Adam said, "You did all right, Junior."

"Well," Francis Jr. said, "I guess I'd better go in. So long. And thanks again." And now he took his hand from the car door; he turned and started to go up the front walk. He stopped almost as soon as he had started; for a long moment he stood staring at the house, not moving at all. Then he began to walk, very quickly, the slim figure moving faster as it neared the house, as if it would stop altogether if it slowed down. Finally the front door was reached, it was opened, and Francis Jr. disappeared.

"Oh, *Adam!*" Maeve breathed. She had been gripping the front edge of the car seat so tightly that there were deep grooves in her palms; now, relaxing, she shook her head and said: "Adam, it was so cruel! We should have *made* him come home with us!"

"Well, maybe," Adam said, starting the car, "but, as he said, he'd still have to come back sometime, wouldn't he? I don't know that it would be any less cruel tomorrow. Or next week." He edged the car out into the stream of inbound traffic, and added thoughtfully, "And there is this: at least he could make himself go in. For Junior, that's not so bad. It may even be a good sign. Anyway, let's hope so." He looked across at his wife and smiled; he put one hand on hers. "A rough few days," he said. "And, in the words of Junior, thanks for everything."

Maeve said nothing; she smiled back and held his hand tightly. They drove home.

At the house, Adam got out of the car with Maeve and said, almost too casually, "I'll tell you what I thought I might do. I thought I might leave the car here and walk down to the paper this morning."

Maeve looked up at the dull, threatening sky, and felt the uncomfortably sharp sea wind. It was a remarkably unpleasant day for such a walk, but she said immediately, "All right, darling. Do you want me to come in and pick you up tonight?"

"No, I'll grab a cab." He had seen the upward glance at the sky, and he knew that his casualness had been a poor mask. He gave her an embarrassed grin and said, "The well-known therapeutic treatment. The long walk in foul weather. Anyway, I won't be late. Let's have an early dinner tonight."

She nodded, and he kissed her good-by; he felt the sympathy and love in her warm responsive body as she pressed against him. He released her at last, and began the walk through the dismal morning into the center of the city.

It was a curious walk, and not at all what he had expected. Everything had happened so quickly, and he had been so busy, that he found himself now unable to think clearly about his uncle. A kind of fatigue had set in, a numbness, and he thought that by walking fast through the cold damp morning, he could beat back fatigue, that he could introduce some order into the jumble of thoughts that had plagued him all morning. And as he walked, he thought now of Skeffington, but not at all clearly, not in the logical, sequential way he desired to. For he wanted to think, quietly, about his uncle as he had known him; instead, he found that these thoughts were overwhelming him. He felt that suddenly, into his head, had come rushing an army of impressions of his uncle, each one vivid, each one different, each one struggling against all others for the dominant place in memory. He found that, try as he might, he could not focus steadily on any one impression; it was as if he could see his uncle all at once and quite clearly in a thousand different moments of their association together, yet was powerless to take any one moment and separate it from the rest. These images kept coming, swift, elusive and confusing; he walked faster, hoping that by the acceleration of his pace he could somehow work his way into clarity and order. But the kaleidescope continued as before; he found that he could not even concentrate for more than an instant on Skeffington's death, for Skeffington alive, in multiple, unforgettable guises, kept getting in the way.

He reached the newspaper building and went up to his office. He met no one on the way; entering, he closed the door behind him. He had been in very little during the past week; his desk was in some disarray, and he was far behind in his work. He sat down and began to sketch aimlessly. Little Simp, he thought, the anodyne to care.

He worked at the comic strip most of the afternoon, trying to get back on schedule. He worked well: drawing the diminutive figures rapidly, almost automatically, around the ridiculous story line, filling panel after panel with poet, chipmunk, and the vacant-faced little boy, he succeeded in accomplishing more than he had for weeks. It was useful drudgery; in the chore of preposterous creation, the hours passed by.

It was nearly six o'clock when he quit for the day. He straightened the pile of finished cartoons on his desk, switched off the office light, and went down into the street. It was dark, and the street lights were on; he saw that the snow had begun to fall again. He called a cab, and when he gave his address to the driver, he added, "Go by way of the Boulevard. I'll tell you when to turn off."

"It's the long way, mister," the cab driver objected.

"I know. But it's the way I want to go."

They drove off; Adam sank back wearily against the rear seat. He was tired. His bones ached; he had been working in the same position all afternoon. But more than that, he knew that it was the past week catching up with him. It had been a hectic as well as a sad time; he had had little sleep. Maeve, too, was tired; it had been evident this morning. She had worked hard, he thought. Now, however, it would be easier; the pressure would be off. They would go to bed early tonight; they would rest. . . .

The cab swung onto the Boulevard. And now, as he traveled along this route which had become so familiar to him in recent weeks, the thoughts that had been drumming away all day at the base of his brain, resisting all efforts to smother them in labor or fatigue, blazed through. Adam closed his eyes; once again he was riding with his uncle along this street at night, making still another swift, striking foray into that strange and heady world of John Gorman, Sam Weinberg, Ditto, Cuke, Charlie Hennessey and Mother Garvey. And in his memory, he heard once more the deep, musical voice, he saw the wave of the hand, the gleam of the eye, he heard the laughter and cheers of delighted, excited, jubilant crowds. . . .

He shook his head savagely, and opened his eyes. They had

been moving swiftly, and were now approaching the wide turn; they swept around it, and now the house was visible.

"Up there on the left," the cab driver said. "That big house, there. That's where Governor Skeffington lived."

"I know," said Adam.

"They buried him this morning," the cab driver said. "What a funeral! I never see anything like it." He waggled his head in admiration. "It tied up traffic downtown more than an hour. They all come out to see him, I guess. A great guy. I drove him around a couple times. You want to know what he did, one time?"

"Yes," said Adam. "Slow down, will you?"

"Yeah. O.K." The cab slowed; they were only fifty yards or so from the house now. "Well, one time," said the cab driver, "it must of been maybe twenty years ago, maybe more, I got him in my cab and he starts talking to me. You know, asking me questions, like how long I been driving a cab, how many kids I got, and like that. So anyways, I tell him about my kid, he's only ten years old, and he's a baseball nut. You know, reads them up in the papers, knows all the batting averages, and the big deal is naturally Babe Ruth. So he listens all the time, you know, just like he was just another guy, and then I let him off, and he says so long. *One week later,*" the cab driver said impressively, slowing down even more, and turning around, "one week later, you know what my kid gets in the parcel post?"

"No," said Adam. They were abreast of the house now; he leaned forward, peering out the window. The snow was still falling, not hard; the street light beamed faintly against the front of the house. The house itself seemed dark; Adam could see no lights.

"A autographed baseball," said the cab driver, "by BABE RUTH! Whaddaya think of that? And I don't even know he's got my name! The Governor, I mean. What a great guy! Right?"

Adam nodded. "A great guy," he said absently. They were pulling away from the house now; the cab was picking up speed. Suddenly Adam saw, in the second story, a single lighted window; it was in Francis Jr.'s room. Then this was blotted out by an intervening tree. The cab drove on down the long straight stretch; the house was still visible, and Adam, through the rear window, saw the dark bulk of the big house, and then, suddenly, for just an instant, and through some queer trick of the imagination, it seemed to him that through the dim light and the softly falling evening snow, he could see the ghosts of the lines that had once formed at the door, and now would form no more. And he knew, with one, quick, final ache, that he would miss his uncle very much, in ways he did not yet know, and he knew too, that in missing him, he would never be alone.

The cab swerved around another bend; the house was gone. Slowly Adam turned away from the rear window; to the driver he said: "All right. You can cut over on the next left."

The driver nodded; Adam sat back once more against the cushions, his eyes closed. The pilgrimage, and with it, a part of his life, was over; he was going home.